Catherine wat[...] juice escaped the corner of his mouth, and he retrieved it unself-consciously with the tip of his tongue.

Aware that she was staring, Catherine lowered her eyes, swallowing and licking her lips in unconscious imitation.

"Not eating your grapes?" Crispin said lightly. "Are they too sour?"

"No," said Catherine hastily. "I...ah..." Embarrassed, she fumbled with the grapes.

"Let me do it for you," Crispin said kindly. Taking up the bunch of grapes, he began to pluck them from the stem one by one and pop them into her mouth.

Crispin's thumb brushed across her lips, more or less by accident. And then, suddenly, Catherine felt quite breathless, and her heart leaped up into her throat. What kind of magic spell was he working on her? she wondered helplessly.

Other *Leisure Books* by Sue Deobold:
SAVAGE SPLENDOR
THE MILITANT HEART

THE LOVE KNOT

SUE DEOBOLD

LEISURE BOOKS NEW YORK CITY

*To my husband, Dan, without whose unfailing patience
this book could not have been written.*

A LEISURE BOOK®

March 1995

Published by

Dorchester Publishing Co., Inc.
276 Fifth Avenue
New York, NY 10001

Printed in the United States of America.

THE LOVE KNOT

Chapter One

Freedom! How infinitely precious it was. The slender girl in the grass-green kirtle tossed back her heavy mane of hair and gave a little skip of pleasure. This was her favorite time of day, a time when she could escape her duties, lessons, and the continual exhortations of her old nurse and her lady mother and be free, free, free—if only for a little while.

As she emerged from the shadowy woods into a verdant meadow, the sun's rays caught her tangled mass of reddish-brown hair and turned it into a coppery nimbus of light. Impatiently, she pushed the heavy hair back from her flushed face and pursed her lips in a boyish whistle.

A great dapple-gray destrier grazing peacefully on the lush meadow grass perked up his ears, lifted his massive head, and whinnied. Snorting and blowing through his nostrils, he trotted to the wattle fence where the girl was waiting, and nuz-

7

zled her for the apples and carrots she habitually brought him.

"Bonjour, Bayard. Comment ça va?" Catherine murmured affectionately in the French that was as natural to her as her own English tongue. Clambering over the fence, she offered him a wrinkled apple, slung a bridle over his head, deftly slipped the bit between his teeth, and scratched him between the ears as his strong yellow teeth crunched the treat.

Wiping the horse's slobber from her hand onto her skirt, she sprang lightly onto his broad back, her legs gripping tight as she felt the powerful beast's muscles gather and ripple beneath her. Then she leaned over to open the gate and turned his head toward the open downs.

As always, whenever she mastered the great gray stallion, Catherine Clifford felt a surge of triumph. She would be punished if her mother or her nurse knew that she dared to ride her late father's warhorse, but she didn't care, or rather—her full red lips curled into a rueful smile—she took special care that they did not know! Only the peasants of Clifford Manor knew or suspected—and they would not betray her, she was certain. She had played among the manor children in her childhood, worked beside them in the fields at harvesttime, and brought her mother's herbs and simples from the still-room to cure their ailments. No, they would not betray her, she thought contentedly. They regarded her as one of their own.

After a bracing gallop across the downs—a ride that left her spent and breathless, though exhilarated—she reluctantly turned toward home.

Patting her mount's sweaty neck, she felt a moment's compunction. Bayard was too old for hard riding, she reflected. He had carried her father on many a campaign and had battle scars aplenty. Geoffrey Clifford had followed his lord, the Black Prince, into France, had fought bravely and distinguished himself at Crecy and Poitiers. These had been great English victories, but the greatest prize Geoffrey had won for himself was his beautiful French bride, a member of a minor branch of the royal house of France.

Yet Marie de Valois had not brought her husband a dowry. Although she was the French king's cousin and ward, hers was a runaway match. In the uneasy truce that followed, Charles V, King of France, had demanded just compensation for her loss. Geoffrey Clifford had stripped his estates bare in order to pay the heavy indemnity required.

Finally, in an attempt to make his fortune through the plunder and spoils of war, Geoffrey had left his pregnant wife to go adventuring again, following the Black Prince into Spain. But the Spanish campaign was a failure and, in the Pyrenees, the Black Prince picked up a lingering malignant fever that rendered him a helpless invalid, while Geoffrey himself suffered a battle wound that stank and suppurated and refused to heal. He had come home to die, with only a last glimpse of his French bride and a first and final glimpse of his newborn daughter to ease his passing.

She, Catherine Marie Clifford, was his only heir—heiress to his encumbered estates and to his debts.

Ever since her father's death, her mother had been scrimping and saving to pay off those debts. That they had been largely paid was primarily due to Bayard, whose services at stud were greatly in demand. When the old stallion grew too old to service mares, Catherine wondered what she and her mother would do for an income.

"The Good Lord will provide," Catherine's old nurse always said comfortingly. But her mother was worried, desperately worried. For years the older woman had lived in hopes of being called to court, where preferment might be obtained. But as year followed year, and Catherine grew to womanhood, her hopes faded and finally died.

"If only you had a dowry," Catherine's mother would fret. "You'll never find a husband while you're hidden away in the country like a peasant." Then she would sigh. "And you have no beauty to recommend you." The petite, fine-drawn Frenchwoman was wont to eye her long-legged, redheaded daughter in despair.

As a child, Catherine had been nurtured at her mother's knee on reminiscences of life at the royal court of England and the even more splendid court of France, on tales of knightly valor and deeds of chivalry. With shining eyes, the little Catherine listened to her mother's descriptions of regal King Edward III (grandfather of the present king) and his stalwart brood of tall blond Plantagenet sons: Edward, the Black Prince, whom Catherine's father had so loyally served; Lionel, Duke of Clarence; Edmund, Duke of York; John of Gaunt, Duke of Lancaster; Thomas, Duke of Gloucester. Together with their retainers they had formed a veritable

Round Table of Knights of the Order of the Garter, the highest order of knighthood that King Edward himself had instituted, perhaps with his bevy of sons in mind.

No less entrancing to Catherine's mind were her mother's stories of the handsome Sir Geoffrey Clifford, who had swept her mother off her feet under the French king's very nose and carried her across the sea to England, where their marriage had been celebrated in song and story, at banquets and tournaments and jousts contrived in their honor.

Because the Frenchwoman lived so much in the past, reliving her memories over and over and recalling past glories, she neglected to warn her daughter that love matches, such as that between herself and Sir Geoffrey, were exceedingly rare— so rare as to occasion fetes and celebrations and inspire ballads and stories. But harsh reality caught up with the lovers when the old French king's minions intruded on their idyll, demanding harsh reparation payments in his name.

Their daughter, only dimly aware of the real circumstances and serenely untroubled by her lack of a dowry, spent her childhood dreaming of the day her own handsome knight would come to sweep her off her feet. She wove girlish dreams and fancies about him, but as the years passed and she grew older, he began to seem more and more like a figment of her imagination and less of a distinct possibility. So she had dismissed him from her mind and begun to resent her mother's grooming her for a role that, in all likelihood, she would never fulfill.

She didn't care, she told herself with a toss of

her red head. She loved her home passionately and never wanted to leave it. She couldn't imagine leaving her home and her own country for love of a mere man as her mother had done, living forever in exile from the place of her birth and upbringing.

At least that was what she told herself as the years of her girlhood slipped away. And since it was pointless to pine for what she could not have, she told herself that she didn't really want it after all! She was, she assured herself, content. She had Clifford Manor, her beloved home, and that was all she wanted from life. Here she had grown from childhood to womanhood. Here was the gray stone manor house, its furnishings and draperies shabby and worn but much loved. Here were the fields and the peasants, each one of them her friend; here her garden with its espaliered fruit trees, the good earth, and green growing things; here her father's beloved old warhorse, Bayard. How could she bear to give it all up—even if she had the opportunity!

But her mother had never quite given up hope and, to her daughter's annoyance, persisted in drilling the girl in the niceties of deportment and the etiquette of good breeding—courtoisie, as it was called.

She taught Catherine to sit straight in her chair instead of slouching, how to make a proper obeisance to royalty, the use of cosmetics and lotions to improve her complexion, and she corrected Catherine's free-swinging boyish stride. She spent hours teaching her daughter fine needlework, and how to play the lute and sing French songs. She also taught her how to play chess—to lose gracefully—and to win graciously.

Catherine loved to watch her mother's long, slender aristocratic fingers with their shapely polished nails move about the chess board as she exchanged pawn for rook or bishop for knight. Catherine's own fingers were neither long nor especially aristocratic—all too often they were grimy at the knuckle and stained under the short-cropped nails from too much grubbing about in the garden. Nor were her hands soft and supple like her mother's, but instead they were roughened by riding and overmuch field work, and sometimes marred by unsightly blisters.

One such blister had broken during the course of her current ride, and being painfully reminded of it, Catherine put her finger to her mouth to suck at it childishly, the reins lying loosely across Bayard's neck as he ambled peacefully along.

Suddenly, the peace of the afternoon was shattered as the blast of a trumpet horn shrilled in the still air. Bayard, old warhorse that he was, screamed a stallion's challenge and reared up, his huge hooves that could shatter a man's skull like an eggshell, pawing at the sky.

Taken unawares, Catherine went down, down onto the earth, which rose up to meet her, or so it seemed. She lay prone for a moment, stunned, shaking her head dizzily and listening to the thud of hooves as Bayard galloped off.

Fortunately, the ground was soft in that particular spot, and after taking a moment to gather her scattered wits, Catherine scrambled to her feet, rubbed a painful bruise on her thigh, and limped off after her runaway mount.

In the distance, she heard a cacophony of noise—the neighing of horses, the barking of dogs, the cracking of whips—all mingled with loud voices and some varied and colorful cursing.

Her curiosity piqued, Catherine quickened her pace, ignoring the pain in her hip, and bent on discovering the cause of the commotion, rounded the crest of a hill.

Just breasting the hill, a party of riders had become entangled with a large flock of sheep herded down the narrow path by a wizened old shepherd and a couple of sheepdogs. Sheep, being notoriously stupid animals, baaing and bleating, milled around the riders, while black-faced lambs gamboled in and around the melee.

Catherine watched two or three great hounds belonging to the horsemen snap at the sheep's flanks, cutting them off from their lambs. The sheepdogs, sensing danger to the flock, leaped at the hounds, teeth bared, snarling. Members of the party were cracking whips at the dogs to separate them, while a young page blew shrill trumpet blasts in the hope, if not the expectation, of accomplishing something useful.

Into the fray galloped Bayard, neighing joyously. A powerful kick from his hooves sent first one hound, then another flying through the air, yelping in pain.

A man-at-arms leashed a third hound at the crisp direction of a horseman who was evidently the leader of the party, such an obvious air of command did he possess. Leaning from the saddle, the leader directed a volley of imprecations at the old shepherd, who gaped at him, bemused, then cupped

14

a knarled hand around his ear and mumbled, "Eh, master? What's that you say?"

Catherine giggled, in spite of herself. Yelling at the shepherd would afford Sir High-and-Mighty very little gratification, she thought with amusement. Old Will was as deaf as a dead man. He was past 70 and had survived the French Wars, the Black Plague, and the deaths of his wife and children. He would not be intimidated by a few shouts, curses, or even a well-aimed blow.

Nevertheless, she stepped forward to forestall any such contingency. The horseman, catching sight of her, dismounted, tossed the reins of his fine-blooded stallion to his page, and strode toward her.

"You, wench, come here!" he snarled.

Catherine gaped at him. She was not accustomed to being addressed in such an insolent fashion. An equally insolent retort leaped to her lips, but wisely she held her tongue.

The man was tall, she noted, since he towered over her and she was considered tall for a woman. He was strongly built and muscular, though with a horseman's lean hips, clad in particolored hose. His garments were rich and resplendent, his hair a burnished pelt of gold, and his eyes a piercing blue. A fierce hawklike nose jutted from the hard planes of his face, and all in all, he displayed an astonishing air of authority and command. Ignoring her for the moment, he threw a rapid-fire volley of orders over his shoulder—orders that dissipated the chaos and quieted the din almost instantly, as his men-at-arms leaped to obey him.

"You, wench," he said again, in a more moderate

tone. "Can you tell me the wherebouts of Clifford Manor?"

"Yes," Catherine said slowly, as if much thought were required. She had just noticed that the badge of the White Hart was sewn to his scarlet tunic, denoting, she supposed, that he was a king's man. But what was a king's man doing here in the back of the beyond? Bemused, she was silent.

"Well, I'm waiting," he said impatiently. He wore a jeweled cap with a jaunty feather, and he did not bother to doff it when he addressed her, which irked Catherine.

Doubtless he thought her a peasant wench and not worth the courtesy. She knew she looked the part. Her feet were bare, her legs scratched by brambles, her kirtle torn and mud-spattered, her hair a tangled mass tumbling about her shoulders. But she was a Clifford of Clifford Manor and the blood of stout English gentlefolk and of French kings ran hot in her veins.

"The manor's over there." She pointed. "Just beyond those hills. It nestles in the valley. What's more," she added pertly, "it's as plain to see as the nose on your face!" She lifted her chin and stared pointedly at this feature as she spoke.

His thin lips tightened. "Take care you don't provoke a taste of the whip, wench!" he rapped out. With a snap of his fingers, he summoned the page, who ran up leading his horse.

Tapping his riding crop against his thigh-high boots of fine Spanish leather, the man swung into the saddle and clattered away.

Chapter Two

The hour was late when Catherine returned to Clifford Manor. She had first to catch Bayard and then turn him out in the meadow before making her way home, sore-footed and weary.

The courtyard was astir and the kitchen bustling with unwonted activity. Catherine slipped in by a side door and ran up the narrow back stairs, which were normally used only by the servants, hoping thereby to pass unseen.

But her old nurse, well accustomed to her charge's tricks, cornered her at the top of the stairs. The woman's face was red as a turkey's wattles, her coif pushed askew, revealing limp strands of graying hair. Her hands were on her ample hips, her toes tip-tapping with impatience.

"Back at last, are you, my girl?" She scolded, "And not before time. Your lady mother has called for you over and over again. She is not best pleased that you could not be found. You may be sure of that!"

Grumbling steadily, she followed Catherine to her chamber. "There are guests in the great hall, and you have been summoned to dinner, and how can you show yourself looking like a ragamuffin or a peasant wench?" She clucked her tongue against her teeth in disapproval. "But there now, my lamb. I have been looking out for you. There is a bath all set out." With a clap of her hands, she sent the maids scurrying for buckets of hot water to fill the battered tub. "Now off with those clothes!" She sniffed. "Rags, more like—not fit for a tinker's lass nor a beggar wench!

"God save us, girl!" she grumbled as Catherine fumbled with the tangled laces of her bodice. "This is no time for niceties!" Seizing a dagger, she slit the gown from bodice to hem. As Catherine stepped out of the tangled folds, the old woman gasped. "Whatever have you done to yourself, child? You look as if you'd been beaten!"

Catherine craned her neck to look over her shoulder at the ugly purplish bruises spreading across her thigh and backside. "I fell," she stammered.

The nurse clucked her tongue and bustled away to find a salve while Catherine sank gratefully into the steaming water, which eased the soreness of her strained muscles.

She would have liked to linger there until the water cooled, but her nurse would have none of that. Soaping and rinsing the girl's hair, she towled it briskly, and rose from her knees with a groan. "Come, child. Dry your hair by the fire while I set out your best gown. I've mended the rent so that it barely shows. Now mind you don't rip out the stitches," she warned.

Catherine's best gown was of green velvet, a color vastly becoming to her, she knew, though it was a little faded. But the fur trim was still good, and the velvet scarcely worn at all, though the gown itself was a trifle short since she had grown so tall.

While the nurse drew the gown over her head and tugged the laces tight, Catherine stood still and silent, wondering what excuses she could concoct for her tardiness and who the visitors might be. Guests were few and far between, and travelers correspondingly rare, so it was obvious to the meanest intelligence that Sir High-and-Mighty and his party were the guests awaiting her presence in the great hall. But what would a king's man want with her? Unless . . . She drew in her breath sharply. Unless . . .

The nurse, who was dragging a comb through the tangled snarls of still-damp hair, frowned and warned her sharply to stop fidgeting.

"There. Now let's take a look at you." The old woman put down her comb and, taking Catherine by the shoulders, drew her to a mirror. Her sharp eyes softened. "My nurseling . . . my lamb . . ." She smiled, revealing the loss of several teeth. "My little lady, you are fair to look upon."

Catherine couldn't see it herself. She squinted doubtfully at her wavery reflection in the crooked

19

mirror which a crusading ancestor was said to have brought back from the Holy Land.

In the first place, she was no little lady, but a tall girl whose long limbs gave her an awkward coltish look. Her waist was thin enough, its slenderness emphasized by a belt of gold chain links which her nurse had looped around her. Yes, overall her figure was good, she judged, though perhaps a trifle . . . top-heavy? For her bosom was deep and full, straining the bodice of the green gown and revealing the cleft between her breasts. Her figure had "developed," she feared, since last she wore the gown, and she wondered if her lady mother would consider it improper or immodest. Oh, well, it couldn't be helped, she thought with a shrug. It was all she had.

Her face was broad with high cheekbones, and it tapered toward a pointed chin. She had good bone structure, Catherine admitted to herself, but, oh, that mass of freckles! Sprinkled generously across her tip-tilted nose, they gave her a mischievous gamine look.

Her eyes were bright and wide-spaced, fringed with curling dark lashes and flecked with golden lights. They were an indeterminate color, she thought critically, changing from brown to green according to her mood.

Her hair was equally changeable—autumn-leaf brown at times, at other times its coppery reddish highlights predominating. It had been carroty red when she was a child, and she acknowledged that time had wrought some improvements at least.

The nurse twitched straight a fold of her gown, then patted Catherine's shoulder encouragingly and gave her a little push. "You must go, child. They are waiting for you below. Go down, my lady, to meet your destiny!"

"Ah, Sir Crispin, here is my daughter, Catherine." Her mother, who bore an air of suppressed excitement, stretched out a slender white hand and drew the girl to her side. "Catherine, I would like to present to you Sir Crispin."

As her mother performed the introductions, Catherine dipped low in a curtsy, so low that her modest decolletage was exposed to the man's bold blue gaze.

They were the same pair of piercing blue eyes that she had encountered earlier in the day, and they exhibited, Catherine thought indignantly, far too much interest in her decolletage. Flushing, she straightened and stood quietly at her mother's side, striving to project an image of ladylike dignity and cool hauteur.

Catherine had had ample opportunity to steel herself for the expected confrontation. But would he recognize her? Would he see beneath her finery and detect the pert peasant wench in her guise of young lady of the manor? Fervently, Catherine hoped not. After all, their previous encounter had been brief and over in a matter of minutes.

His expression was noncommittal, though a mocking smile played about his lips. "You have a charming daughter, madame," he observed. "Charming."

Catherine's mother smiled. "Thank you." She slipped an arm through her daughter's and squeezed it. "Sir Crispin brings us good tidings, my dear.

That which I have long prayed for has come to pass. You are summoned to court as lady-in-waiting to the French princess who has already been married by proxy to the king. Sir Crispin and his men-at-arms will escort you to London. Within a few weeks, you will sail for France. You are to go in King Richard's entourage to bring the new queen home!" Her mother beamed. "Is that not wonderful news and a cause for rejoicing, my child!"

Catherine gaped at her mother, thunderstruck. "Me?" she stammered when she could find her voice. "But why me?"

Sir Crispin was ready with an answer. "The king is pleased to remember your father's service to his father in France and Spain," he said smoothly. "Furthermore, your mother is a member of the French royal house—"

"A minor branch of the family," her mother interjected modestly.

"But family nonetheless. I have the king's ear, and he believes that a princess of France will feel more at home with a member of her own family, no matter how distant the connection, to wait on her . . . the more so because France and England have long been at war."

"It is hoped that this marriage will cement a long-lasting peace between our two countries," her mother explained. "It is a political alliance, and for some years must be a marriage in name only, as the little queen is but seven years old."

"Seven years old!" Catherine echoed in amazement. "Why, the king is a grown man. He must be nearly thirty years old and a widower to boot!"

"It is a political alliance, and in no way a love match," her mother reminded her. "The disparity in age will be less significant as the queen grows older. Arranged marriages between members of one royal house or another are the rule, rather than the exception. Their purpose is to seal political alliances." She shook her head. "Surely you know, Catherine, that love matches, such as mine with your father, are exceedingly rare."

"That is true," Sir Crispin said in agreement. "Few of us are free to choose our own mates." He shrugged with seeming indifference. "It is just the way things are."

But not the way they ought to be! Catherine thought rebelliously, though she bit her lip and held her tongue.

"As a matter of fact," Sir Crispin remarked, "there are those who object to the French marriage, not because of the queen's extreme youth, but because they are profiting from the French war and wish to see it prolonged. They would wreck the alliance if it were in their power to do so . . . which is but another reason for the king to look far afield for a young woman to wait on the queen. He requires someone who can speak French like a French woman, someone who has no political axes to grind, someone young enough to entertain and amuse her. . . ." He cocked a quizzical eye at Catherine. "Which, I daresay, madame, your daughter will do admirably."

"In other words, I am to be a glorified nursery maid to a political pawn!" The girl spoke impulsively, as she so often did, blurting out what was in her mind before she thought it through.

"Catherine!" her mother said sharply, with a frown of disapproval darkening her face.

Sir Crispin, however, was imperturbable. "The queen is young in years. That is true. But she is mature beyond her age. I was with the party of English ambassadors who brought her the king's offer of marriage. When we knelt before her, she took a step forward and without anyone prompting her, said, 'Sirs, if it please God and my lord and father that I be Queen of England, I shall be well pleased, for I have been told that then I shall be a great lady.'"

A servant was passing round glasses of wine, and Sir Crispin paused in his narrative and accepted a goblet. "To my mind," he said thoughtfully, "she already *is* great lady, though young, and moreover, is one of much sweetness and presence of mind." With a flourish, he raised his goblet high, "To the Queen, God bless her!"

"To the Queen!" Catherine and her mother echoed dutifully, raising their goblets to clink against his in a toast of loyalty.

Catherine's hand shook a little as she raised her glass, and ruby droplets of wine flew out to splatter against the once-spotless, though well-darned, white linen tablecloth. Her sharp-eyed mother shot her a look of reproof and quietly summoned a servant to soak up the wine stains.

The girl's face flamed in embarrassment. How could she be so clumsy in front of a guest? And such an important guest, at that! Miserably she looked down at her plate.

Sir Crispin eyed her flushed face thoughtfully. It was a most becoming flush, he mused, accentuating those high cheekbones and soft round cheeks upon which her thick, dark lashes lay, soft and spiky as a child's.

Poor child, he thought, she has much to learn about life and the ways of the world. And then his eyes traveled downward to her well-filled bodice, where her thrusting breasts strained against the worn fabric of her gown. She was not such a child after all, he realized, and idly began to speculate on what he could say or do to bring that most becoming flush to her face again and again.

All through dinner, Catherine kept her eyes fixed firmly on her plate, for whenever she peered across the table she was disconcerted to discover Sir Crispin's penetrating gaze upon her. It was as if the man were devouring *her,* instead of his dinner. She told herself that she was imagining it, but she was sure he was assessing her, in his bold way, and finding her wanting. Flustered, she wondered that she had any appetite at all, but the food was good and, in honor of their guest, there was a more plentiful repast than her frugal mother ordinarily served. Somewhat to her surprise, Catherine found herself able to do full justice to it.

Her mother kept up a gentle flow of conversation to which Sir Crispin responded with absentminded politeness, though each time her mother had touched on his origins or antecedents, Catherine noticed he had deftly turned away the conversation into other channels. This piqued the girl's curiosity. It made their guest a man of mystery, a man with a past that intrigued her.

Later, after dinner had been cleared away, the talk turned to the state of the country, impoverished as it was by the wars and decimated in population because of the Black Plague. "Times are not good," said Sir Crispin with a shake of his head. "England is caught up in a contagion of lawlessness that was spawned on the Continent during the incessant wars. Soldiers returning with the habit of pillage are forming armed bands and live by lawlessness and highway robbery."

"My heart bleeds for the wounded and the maimed," Catherine's mother remarked. "Even here, in our little district, we see them dragging themselves along these backcountry roads, begging alms from house to house, homeless and friendless."

"The country is full of them," Sir Crispin admitted. "Yet war is profitable to some. I myself am a landless knight with only my sword to make my fortune."

Catherine pricked up her ears. Ah, here was a chance to assuage her insatiable curiosity. "You have no lands, sir knight?" she blurted out.

"I am, in a manner of speaking, a soldier of fortune, lady, whose only hope of fame and fortune is in the king's service. The king's peace will go hard on such as me," he admitted.

"War enriches only a lucky few," Catherine's mother remarked. "While for others, and for their widows and orphans, such as me and my daughter, there is only poverty and hardship."

"Yet the land is rich enough hereabouts." Sir Crispin twirled his wine goblet. "Perhaps you need a new bailiff or steward, madame, to bring the land into greater productivity and thus mend your fortunes."

"Think you so?" Catherine's mother was doubtful.

"I have observed that here, as elsewhere, good land lies fallow, and I suspect your harvests are small."

"True enough," Catherine's mother agreed. "And the peasants are often unruly, now that there are fewer of them and laborers are in demand."

"Exactly," said Sir Crispin. "Why, I myself met with impudence from a daring peasant wench when I asked directions on the road."

Catherine, who had been half dozing by the fireside, surfeited with food and unaccustomed wine, opened her eyes wide and found herself staring into Sir Crispin's bright blue orbs.

"Describe her, sir. She shall be found and well whipped, I assure you," Catherine's mother declared, eager to set right an affront to her guest.

Sir Crispin locked eyes with Catherine, who trembled. "Oh, one peasant wench is much like another," he said lightly. "I doubt I could tell one from another beneath the dirt." He frowned thoughtfully. "She was taller than is common, I believe, lithe as a cat, with greenish cat's eyes and with hair as tangled as a horse's mane." His eyes shifted to Catherine's mother. "But do not trouble yourself on my account, madame. It was but a piece of childish impudence, which I used merely to illustrate my point. Seeking her out to discipline her is not worth the bother," he said easily.

His hostess looked unconvinced, and while they argued politely back and forth, Catherine was in a dither over whether to stay or take flight. She wished miserably that the earth would open and swallow her up, but failing that unlikely contingency, she would gladly settle for the safety of her own room, where she could ease her tight lacings and collapse upon her bed. But if she rose and excused herself at this particular moment, wouldn't she just be calling unwanted attention to herself?

Grabbing her wine goblet, she drained the contents at a gulp. The wine gave her false courage, and she decided to stay, but its potency made her light-headed. When finally the conversation turned to a topic less fraught with risk to herself, Catherine rose unsteadily and excused herself.

Unfortunately, she blundered over the long booted legs of Sir Crispin, and would have tumbled over in an undignified heap had not the man stretched out a hand to set her back upon her feet. "Steady on," he warned her, his strong arm encasing her back, his lips close to her ear.

Instinctively, she stood within the circle of his arms, bracing her hands on his shoulders for support until her head cleared. His hands encircling her trim waist had a hard strength and were so warm they seemed to sear her skin right through the material of her green velvet gown. With a little gasp, she jerked herself away.

Her mother, mortified, said, "You must pardon my daughter's rudeness, Sir Crispin. She is unused to wine at dinner and to keeping late hours. We are but simple country folk hereabouts. I do not know how she will go on at court," her mother added, vexed.

"Oh, she will do well enough," he said lightly. "She is but a green girl yet. A green-eyed girl," he muttered sotto voce for Catherine's ears alone. His own eyes danced with merriment as Catherine flounced away.

Alone, in the privacy of her room, Catherine found to her consternation that she was too excited to relax now that she had the chance. The nurse, who would ordinarily have been there to help her undress, was gossiping in the kitchen with Crispin's men-at-arms, and Catherine had the room to herself. Restlessly, she paced back and forth, re-living in memory every word and look that had passed between herself and Sir Crispin. Her face burned. She had shamed her mother with her clumsiness and gaucherie. Worse yet, she had made a fool of herself in front of Sir Crispin. What would he think of her?

Oh, why did she care what he thought of her? The man was an arrogant brute who had mocked her and teased and taunted her right under her mother's nose! The nerve of him! Oh, it was not to be borne!

But she would have to bear that and more, probably, for he was to be her escort to the king's court—he whom she wished never to see again!

At the thought of going to court, she brightened. It was a dream come true, and her eyes began to sparkle at the thought. King Richard's court was said to be the gayest and brightest and most lavish in Christendom. It drew knights and ladies, noblemen and noblewomen, and artists and craftsmen whom the king held in high regard. There was even a court poet, Geoffrey Chaucer. She had read some of his tales and enjoyed them, though her mother frowned on the poet's bawdiness and irreverence.

Her mother . . . how could she bear to leave her mother, who was in poor health and who needed her?

But when kings command, Catherine reminded herself, subjects must obey. Besides, it was her mother's wish that she should go to serve the House of Plantagenet as her mother had the royal house of Valois.

But a child-queen. Catherine sighed. The princess would be a spoiled and demanding brat, no doubt, accustomed to having her own way. She would require constant attention and Catherine would be at her beck and call.

On the other hand, there was the glittering prospect of a royal wedding with all the lavish amusements and entertainments attendant upon it. Lavish dinners, gala festivities, colorful and exciting tournaments beckoned alluringly. And she, Catherine Clifford, would be in the thick of it all! A part of the glamorous panoply of life at court.

If only her escort to this latter-day Camelot were not to be that odious Sir Crispin!

Chapter Three

"Up! Up! You slugabed!" It was barely dawn and already Nurse was bustling about Catherine's room, picking up garments the girl had thrown helter-skelter when she disrobed the night before.

Catherine groaned, sleepily opening first one eye and then the other and scowling at the old woman. "Oh, Nurse, what hour is it?" she asked with a sleepy yawn.

"Time for you to be up and doing," Nurse replied briskly. "Your lady mother has been up for hours, cutting out new garments for you and refurbishing old ones, straining her eyes by candlelight. She wants you in her chamber for a fitting as soon as you have broken your fast." Ruthlessly, she stripped the bedcovers from Catherine's body, destroying her warm little nest. "Up, girl! Up, I say!"

Reluctantly, Catherine scrambled out of bed and made for the basin of water that Nurse had brought her to bathe her face and sleep-sticky eyes. As she splashed in the basin, Nurse held up the gown Catherine had ripped off the night before and tsk-tsked over it.

"You didn't come up to help me with the lacings," the girl said guiltily, drying her face on a towel. "Besides, it was far too tight. I couldn't have worn it again."

"Ah, well, it can be repaired and given to one of the maids, I suppose," said Nurse. "You won't need it, not where you're going. You will have far grander clothing." She picked up a comb and began to drag it through the girl's tangled curls. "Oh, my little lamb! Is it not wonderful news!" she said enthusiastically. "There was talk of nothing else in the kitchens last night. How you are to go to court to serve the new queen. What an honor!"

"Hmmm." Catherine was still more than half asleep, but at the mention of court she jerked wide awake, the events of the preceding day flooding back into her mind. So it was really true after all, and not, as she had first thought, a half-remembered dream.

Nurse burbled on as she straightened the tangled bedcovers and plumped up Catherine's pillows. "And your escort, my lady!" She sighed. "Ah, what a man he is! So handsome! Such piercing blue eyes! Such a strong muscular frame! I have not seen his like in many a long day. Not since your father brought your lady mother home, God rest his soul." She crossed herself.

"From what I have heard of my father, he and Sir Crispin are nothing alike," Catherine remarked a trifle sharply, twitching a fold of her gown straight and coiling up her fiery braids of hair.

"Not in looks, perhaps," Nurse agreed. "Ah, but in all that makes a man a man..." she breathed. "Such vigor and potency as he projects... such an air of command... such..." Glancing at Catherine's innocent face, she broke off rather hastily. "But there, my lamb, you do not know what I am talking about." She cackled. "But you will... you will..."

Catherine, tired of hearing Sir Crispin's praises sung, made a hasty departure. In the kitchen, she snatched an apple and a bit of bread. Pocketing the one and munching the other, she made her way to her mother's chamber.

Her mother, who was closeted with the best sewing woman the estate could provide, looked a trifle harassed, as did the two maids she kept busy running hither and thither to fetch this and that and digging deep into chests to bring out long-forgotten bits of finery.

"Catherine, where have you been?" her mother asked sharply. "Come, child, try on this gown." She handed her a length of soft apple-green velvet. "Joan has basted it together, but it needs to be fitted."

Meekly, Catherine shed her clothing and stood like a statue as the new gown was drawn over her head and pulled down. She smoothed it over her hips as the maids knelt at her feet, marking the hem.

"Stand up straight, child. Don't slouch," her mother admonished through a mouthful of pins. "I don't know... what do you think, Joan?" she asked doubtfully, standing back to take a critical look.

Joan shook her head. "Too tight across the bust, my lady. We'll have to take it out some more," the sewing woman advised.

"I believe you're right," Catherine's mother agreed. "Take it off, child . . . carefully, mind," she ordered, "and try on the blue silk."

Patiently, Catherine submitted to the women's ministrations, being pushed, poked, and prodded until she was ready to scream for relief. At last, sensing her impatience, her mother relented.

"That'll be all for the time being." Her mother waved her away, and Catherine gladly seized the opportunity to escape. She was on her way out the door when her mother called her back. "Not so fast, girl. You are not to go running off on your own. We have a guest," she reminded her daughter. "When you are not needed for fittings, you should be mindful of that, Catherine, and see to his comfort and entertainment. Sir Crispin has expressed an interest in the estate. You can be his guide."

Catherine's face fell. She nodded obediently, but without enthusiasm.

"He appears to be a pleasant, well-spoken young man," her mother remarked with asperity, seeing her downcast expression. "It should not be an onerous duty. In fact, it will give you an opportunity to get to know him better before you embark on your journey."

"Do you know when we are to leave, madame?" Catherine ventured.

"Not for several days at least. Perhaps a week or so," her mother said vaguely. "Sir Crispin understands that I want you to be outfitted with the best we can provide on such short notice and is agreeable to delaying the journey. He expected no less." The older woman's face took on an anxious expression. "On the other hand, providing hospitality for him and his men-at-arms will strain our limited resources to the uttermost. The day of your departure cannot be unduly prolonged." Her mother sighed. "Run along now, child. There is much that I must see to, and little time to waste."

Remembering her humiliation of the previous evening, Catherine was reluctant to seek out Sir Crispin, but seeing her frail mother put so much effort into outfitting her properly reminded her of her own duties and obligations as a daughter of the house. Moreover, as her mother rightly pointed out, the two of them were going to be traveling together. Catherine knew she must try to develop a more cordial relationship with the man, detestable as he was. Catherine sniffed. Sir Crispin, indeed! Sir High-and-Mighty was more like it.

With lagging steps, she made her way to the courtyard, where Sir Crispin, like a prudent commander, was reviewing the condition of his travel-weary troup of men-arms and their hard-ridden mounts. Catherine, standing quietly back in the shadows cast by the gray-stone manor house, took the opportunity to observe him more closely.

Oh, the man was handsome enough. Grudgingly, she had to admit it to herself. Even his fierce, hawklike nose did not detract from that impression, but rather added strength and boldness to features that might otherwise have been too symmetrical. It might also have added a dimension to that air of arrogance that she found so alarmingly challenging.

He had an authoritative stride as he moved among his men, reviewing their arms, accoutrements, and horses. As he strode along, his hair, ruffled by a vagrant breeze, caught a shaft of sunlight and gleamed with the richness of dark gold.

One of the men spoke up, evidently asking a question, for in response Sir Crispin hunkered down by the man's horse, lifting its forehoof and bracing it against his own muscular thigh as he probed the hoof for foreign material. Catherine saw him shake his head, and the words "nothing lodged in the hoof" drifted back to her on the wind. He straightened, letting the hoof drop, and ran skillful hands almost caressingly down the animal's leg, from elbow to fetlock. "A swelling in the joint," she heard him say. "Apply hot fomentations twice a day until . . ." The rest was lost to her by a shift of the wind.

She was impressed by his equine expertise as well as by the caring and concern he evinced for the well-being of his men, as evidenced when the next man stepped forward, his fist clenched against a swollen jaw, to report a toothache. His commander sent him to the manor kitchen to beg oil of cloves from the cook. As the man shambled away, Crispin turned to call after him, "If all else fails, man, you have my leave to go down to the village and find a barber-surgeon to pull that aching tooth. Rotten as it is, it may be the only remedy."

Catching sight of Catherine, he dismissed his men and came over to where she was standing in the lee side of the wind, sheltered by the gray stone walls of the manor house. "Good morning, lady," he greeted her, his boldly handsome face smiling down at her, for though she was tall for a woman, he topped her by several inches.

He had all *his* teeth, Catherine noted, and they were sparkling white and very even—the better to eat her up, she thought with an inward shiver.

"Good morning, Sir Crispin," she responded, banishing the wayward fancy from her mind. "Don't let me interrupt you in the performance of your duties," she added a trifle shyly, for she felt awkward and ill at ease with him.

"You interrupt nothing, lady. My inspection is over for the day." He snapped his fingers to summon a subordinate. "As a matter of fact, you are here in good time. I have something to show you."

"Oh?" In spite of herself, Catherine's curiosity was piqued.

Sir Crispin muttered a word in the man's ear, and he went off to the stables, reappearing a few minutes later leading out a pretty dapple-gray palfrey. Affixed to the horse's bridle was a set of tiny tinkling silver bells that jingled merrily with the animal's movements.

Catherine was charmed. The placid palfrey could not compare to her beloved Bayard, of course, but it was a pretty little animal all the same. Stroking the palfrey's velvety hide, she awkwardly mumbled her thanks, but Sir Crispin brushed them away. "It is the king's gift, not mine," he explained candidly. "It is he to whom thanks are due, for he authorized the purchase."

"Still, you chose the gift, did you not?" she asked, liking the man's candor.

"I did," he acknowledged, well rewarded by her exclamations of pleasure. Her greenish cat's eyes sparkling like emeralds, Catherine rubbed the palfrey's soft nose affectionately and led it about the courtyard, its bells jingling merrily with every step it took.

"Would you not like to try out its paces?" the man asked. "I'm told it's a very smooth-gaited beast."

Catherine nodded eagerly, and Crispin gave orders for the palfrey to be saddled.

"Would you care to ride with me?" she asked, extending the invitation in a spirit of reconciliation. "My lady mother tells me you have expressed a desire to be shown round the demesne."

"Nothing would please me more, lady," he responded heartily, amending his orders to include the saddling of his own blood-bay stallion.

While they were waiting, they chatted amicably enough, finding common ground in their mutual love of good horseflesh. But Catherine's pleasure in her new mount was short-lived, for when it was led out again, it bore upon its back, in place of the conventional saddle, a curious contraption. It appeared to be a kind of bench with a step hanging down upon one side. "What on earth is that?" asked Catherine in a voice brittle with astonishment.

"That? Oh, that is a sidesaddle." Sir Crispin smothered a smile at her obvious dismay. "It is a recent innovation, introduced into England by Anne of Bohemia, the king's late wife."

Catherine eyed the contraption dubiously. "Is it safe?" she demanded.

"So I'm told. It has become all the rage at court," Sir Crispin assured her. "Gentlewomen no longer ride astride. It is not considered ladylike."

"Is that so?" Catherine eyed the sidesaddle suspiciously. It didn't look safe to her, nor particularly comfortable, and she was about to reject it outright, but the man coaxed her into trying it, pointing out the advisability of her getting accustomed to it before they embarked on their journey.

"Oh, very well. If I must, I must," said Catherine ungraciously, not wanting to give the appearance of a country bumpkin when they entered London town.

A man-at-arms sprang forward to assist Catherine into the saddle. To her surprise, she felt a little pang of disappointment that Sir Crispin did not offer to perform that function. Surely she was not so light-minded as to pine for the hard strength of his hands round her waist, she thought crossly.

"That's right. Both feet on the footrest," he advised her as she settled herself. "Are you comfortable?"

"Quite," fibbed Catherine from her precarious perch, too proud to admit she was anything but comfortable. She would learn to ride like a lady or die in the attempt, she thought grimly.

Sir Crispin swung lithely into his own saddle, the hard muscles of his thighs rippling as they gripped the horse's sides. The bay stallion was a mettlesome mount that frisked and danced about, and he checked it with a firm hand.

Catherine gnashed her teeth with envy. How ridiculous that she, who was accustomed to riding her late father's warhorse bareback, was now relegated to perching insecurely on a curious contraption atop a placid palfrey. Petulantly, she kicked at the palfrey's plump posterior, and the animal advanced at a sedate walk. She kicked it again, a little harder this time, and it picked up speed, moving a bit more briskly, its set of silver bells jingling merrily.

Sir Crispin fell back, allowing her to take the lead and set the pace, and they embarked on a tour round the estate.

The spring day was sunny and fine, though the wind blew brisk, and gradually Catherine's mercurial spirits rose. At least she was out of the house, free of the bustling maids, the grumblings of old nurse, and the tedious fittings for new garments that she had endured all morning. Being out of doors had ever provided her with a measure of freedom, and usually had an uplifting effect upon her spirits.

Today, however, a new element was added. A handsome young knight rode by her side. Gradually, it was borne upon her that his presence added an extra fillip of zest to a fine day. The sun shone just a trifle more brightly than was its wont; the sky seemed bluer; the scent of the spring breeze smelled fresher to her nostrils; birdsong sounded sweeter to her ears. It was as if all her senses were sharpened and intensified.

The beauties of nature were lost on the man, however. Considerations of a more practical nature loomed larger in his mind, as Catherine soon discovered, to her annoyance. He surveyed every field of grain and vegetable patch and bit of pasture, assessing each for its productive capacity and freely offering opinions as to how the yield of each plot of ground might be increased and rendered more productive, suggesting that oats might do better in this field and barley in that one.

"How many serfs have you?" he asked abruptly as they skirted a field where back-bent peasant laborers stooped to plant and sow a crop.

His query brought the girl back to earth with a jolt. "Why, I don't know offhand." She wrinkled her brow in thought. "Fifty or sixty, I believe."

"Sufficient to support a manor in comfortable circumstances, if properly administered," he remarked.

Catherine stiffened. "My father once held other lands to supplement his rents, but my mother was forced to sell them off to pay his debts. Times are hard too, and my lady mother is too kindhearted to exact full payment for overdue rents and fines when doing so will cause hardship. Our vilains give us a half day of labor for every day they spend on their own plots and boon work at haymaking and harvest, and that is all that can be expected."

"The peasants doubtless take advantage because there is no lord of the manor." Sir Crispin shook his head. "You need a good bailiff to manage your estate and obtain from them the requisite labor."

"Our people do the best they can." Catherine flared to the defense of the peasants she had known from childhood. "Most of them are well along in years, for the young men go off to the wars or run off to the towns to seek service for wages, hoping thereby to better themselves."

"In such cases, the families should pay 'chevage' to offset the loss of their services," Sir Crispin insisted. "Other feudal dues should be upheld as well: the 'merchet,' when a son or daughter marries; 'lehrwite,' if an unmarried daughter becomes pregnant; 'heriot,' payment of the best beast or chattel of his holding when a peasant dies."

Catherine ground her teeth. By now, she was in a fine rage. How dare he presume to tell her how the estate should be run! How dare he!

"You are knowledgeable for a landless knight, Sir Crispin," she said between her teeth, resorting to sarcasm.

"Ah, but I don't intend to remain a landless knight, my lady," he retorted. "As I told you last evening, I have my fortune to make."

"Your father had no demesnes to leave a younger son?" she asked boldly, not liking to be reminded of the previous night and determined to satisfy her insatiable curiosity, if she could.

The man's face hardened. "My father expected his baseborn son to win his fortune with his sword, lady."

"Oh," said Catherine in a small voice, taken aback by his blunt reply. She felt embarrassment and no little compunction at having inadvertently touched upon the sensitive topic of his bastardy. But how could she have known? Now she understood why he had evaded her mother's polite probing into his family and origins.

While she was wondering how to make amends for her clumsiness, he asked gruffly if she had grown accustomed to the new saddle.

"Tolerably," she admitted, gratefully seizing on the topic as a way to change the subject. "Though, I can't help wondering . . . Queen Anne did not die from a fall from a horse, did she?"

The thunderclouds disappeared from his face, and he threw back his head in a hearty laugh. "Indeed no. She died of plague, in the same epidemic that carried off the Duchess of Lancaster and the Duchess of York, her younger sister. Plague is no respector of rank and privilege."

"They say that King Richard was heartbroken at the queen's death," Catherine ventured. "He must have loved her very much."

"He was bereaved to the point of madness, if that is a reliable sign of love," said Sir Crispin dryly. "To my eyes, it was rage at being deprived of one of his most prized possessions—an act of lèse-majesté committed by the Lord."

Catherine was shocked. "You . . . you do not like the king!" she gasped.

"I serve the king loyally. It is not required that I like the man as well."

The open expression of shock and horror on Catherine's face set the man to laughing again, laughter that was bitter and held more than a note of cynicism. "Lady, you will have much to learn at court, not the least of which is how to conceal your feelings," he said grimly.

"You . . . you disapprove of the court as well?" Catherine asked faintly, though this was more understandable; she had reservations about the court herself.

"Life at court is composed, in equal parts, of hypocrisy, flattery, betrayal, pandering, lying, and falsity; it is where calumny and cupidity meet, where common sense is rejected, where truth dare not appear. To survive at court, lady, you must be blind, deaf, and dumb."

"Then, how shall I survive?" mourned Catherine. She felt dispirited and chilled to the bone by the man's grim assessment, yet instinctively she knew he was telling her the truth as he saw it. "How shall I know whom to trust?"

"You can trust me, lady," he assured her. "I have not betrayed your secrets, have I?"

"Secrets?" Catherine hedged, suddenly wary. "What secrets?"

He smiled. "The secret of the young lady of the manor who disguises herself as a peasant wench and rides a great gray warhorse."

"How do you know about Bayard?" Catherine gasped, too surprised to deny his accusation.

"Once I recognized the green-eyed peasant girl in the green-eyed lady of the manor, it was a simple deduction," he told her a trifle smugly. "I assumed when I saw you with the stallion yesterday that you had been given the task of leading him from one pasture to another or were taking him to service a mare, though I did wonder why a stable lad was not entrusted with the task. But when I saw you again last night and recognized you, my suspicions were aroused, suspicions confirmed by one of your servants. You had been riding him, hadn't you?

"Well, hadn't you?" When Catherine obstinately refused to answer, he grabbed her palfrey's bridle and jerked it to a halt, swinging his own mount in front of her to block her way. "Answer me."

"*Yes!*" Catherine snapped. "But what if I had? There is no reason why I should not, if I choose. He is my father's horse."

"Your father's warhorse," he corrected her. "An animal trained to fight with hooves and teeth. To kill, if necessary."

"Bayard is as gentle as . . . as a kitten. As gentle as this sluggish palfrey."

"I doubt your lady mother would agree with you. Or with your impudent way of greeting guests. I saved you from a beating last night, my girl," he reminded her. "A well-deserved beating, I might add."

"And are you going to betray me now?" Catherine stared at him defiantly.

"I have said that I will not. I have said that you can trust me." He shrugged. "Your impudence in your peasant guise means nothing to me. But heed this warning well. You are *not* to ride the stallion again. From now on, until we reach the court, I am responsible for your safety to the king. It would go hard on me if aught befell you now. So, there will be no sneaking off for one last glorious gallop before we leave."

Catherine drew in her breath sharply. How could he know she had been planning that very thing as soon as his back was turned? Could the man see into her mind?

"No stolen rides on Bayard," he insisted. "I want your word on that, Catherine."

"And if I do not give it?" she asked sulkily.

"Then, my lady, you will find I am capable of administering a whipping myself, should the need arise!"

Stormy-eyed, Catherine reluctantly pledged her word.

Accepting it, he released his grip on her horse's reins.

Freed at last, Catherine dug her heels into the palfrey's plump sides and set off at as fast a pace as her sluggish mount could muster.

For the rest of the day, Catherine managed to avoid their unwelcome guest, who, not a whit abashed at being left to his own devices, poked his long nose into every nook and cranny of the estate, making exploratory forays into the various outbuildings—the blacksmith shop, the dairy house, the bake house, the weaving sheds. Even the tumbledown dovecot, woodsheds, and spidery cellars did not escape the man's sharp-eyed inspection.

Catherine, who was embarrassed by the estate's air of genteel dilapidation, complained of his prowling to her mother, but received a sharp rebuke.

"What ails you, girl?" The mother was mystified by her daughter's ungracious attitude towards their guest. "I myself have given Sir Crispin leave to make himself at home while he is with us. In fact, I have specifically invited him to roam around to his heart's content and make such suggestions for modifications and improvements as he deems advisable. It has been years since we have had the benefit of a man's advice," she reminded her daughter, "and Sir Crispin appears to be a forward-looking young man with a fund of sound common sense and a good working knowledge of estate management. I value his advice and so should you, my girl," her exasperated mother said tartly.

Catherine retreated to her own room to sulk.

It was not the refuge she had hoped to find. For, almost immediately, her old nurse cornered her and coaxed her into trying on myriad bits and pieces of long-forgotten finery that her mother had put by long ago. Diving deep into chests and wardrobes, Nurse retrieved embroidered riding gloves (a size too small for Catherine's hands), slippers (a size too small for Catherine's feet), bodices (too tight for Catherine's well-developed bust), and kirtles (too short to cover Catherine's long slender legs).

"I cannot wear my lady mother's discards," the girl protested impatiently, shoving aside an array of such fripperies. "It is not that I disdain them, Nurse. Everything is at least a size too small. Surely you can see that."

Surveying Catherine's long slender feet cramped into a pair of tiny slippers and a skirt that bobbed about her knees, the old nurse was forced to agree. "You are not so dainty as your lady mother, more's the pity," she said with a sigh of resignation. "Ah, well, we can pick the fine lace off this bodice and set it to bleach in the sun. It will be as good as new and fit to adorn one of your new gowns. And the fur trim from this kirtle can likewise be removed and sewn to another garment." She set her charge to picking out stitches and sewing new ones, but she could not endure Catherine's fidgeting and awkward stitching for very long.

"God save us, girl!" she grumbled when Catherine pricked her fingers and tiny ruby droplets bubbled up. "If you are not careful you will get bloodstains all over the lace!" Grumbling, the old woman snatched the delicate webbing from the girl's hands and shooed her from the room. "Be off, girl. Away with you. I will do it myself. Though my fingers are gnarled and my eyesight none too good, I still can do better than you."

Sucking drops of blood from her pricked fingers, Catherine, who was thankful to be released from the tedious chore, wandered out into the garden, where she hoped to find a quiet sanctuary.

But it was not to be. Spotting Sir Crispin strolling among the plants along a flagstone-paved walkway, she would have beaten a hasty retreat, but it was too late. He had already seen and hailed her.

Coming up to where Catherine stood irresolute, skittishly poised for retreat, he said courteously, "I must compliment you upon your garden, lady. It is very fine."

"Oh . . . why, thank you." His unexpected approbation took Catherine by surprise. Pleased and flattered, she let down her guard. "With good mulching I did not lose many plants to winter-kill, but still, there is little to see and admire so early in the season."

"On the contrary, I can see that the beds are well tended and the plants healthy and flourishing." As they spoke, they moved slowly along the neat beds of mint, sage, thyme, parsley, fennel, and hyssop,

Catherine enumerating the culinary or medicinal properties of each plant.

"Your skill at growing plants does you credit, lady, as does your knowledge of their uses." Seeing her absentmindedly put her finger to her mouth to suck away a drop of blood, he frowned. "Have you pricked your finger upon the thorns of a rosebush, lady?" The ruby droplets upon her fingers were no less red than her soft red lips, he mused, watching in fascination as they parted to envelop her finger.

Feeling his eyes upon her, Catherine colored and self-consciously snatched her hand away, hiding it behind her back. "Not a thorn, but a needle. It is naught but the prick of a sewing needle," she stammered.

"Let me examine it," he demanded.

Catherine drew her hands forth from behind her back reluctantly, for her fingers were stained and her hands rough from riding and gardening without gloves. "It is naught but the prick of a needle," she reiterated.

"I can well believe that sewing a fine seam is not your forte, lady," Sir Crispin remarked, his eyes dancing and his well-shaped lips twitching in amusement. "It is altogether too tame a pastime for you."

He was mocking her again, Catherine feared, but the touch of his hands on hers, strong and firm and cool, was so unsettling to the girl that she could be sure of nothing.

His head was bent low over her hands, his keen eyes searching her fingers for pin-pricks, and a vagrant lock of tawny-gold hair fell forward over his brow. She drew in her breath sharply, nearly giving way to the impulse to reach out and smooth it back, but fearing to touch him in such an intimate way.

Her hands were clasped between both of his, and he held them longer than was strictly necessary to make an examination, turning them over, palm upwards, and splaying the fingers. "The bleeding has stopped," he announced almost regretfully, for he would have welcomed an excuse to bring her fingers to his lips and suck the ruby droplets from them himself.

"As I told you, it . . . it was nothing," Catherine murmured. Withdrawing her hands from his with difficulty, she turned back to the garden. The moment was fraught with a kind of curious tension that she wanted to dispel if she could.

"What . . . what think you of my hanging baskets, Sir Crispin?" she gabbled nervously, referring to the hanging wicker baskets which held young plants she had rooted from cuttings. "Do you not think it an excellent way to start young plants? The increased exposure to sunlight and fresh air gives them added strength and vigor, I do believe."

Sir Crispin, amused by the girl's naive discomfiture, agreed with her absently, though he knew little about the techniques of rooting cuttings and cared less. Idly, he dropped down on a convenient bench, and with a contented sigh, sprawled comfortably against the backrest, his long muscular legs spread wide, one ankle crossed over his knee, and an arm stretched across the back of the bench.

"Will you not come and sit beside me?" he asked after a while, patting the bench invitingly. "It is too warm an afternoon for so much industry."

Catherine's eyes skittered to where he sprawled his manly form in indolence, taking his ease in the warm sunshine, an elbow propped on his knee as, chin in hand, he watched her at her work. He certainly had a way of making himself right at home, she reflected, as well as making himself master of any situation in which he found himself.

"No, thank you," she said primly, obstinately making a great business of plucking stray weeds from her hanging wicker baskets and stretching on tiptoe to give thirsty plants a drink from her long-spouted watering pot. It gave her an excuse to avert her eyes from the man's too-compelling gaze.

"As you wish," he said easily. Silence fell between them, broken only by the droning of bees buzzing round a few early blossoms.

The morning's breeze had long since died away, and the westering sun made the late afternoon air heavy and somnolent. The man's broad chest rose and fell regularly with his deep and easy breathing and his eyes were heavy-lidded. Peering between fronds of greenery, Catherine sneaked a peek at him. So indolent did he appear that she supposed he had fallen into a doze.

But she was wrong. His lazy-lidded eyes, narrowed to slits by the sun's glare, were upon her, even as his keen mind was at work assessing her qualities and capabilities.

The girl was attractive, he mused, for all her pert waywardness. Doubtless she had been spoiled and overindulged by her ailing mother and her doting nurse. Certainly she had been let run wild far too long. As was customary for the children of gentlefolk, she should have been sent from home

51

years ago to learn manners and decorum in one or another of the great manor houses of the gentry. He himself had been taken from his mother at the tender age of five and sent to the household of John of Gaunt for his training, and it had done him a world of good, he considered. Despite the pummeling and the hard knocks he had received at the hands of the older boys in the household and the harsh lessons of a stern taskmaster, the experience had opened up opportunities for him that would otherwise not have been available to a base-born son, and he had made the most of them.

But Lady Catherine, coddled and cosseted by her mother and old nurse, had had no need to develop self-discipline and self-restraint, no opportunities to develop poise and social skills and savoir-faire. The girl was as green as the flourishing plants that grew in her garden and as skittish as a green-broke filly. But she was quick-witted and capable of learning; she came of good stock, and there was good stuff in her. If he was any judge, she would make an excellent companion and playfellow for Richard's little queen, for Isabella was mature beyond her years and Catherine young for her age. The two of them, he shrewdly suspected, would get on famously together. Moreover, Catherine would undoubtedly bring a breath of fresh air to the stuffy confines of the court. And in time to come, when experience and exposure to a wider, more sophisticated world had worn off her rough edges, tamed her impetuous tongue, and smoothed her awkward coltishness into elegant grace, she would, he could foresee, become a stunning woman, a woman any man would be proud to claim as his own.

Any man, that is, who did not bear on his escutcheon the mark of bastardy, as he did. Such women, Crispin harshly reminded himself, were not for him and could never be.

Seeing Crispin, as she supposed, dozing in the sunshine, Catherine put down her watering pot and tried to slip quietly away without disturbing his slumber. But the man forestalled her. His slitted eyes instantly popping open, he rose and lazily unfolded and stretched his long limbs like a great tawny tiger awakened from his nap.

"Oh, I . . . I thought you were asleep!" Catherine stammered, startled by this manifestation.

"Ah, but as you can see, I was not," he said pleasantly. "I was merely resting my eyes, shielding them from the glare of the setting sun," he explained glibly. "If you have done with your labors, we should go in, my lady." He offered Catherine his arm. "It grows late and must be near to dinnertime. We should not keep your lady mother waiting," he reminded her.

"No . . . no, of course we should not." And Catherine meekly took his proffered arm with a sigh of resignation. "By all means, let us go in to dinner, sir knight."

"Check!"

Catherine frowned over the exquisite set of carved ivory chess pieces her mother had brought from France as a bride. Although she considered herself a tolerably proficient chess player, Sir Crispin was a skillful opponent who put her on her mettle. Already, he had beaten her two games out of three.

And to her utter humiliation, she suspected he had let her win the third.

But chess was a pleasant pastime, a way of whiling away an evening in a pleasurable fashion, and Catherine thanked her lucky stars for the game. Her ailing mother, exhausted by the day's unwonted activity, had excused herself early in the evening and, with a murmured apology, had betaken herself to bed, leaving Catherine to entertain Sir Crispin. Weary herself and ill at ease with the man, Catherine, who was unused to entertaining company on her own, had been at her wit's end. Conversation had lagged until Sir Crispin, taking pity on her gaucherie, had spotted the game board set up in an alcove of the chimney corner and suggested a match. It was an alternative to conversation that Catherine had seized upon with alacrity.

She gave her full attention to the pieces on the board, weighing her options with more care than usual, for she was bent on distinguishing herself in some way and was determined to give the man as good a game as she was capable of playing, if not a beating! If she could not beat him fairly, at least he would not find her an easy opponent!

There were three options open to her to get her king out of check. Her most obvious response was to move her besieged king out of the line of attack. But she had already learned to her cost that the obvious move was seldom the correct gambit to use with Sir Crispin, who invariably had a well-developed strategy worked out to counteract the obvious ploy.

Interposition was another tactic open to her, moving one of her pieces between the attacking force and that of her threatened king. Briefly, she considered just such a move. Her brow creased in thought as her hand hovered irresolute over a pawn.

"Is that your move?" the man asked, in a tone that warned her it was not the best move she could make.

"N-no." Catherine snatched her hand away from the pawn, folding her fingers together under her chin while she mused over her options. Crispin sat back in his chair, watching the mobile play of expressions on her heart-shaped face as she pondered this move or that, and taking delight in the gleam of her fiery hair as it caught the candlelight's glimmer.

"*This* is my move!" she announced with glee, reaching out to capture his attacking rook, which was vulnerable to her knight.

"I didn't think you'd see that move," he remarked with seeming chagrin, as he paused to rethink his strategy. He was a seasoned chessplayer who was adept at spotting an opponent's weaknesses and turning them to his own advantage, and it had not taken him long to learn that Catherine was often over-hasty in her moves and prone to overlook the potential of her knights, whose picturesque L-shaped moves she sometimes ignored.

He put her remaining knight (she had already lost the other) on the run with his diagonally moving bishops, and the game continued.

Catherine's easy capture of Crispin's rook made her overconfident, and she promptly went on the attack with her queen, the most powerful piece on the board, capturing several of his pieces and endeavoring to put his king in check. But forgetful of those treacherous L-shaped moves, she finally lost her queen to his knight. "Garde la Dame," he had warned her, but she had not seen the danger until it was too late.

"You must beware the knight, lady, at all times," he remarked.

"I will remember that in future," Catherine vowed, her eyes flashing green fire, as they so often did when her temper was roused.

Undaunted, she attempted to move one of her far-advanced pawns up the ranks to promote it to queenship status, to "queen the pawn" as the tactic was called. But Crispin called his attacking bishops into play, diverting her, and then attacked her black king with his own white queen, putting her once more in check.

Scowling, Catherine tried to think of a ploy that would threaten his queen, but the powerful piece was protected by Crispin's bishop. This time, there was no possibility of interposition either, nor could she move her king to a less vulnerable position where he would not be threatened by Crispin's queen in combination with one of the man's far advanced pawns.

"Checkmate, I believe," announced Crispin quietly.

Ruefully, Catherine stretched forth a hand and toppled her king, conceding defeat. "You have bested me again, sir knight," she admitted. "Shall we have another game?" She hoped he would decline her offer, for she was smarting over her third defeat of the evening. Despite her best efforts, not only had she not given him a sound beating, she had been soundly beaten herself! Her pride was badly bruised, but mindful of her mother's lessons in losing gracefully, she exerted self-control to conceal her vexation and fixed a pleasant smile to her face.

"I think not." Crispin leaned back in his chair and laced his fingers behind his head, surveying her flushed face thoughtfully.

"Will you have more wine?"

At his affirming nod, she carefully lifted her mother's prized Venetian decanter and poured a measure of the ruby wine into his goblet.

"Will you not join me?" he said.

But Catherine shook her head, remembering all too well the throbbing in her temples from too much wine the night before. Desultorily, she gathered the chess pieces and began setting them up on the board in readiness for another game.

"The queen belongs on a square of her own color," Sir Crispin remarked idly.

"I do know that much at least!" Catherine flared. Her face flaming with a temper that was already high, she hastily jumbled the chessmen about so that each piece sat on his own square.

"I meant no offense, lady," said Sir Crispin mildly. "You take offense too easily. And you are too prone to go on the attack without sufficient provocation." He smiled to take the sting out of his words. "In life, as in a game of chess, it is well to look to your defenses before plunging into the fray."

"Indeed," said Catherine frostily. "And is it now your intention to give me lessons in chessplaying, sir knight?" She added wildly, "Since, by your reckoning, I am such a poor player."

"I never said such a thing," Sir Crispin protested. "Though I will be glad to give you lessons, if you wish me to do so." He added carelessly, "In truth, you play well enough. Sufficiently well to amuse the little queen, which is all that will be required of you."

Catherine gnashed her teeth. So she played well enough to entertain a seven-year-old child, did she? How gallant of him to reassure her on that score at least!

"I appreciate your generous offer to tutor me, Sir Crispin." Catherine's shaky voice dripped sarcasm. "But since you consider my mediocre skill sufficient to amuse the little queen, it should suffice! You need not trouble yourself further." Catherine scraped back her chair and struggled to her feet, nearly toppling table and chessboard in her haste. "And now, sir, I bid you good night." Blinking back tears of humiliation, she blundered from the room, leaving Sir Crispin, the victor of their verbal skirmish as well as of the chess match, in clear possession of the field.

Chapter Four

That first day set the pattern for the days that were to follow. Catherine patiently endured the fittings for new or refurbished gowns and did her share of plain sewing that was entrusted to her. She kept her distance from Sir Crispin whenever she could, and endeavored to treat him with cool courtesy when she was thrown together with him, as was too often the case for her comfort. She supposed it was a timely lesson in dissimulating her feelings that would stand her in good stead at court—to feign the appearance of cordiality towards a man she disliked under the sharp eyes of her mother, who would tolerate no discourtesy towards a guest in her house, and who, in any case, was rapidly developing a fondness for the young man.

Catherine herself could not imagine why. The man was a pompous bullying braggart, she told herself, whose overweening arrogance knew no bounds, and more to the point, he was a long-nosed meddler! For to Catherine's mortification, Sir Crispin continued his inspection tours of the estate, ostensibly to be able to offer her mother sound advice on managing the property efficiently and increasing its productivity.

Catherine sniffed. By bullying the peasants, no doubt. Why, just this afternoon he'd ridden down to the village, rent roll in hand, to look into payments long in arrears.

To be sure, he was not undertaking this venture on his own initiative, as Catherine had to admit to herself, albeit grudgingly. At her mother's specific request, he was acting as her deputy. Nor was he holding a formal manor court. He was merely making an informal inquiry of those whose rents were perpetually delinquent.

Catherine had looked after him resentfully as he set forth on his errand. He had no business meddling in the affairs of the estate.

Sir Crispin, quite properly, had invited her to accompany him, but she had curtly refused. She was not going to lend her countenance to his interference. Or so she'd told herself.

But she was having second thoughts. As young lady of the manor, she *should* be present, if only to protect her peasants from his high-handed methods. Why, without her intervention, Sir High-and-Mighty would be free to browbeat and bully those who were powerless to protect themselves after laboring long and hard all day in the fields. Catherine sighed. Reluctant as she was to confront Sir Crispin again, she knew she should go down to the village herself to make sure that justice was tempered with mercy.

In actual fact, very little in the way of browbeating was going on when she arrived. Sir Crispin, seated on an oak settle in front of the village inn, was dandling Molly Brewster's twins on his knees and listening, with a glazed expression, to a harrowing account of their birth, to which Molly subjected everyone who could take the time to listen. "Big as a house I was last year at this time, sir," she said cheerfully. "Not able to get about properly for months and months. And there I was, brought to bed of the twins just at brewing time. All the village has been telling Ned and me that we should have managed it better!" She giggled.

"Yes . . . yes, I understand about last year," said Sir Crispin testily. "But what about the year before? You are two hogsheads of ale in arrears."

"The year before . . ." Plump Molly gazed off into space for inspiration. "Oh, that was was the year the ale was so thin and sour it wasn't fit to be sent to the manor, sir. Highborn folk could not have drunk it with enjoyment. It was the first year I'd had the brewing to do all on my own, for Ned's old mother died that spring and 'twas she who taught me all I know." One of the twins started to squall, and Molly snatched the infant up, crooning to it wordlessly. The baby had left a damp spot on Sir Crispin's tunic, and he looked down at it ruefully as Catherine stifled a giggle of amusement.

"Here's the lady of the manor now." Molly beamed and bobbed a curtsy. "Wouldn't you like to hold your namesake, my lady?" She transferred the baby to Catherine's arms. "Don't you think she has grown since last you saw her? And she has two new teeth," Molly announced proudly.

"So I see." Catherine took the damp, drooling infant from its mother a bit gingerly and sat down beside Sir Crispin. "Little Christopher is teething on the hem of your tunic," she told him with a grin.

Sir Crispin, who had glanced up with a welcoming smile when she made her appearance, and was now musing over what an attractive picture she made with the baby in her arms, looked down at his lap in dismay. "So he is." Gently disengaging the hem of his tunic from the baby's chubby fist, he hastily transferred the little boy to Catherine's arms. "I'm pleased that you changed your mind and decided to join us, my lady."

"I'm sure you are." Catherine juggled both twins with practiced ease, rubbing their reddened gums with a forefinger as she watched Sir Crispin assume a stern expression. "Now, about this year's brewing, Molly . . ."

"Oh, never fear, sir. We'll send two fine hogsheads of ale up to the manor this year," the woman promised quickly. "It's already arranged that my sister-in-law is to come at brewing time to help me with the brewing and the babies."

"See that you do." Sir Crispin dismissed her with a nod. Glad to be let off so easily, pretty Molly relieved Catherine of the fussy babies. Disappearing into the tavern with them, she reappeared moments later with brimming mugs of ale to refresh the lord and lady.

The next miscreant was Alf Fenton, a man Catherine had never liked. Alf had a sly ferret face and was widely known as a miserly man who starved his wife and children, sending them to the manor kitchen to beg scraps and leftovers from the cook. If Sir Crispin succeeded in extracting a groat from him, she would be much surprised, Catherine thought to herself.

She was. Sir Crispin accepted none of the man's whined excuses, but promptly threatened to distrain upon him, seizing his goods and chattels until such time as he paid what was owed. The perpetually delinquent Alf had ignored the threat of distraint many times in the past, but this time, Sir Crispin's firmly set jaw and glinting eyes told him he had met his match. Without further ado, the man dug deep in a money pouch belted closely around his waist and, extracting the required coins, rubbed them caressingly between his fingers before handing them over.

Sir Crispin dealt as summarily with two or three similar cases, in none of which Catherine was disposed to intervene, for she knew that each man was able to pay his overdue rents without any hardship. But when Tom Fowler stepped up to the bench stating that he could not pay his rents until after harvest, and moreover that his daughter wished to wed and that he could not afford to pay merchet on her, Catherine felt compelled to whisper a word in Crispin's ear. "Old Tom has had bad luck this year. He lost almost a whole flock of sheep to a murrain last fall, and his ailing wife is confined to her bed and is no help to him. I recommend that the merchet be ruduced or excused and the rents remitted until after harvest, at least."

"The rents can be remitted, but the daughter should postpone her wedding and stay at home to help out until her father is able to fulfill his obligations," Sir Crispin decreed.

"Postpone it she can not," Catherine hissed. "She is with child. Her sweetheart is willing to wed her now, but he is a poor lad with no family to help him pay merchet. If it is not reduced or eliminated, Sally will be disgraced and her child will be born a bastard." Catherine hoped that this argument would weigh heavily with Sir Crispin, who himself bore the stigma of bastardy.

It did. Without a quibble, Sir Crispin promptly agreed that the merchet should be eliminated altogether.

Catherine had no such leverage to employ in the case of Wily Willie Watson, however, and she regretted that because Wily Willie was one of her favorite people. Whether he had earned his nickname because he was ever ready with a plausible excuse to get out of working in the fields or because, as was widely rumored, he was a skillful poacher who had never been caught, she never knew. But she was well aware that Wily Willie knew the countryside roundabout and the wildlife in it like the back of his hand. When she was a child, he had taught her how to snare coneys and rabbits and how to tickle a trout, and she had a real fondness for the gentle giant who flashed her a crooked grin as he shambled up to the bench where they were sitting. "Good afternoon, Cath-er . . . milady," he boomed in a deep voice.

"Good afternoon, Wil-er, Willie." Catherine frowned at him, trying to send him a wordless warning to guard his tongue in the presence of Sir Crispin.

"It says here you owe an Easter tribute of a basket of eggs." Sir Crispin glanced up from the rent roll.

"Yes, sir, that I do. But you can't have eggs if the hens don't lay 'em, now can you, sir?" said Willie reasonably. "Molting, they are. The hens, I mean. Hens don't lay when they're molting," he explained cheerfully. "Though I don't suppose a fine gentleman such as yourself, sir, would know much about hens." He grinned crookedly at Catherine. "Her ladyship does, though, don't you, milady. You know all about rabbits and trout and hens and . . ."

"Yes, yes, Willie. But that's enough said," she warned.

Sir Crispin frowned. "I don't like the man's attitude," he said in an undertone. "He is too familiar."

"Oh, Willie's all right," Catherine mumbled uncomfortably. "We were children together," she mumbled by way of excuse. And when Sir Crispin still looked unconvinced, she leaned close to him and whispered, "I . . . I think Willie is a . . . a little simple. You cannot hold him to account." Which was far from the case, for anyone less simple than Willie she had never known.

But Crispin's brow cleared. "Oh, I see." He nodded dismissively at the man. "Very well, Willie, You may bring the eggs up to the manor when you have them. Now you may go."

"Oh, I will, sir. I'll bring 'em as soon as the hens are laying again." The hulking giant pulled a flaxen forelock and then, outrageously, gave Catherine a wink.

Watching the man shamble away, Crispin frowned. He had already taken notice that the peasants seemed to hold Catherine in no awe, seeming almost to regard her as one of themselves, while she, in her turn, had no proper regard for her own station in life, no consideration of the dignity and reserve she should maintain among those who were not her equals in birth or breeding. "I marvel to see you on such friendly terms with the peasants, lady. It has not been so many years since the Peasants' Revolt, you know, though I suppose you are too young to remember it well," he remarked.

"We were too far away from the center of the revolt to have experienced it," said Catherine cautiously. "Though I remember a time of turmoil vaguely and have heard it discussed."

"You can know nothing of what it was like unless you were there," said Crispin feelingly. "I was in London at the time, serving as page in John of Gaunt's great Savoy Palace."

"The Savoy was burned during the revolt, was it not?"

"Indeed it was." Sir Crispin's face hardened. "Looted and burned to the ground by just such men as you see here." He gestured to the departing figure of Wily Willie. "Hulking peasants armed with staves and billhooks, scythes and sickles. They went first to the Fleet Prison, released all the prisoners, and then went to the Temple, setting it afire. The poor fools, in their ignorance, must have thought that if they destroyed the legal rolls that recorded their villenage, they would be automatically freed of bondage." He sighed. "Then they came down the Strand to the Savoy Palace." The man's eyes darkened with the pain of remembrance. "My Lord Duke was in Scotland on the king's business, but my Lady Katherine Swynford and her children were in residence at the Savoy, and I was in attendance on them."

"How did you make your escape?" Catherine couldn't stand the suspense. She had to hear the end of the story first.

"The household was permitted to leave," Crispin admitted. "But before we left, we saw with our own eyes the mob of peasants stripping the Great Hall of its priceless treasures and precious works of art. They'd already broken into the wine cellars, broaching vats of vintage wines, and as they wreaked their havoc, they gulped and sloshed wine about, pouring rare vintages over each other's heads and down each other's throats for sport, filling their bellies to capacity, and then emptying bellies and bladders on priceless parquet floors and precious tapestries like . . . like animals!"

"It must have been heady stuff to men accustomed to drinking only sour ale and small beer," ventured Catherine.

"I suppose so. Still, that does not exculpate them." He frowned. "When they moved on, into Duke John's Avalon Chamber, a treasure trove of invaluable artifacts, we saw them senselessly hack to pieces the room's pièce de résistance, a great marble mantelpiece that was two years in the carving. Not content with destroying such a work of art, they ground priceless jewels into powder, chopped up inlaid furniture, and carved ivory prie-dieux into bits. There was nothing we could do to prevent it. We were helpless. I remember being thankful that in their frenzy they did not hack *us* into pieces too!" Crispin exclaimed.

Tentatively, Catherine reached out and put a comforting hand on his arm, though she sensed he was unaware of the soothing gesture, so deeply had he traveled back into the troubled past. Hearing in the man's tortured exclamation an echo of the powerless and frightened young boy he had once been, she found herself beginning to like him a little better, and she began to understand the forces that had molded him into a hard and sometimes arrogant man.

As if to confirm her thoughts, he said hoarsely, "On that day, I swore never again would I let myself be powerless and helpless in the face of threats or danger, that I would find some way to control the situation before it could put me or mine in jeopardy."

"Yes . . . yes . . ." Catherine murmured soothingly. "What happened next?" For now that he was caught up in the remembrance, she thought it best that he purge himself of the bitter recollection if he could.

"Fire!" said Crispin laconically. "Wat Tyler himself, one of the ringleaders of the revolt, threw the first torch, setting the ruby velvet bed hangings in the Avalon Chamber alight. Some of the others ran for more torches, all the while chanting that hedge-priest John Ball's accursed couplet, 'When Adam delved and Eve span, who then was the gentleman?' "

Crispin paused in his recital to wet his lips with a sip of ale. "Bonfires blazed everywhere," he continued hoarsely. "The ignorant fools dragged out coffers of gold and silver and priceless pieces of art and piled them on the fires in heaps. Gold and silver plate was melted down, though some among the mob hacked pieces into small bits to carry them away as souvenirs of the day. Whatever could not burn readily or be carried away, they ground to powder on the great paving stones of the courtyard.

"By then, flames were licking everywhere, in the Monmouth Wing and in the Beaufort Tower, in Duke John's Privy Suite and in the Outer Ward. I remember the licking flames and the thick choking black smoke. . . ."

"And then?" Catherine prompted.

"When the mob tired of venting vengeance and spite on the duke's treasures, they exploded barrels of gunpowder in the wreckage. By nightfall, nothing was left of the once-magnificent Savoy Palace but a pile of rubble." Crispin sighed. "Even some of their own men who had drunk themselves into a stupor in the cellars were forgotten by the mob. When their cries were heard at last, it was too late for them to be rescued from the inferno. They were burned alive."

Catherine made a little wordless sound expressive of horror and pity.

"Such destruction was futile," Crispin brooded. "Mindless . . . useless . . . senseless . . ."

All of that and more, thought Catherine, but perhaps also understandable, given the harshness and poverty of peasant life. The sight of all those priceless treasures must have driven to frenzy men who lived in dark little dwellings, labored in poverty for bare subsistence, and went clothed in rags with empty bellies all their lives. But she knew better than to voice such thoughts to Sir Crispin.

Seeking to divert him from his brooding, she asked brightly, "Did not the king distinguish himself during the revolt in some way?"

"By God, he did indeed!" exclaimed the man. "Though he was but a lad of fourteen years, it was perhaps Richard's finest hour!"

"Tell me about it," Catherine coaxed.

The man did not need overmuch persuasion. Tossing off the last of his ale, he embarked on the tale enthusiastically.

"The final stage of the Peasants' Revolt was to march on the Tower of London where the king and his courtiers had taken refuge, and camp round about it, virtually putting the Tower under siege.

"Richard rode out from the Tower early the next morning and met with the insurgents at Mile End. He was a resplendent figure, clothed in a tabard of blue and silver and mounted on a white stallion, the better to be seen by the multitudes. He conferred with Wat Tyler and Jack Straw, another of the ringleaders, and strove to conciliate them. They were appeased by his promises, and clerks were summoned to take down the terms of the agreements, for a copy was to be provided for each district represented by the various factions among the rebels," Crispin explained.

"But while Richard was conferring with the ringleaders, the rank and file swarmed under the portcullis of the Tower and broke into the royal apartments, frightening the king's widowed mother. They seized two royal councilors, Sir Robert Hales, the treasurer, and Simon Sudbury, the Archbishop of Canterbury, dragging him from his very altar."

"Sacrilege!" gasped Catherine.

"Worse was to come," said Crispin grimly. "Both the treasurer and the Archbishop were beheaded on Tower Hill. Meanwhile, one of the city gates was opened by treachery, and the mob swarmed through it, roaming the streets, looting and pillaging, putting buildings to the torch and beating and killing all who opposed them. They were drunk on power and blood, as well as on wine and ale. All was anarchy and London cringed under a reign of terror.

"The next day, the king agreed to meet with the rebel leaders again, this time at Smithfield, in an attempt to appease the frenzy of the mobs and lure them out of the city."

"It must have taken uncommon courage for the boy king to confront the rebels, not once, but twice!" Catherine marveled.

"Courage is a quality Richard possesses in abundance," Crispin agreed. "He rode out boldly, demanding to know why the peasants had not returned to their homes, in view of the concessions he had made to them the day before. Wat Tyler, the ringleader of the revolt, hemmed and hawed, and finally ended by demanding more sweeping concessions and reforms, even to the abolition of rank and privilege among men, save the king alone."

"Did he so?" Catherine gasped at the outrageous nature of the claim which struck at the very foundations of the social structure. "But surely he must have known he was asking for the impossible."

Crispin shrugged. "Who knows what was in his

mind? By that time, he must have been crazed on power, for the multitudes had been proclaiming him 'King of London,' as indeed, for three days, to all practical purposes, he was." Crispin added shrewdly, "More than likely it was a way of buying time, for to disband his followers and go quietly home would have meant surrendering the upper hand. He needed a pretext for the peasants to remain under arms and keep control of the city."

"What happened then?" Catherine asked breathlessly.

"Sir William Walworth, the Lord Mayor of London, who was a member of the king's entourage, was so outraged by Wat Tyler's insolence that he unsheathed his sword, swung it, and with one mighty blow, severed Tyler's head from his shoulders.

"All might have been lost, and the king's entourage swallowed up by a surging mob of enraged peasants, had not Richard kept his head and saved the day," Crispin said, continuing his story. "The peasants swarmed across the field, yelling and shouting, waving their staves and sickles, those of them armed with bows and arrows fitting them into the notches as they ran. The king's party, stunned and appalled by the unexpected turn of events, faced instant annihilation. But Richard rose to the occasion superbly. Spurring his white stallion into a gallop, he rode out across the fields alone to face the angry mob, calling out, 'Seek you a leader? *I* am your captain and your king. Follow me!'"

"And they did?" said Catherine softly.

"And they did. They might well have pulled him

down from his horse and torn him limb from limb, but they did not. He pointed to the fields north of the city and said, 'Follow me!' and they followed." Crispin paused, then said, "By King Richard's courage and coolness in such a crisis, he recovered his heritage and the realm of England."

Catherine's eyes glowed. "Such panache! Such shining courage!" She felt stirred to the depths of her soul. "He is a king to die for, is he not?" she exclaimed enthusiastically.

Crispin stirred in his seat. "Perhaps," he said evasively. "But boys grow up, and life has a way of shaping and molding each of us in ways we do not expect or wish. Let us just say that Richard has not fulfilled his early promise." Seeing her shining eyes and exalted expression, Crispin forbore to say more for he did not want to disillusion her. It was fortunate, he reflected, that given her feeling for her own peasants, she did not think to ask the fate of the peasants who had followed after Richard so blindly out into the fields beyond the city limits. For a swift and bloody retribution had befallen many of the rebels, infinitely more terrible than even the bloodiest days of the revolt. Following the "Bloody Assizes" of Judge Tressilian, the trees of England had begun to blossom with a grim fruit, the bodies of hanged rebels dangling from their branches. Appalled as Crispin had been by the revolt, the days of savage repression that followed it stuck in his craw.

But Catherine knew nothing of those days, and it was just as well that she remain in ignorance, he decided.

"What a wonderful story with which to regale

the little queen," she said happily, still musing over the role Richard had played in subduing the rebels. "For sure, King Richard will win her heart when she has heard it. I must be sure to tell it her, just as you have told it to me."

"I expect he will win her heart, for he has much charm of manner, and it is a stirring tale," Crispin said noncommitally. "Come, let us finish our business here," he added. "The hour grows late."

He picked up the rent roll and consulted it briefly before calling out a name at random, and the line of delinquent peasants who had been waiting patiently (for was it not a peasant's lot in life to wait in patience on their betters?) began to move again.

Catherine had hoped that Sir Crispin would weary of the chore long before he reached Ralph Wright, for his was a particularly thorny case, and the man himself was of a sullen and truculent disposition, which she foresaw would be bound to aggravate Sir Crispin. To be sure, poor Ralph had reason a plenty for his disaffection, Catherine reflected. Ralph was a hardworking man who strove constantly to better himself, but the lands he tilled were perhaps the poorest on the manor, as was his tumbledown hut which he shared with an ailing wife, five children (all of them girls), and a sharp-tongued mother-in-law. His old father had died two years ago, and he still owed heriot duties, which could take the form of the deceased tenant's best single beast or a money payment. But Ralph had no coins to spare, and he was using his deceased father's ox to clear a nearby field that had grown up to brush and brambles, in hopes of ameliorating his condition. When he began the project, he had had the help of his only son. But the boy had run off from the manor, for he had his father's itch to better himself, and since he had been gone more than the required year and a day to win his freedom, Catherine doubted that any of them would see him again. If Sir Crispin, who was ignorant of the circumstances, dunned Ralph to pay the boy's chevage fine as well as heriot dues, Catherine did not know what the poor man would do.

Before Ralph's name was called, she tried to explain the circumstances. "This is a special case," she told Crispin urgently.

"All of them are special cases according to you, my lady."

"That's not fair," Catherine protested. "I did not intervene in the case of Alf Fenton or half-a-dozen others who are well able to pay what is owed."

The man's brows drew together in a frown of displeasure. "Are you now accusing me of being unfair?" he asked haughtily.

"No . . . no . . . of course not," she responded quickly. "I only meant . . ." It was obvious that Sir Crispin was fast losing patience, and Catherine wisely subsided. "Here is Ralph Wright now," she said weakly. "You must determine his case as you think right and proper." So pleasant did she find the atmosphere of accord and amity that had developed between herself and Sir Crispin during the course of the afternoon that she was loathe to disrupt its harmony by acting as advocate for a particularly surly peasant.

Unfortunately, Ralph Wright was ill equipped to be his own best advocate. The victor of many a village wrestling match, he was abnormally broad-framed and muscular from years of toiling in the fields, his massive sinews rippling and bulging through his ragged jerkin. His face, through no fault of his own, was equally grotesque. He had lost several front teeth so that the one remaining gave the appearance of a fang, and the thick dark brows that were knotted over his broken nose gave him a perpetual scowl.

Nor was his manner calculated to appease authority. He approached the bench with his head held high, looking lord and lady squarely in the eye, and Catherine knew that he would neither bend the knee nor grovel and beg. She feared for him and his, should he arouse the wrath of Sir Crispin, for though he walked with the proud stride of a free man, Ralph was as much in bondage as any of the other serfs.

His wispy little wife trailed after him at a respectful distance, and Catherine exchanged a look of commiseration with her as she put her flock of scrawny little girls in the charge of the eldest and hurried after her husband.

Sir Crispin reeled off the figures on the rent roll and then summed up the case. "Ralph Wright, you are in arrears on your rent and you owe heriot duties, as well as chevage on your runaway son. What do you have to say for yourself, man?"

Bold dark eyes freely met Sir Crispin's eyes of piercing blue. "My land is the poorest on the manor, as my lady can tell you." He glanced at Catherine, who nodded in confirmation. "I've worked from dawn to dusk to bring a new field under cultivation, and it's nearly ready for the plow. When it's producing crops, I'll be able to pay my rents, but not if my father's best ox goes to pay his heriot duties." The argument was reasonable enough, and Sir Crispin nodded, though he disliked the surly peasant's aggressive tone and manner and felt challenged by the bold look in his eye. "But the payment of chevage is a custom that's been allowed to lapse on this manor, and I won't be held accountable for my son's actions," Ralph said daringly, in a tone of bold defiance.

Sir Crispin was thunderstruck. "Do you mean to say you refuse to pay chevage at all and will pay your other dues only at your own convenience?"

"That's right," the man said doggedly, meeting Sir Crispin's icy glare straight on.

"Ralph . . . Ralph . . ." His timid little wife plucked at the man's jerkin. "Please don't antagonize his lordship," she whispered.

Sir Crispin's face was an icy mask of sternly repressed anger. "And if I distrain upon you, seize your property for the chevage fee . . ."

The peasant thrust his beetle-browed face aggressively close to Sir Crispin's. "My boy is gone and will not be back, nor would I have him back in villenage," he snarled, inadvertently spraying fine droplets of spit into the air. "Were I young again, without a wife and family dependent on me, I'd be off myself." His wife timidly laid a restraining hand on his arm, but he shook it off roughly. "Despite my years of toil on this manor, I've nothing to show for it and naught in my poor hut of any value. Distrain," he blustered, "and . . . and be damned to you!"

A stunned silence followed the man's outburst. Catherine was appalled. This was much worse than anything she had envisioned. Sir Crispin would be well within his rights to set Ralph in the stocks for such effrontery, to order him whipped or even branded. She held her breath, waiting for the storm to break, hardly daring to peep at Sir Crispin's steely face, in which anger vied with amazement.

"Oh, sir . . . sir!" Ralph's wife, so colorless a woman that Catherine could never remember her name, flung herself down before Sir Crispin. "Please, sir, don't punish my man too severely. He's been out of his mind with grief and sorrow ever since our boy left home. He don't know what he's saying, sir!"

"I'll give him something to be sorry about!" growled Sir Crispin, wiping dewy droplets off his face. "A touch of the lash, mayhap, that would serve to bring him back to his senses." He transferred his icy glare to Ralph, who stared back at him truculently, standing his ground with an air of bravado. "I could have your tongue cut out for your insolence, churl!"

Ralph's wife uttered a long heartrending wail. She dragged herself to Catherine and clasped her about the knees. "Please intercede for us," she begged. "Please, my lady . . . !"

Catherine bit her lip. Her heart was touched, but she hesitated to intervene for fear of making a bad matter worse.

The poor, work-worn woman jumped to her feet and gathered her children round her. Her wide-eyed little girls clutched her with grubby fists, the oldest balancing the youngest on on her skinny hip. "If my man is maimed or disabled by too harsh a punishment, I don't know what will become of us. It is these little ones who will suffer the most," their mother averred. "We're hard put to it to clothe and feed them as it is, let alone pay overdue rents and fines. Why, we've none of us eaten aught but watery cabbage soup for weeks, and are likely to have nothing better till harvest time."

"Why have you not come up to the manor kitchen to ask for help?" asked Catherine, who had not known their plight was so desperate. "Many do."

"Ralph won't have it, that's why. He is too proud a man to humble himself. He'd rather go hungry and see his wife and children do likewise," the woman responded, not without bitterness.

"Is this true?" Sir Crispin gruffly demanded of Ralph, who nodded shamefaced.

"Our situation is desperate, sir." Ralph admitted despondently. "My plot of land is worn out. It won't grow aught but a few cabbages and onions. I'd hoped to get the new field under the plow long before this." The man's face crumpled, beginning to work with the stress of his emotion. "But when my boy took off, I'd no one to help. My boy," he added brokenly, "that I will never see again."

"Oh, sir, what are you going to do to Ralph?" asked his wife timidly. "He is a good man, though a hard and stubborn one."

Sir Crispin meditated for a few moments before answering. "Lady Catherine will take you and the children up to the manor kitchen to see you fed," he decreed. "You should have applied for help long before this—before things got to such a pass," he said to Ralph in a severe tone. "And when I have done with you, you will yourself go and beg a crust of bread from the manor cook, as you will continue to do each day until the harvests are in. To do so will humble the haughty pride so unseemly in one of your station."

He was a fine one to talk of haughty pride, thought Catherine with an inward sniff, though she was glad Ralph was to be let off so lightly.

"I wish to see for myself this field upon which you have expended so much effort and assess its productive capacity," he continued. "If it is not worth the effort you expended on it, it may be that we can find other work for you—a means by which you can support your family and pay your debts, subject to the approval of the lady of the manor, of course."

He glanced briefly at Catherine. "And now, my lady, if you will excuse us . . . I will see you back at the manor presently." Sir Crispin bowed politely to her and strode away, followed by a chastened Ralph.

Looking after him, Catherine decided that she liked and understood him very much better than she had hitherto. Arrogant himself, a very tower of arrogance against anyone, man or woman, who set himself up in opposition to him, or who contested his strong will, he yet could be moved by a genuine show of weakness or need. Nor was he immune to tender persuasion, if it were presented in the right way. All in all, he was surprisingly tender-hearted, much more so than Catherine had supposed. It might be, she mused, that she had misjudged him all along, and in so doing had created unnecessary grief for herself. It was a thought she pondered much on as she shepherded the peasant woman and her children back to the manor kitchen, mulling it over in her mind. It also occurred to her that in a kinder and gentler world, he might have been a very much kinder and gentler man.

They did not meet again until the evening meal, at which Catherine's mother was gratified to notice that her difficult daughter and Sir Crispin appeared to be on much more amicable terms than formerly. She was pleased by this new and welcome state of affairs, for she had been troubled by the fact that each one seemed to strike sparks off the other, and had been loathe to entrust her daughter to the keeping of a man for whom (for whatever freakish and distempered a reason) she appeared to have a strong aversion. That Catherine appeared to be well on the way to overcoming her antipathy was particularly gratifying just now, for preparations for their departure were well advanced and there was little more the mother could do for the daughter to see her well provided for.

It was also gratifying, she reflected, that Sir Crispin had succeeded in collecting some of the long-overdue rents so that she might send the child to court with a few pennies in her slender purse. The manor was largely self-sufficient, but cash money was hard to come by. It had once been the duty of her late husband's bailiff to collect the rents, but when he too died a few years back, the Frenchwoman, feeling ill equipped to cope with sturdy English peasants, had turned the task over to her daughter, who was, she feared, singularly prone to lend a sympathetic ear to hard-luck stories. She was pleased that Sir Crispin, an astute and capable man not easily deceived, had taken an interest in their affairs. As well as collecting overdue rents, he

81

had set up an easy payment schedule for delinquent peasants so that she could count on a small but steady income trickling in for the future, and for that she was grateful.

She tried to express her gratitude to Sir Crispin over dinner, but he brushed aside her thanks. "Think nothing of it, madame," he assured her. "I am happy to do what little is in my power to assist you." He frowned thoughtfully. "It appears to me, madame, that you need a man about the place upon whom you can rely to oversee the hay-making, the harvest, the collecting of rents, and so forth."

"That is so," Catherine's mother admitted.

"I will look around for a new bailiff for you if you wish, but in the interim, I recommend that you promote Ralph Wright to a position of responsibility. He has done wonders with the new field and is a capable, hardworking man, anxious to improve his lot in life."

Catherine pricked up her ears and shot Sir Crispin a look in which surprise was mingled with gratitude.

Her mother thought it over carefully. "The man is an ill-favored brute," she said uneasily. "And I have heard he is a troublemaker as well."

"In faith, madame, the man cannot be blamed for his looks!" Sir Crispin exclaimed with a touch of humor. "As for being a troublemaker, I suggest to you that the more content a man is, the less trouble he is likely to make."

"That is so," Catherine's mother agreed.

"If you can provide him with a small pittance for his labor, and perhaps a dwelling more suitable to his new status than the hovel he and his family presently occupy, you will earn his loyalty and his trust," Sir Crispin predicted confidently.

"Very well, Sir Crispin. I am agreeable to your recommendation," she said, though a bit dubiously. "Will you notify the fellow of his good fortune and find him better accommodation?"

"I will indeed, madame, and I thank you."

Catherine's mother shook her head. "It is I who should be thanking you, Sir Crispin, for all you have done for us."

But it was Catherine's bright face, glowing with satisfaction, that gave him all the thanks he needed; though he disclaimed his own magnanimity when, after her mother had retired for the night, she taxed him with it.

"If the peasants are content, they are of more value to your lady mother and will serve her with a better will," he pointed out. "Discontent at best breeds surliness and ill will; at worst, rebellion and revolt. So you see, lady, my seeming magnanimity towards poor Ralph is but mere good sense."

Catherine shook her head. "Call it what you will. Nevertheless, it was a generous and kindly act towards one who, though of humble birth, dared offer you such an affront, and who is all undeserving of your favor." A warm, soft light in her eyes, she gazed at him with awed admiration and respect.

"Not so." He smiled, basking in her approbation for his good deed. "Though my temper was roused at the time," he admitted, "it would be folly to hold a grudge, for the man, though surly and insolent, is competent and hardworking. From now on, it will be to his benefit to serve your mother well, for his interests will more nearly coincide with her own, and if he sees his interests bound up more closely in the prosperity of the estate, he will do his best by it. Indeed, in the long run all will benefit, for with *his* increased prosperity, he will be able to pay off his rents and dues." Sir Crispin's smile broadened. "Even, in due course, pay merchet when his daughters grow up and wish to wed."

Catherine's ripe red lips curved upwards in delighted laughter. "Imagine poor Ralph paying merchet fees five times over!" She gurgled in amusement. Her mirth was contagious, and Sir Crispin's deep, rumbling chuckle mingled with hers as the gulf that had yawned between them was bridged with healing laughter.

Catherine's last few days at home sped by on wings, or so it seemed to the girl, in whom eager anticipation was mixed with a certain reluctance to part with the dear and familiar. However glittering her future prospects at court might be, still, she was leaving behind all those she loved and who loved her and exchanging the known for the unknown. The only link between the world she had known and the world she was about to enter was Sir Crispin, who would serve as her escort from the one to the other, and her feelings about him were as confused as her state of mind in general. Only a few short days ago she had detested him and anticipated embarking on the journey in his company with considerable trepidation. Now she wasn't so sure. She was beginning to wonder if she hadn't misjudged him all along, and she was actually starting to look forward to making the journey in his company, anticipating it with pleasure instead of with dread. The man was not as arrogant and ill-tempered as he had first seemed to her; he had unexpected facets to his character which it would be intriguing to explore as they traveled together, as intriguing as the new world she was about to enter.

On her last day home, Catherine slipped away from the bustle of preparation for departure and made her way to the meadow to bid farewell to her beloved Bayard. Hitherto, she had avoided the old warhorse, for she did not want to be tempted into breaking the promise Sir Crispin had extracted from her—that of not riding the great destrier again. She'd filled her pockets to sagging with wrinkled apples and wizened carrots, and she fed them to him one by one, rubbing his soft nostrils as his yellowed teeth crunched the treats. When he'd eaten his fill, she brushed and curried him until her arms ached and his dappled hide gleamed in the sun.

"He must have been a magnificent animal in his prime," a familiar voice remarked.

Catherine, who was plaiting Bayard's mane, let the coarse strands slip through her fingers and swung round to face the man who had taken her by surprise, for she'd been too engrossed to hear his approach. She stared up, resentful of his intrusion on her farewell, to where he sat astride his own mettlesome blood-bay stallion. "Bayard was once . . . in fact, he still is . . . the finest horse in Christendom!" she choked out, not caring if he ridiculed her for her devotion to the old warhorse.

"And in case you're wondering," she added defiantly, "I wasn't going to break my promise. I won't ride him. I . . . I only came to say good-bye." She bit down on her lower lip, which was quivering uncontrollably. "I . . . I sometimes think he is my dearest and only friend."

"Surely not. You have many friends," Crispin responded. "There are the peasants you have befriended . . . your old nurse . . ."

"Yes. And all of them to be left behind," Catherine blurted out. To her horror, her face crumpled, and her eyes stung with tears. Abruptly, she swung around to bury her face in the destrier's plaited mane while fighting to regain her self-control.

"*I* am not to be left behind, and I will be your friend if you will let me, Catherine," said Sir Crispin gently. In an attempt to brighten her spirits, he added whimsically, "And a friend at court, so they say, is better than a penny in the purse."

She knuckled her eyes like a child and turned round, leaning her back against the old warhorse as she attempted a watery smile. "For sure, I will need all the friends I can get, for I have few enough pennies in my purse," she jested, attempting to meet his sally with one of her own.

"That's better," the man said encouragingly. "Now, my lady, what say you to one last gallop on the downs? I am responsible for you to the king, and God knows, it will go hard on me if any harm befalls you now. Yet I would like well to see you clinging like a cat to the stallion's broad back, your hair flying in the wind. If you like, I will release you from your promise and will ride with you to see that you come to no harm."

If she liked! Catherine could hardly believe her ears. Needing no further invitation, she scrambled onto the stallion bareback, before the man could change his mind. And then, they were off and away across the downs. Catching a glimpse of the sparkle in her eye and the joyous expression on her face, the man was well content, thundering along beside her until both their horses were winded and spent.

So Catherine had her one last wild gallop on her beloved old Bayard, a ride made more poignant because she knew in her heart it would be her last. Well content, she afterwards went sedately home, seated on the blood-bay stallion behind Sir Crispin. As she wound her arms round the man's waist and tucked her soft cheek on his broad shoulder, she felt a little tremor of a new and different kind of excitement ripple through her. Could it be, she wondered, that in Sir Crispin she had truly found a new friend—and perhaps even more than a friend?

Chapter Five

The parting from her old nurse and her mother was equally harrowing. Nurse was noisy and shrill in her lamentations, while Catherine's mother was subdued and restrained, as befitted the lady of the manor. But as she said her good-byes, Catherine was jolted into a realization of how much she would miss each woman, who, each in her own way, had had a powerful effect on her life. Nurse had bullied and scolded her and even cuffed her occasionally, but only for her own good. Moreover, she had been the source of much comfort, especially in Catherine's younger days, providing a soft lap to clamber into and warm arms to cuddle a child, easing childish ailments and small hurts with common sense and cozy comforting.

Her mother was a more remote figure, austere and less approachable. Catherine held her in awe, and living up to her mother's expectations had sometimes put a strain on their relationship. The woman was less a source of comfort than an example and a teacher, imposing a regimen on the girl and drilling her in lessons of deportment, reading, needlework, and the other accomplishments of a lady.

But in recent years, as the older woman's health declined, their respective roles had, in some measure, become reversed. Catherine had attempted to transfer some of the burden of running the estate to her own shoulders, protecting and shielding her mother as best she could from worries, while yet maintaining a modicum of freedom and independence for herself. And while they had not enjoyed an easy relationship, Catherine knew her mother would miss her companionship.

"Take care of my lady mother," she begged Nurse at parting, throwing her arms around the woman's ample form.

"I'll do that, my lamb," Nurse promised, clutching her former charge to her capacious bosom in a hug that nearly squeezed the breath out of the girl. "And if she should have need of you, I will manage to get word to you some way or other." She sniffled and wiped her eyes on her apron. "My lady will miss you sorely, but she is proud, and her pride will sustain her, as it has all these years since your father died. Now go and make your farewells to her. She is waiting for you."

Catherine found her mother kneeling at her priedieu. When Catherine knocked timidly at the open door, her mother crossed herself and got up from the kneeling bench.

"I have been asking God's blessings on your journey," she said without preamble. "May He keep you safe from harm." Her pale face creased in a frown of concern. "I wish I could spare a waiting woman to accompany you. It is not proper that you should travel with Sir Crispin alone."

"He is responsible to the king for me," Catherine assured her, wishing that her mother did not look so wan and weary. "He told me so himself. He will let no harm befall me. You can be sure of that."

"That's true," her mother admitted. "I am sure that Sir Crispin is a man who takes his responsibilities seriously. He is a man of honor and chivalry, such as your father was."

Catherine wondered how her mother had arrived at that assessment of Sir Crispin's character but forbore to ask.

"I wish your father were here," her mother fretted. "He would have known what to say to you . . . what advice to give you." She eyed her daughter dubiously. "You are so young and inexperienced and untried." She sighed. "And often so impetuous. You must learn to think before acting and, above all, guard your tongue." She smiled faintly and placed a warning finger at Catherine's lips. "You will learn that things are not always what they seem, that the ideals of chivalry are more often honored in the breach than the observance, that the court, though full of splendor, is often corrupt, that it is not always easy or even possible to tell friend from foe." She bit her lip. "I think that is what your father would tell you, were he still with us."

She unclasped a small gold brooch from her shoulder and pinned it to Catherine's bodice. "This was his last gift to me. Now it is yours."

Catherine examined the brooch reverently. It bore her parents' initials entwined in a heart shape. On the back was inscribed the motto "Amor Vincit Omnia." Laboriously, Catherine, whose Latin was not good, translated the motto. "Love Conquers All." Did it? she wondered.

Her eyes blurred. "But I have never seen you without it," she began to protest, but her mother stopped her.

"I want you to have it, my child," she said firmly. "Wear it in memory of both your father and myself. Though it is of little real value, it is all I have to give."

"You have given me much," Catherine said huskily. "Much more than this. And I thank you for it." Impulsively she bent and gave her mother a kiss, though they had never been openly affectionate.

Her mother enfolded Catherine in her arms and kissed her on both cheeks in the French fashion. "Now you must go, my child, for we are keeping Sir Crispin waiting and he has been patient long enough." She smiled through her tears. "You will find that men, whatever their other virtues, are seldom patient."

Sir Crispin was waiting in the courtyard, which was bustling with activity. His men-at-arms were already mounted and ready to set forth. Horses stamped and neighed, their bits and bridles jingling. Dogs barked and darted between the horses' legs. House servants and peasant children gathered in the courtyard to offer good wishes and gape at the scene, while Nurse bustled up at the last minute with a package of bread and cheese and sweet cakes that had been prepared by Cook especially for the journey and had nearly been forgotten.

Sir Crispin greeted Catherine and her mother courteously without any visible signs of impatience, though the hour he had set for their departure was already long past. Tactfully, he stood a little apart while they made their final farewells, then assisted Catherine to mount her palfrey. At her mother's request, he walked about the courtyard with her for a moment, conferring privately. Then he bowed low over her hand, strode to his horse, and swung into the saddle.

Amid cries of "Godspeed" and "Farewell" from the spectators, Catherine smiled and waved good-bye, fiercely determined to hold back her tears. As the little cavalcade set forth, she craned her head around for one last bittersweet look back, then set her face forward into the future.

Before long, Catherine forgot her misery and heartache, so great was her interest in her new surroundings. The air was fresh and sweet, birds sang melodiously, and wildflowers bloomed in the meadows. Since she had never been far from home before, and was, moreover, of a naturally curious disposition, she began to revel in the new sights and sounds confronting her around each bend in the road or over each hill. Sir Crispin smiled to himself, seeing her naturally buoyant optimism revive, and though he was a seasoned traveler, he began to take a renewed interest in their mundane journey, seeing the world afresh through her eyes.

At noon, they stopped for a hasty bite of bread and cheese and then pushed on, as Sir Crispin was anxious to reach the convent of St. Mary-in-the-Wold before dark. He had planned to halt there overnight, as the convent routinely provided accommodation for travelers in lieu of an inn, which was hard to find in these parts. But their late start had delayed them. Then Catherine's palfrey picked up a pebble and developed a limp, and as dusk fell, they were still far from the convent, finding themselves on a lonely windswept heath with little or no shelter.

Sir Crispin was undismayed, for he was not unprepared for the contingency, calmly bidding his men make camp and strike up a tent for the lady.

Strolling about to ease limbs cramped from so many unaccustomed hours in the saddle, Catherine marveled as the green satin pavilion went up effortlessly. Pillows and cushions were unpacked and strewn about inside the tent for her comfort. There was even a fur rug to cover the floor of the tent, and ample supplies of blankets and bedding.

"I trust that these accommodations meet with your approval, lady," said Sir Crispin, ushering her in with a low bow. "All has been done that can be done to secure your comfort."

Catherine was a trifle awed. "Indeed it is a pavilion fit for . . . for an Eastern potentate, sir knight," she assured him.

"One of my men will fetch wash water from the stream, should you desire to bathe. As for provisions, there is wine in plenty, but little food, I fear," he said apologetically. "Only bread and cheese."

But Catherine dived into the packet of food her nurse had provided and retrieved a pigeon pie, which she insisted on sharing with Sir Crispin. "Though your men will have to make do with bread and cheese," she said regretfully. "There is not enough for everyone."

"They are journey-hardened and expect no better fare," he said callously. "Nor do I," he added, refusing her offer of pigeon pie, though she coaxed him to sample it.

So Catherine ate her pie in lonely splendor, and afterwards, finding the tent stuffy and growing a little bored with her own company, emerged to sit by the flickering campfire, listening to a nightingale singing its heart out in a clump of willows by the little stream.

Sir Crispin, who had been posting guards round the camp, strode up to the fire and, removing his cloak, draped it round her shoulders. "You should move away from the fire, lady," he advised her.

Catherine looked at him in surprise. "Why? There are no sparks nor smoke." The evening had grown chill, and she snuggled into the cloak, which was warm from Sir Crispin's body.

"Because you are visible in the firelight, lady, and birds of quite another feather, birds of ill omen, flock in the fading light and ply their trade in the dark," he explained patiently.

"Do you expect trouble?" Catherine peered into the shadows, straining her eyes in the dim light for a glimpse of menacing forms gliding towards them. There were none visible, and she laughed, a trifle nervously.

"I do not expect trouble, lady, but I prefer to be ready for it if it comes."

He offered her his arm, and escorted her back to her tent. "I will roll up in a blanket tonight and sleep directly outside the tent," he assured her. "You need have no fear."

A few minutes later, Catherine found herself in a state, not of fear, but of exasperation. Accustomed as she was to having Nurse or one of the maids undress her for the night, she had given no thought as to how she would manage without their assistance. She twisted and turned in vain, trying to reach the back buttons and ties of her riding dress, but the garment was so constructed that she could not manage without help.

Briefly, she considered giving up the attempt and sleeping in her clothes, but she rejected the notion almost as soon as it crossed her mind. The garment was new, having been sewn by her nurse from a length of material her mother had long been hoarding for her. It would be rumpled and wrinkled past mending if she slept in it. Moreover, while the garment was comfortable enough for daily wear, she knew she would not sleep a wink if she lay down in it.

She persisted in her futile attempt a little longer, tugging at the ties and lacings until, in desperation, she cast modesty aside and called softly through the tent flap to Sir Crispin.

He was beside her in an instant. "You called, my lady? Is aught amiss?"

Her cheeks aflame with embarrassment, Catherine explained her predicament.

He laughed softly. "Is that all? It is a problem easily remedied, lady, though I must admit I have never before served as a lady's maid."

Catherine presented her back to him. "You . . . you must promise to close your eyes," she choked out in a paroxysm of embarrassment.

His voice quivering with amusement, Sir Crispin swore, and then swore again, in a different context, as he found the task presented more of a difficulty than he had anticipated. "You have gotten these lacings into a hopeless tangle, lady." Scowling at the tangled laces, he bent his head to the task, and Catherine could feel his breath warm on the nape of her neck as he exhaled. Patiently, he worked at the tangles, picking out the snarls, and Catherine, for some unknown reason, found herself trembling at his touch.

Presently, he met with success—the laces disentangled and the material gave way. Catherine caught her breath as she felt his hands on her bare skin, their warm hard strength sending little quavers through her flesh as he quite unnecessarily slid the garment down her shoulders.

"I . . . I can manage quite well now," Catherine said in a breathless tone. "Thank you for your help," she added in a voice that she hoped was sufficiently cool and dismissive.

"Wait. There is one more button. . . ." His voice was thick as his hands slid slowly and caressingly from her shoulders down to the small of her bare back, his thumbs tracing the indentation of her spine.

"That will do . . . I can manage," she reiterated. Crossing her hands over her breasts and pulling the material high, Catherine swung round to face him. She saw laughter in his eyes, but something more, something she was quite unable to define. "You promised to keep your eyes closed," she said, reproaching him.

"Alas, lady, I am forsworn," he confessed without an ounce of contrition. "You could not expect me to disentangle that snarl unseeing," he explained.

Catherine shrugged her shoulders, an unwise gesture since it caused her bodice to slip further down, revealing that which she wished to conceal. Her face flaming, she clutched at the garment hastily. "I bid you good night, sir knight," she said pointedly.

He took her meaning, bowing low before opening the tent flap to step outside.

Catherine drew a shaky breath, vowing that on the morrow she would wear her old riding clothes. Though they were frayed and well worn, she could get into and out of them without help.

Surprisingly, she slept well that night, lulled to sleep by Sir Crispin's deep, even breathing as he lay before her tent within call.

In spite of the little contretemps that had occurred, she felt safe in his custody, certain that she would come to no harm. After all, Sir Crispin was a man of honor and chivalry. Why should she fear?

She would not have felt so safe could she have read Sir Crispin's mind as he lay before her tent, willing his twitching limbs to lie motionless, willing his chest to rise and fall rhythmically with the deep, even breaths he took to calm his stirred senses.

He groaned softly to himself, aching with a need that was old and familiar and yet contained elements that were altogether new to him.

The girl was half witch, half wench, he told himself roughly, and he must put her out of his mind once he had delivered her safely to the king. That she had a strange power to stir his senses meant nothing. She was no peasant wench to tumble at will, and he would find no ease in her, either of body or mind.

He had been too long without a woman, he mused, trying to convince himself that was all that ailed him. He had been too fastidious for too long. Well, at the first opportunity he would slake his needs with the first likely-looking wanton to cross his path. One woman was as good for the purpose as another. All cats were gray in the dark . . . wasn't that what they said? He had his way to make, and no need of a willful wench with gleaming cat's eyes who, in any case, was well beyond his reach, well born as she was and earmarked for the queen's service.

At long last, his clamoring body yielded to the discipline he imposed upon it, and he slept.

Chapter Six

In the gray light of dawn, Catherine woke to the clash and clangor of arms. She threw back the tangled bedding, scrambled to her feet, and pulled on a robe. Knotting it about her slim waist with fumbling fingers, she scurried to the tent flap and peered out.

Sir Crispin had disappeared, though his blankets lay in a tangled heap nearby. Farther off, shadowy forms engaged in combat. Catherine could hear the clash of steel on naked steel, the clamor of hounds who had been unleashed to leap snarling on the intruders who swarmed through camp daggers drawn. One of the hounds sprang for a man's throat, only to collapse in a pool of blood as the intruder thrust his dagger deep into the hound's belly. It thrashed about in its death throes, blood spurting from its entrails.

Catherine watched, horrified, but unable to drag her eyes away from the gory sight. She clapped her hands to her ears, for the din was frightful. A trumpet blew a belated alarm, men and dogs alike howled in pain, and men grunted with effect of blows given and received. At the horse lines, tethered warhorses neighed and plunged against their ties.

A dirty hand clasped Catherine's mouth and, from behind, a wiry arm pinioned Catherine's to her side. She struggled, twisting and turning and kicking backwards, but to no avail.

Intruders swarmed into the tent, which had been slit open from the rear. She could hear them rifling her belongings and grumbling at the scarcity of the spoils. She could smell sweat and dirt and fear (possibly her own) and incongruously, the stink of onions on the hot breath of her captor.

The man dragged her backwards through the gash in the tent, muttering, "Come on, lads, let's make our getaway. We got a prize worth ransoming."

A pockmarked face leered into Catherine's frame of vision. "Right you are, Cob. She is a prize. A virgin, I'll wager." The man licked lean and lustful lips. "Wot say we all take a turn with her before she's ransomed? You can have her first," he added generously.

"None o' that before we're well away from here." The man incautiously lifted a hand from Catherine's mouth to swot at his too eager companion, who had ripped her robe open.

Catherine seized her chance and screamed long and loud.

The man swore a vile oath and clapped her hand back over her mouth. She bit his grubby fingers hard, tasting blood. He tore his hand away and held it up, dripping.

"Bitch!" he cried, clouting her in the head. She shook it dizzily, fighting to retain consciousness, black specks dancing before her eyes.

They were at the perimeter of the camp by now, and Catherine saw a guard slumped at his post, a feathered arrow quivering in his throat.

English longbows, she thought dully. These men must be English archers, former soldiers home from the wars who preyed on defenseless travelers in lieu of foreign prey. If only she could scream again and call attention to her plight, she thought despairingly. But her captor had stuffed a dirty rag into her mouth, half choking her. She nearly swooned, but fought off the blackness that threatened to engulf her.

Blood was pounding in her ears, thundering in her ears. Or was it the thunder of hooves she heard? Hardly daring to hope, she opened her eyes wide.

Sir Crispin, pounding up on his blood-bay stallion, rode bareback, clad only in tunic and boots. The rising sun glinted on his tawny-gold hair and on the sword he brandished high.

The little band of miscreants scattered in all directions, fearing to be ridden down. Only her captor stood his ground. Thrusting Catherine behind him, he drew a short sword from its sheath and prepared to defend himself.

Suddenly released, Catherine staggered and nearly fell headlong. Her outstretched hand curled about a stave that one of the bandits had used as a cudgel and dropped in his hasty flight. Catherine groped for it, using it as a staff to lean upon, for her strength was nearly spent.

Gagging and choking, she spat the filthy rag from her mouth and peered through watering eyes. Sir Crispin was unhorsed. Perhaps he had leaped down to fight afoot while her back was turned.

She watched as the two antagonists circled each other, warily sparring. Swords clanged as steel met naked steel. The combatants were about the same height and weight and appeared evenly matched.

As they feinted and parried Catherine, in horror, spied a bandit creep up on Sir Crispin, dagger drawn. He raised it high to plunge the weapon deep into Crispin's unprotected back.

Gritting her teeth, Catherine, using her stave as a cudgel, thwacked him with it. The bandit yelped, his upraised knife dropped from nerveless fingers, and he turned to flee. Catherine, her blood up, followed him, belaboring him about the head and shoulders with her cudgel.

A great shout of laughter startled her as Crispin came up and pinioned her flailing arms in his. "Sweetheart, do you mean to pound the poor wretch into a jelly?" he remonstrated. "Peace," he soothed her. "Have done!"

Catherine watched the little runt run off whimpering. Looking over her shoulder, she perceived that Crispin's antagonist was down, a sword embedded in his chest, his sightless eyes rolled upwards, staring into the sun.

Catherine shuddered and swallowed convulsively. She swayed and would have fallen had not Crispin cradled her in his strong arms. "There, there, sweetheart," he soothed, stroking her tangled hair, smoothing it over her shoulders. "My good brave lady . . . my little wildcat." He rubbed her back in broad circular soothing strokes. "It's all over. You're safe now."

Catherine heaved a sigh and snuggled closer, savoring his strength, for she felt unexpectedly weak at the knees. Yet never had she felt so safe. "Crispin," she said wonderingly, "Crispin . . ."

"Yes, my dear . . . what is it?" he murmured encouragingly.

"I . . . oh, nothing. Only that I . . . I like your name," she said childishly.

He threw back his head and laughed. "And I like yours, Cat," he teased. "I like it well, for you are a little wildcat, I think, and so I shall call you henceforth. Will you like that, my Catherine?"

While Catherine was thinking this over and secretly deciding that she preferred "sweetheart" as a term of endearment, one of Sir Crispin's men-at-arms ran up.

"All of our men are present and accounted for, sir," he reported. He rattled off the names of the dead. "The bandits have taken to their heels, sir. Shall we pursue them?"

"I think not," Sir Crispin decided. "Let them go, poor wretches. They are homeless, desperate men. Mayhap they have learned their lesson."

The little page trotted up with his horse, and Crispin scooped Catherine up and sat her on the animal's broad back, then mounted behind her. "I'll take my lady back to camp, Gervaise. Strap our dead across their saddles. We will take them to St. Mary's convent so they may rest on consecrated ground."

The rest of the trip passed in a blur for Catherine.

She never afterwards remembered a detail of it, only that Crispin rode beside her, murmuring little words of support and encouragement the whole way. He offered to take her up behind him, and though she longed to lean into his hard strength and rest her aching head upon his shoulders, her pride would not permit it.

The nuns clucked over Catherine, shocked at her white face and battered appearance, at the two dead men slung over their saddles, and at the battle-weary look of the little company. Three slightly wounded men-at-arms were treated at the convent's infirmary, and their wounds dressed. The priest who was chaplain at the convent was summoned to bury the dead and say Masses for their souls, and Catherine was led off to be bathed and fed and put to bed.

She slept all the rest of that day and straight through the night as well, waking refreshed and revived early the next morning.

A nun who had peered in on her earlier and found her stirring, came in to help her dress and conduct her to the refectory, where she found Crispin breaking his fast with the lady prioress.

To her surprise, Catherine found the prioress very grand, as elegant as a queen with a black silk habit, starched white coif, and a bejeweled cross suspended from a heavy gold chain upon her breast. But she was courteous and kind, though Catherine suspected that she ruled her little flock of nuns with a rod of iron and would not be crossed or contradicted with impunity.

When Sir Crispin introduced them, she smiled a welcome. "Ah, yes, I remember your parents well.

They stopped her on their wedding journey many years ago. You do not resemble your mother in the least. A pity, for she was a great beauty."

Catherine heard Crispin stifle a snicker at this insult, which she assumed was unintentional. She shot him a reproachful glance.

The prioress was studying Catherine intently. "You *do* put me in mind of your father, though. Something about the eyes . . . the mouth . . . the hair." She sighed. "Ah, he was a 'true, perfect, gentle knight' as Master Chaucer says. He had a wild, free look about him too. And a bold, brave warrior he was."

"Courage his daughter has inherited in full measure," Sir Crispin interjected.

"Ah, yes, my dear. Sir Crispin has told me of your misadventure on the road and of the part you played in it." The prioress shook her head. "These bandits . . . indeed I don't know what the country is coming to. It was not so in my young days."

Crispin moved restlessly, pushing back his chair. "Have you finished your breakfast, my lady?" he inquired of Catherine. "If so, we must be on our way."

Catherine nodded, hastily cramming the last bite of bread, thickly buttered and spread with honey, into her mouth and washing it down with a mug of ale.

"Madame, I thank you for your hospitality." Crispin bowed to the prioress and handed her a small bag of coins. "A small donation towards the chapel roof. It would be a shame if the rain should ruin those Flemish paintings of which you spoke."

Catherine lingered, loath at the last minute to leave the peace and tranquillity of the convent for the hazards of the road.

"Not thinking of taking the veil as a result of our little misadventure, are you?" Crispin teased her later. "Fie on your faint heart, my lady!" He shook his head dolefully. "And to think that only moments ago I was bragging of your bravery to the prioress!" He grinned. "Though, on second thought, it would take courage of a rare sort of place yourself under that redoubtable lady's thumb!"

Catherine could not restrain a gurgle of amusement. It was exactly what she had been thinking herself.

So, after all, they set off in a spirit of harmony. Catherine's earlier misgivings melted away entirely with a change of scene and with Crispin's assurance that further on the roads were well traveled and the risk of robbery correspondingly reduced.

In fact, by midday traffic on the road had picked up considerably, and Catherine found that her greatest danger lay in appearing to be a gawky rustic as she craned her head to look this way and that.

Their fellow-travelers were a varied lot, she discovered. There were beggars, clad in rags thrusting out their begging bowls for alms, gaily dressed squires, richly dressed merchants, poorly dressed scholars, and churchmen of varying degrees, ranging from haughty prelates with an entourage of lesser clergy in attendance to humble parish priests.

What an exciting, invigorating world it was, thought Catherine, who sat sedately on her palfrey, doing her best not to gape and failing utterly in the attempt.

As their route converged with that of a party of pilgrims bound for the shrine at Canterbury, Catherine, who was fond of Master Chaucer's tales, diverted herself by picking out people in the gay cavalcade and trying to match them with the storyteller's characters.

Which led her, not unnaturally, to speculate about Sir Crispin, whom she found something of a mystery. He did not fit into a neat category, nor was he a typical knight, she felt sure. Though a bold fighter when action was called for, he lacked the bloodthirstiness and insensitivity of the breed. Witness his compassion for the fleeing bandits yesterday. "Poor wretches" he had termed them, and so she supposed they were. Misfits in a society that no longer needed their particular skills.

That he was intelligent and perspicacious was obvious to her. Judging from his conversations with her mother and the prioress, it was evident that he possessed remarkable political sagacity, not unmixed with a deep and abiding cynicism.

From his relations with herself Catherine deduced that, underneath a somewhat forbidding exterior, he possessed an abundance of humor, wit, and charm. Undeniably, he also possessed physical attraction in large measure, a physical attraction that made her more than a trifle uneasy. Inevitably, she wondered about his relations with other women who were more experienced than herself. Did they too find him irresistibly appealing? she wondered. She also wondered what combination of factors made him the man that he was.

Preoccupied with such speculations, she barely noticed that foot traffic was increasing as they jogged into a little market town where gaily decorated booths were set up on the town square. Vaguely, she realized that it was market day.

Abandoning her speculations, Catherine looked about her with undisguised eagerness. Eagerly, she sniffed the air, which was redolent with the odor of roasting meat and spicy gingerbread. Much to her chagrin, her stomach growled loudly.

Crispin looked amused. "Hungry, Cat?" he teased. "There's quite a decent inn here. The White Hart." He gestured to a gabled edifice with a creaking sign out front depicting a gamboling white deer with a jeweled collar. The building was not far from the town square. "We'll spend the night at the inn in comfort. As soon as the horses are stabled, I'll take you round to the booths and buy you a hot pie and a fairing."

Catherine assented to this proposal with enthusiasm, quite forgetting the ladylike reserve she had been bred to display on all occasions.

They went first to a booth selling hot meat pies, and Catherine devoured every crumb of the crusty treat. Still munching the last few bites, they strolled round the square, and her eyes grew round to see the tumblers performing their acts with incredible agility. She was particularly entranced by a juggler who did tricks with a small animal that she assumed must be some strange kind of small dog.

"On the contrary," said Sir Crispin with a chuckle. "It is a monkey, brought from the East. It's not uncommon for great ladies to keep them as pets.

Perhaps the queen will have one," he said, disengaging the monkey from Catherine's neck. She had fed it bits of hot pie, and it had promptly leaped upon her shoulder, wound its little arms around her neck, and then chirruped indignantly at being restored to its master.

"What a child you are, Cat," said Crispin indulgently, throwing the monkey his last bite of pie by way of consolation.

Catherine refuted this charge indignantly. "I just like animals," she protested as she was led away.

Sir Crispin led her to a stall where small trinkets called fairings were temptingly displayed. Catherine chose a length of bright ribbon with which to bind back her tangled tresses, while Crispin browsed through a selection of intricately tied bow knots.

Did he recognize the significance of the stylized knot? Catherine wondered. It was generally regarded as an emblem of love, and she felt a small pang of irrational disappointment when he replaced the true lovers' knot on the tray of goods and turned away.

Suddenly, a small brown-skinned girl darted from the neighboring stall and seized Catherine's hand.

"Cross my palm with silver, lady, and I will tell you a fortune such as you have never dreamed," she wheedled. A tiny creature, she grinned impudently up at them, a flash of white teeth gleaming in her sun-browned face. She wore a many-flounced kirtle and a low, scooped-neck blouse. A bright orange scarf twined through a tangle of jet-black curls, and huge golden hoops dangled from her ears. She was older than Catherine had at first supposed, for she swayed her hips provocatively and eyed Crispin knowingly. "And you, sir knight," she taunted. "Will you not part with a penny or two so that your lady may know her fate?"

Crispin gazed at the girl thoughtfully and with more appreciation than Catherine thought was warranted. Then, extracting a coin from the pouch that hung at his belt, he tossed it to the girl. "Here, wench. See you tell my lady a good fortune."

She caught the coin expertly in mid-air and slipped it into her low-cut bodice, where Crispin watched it disappear. His face was impassive, but as Catherine looked from one to the other, she sensed a spark pass between them.

To her surprise, the girl suddenly reached upwards and caught Catherine's chin in her slim brown hand, studying her face earnestly. "It is a good face . . . a kind face," she muttered, more to herself than to the others.

"You are supposed to read palms, girl, not faces," said Catherine sharply, jerking her chin away.

"Sometimes the one reveals more than the other," remarked the girl placidly. "And my name, lady, is Chantal."

The girl half-smiled, a secretive smile, Catherine thought, as she bent low over Catherine's hand and gabbled a fortune consisting of a handsome stranger, a trip across water, a reunion after long parting, a happy marriage blessed with many children, and a long and prosperous life.

"You see all that in my palm?" asked Catherine skeptically.

"That and more, lady." But what else the future held in store, the girl refused to divulge.

Crispin, who was strolling about in a seemingly aimless fashion while this all was going on, sauntered up to the Gypsy girl's ramshackle cart and swaybacked horse tethered nearby. He pursed his lips, whistling an almost soundless tune while surveying the rickety equipage.

The girl dropped Catherine's hand and went to stand beside the horse and cart, as if to defend her property.

"You travel alone, Chantal?" the man asked idly.

"I do . . . for the time being." She tossed her head until her black curls bobbed. "I left the band I traveled with three days ago." she explained glibly. "There was a man . . . he wanted me but I . . . I did not want him." Her bold black eyes stared disdainfully into Crispin's. "I, Chantal, choose my own man."

It was more than a statement of fact; it was a challenge, a challenge so blatantly tendered that Catherine gasped.

But Crispin's face was impassive. "Indeed," he remarked coolly. Then, harking back to his original topic, he added casually, "I gather you have come far?"

The girl nodded. "Far enough. And farther still to go. I travel to London to seek my fortune. There will be celebrations a plenty when the king brings home the new queen, and money to be made." She smiled wickedly. "When wine is in, wits are out!"

"True enough," Crispin admitted. "We also go to London. Perhaps our paths will cross again?"

"Perhaps." Chantal's lips curved into a provocative smile and her bold black eyes, roving over the man's face, held out an invitation . . . and a promise.

Catherine, who had been a silent spectator of this, had had quite enough. Seizing Crispin's arm, she steered him toward the next booth, where a beguiling array of silks from the East were temptingly displayed. She exclaimed loudly at their beauty and rarity, pretending an interest she did not feel, while the girl's mocking laughter rang in her ears.

Crispin meant nothing to her, she told herself angrily, as she rummaged through the silky bolts of cloth. Why should she care if a Gypsy wench made bold eyes at him? Or if he responded to her overtures? He meant nothing to her. Nothing at all.

Chapter Seven

But Catherine's ill humor soon dissipated in the novelty of market day. There was a feeling of excitement in the air, and she allowed herself to be caught up in it.

Young men loitered about the town square, idly watching young girls who watched them out of the corner of their eyes, seemingly demure yet flirtatious. Peddlars cried out raucously, offering their wares, and plucked at the sleeves of passersby to get their attention. "A gaud for your lady, good sir? A bauble for your lady?" they wheedled as Crispin passed by with Catherine on his arm.

A wandering minstrel wearing a jaunty belled cap threaded his way through the throng, strumming his instrument and playing for pennies tossed into his cap. He must know every song ever written, thought Catherine, for whenever he was challenged by this person or that to play a particular tune, he rose to the occasion superbly, never missing a beat as he swung from a lilting love song to a bawdily humorous tune that made the men in his audience roar with laughter.

Catching sight of the couple who were so obviously above the station in life of the townsfolk clustered about him, the minstrel doffed his cap with a merry jingle of bells and, without prompting, thrummed a lovely ballad of a brave knight, his hawk, his hound, and his lady fair which enchanted Catherine. She smiled and clapped, calling out her appreciation to the musician, while Crispin tossed a coin his way. Snatching it up expertly, the man grinned and executed a deep bow by way of acknowledgment.

At the corner of the square, a stand piled high with luscious fruit proved an irresistible attraction. After much jesting discussion of the merits of particular fruits, Crispin selected a ripe apple, Catherine a bunch of grapes. Holding her grapes desultorily, for she was not really hungry, Catherine watched Crispin bite into his apple. His white, even teeth crunched the juicy treat, and the muscles of his sun-browned throat worked as he swallowed. A drop of juice escaped the corner of his mouth, and he retrieved it unself-consciously with the tip of his tongue.

Aware that she was staring, Catherine lowered her eyes, swallowing and licking her lips in unconscious imitation.

"Not eating your grapes?" Crispin said lightly. "Are they too sour? Would you like something else in place of them? Perhaps one of those pears from Anjou?"

"No," said Catherine hastily. "I . . . ah . . ." Embarrassed, she fumbled with the grapes, twisting them but not succeeding in parting even one from its tough, wiry stem.

"Let me do it for you," said Crispin kindly. Taking up the bunch of grapes, he began to pluck them from the stem one by one and popped them into her mouth.

As Catherine obediently chewed and swallowed, the man's thumb brushed across her lips, more or less by accident. And then, as if his hand liked the feel of them and could not resist repeating the sensation and enlarging on it, his fingers more deliberately traced the outline of her lips, then trailed down her cheek and chin and finally her throat in a lingering caress.

Suddenly, Catherine felt quite breathless, and her heart leaped up into her throat, so that she was sure he could feel it beating there. What kind of magic spell was he working on her? she wondered helplessly, gripped by powerful emotions and intensely strong sensations she did not in the least understand.

He plucked another grape, bit into it until the juice spurted, then rubbed the fleshy fruit over her lips, wishing he could sample their ripeness.

Catherine whimpered softly, savoring the contrast between the cool firm skin of the grape and the warmth of the fleshy pad of his thumb as it caressed her lips. Her tongue flicked out to gather in the grape, and then some instinct prompted her to nip delicately at the flesh of his thumb.

He made a low, growling sound deep in his throat, and the hand that caressed her face trembled ever so slightly.

Half-closing her eyes in order to savor the sensations his sensual spell was evoking, Catherine swayed toward him, then clutched his tunic for support as her knees buckled and the magic spell was rudely broken.

An urchin who had filched a piece of fruit from the stand careened around the corner and collided with them, the vendor of the fruit in hot pursuit.

"You imp of Satan, I'll have you whipped!" the merchant shouted. He came to a skittering stop in front of Catherine, where the boy cowered, clutching her skirts.

"Oh, begging your pardon, my lord, milady," the man mumbled, excusing his intrusion as best he could. Grabbing the lad by the ear, he tried to haul him away to the magistrate.

The boy howled loudly and clasped Catherine's knees in a death grip.

"It was but a boyish prank," Crispin said, his lips twitching in humor in spite of himself. "Let the lad go," he offered. "I will pay for the fruit."

Grumbling, the merchant pocketed his money and stalked back to his stall. Gabbling his thanks, the boy scrambled to his feet and made off as if demons were at his heels.

Catching Crispin's eye, Catherine began to laugh hysterically. In a swift reversal of her earlier mood, she caught up the dusty grapes which had fallen to the dirt and began pelting the boy with them, and then, when he was out of range, Sir Crispin.

He seized her by the wrist, staying her hand. "You, wench, are as much an imp as that lad," he growled. "And as much in need of discipline."

"Pooh!" she said airily. "I do not see you as a disciplinarian. You let the boy go, after all."

"You may not fare as well," he growled. "You, my lady, I intend to hold fast."

Crispin proved as good as his word, escorting her round to the other booths with her hand clamped firmly in his.

It was late in the day, and many of the vendors were packing up their unsold goods and setting out for home. But a small crowd still lingered around a juggler, clad in motley, who kept three knives going in the air at the same time. Catherine and Crispin paused at the edge of the crowd to admire his skillful performance. Along with everyone else, Catherine breathed "ooh!" and "ah!" at the juggler's demonstration of skill, for his fingers flashed flawlessly among the flickering blades of steel.

"Well done, fellow!" called Sir Crispin, tossing the man a coin, and then they moved on hand in hand.

They might be any young couple, thought Catherine wistfully, like the ones they now saw pairing off together and slipping away into the twilight. Suddenly, she wished passionately that this day would never end—that she and Crispin were not king's man and queen's lady, but were, in fact, one of those comfortably anonymous couples and that they might always be together as they were now.

She shivered, and Crispin, ever solicitous, noticed and draped an arm about her.

"Are you cold?" he inquired. "It is a trifle chilly now that the sun is going down. We should go back to the inn. The host of the White Hart puts on a good dinner for his guests, and you will be able to warm up beside a roaring fire." He added practically, "We should turn in early tonight, in order to get an early start in the morning. If we push on tomorrow, we should make London by nightfall. I don't suppose you are eager to spend another night on the road."

"No . . . n-o-o, of course not," Catherine said slowly, but her thoughts were suddenly bleak. What would his reaction be, she wondered, if he knew how reluctant she was to see their journey end?

But their journey was not over yet, not by any means, Catherine reminded herself, resolving to wrest every bit of enjoyment she could from it while it lasted. "Come on," she said merrily, seizing his hand in a sudden swift reversal of mood. "Let us turn our steps towards the White Hart, for I am ready, and more than ready, for the good dinner and warm fire that you promised me!"

The White Hart Inn was a crooked black-and-white half-timbered building that had provided accommodations for travelers on the London Road for generations, though not always by that name. The creaking signboard that hung over the front gate had been re-painted many times with differing devices. Since the inn's current landlord was an ardent supporter of the king and had been so since the days of the Peasants' Revolt, he had re-named his hostelry the White Hart and re-painted his signboard with king's own emblem out of compliment to King Richard, whose chosen device from the College of Heraldry was a little white deer. The heraldic beast in the emblem wore a jeweled collar to which two long chains were attached.

Catherine paused before the heavy oak door,

looking up at the device painted on the weathered signboard. The device was an artistic rendition of the device emblazoned on the king's livery that was worn by Sir Crispin and his men-at-arms. In idle speculation, she wondered aloud why the king had chosen a chained and collared deer for his emblem, rather than some fierce heraldic beast— lions rampant or couchant, a fiery cresset or a fierce wild boar. "It seems rather a tame device for a king to choose," she remarked, voicing a thought that had occurred to her several times since she had first seen the device emblazoned on Crispin's livery.

Crispin shrugged. "Who knows what goes on in the king's mind?" His mouth twisted wryly. "Richard is a wily and subtle man, as you will find. I believe his choice was deliberately designed to spite the royal dukes, his uncles, who kept him on leading chains during his minority." He pushed open the heavy door and stepped back, waiting for Catherine to precede him into the inn.

A stone-flagged passage led to a large, low-ceilinged room with broad oak beams overhead, hand-carved paneled walls, and a huge brick fire-place large enough to roast an ox. Succulent joints of meat were roasting on spits rotated over the fire by a spit-boy, and their delicious aroma made Catherine's mouth water, even as her ears were assailed by the cheerful hubbub of merrymakers who thronged the room—in the aftermath of market day, she supposed.

She looked at Sir Crispin inquiringly. "Shall we find a seat?" she asked, taking a hesitant step toward an eight-foot-long refectory table that was crowded with revelers, among them Crispin's men-at-arms.

But Crispin shook his head. "I bespoke a private parlor for us when I stabled our horses earlier today. This is altogether too boisterous a place for a lady." Catching the eye of one of the buxom maids who was distributing brimming tankards of ale, he sent her scurrying for the landlord.

While they were waiting for the host to make an appearance, Catherine had the opportunity to take a good look around. She was enjoying the cheerful din and wished, rather wistfully, that they might linger in so convivial an atmosphere. But even her inexperienced eye could perceive that a good many of the merrymakers were far gone in inebriation. Sir Crispin's mind was evidently running along the same lines, for he muttered in resignation, "I shall have the devil of a time rousing the men at dawn. Oh, well, it can't be helped, I suppose."

Just then the landlord came bustling up with many apologies for his tardiness. With an obsequious bow, he led Catherine and Crispin down one of the many twisting corridors that branched off the flagstone passageway. "We have been expecting you, my lord, and my daughter has already laid a fire in the grate," he said, opening a heavy door and ushering them into a pleasant octagonal-shaped room the charm of which went far towards reconciling Catherine to her exclusion from the common room. It had tapestry wall hangings finer than any the manor at home could boast, an ornately carved oak table and sturdy chairs with tapestried seat coverings, and a beamed inglenook fireplace in which a cheerful fire crackled against the evening chill.

The landlord looked well pleased at Catherine's exclamation of delight and assured them, "I will send Meg in with your dinners directly, and she will herself wait upon you. If you require anything further, you have only to ask."

The dinner, when it came, was every bit as good as Crispin had predicted, though Catherine was a bit unnerved at sharing a plate with him for the first time. At home, her mother, as hostess, had shared a plate with their honored guest. Catherine knew it was an old custom when dining in company, but she found it produced a curious sensation of intimacy, and she couldn't imagine sharing her plate with a stranger, as she might be required to do in the king's hall. Though, upon further reflection, she thought it might be easier, for whenever their hands now brushed against each other, as they inevitably did, she felt a tingle of pure pleasure at his touch.

The man appeared unaffected, however, casually feeding her tidbits of his roast boar's head with brawn pudding in exchange for a piece of her roast goose with herbal stuffing.

But Crispin was not as unaffected as he appeared. Why had he never noticed before how daintily she ate? he wondered. She did not dip her fingers too deeply into the sauce as she delicately separated the flesh from the bone of her bird, letting not a morsel drop from between her fingers as she daintily coveyed it to her sweet red mouth. Afterwards, she neatly wiped her lips with a napkin so that not a trace of grease remained upon them, and then dabbled her fingers in the bowl of rosewater provided for the purpose of cleansing them between each course. And yet, with all her daintiness, she'd attacked her fowl with gusto, for she had a hearty appetite and relished her food.

As he watched her sink her tiny white teeth into a fruit tart and tidily lick a crumb of the pastry from the corner of her mouth with the tip of her little pink tongue, he found himself wondering if she would enter into all such sensual pleasures with like abandon. He decided that, being Catherine, she very likely would, for she had an unconscious way of throwing herself wholeheartedly into all that she did that he found utterly endearing.

Endearing? The man roused himself from such wayward speculations with a start. Good Lord, what *was* he thinking of?

The girl meant nothing to him, he told himself sternly. She was naught but a charge with which he had been entrusted, and it was his responsibility to convey her to court in as pure and untouched and virginal a condition as when she had left her mother's manor.

At the last minute, her mother had reminded him of her daughter's innocence and inexperience, and he had soothed her maternal anxieties without a qualm, promising to take the greatest care of Catherine, for such was his obligation to the king. It was perhaps, he reflected, why he had been selected for this particular task, for his sense of honor was well known to be strong and incorruptible. Nor did he go in for casual dalliance with maidens of high degree as a rule, or indulge in lighthearted flirtations with ladies of the court. Hitherto, he had always kept a strong rein on his passions, indulging his masculine needs infrequently and then only with women of lesser degree, such as

the simpering maidservant who now made bold
eyes at him as she served their dinners. Doubtless,
she would be available for an assignation later in
the evening, he told himself, or if she was not, he
could seek out the Gypsy. The Gypsy! There was
something about that little wench that did not ring
true—something he could not quite put his finger
on. He frowned. It behooved him to keep an eye
on the wench strictly in the line of duty, and if in
so doing he could assuage the physical needs that
bedeviled him into the bargain, why, so much the
better; he could thereby kill two birds, as it were,
with one stone. Especially if a casual dalliance
with the Gypsy wench served to dull his dangerous
desire for Catherine, a lady quite out of the reach
of a landless baseborn knight such as he.

And yet, as Catherine took a sip of wine and
with a smile offered him the cup, and as he took
it from her, placing his lips to the rim where hers
had so lately touched, his hitherto invulnerable
heart began to pound like that of a lovesick squire,
and he began to wonder if any woman, no matter
how wanton or free with her favors, could dull
his desire for the bewitching redheaded beauty at
his side.

With another frown, he tossed off the dregs of
the wine. There was, he told himself, only one way
to find out.

Observing his frown and his air of preoccupation,
Catherine was piqued. Was it something she had
said or done? she wondered. Was he bored with her
company? Impulsively, she jumped to the conclusion that he was, and made up her mind to relieve
him of the tedium of her presence. Professing her-

self more tired than she really was, she suggested an early night.

Sir Crispin raised his eye brows. "This early?" he sounded disappointed.

But Catherine pushed back her chair and rose, forcing him, out of politeness, to do the same. "You said you want to get an early start in the morning," she reminded him.

"So I did." Summoning the maidservant to light them upstairs, he took Catherine's arm. "I will myself escort you, to make sure your chamber is all that it should be."

"That's not necessary," Catherine demurred.

He knew it was not, knew that the White Hart's accommodations would be adequate and that Catherine could find her way perfectly well with Meg as guide, but it was a ready excuse to prolong their intimacy, to tuck her hand into the crook of his arm and draw her slender form closer to him than was necessary.

"Nevertheless, I insist," he said in a tone that brooked no argument.

With Meg preceding them with a lighted candle, they went out into the dim passageway, lighted only by a few scattered rushlights at infrequent intervals, and up a massive staircase of dark oak that sloped up between paneled walls, then branched and curved away to right and left.

"Your room's to the left, sir," Meg said, taking the branch to the right. "We put ladies to the right and gentlemen to the left, them that can afford private rooms, that is. Your men-at-arms will be bedding down on pallets below in the common room, I take it."

"I believe so." Crispin took the candle from her as she jiggled with a door latch, and she flashed him a startled smile of gratitude. "Thank you, sir," she breathed with a simper. "It sticks a bit, that latch does."

Retrieving the candle, she ushered them into a cozy little room tucked away under the eaves of the inn's steep, gabled roof. The room was scrupulously clean but bare and devoid of ornament. Its most prominent feature was an enormous bed, which was, Crispin could not help but reflect, plenty large enough for two, with curtains that could be drawn around to insure its occupants ample privacy. It definitely was not a bed for sleeping in alone, and he rather regretted the waste.

Dragging his eyes away from contemplation of its delights, he said formally, "The room suits you, my lady?"

"Oh, quite," Catherine assured him, taking it in at a glance. Inevitably, her eye too was drawn to the bed, for it dominated the small room. "The bed looks very comfortable," she remarked innocently. Unself-consciously, she threw herself down upon it, setting the feather-filled mattress to rustling and the bed itself to jiggling as she bounced upon it to test its firmness.

Crispin averted his eyes from the sight. "I will leave you now, with Meg to attend upon you. She will bring up your belongings and see to your needs, I am sure."

Catherine nodded. "Will you also bring up hot water from the kitchen, Meg? I would like to bathe away the grime of travel."

"Certainly, my lady. I'll see to it right away." The

maidservant bobbed a curtsy and scurried out.

Catherine lay back upon the bed, continuing to bounce gently on it. "I hope your bed will be as comfortable, sir knight," she said demurely.

"I trust it will be, lady," he said in a strangled tone. Her languorous position upon the bed was innocently provocative, fairly inviting him to tumble her upon it, and yet he knew it was a sign of her youth and inexperience and of the trust she reposed in him that he was admitted to her bedchamber at all.

"You will be just across the hall?" she asked, pursuing her line of thought.

"Yes . . . presently . . . that is . . . ah . . . there are matters requiring my attention before I can seek my rest."

"Ah, yes, you must, of course, see to the welfare of your men," she remarked innocently.

"That, of course, among other things." He was deliberately vague. "And now, if you will excuse me, lady, I will bid you good night."

Though her lips bade him a chaste good night in return, the eyes she raised to him were deep green pools of allure that were very nearly his undoing. Turning on his heel, Sir Crispin fairly bolted from the room.

On his way downstairs, Crispin passed Meg trudging up them, laden with pails of steaming bathwater, and an irrational pang of envy shot through him. How willingly would he take her place as lady's maid tonight—to take down the shining tresses of his lady's hair, to lovingly divest her of her clothing, garment by garment, to bathe her long slender limbs and the melting softness of her shapely body. At thought of such sensual delights, he very nearly groaned aloud.

But Catherine was not his lady and could never be, he reminded himself sternly—except, perhaps, in the way of "courtly love," a chivalric ideal in which a knight was permitted to worship and adore an unattainable lady from afar, a pursuit that was considered to be elevating and ennobling and an inspiration to a man, making him a more valiant and gallant knight, a virtual chevalier preux.

Crispin, however, rejected the notion almost as soon as it crossed his mind, a rueful smile tugging at his lips in spite of his perturbation, for willful Cat was no lady to be put on a pedestal and worshipped from afar! She was too irritatingly faulty, too endearingly human for such treatment. She was a bewildering mixture of child and witch and woman, all rolled into one. As he mused, random images of her began to flash into his mind—of her as ragged peasant wench impudently taunting him—of her straddling her father's old warhorse, her bare legs gripping the horse's barrel and her skirts flying—of her pouting because, forsooth, he had beaten her in a chess game—of her on her knees, grubbing about in her garden, unearthing weeds. She was of the earth—earthy—not an idealized version of woman to be worshipped from afar, but a very human one. Her very faults endeared her to him.

Nevertheless, he must guard her honor and his own, and to that end he bent his steps towards a woman who *was* attainable, and with whom he could ease the base desires of his body, the better to guard his lady's honor.

Sue Deobold

Sir Crispin, though absent from Catherine's chamber, was ever present in her mind and in that of Meg, the innkeeper's daughter, as well. The girl was a comely lass with an eye for a handsome man, and she expatiated upon Sir Crispin's good looks, charm, and courtesy at quite tiresome length while she was helping Catherine get ready for bed.

"Oh, my lady, how lucky you are to have such a handsome knight at your beck and call!" she exclaimed, puffing into Catherine's chamber with her brimming buckets of water. "I passed him just now on the stairs . . . what a handsome face he has!" Meg giggled. "My Jack is a likely-looking lad, but nowhere near as good-looking as yonder knight." She uplifted the buckets and poured their contents into a tin tub that had been stowed away under the bed. "The water will be cool enough for bathing by the time you get undressed," she observed. "Shall I help you with your lacings or do you want me to brush out your hair first?"

"The hair, I think," Catherine decided, taking out the pins that bound it and shaking it down her shoulders.

"Oh, my lady, you have such beautiful hair!" said Meg admiringly as she began to comb it out. "Such a color! I have not seen the like before." Gently she tugged the comb through a riotous tangle of curls, chattering all the while and resuming her enthusiastic appraisal of Sir Crispin, whom she referred to as "your knight."

"He is not 'my knight,'" said Catherine with annoyance, for she was growing tired of hearing

Sir Crispin's praises sung. "We are merely traveling together, for he is acting as my escort to London." It was a fact she herself would do well to remember, Catherine told herself a bit ruefully.

Meg, who was re-braiding Catherine's hair so that it would not dabble in the bathwater, giggled. "Ah, but he has an eye for you, my lady."

"Think you so?" Catherine could not help asking doubtfully.

"I do indeed." Expertly, Meg undid Catherine's troublesome back lacings. "I can always tell, for I see enough of the of the world and its ways with all the people that pass through here on their way to London." She sighed. "And seldom have I seen such a handsome, gallant gentleman as your—as yon knight."

Catherine stepped into the tub. "Beware you do not make your lad jealous with your languishings," she warned, half in jest.

Meg tossed her head. "We are betrothed, my lady. But betrothed is not wedded, though it is close enough." She giggled again. "Close enough to be bedded," she confided, soaping Catherine's back.

Seeing that she had a captive audience in Catherine, Meg went on with her confidences. "My da was bound to wed me off to Simon the Miller, all in the way of business, for the inn would get a discount on all its grain. But Simon is a widower twice my age with grown children, and I told Da I'd have none but Jack the Archer, for I'm with child by him."

"And your father gave his consent?" asked Catherine.

129

"Oh, he beat me first," said Meg airily. "But he came around, for he is strong for the king, and Jack is a king's archer and wears the king's livery, like your man."

Catherine sighed. "He is *not* my . . ."

"I know . . . I know . . ." said Meg penitently. She held out a big soft towel for Catherine. "But he is just across the hall, my lady." She grinned wickedly. "And if he came knocking on your door tonight, my lady, would you bar that door?"

It was a question for which Catherine had no ready answer, nor was she put to the test, for Sir Crispin did not come knocking on her door. Nor had she expected him to, for she knew his sense of honor was strong. Whether she wished he would was something she would not admit, even to herself.

In any event, she slept well and soundly, though her sleep was colored with vivid dreams in which she and Crispin were not knight and lady, encumbered with the duties and responsibilities of birth and breeding, but a peasant lad and his lass, idyllically happy with each other in a sylvan paradise, rather like Adam and Eve in Eden, she imagined.

But in the clear light of day, Catherine's dreams seemed like the wild flights of fancy that they were—ephemeral, evanescent, and even a little bit silly. She blushed to think of them. What nonsense it was to dream of herself and Sir Crispin in that particular context. Did she really wish either of them to be peasants, free to choose their own destinies? Of course she did not! Peasants, as nobody knew better than she, led hard lives, and they were no more free to make their own choices than she was. In most cases they were villeins, bound to the land and at the mercy of their lords and masters, much as their betters were at the mercy of the king. Everyone had his own station in life, to which it had pleased God to call him. There was no getting around that. And no evading one's responsibilities either. It was her duty in life to please her new mistress, the little queen, just as it was Sir Crispin's to serve the king loyally. And if, perhaps, at some point their destinies were to coincide . . . to intertwine . . . but she refused to speculate about that any further.

Meg had roused her at the crack of dawn as ordered, bringing bread and cheese to her room to break her fast and helping her to dress. At parting, Catherine pressed one of her few coins into the girl's palm and wished her well upon her wedding day. Then, humming a happy little tune, for she was anticipating just such a pleasant day of travel as the preceding one had been, she descended the massive staircase and made her way out into the courtyard, where Sir Crispin and his men, already mounted, were waiting for her. Some of the men-at-arms looked rather the worse for wear after their evening of self-indulgence, she noted with amusement.

Sir Crispin wished her a hearty good morning and helped her to mount her palfrey, waiting until she was firmly seated in the detested sidesaddle before putting his foot in the stirrup and swinging lithely onto his own mettlesome blood-bay stallion.

There was a neighing and stamping of hooves as the mounted men milled about the courtyard, preparing to move out. Catherine swung her palfrey's head around and urged the animal up beside Sir Crispin's stallion in order to take her customary place at his side.

And then her eyes widened, and she gasped aloud. At Sir Crispin's far side, mounted on one of their spare horses, was the Gypsy girl, Chantal.

Catherine stiffened in the saddle, her eyes shooting sparks of greenish fire. "What," she asked frostily, "is *she* doing here?"

There was a moment of uncomfortable silence. Sir Crispin had the grace to look a trifle abashed, as well he might, thought Catherine sourly.

"Chantal's horse has gone lame and her cart is broken down," he explained glibly. "I have given her leave to ride with us for her protection, as we are all going in the same direction."

Catherine's brows rose sharply. "To court?" she said in a skeptical tone.

"Only as far as London Bridge," Chantal, who was looking mightily amused about something, said. "I have friends who live upon the bridge and will take me in for a time and give me shelter."

"Indeed." *Male* friends, no doubt, surmised Catherine, who took note how the men-at-arms were ogling the Gypsy wench. She bestowed her smiles upon them all impartially and, unencumbered by the requirements of being a lady, rode astride, with her skirts bunched up and her shapely, sun-tanned legs bare for all to see.

Catherine kicked her horse into a trot and rode ahead in a sulky silence.

Behind her, she was aware that Crispin and the Gypsy wench rode ever closer together, he leaning towards her and chatting cordially, she looking up into his face and making bold eyes at him. They appeared to be on remarkably amicable terms, thought Catherine, in high dudgeon.

It was an acquaintance that had developed with amazing rapidity, she mused. After all, he had only met the girl in a casual sort of way yesterday afternoon, when she had accosted Catherine to read her palm. But from the scraps of low-voiced conversation she overheard, she concluded, to her dismay, that the two of them had renewed their acquaintance after she, Catherine, had retired for the night.

As, of course, they had. Crispin had fought an inner battle with himself on the way to Chantal's campsite, first detouring to check on the condition of his men. A number of them were drunk and quarrelsome, and he had relieved his frustrations by knocking a couple of heads together and dunking one drunken sot into the horse trough to sober up. But the muffled sounds coming from the stables, of other men, not so far gone in drink, tumbling wanton kitchen wenches in the straw, had aroused his already sternly repressed male urges to fever pitch. He was a man like other men, he had told himself roughly, not a monk who had taken holy vows of chastity. And with a muttered oath, he had turned his steps to the Gypsy's bed.

As he had surmised, she was an experienced partner who knew an infinite variety of ways to please a man, yet even though his sexual instincts were satisfied, he felt, as he rose from her bed, an inner emptiness that surprised him, for always before he had tumbled willing wenches here and there and gone on his way without regrets.

But it seemed he had lost his taste for willing wenches, he thought ruefully as he adjusted his garments, for he had not bothered to undress. Carelessly, he tossed the girl a handful of coins.

To his consternation, she sprang from the bed and began to berate him. "I am no whore," she spat, "to sell myself for a few coins. What I choose to give, I give freely to a man of my own choice!"

She gathered up the scattered coins and handed them back to him with a sly smile. "But if you would do me a small favor, as friend to friend, let us say, I would not take it amiss."

Crispin looked wary. "What favor do you seek?" he asked.

"Only let me go with you." Seeing his face darken, she wheedled, "Just as far as London Bridge. No farther. It is all I ask. Is that so great a favor, after all? Only let me ride pillion behind one of your men for the day, and I—"

"That wouldn't be necessary," he said, interrupting her. "We have spare horses, formerly ridden by men we lost to brigands. But what of your own horse and cart?"

"My cart has broken down, my horse is old and spavined, and the roads are not safe for a woman traveling alone."

All of which was true enough, Crispin supposed. He did not grudge her a place in his little entourage; on the contrary, it was an excellent opportunity for him to keep her under observation. He had already observed that she spoke French as well as English; he had learned that she had traveled extensively in France, which until recently was enemy country, and that she had a consuming interest in Catherine—her antecedents, temperament, and disposition. All this he attributed to a woman's natural curiosity. Still, she would bear watching, and he readily gave his permission for her to join their little party.

It was unfortunate, he thought ruefully as he rode along beside her, that the very sight of Chantal affected Catherine so openly! Her forthrightness was refreshing, but she must learn to dissimulate or she would not survive at court. Eyeing her straight, unyielding back with misgivings, he spurred his horse and, pulling alongside her, attempted to engage her in conversation, but her replies were terse, and eventually he dropped back again beside Chantal.

Catherine knew she was behaving foolishly, but she couldn't help herself, nor could she understand or control the powerful emotions that surged within her. She burned with jealousy, yet she had no claims on Sir Crispin, nor did she want any, she told herself with a toss of her red head. She was a free agent and so was he, free to demean himself with a Gypsy wench if he chose.

But her jealousy was further inflamed when they stopped to eat and she saw Crispin setting out the choicest portions for the girl. He was assiduous in his attentions to her, or so it seemed to Catherine.

Ironically, she, who just yesterday had wished that their journey need never end, now longed for it to be over. By late afternoon, she was weary and heartsick and sore from days spent in the saddle, and not even the towers of Westminster soaring in the distance lifted her spirits.

At London Bridge, Chantal parted from them, and Catherine hoped she had seen the last of the girl, who disappeared into one of the gabled houses leaning over the parapet. Catherine marveled at the dark tunnel of houses clustered together, and wondered aloud why anyone would choose to live upon the bridge.

Crispin shrugged. "The river smells a little, but less than the garbage that swills through city streets. And from the bridge you can see ships from all over the world come in to port. Look there . . . !" He pointed to a great ship, heavily laden and low in the water, passing slowly down the Thames, its white sails swelling in the wind.

The bridge itself was a marvel in stone, built to stand for all time. It was 40 feet wide, starting at the foot of Fish Street by the church of St. Magnus the Martyr and stretching to the far shore, carried by 20 enormous stone piers. At this time of day it was thronged with a colorful variety of traffic—richly dressed city merchants, churchmen, crippled beggars, noisy young apprentices, and pedlars tinkling little bells and crying their wares. Country folk pulling empty carts behind them were returning home after a day at the market, selling their produce in the Chepes.

Two or three women curiously dressed in garments turned inside-out with striped hoods caught Catherine's eye. "Why are they dressed in that curious fashion?" she asked inquisitively. "Are they doing a penance?"

"They are whores," said Crispin shortly, hurrying her along. "They are required by law to dress in striped garments."

When they had paid their toll and crossed over, Crispin advised her to stop and take one last look back at the great bridge that spanned the turbulent Thames, supporting on its massive pillars the weight of the river below and the houses above. Around the pillars, the river boiled and foamed, raging and battering against them and racing through the narrow arches. On the full swelling tide, ships and barges bobbed up and down, greenish water spraying their decks with foam.

"Magnificent!" Catherine breathed.

Behind them the river bubbled and churned. Before them lay London Town. As they turned their faces towards it once again, Catherine caught a glimpse of towers and turrets and crenelated battlements gleaming in the setting sun.

"London," she said softly, "Master Chaucer's 'flower of cities all.'" Suddenly all her worries and disappointments in the day fell away, and she felt uplifted. "How beautiful the world is," she whispered, she who had seen so little of it up till now.

Crispin shared her pleasure in the view that was spread out before and behind them, seeing the familiar sight anew through her eyes.

"Impressive, is it not?" he remarked.

"It is," Catherine agreed, her eyes sparkling green as the turbulent Thames.

Just then, the bells of St. Paul's began to peal, and in deeper, lower tones the great bells of the Abbey of Westminster joined in, tolling the hour.

"Blythe be thy churches, well-sounding by thy bells," quoted Catherine.

"Fair be thy wives, right lovesome, white and

137

small," Crispin said, finishing the quotation, thinking how aptly it fitted Catherine, who surely was "right lovesome," though tall rather than small.

The girl smiled brilliantly, her pleasure in the day renewed and her jealousy of the Gypsy wench utterly dissipated, reduced to the petty and insignificant trifle that it was.

Her smile was like the sun breaking through clouds, thought Crispin, bemused by it. He returned it with a broad smile of his own and, once again in accord and harmony, they turned their horses towards Westminster and the court.

Chapter Eight

Crispin delivered Catherine to the Maidens' Bower and left her there, promising to return on the morrow to escort her to her audience with the king. Catherine merely nodded, too tired to wonder how it was that a lowly baseborn knight had entree to the king himself.

Of the latter part of their journey, she only had a confused recollection of flaring torches, high crenelated walls and towers soaring into the night sky, the crisp exchange of passwords, the clatter of horses' hooves in the courtyard, and her own feet slipping on the cobblestones as Crispin lifted her from the saddle and set her on the ground. After that, his strong arm supported her through seemingly endless corridors until finally they reached the Maidens' Bower, where he bade her good night and turned her over to the ministrations of a kindly waiting-woman who helped her undress and put her to bed like a tired child.

In the morning, that same woman took her to

the Washplace and showed her where to bathe and dress. From there, they went into the Wardrobe, where Catherine's bundles had been stowed away, and unpacked the gown she would wear for her audience.

"Is this your best gown?" The woman held it up to the light and clucked her tongue against her teeth in disapproval. "Well, it will have to do, I suppose."

As she remembered the long hours her mother and old nurse had put into sewing the gown with loving hands, Catherine's quick temper flared, but she bit back the sharp retort that trembled on her lips.

Seeing the girl's face flush, the woman said more tolerantly, "The gown is well made, my dear, and of good-quality cloth and fine sewing, but fashions have changed much in recent years. The king is interested in fashions and sets the mode himself. I daresay he will send a tailor to fashion you a whole new wardrobe as a complement to the queen." She folded the gown over her arm. "Meanwhile, this will do well enough. And it is your color, after all."

But if Catherine's dress would do, just barely, her shoes would not. Exaggeratedly pointed long-toed shoes were de rigueur, and Catherine's simple slippers were rejected out of hand.

Vexed, the waiting-woman called sharply to a group of young women who were sorting finery and stowing it in chests. "Maude, Alys, Joan, come here," she demanded. "This is Catherine Clifford, who is to be presented to the king. Let her try on your shoes for size."

With much jesting and giggling, an exchange was made. Looking admiringly down at her feet in their borrowed finery, Catherine followed the waiting-woman into a dressing room, where her hair was done in the latest mode and her eyebrows fashionably plucked.

"Now you are fit to meet the king," declared the waiting-woman, with more warmth than she had yet displayed. "Come, we must hurry. The hour for your audience is set, and your knight is waiting for you in the solar. He will conduct you to the audience chamber."

Crispin's eyes lit up when he saw her. At least *he* had not been put off by her outmoded gown, she noticed, and the thought consoled her.

There was no time for pleasantries. Crispin hurried her along one corridor after another, each more resplendent than the last, or so it seemed to Catherine's country-bred eyes. Here and there, heads turned among servingmen and pages to see the country girl come to court to serve the queen.

Crispin's strides were long, but Catherine's long legs kept pace with him, though she was a trifle breathless by the time they reached their destination.

Low-voiced, Crispin spoke to a guardsman, who nodded and relayed a message to a waiting page. The boy darted off. "There will be a little delay before the king will see us," Crispin explained.

Catherine wondered if this was to be the pattern of her life from now on—to hurry up and wait. Doubtless, this was how the term "ladies-in-waiting" had originated, she thought, amused.

While they were waiting in the antechamber, she

141

commented on the scarcity of women about the court, and even in the Maidens' Bower.

"The late queen's ladies were dispersed after her death, and new ones have not yet been appointed," Crispin explained. "The process of selecting new ladies is ongoing even now, as well as the selection of those who will have the honor of accompanying the king to France." Crispin chuckled. "Of these, the only candidate chosen thus far is the new Duchess of Lancaster, and if that doesn't set the cat among the pigeons . . ."

Seeing Catherine's bewildered look, he explained. "The Duke of Lancaster's new wife is Katherine Swynford, she who was governess to the children of his first wife and his mistress for a number of years."

Catherine nodded impatiently. Even in her rural retreat she had heard gossip of the splendid John o' Gaunt, Duke of Lancaster, and his beautiful but notorious mistress.

"Their marriage has legitimated the Beaufort bastards, the children she bore him, and made her first lady of the land, outranking all others. You may well believe that this does not go over well in certain quarters," Crispin said wryly.

His face had acquired a dark and brooding expression when he spoke of the legitimation of the Beauforts, but Catherine had no time to wonder about it, for suddenly the doors of the audience chamber swung open and both their names were announced.

"Come." Crispin took her on his arm. Feeling her tremble with nervous anticipation, he patted her hand and murmured, "Don't be frightened. Despite

his high office, the king is but a mortal man."
Under his breath, he muttered, "Sometimes very
mortal."

They advanced slowly into the audience chamber,
for Catherine's knees were shaking from excitement. When Crispin made his obeisance, Catherine
sank into a curtsy, thankful of the court manners
that her mother had taught her with such pains.

The king gave them the nod, signifying permission to rise, but Catherine's head was bent, and she
did not see it. Amused, the king gave permission
verbally, in a voice that was higher-pitched than
Catherine expected. Timidly, she glanced upward
and could not repress a start of surprise. The man so
superbly arrayed in royal regalia, the man who controlled the destinies of all Englishmen and wom-
en, looked enough like Sir Crispin to be his twin!

When she dared look more closely, however,
Catherine realized that there were distinct differ-
ences between the two men, other than that of
costume, for compared to the king, Crispin was
plainly dressed.

Both men shared the long, lean Plantagenet build,
but while Crispin was muscular, the king was as
willowy and supple as a youth. Their features were
similar, but while the king's nose was straight and
delicate, Crispin's was large, fierce, and hawklike,
that same jutting nose Catherine had twitted him
about when first they met. His face was harder
too, she realized, with sharper planes and angles,
while the king's face was soft and puffy with self-
indulgence, or so she surmised.

But their eyes were the same piercing Plantagenet
blue, though she fancied the king's were a trifle

Sue Deobold

shifty by comparison. And though they both had the same well-shaped lips, the king's mouth had a sly twist, or so it seemed to Catherine.

Slim, soft fingers laden with glittering gems took her by the arm, and the king said, "Come. Let us walk a little. I would question you as to your fitness to serve the queen." He waved away a bevy of sycophants clustered about him and took Catherine a little apart from the horde.

Catherine gathered her scattered wits and answered a rapid-fire volley of questions in French, for which fortunately she was well prepared. Yes, she could dance, and play chess, and ride quite well, though she had never gone hawking.

"I fancy we can remedy that. Sir Crispin can be your hawking master." He continued his slow progress about the room, Catherine still on his arm. "I am told the queen loves music above all things. Do you play an instrument? Or sing?"

"Both. I . . . that is, I sing very well. French songs taught me by my mother," Catherine said proudly. "And I play the lute, though not so well," she added honestly.

The king waved a languid hand, the gemstones of his many rings glittering. "We will send you a music master." He eyed the old-fashioned cut of her gown with disapproval. "And a tailor."

Catherine felt she had been given a thorough examination and found wanting. Sensing her discomfiture, the king smiled a little, and when he smiled Catherine was caught up and held captive to the famed Plantagenet charm, a charm, she suddenly realized, that Crispin shared in full measure.

Still smiling, the king raised his be-ringed hand

144

and tilted her chin, subjecting her to a piercing scrutiny. Catherine met his searching gaze proudly, neither blinking, nor looking away.

"It is a good face," the king mused aloud. "Not beautiful, perhaps, but kind and honest and caring." His hand fell away. "Watch over my little queen well," he ordered. "And make her merry." Beckoning Sir Crispin, he nodded dismissal with a curt "She'll do."

"You might have *told* me!" Catherine raged.

"Of our relationship?" Crispin shrugged. "What does it matter, after all?" His face hardened. "Yes, the king and I are brothers," he admitted. "But I was born on the wrong side of the blanket. A bastard, never openly acknowledged by my father. By *our* father," he corrected himself. "The Black Prince indeed." His mouth curled wryly.

"And your mother?" Catherine couldn't help asking.

"A court beauty married to a complaisant cuckold, fool enough to feel flattered that his lovely faithless wife caught the prince's roving eye, fool enough to let them pass off her bastard as his own, though everyone knew the truth of the story and tittered behind their hands," he said savagely.

"You *claimed* to be a landless knight," Catherine said accusingly.

"And so I am," Crispin asserted. "My mother's husband was not so besotted as to let family property slip through his fingers, though he gave me his name. The Black Prince left no provision for me, and in any case, bastards cannot inherit. I have no estates, nor am I likely to have, unless my brother chooses to bestow something upon me at his whim." Crispin's mouth curled cynically. "So far, he has chosen to bestow little except the spurs of knighthood, and those," he said proudly, "I won for myself." He sighed. "Sometimes I think the king chooses to keep me at court, almost his mirror image, as a plaything, for his own amusement."

"Surely not," Catherine protested. "What you said about the laws of inheritance is true enough, I suppose," she said haltingly, for she knew little of such matters. "But . . . but take the Beauforts, for example . . ."

"A special case," said Crispin dismissively. "The Black Prince is long dead. The Beauforts had nothing until John o' Gaunt married their mother and legitimated them. It took a papal decree and a special act of Parliament, I believe. But now young John is Earl of Somerset, Harry is well on his way to becoming a cardinal, and Joan is to wed Ralph Neville of Raby, the Lord of Westmoreland."

He brooded briefly. "I suppose my Uncle of Lancaster is the best of the Plantagenets. Of them all, he has been the kindest. In fact, his son, Henry of Bolingbroke, helped me win my spurs and offered me a position in his household, but the king will not release me from his service."

The Duchess of Lancaster too was kind, Catherine recalled. She had, in a manner speaking, taken Catherine under her wing during the past few days, doing all in her power to make the girl feel at ease in her new surroundings. "After all, we share the same saint's day and the same name, though we spell it differently," she'd said with a smile. "And we are both redheads." Though Katherine

Swynford's auburn hair was flecked with gray and the younger Catherine's autumn-leaf brown.

"The Lancasters *are* kind," Catherine now admitted. "Though I do not like Henry of Bolingbroke overmuch." She spoke hesitantly, remembering too late that he and Crispin were cousins. "They say he has an eye for King Richard's throne."

"Oh, they say . . . they say . . ." said Crispin mockingly. Irritated and impatient, he spurred ahead over the moorland to loose his hawk at a smaller bird winging its way through the air.

Catherine sighed. Though she loved to ride, she did not like hawking, deeming it a cruel sport. The bird on her wrist blinked beady yellow eyes at her and flapped its pinioned wings, and she made a rude face at it.

This, however, was her first opportunity to talk with Crispin in private since her audience with the king, and she wanted to make the most of it. On their way from the audience chamber, she had been burning to question him, but they had been detained by courtiers, eager for an introduction to the queen's newest lady. And ever since that day, she had been beset by tutors and tailors and shoemakers sent by the king, while Crispin himself had been in attendance upon him. And since the king and his household had flitted from Westminster to Windsor, then to Eltham and Leeds Castle, she had seen nothing of Crispin for days.

But she had had much to occupy herself in the interim. By now, she had a lavish new wardrobe, the likes of which she had never imagined, consisting largely of houppelandes and sideless surcoats, fur plastrons and silver hip belts, with gold or silver cauls for the hair.

She had also learned all the latest dance steps, she could trill a tune set by her music master, and in addition she had been taught the skills she would need to wait upon royalty. She had been taught how to comb a lady's hair without pulling it, how to lace up a gown properly, how to fold back the bedding in an attractive fashion, and how to serve food and drink to the queen with all the proper courtesy.

When she had a few minutes to herself, which wasn't often, she liked best of all to explore the palace. Westminster was a self-contained little city in itself, she had discovered, with its many roofs and spires, halls and chambers, and galleries and corridors without end.

Fortunately, she had a well-developed sense of direction and seldom got lost for long. In any case, there was always someone to show her the way for the palace swarmed with people—craftsmen, cooks and carpenters, architects, jewelers and silversmiths—for the king actively promoted the arts and had a fine appreciation of handicrafts of all sorts.

There were also all the household officers, whom she had come to know by sight—the Master of the Wardrobe, Master of the King's Horse, and innumerable others—ushers, knights, squires, pages, accountants, clerics, and priests.

Occasionally, taking a corner quickly, or wandering in the shrubbery in the gardens, she ran across a lad who reminded her vaguely of the Gypsy girl, and it troubled her. Just the other day, she was sure she had seen him, or her, darting among the pages. She chewed her lower lip thoughtfully. She hated to remind Crispin of the Gypsy girl, but she felt it her duty to confide her suspicions to someone, and who else was there that she could trust?

Clapping her heels to her horse, she set off after Crispin's blood-bay stallion. As she cantered across the moor, she reflected that this was as good an opportunity as she was likely to get to broach the subject to him. His mood was black enough as it was, so she wasn't going to spoil anything by bringing up the girl as a topic of conversation.

But when she asked if he had seen the Gypsy, he denied it. "Why do you ask?" he said absently, calling his falcon in with a lure.

But halfway through her explanation, he snorted incredulously. "You must be imagining it." He frowned. "A lad that resembles the Gypsy girl. What of it? All Gypsies look more or less alike. Perhaps he is kin to her—a brother or cousin."

Abruptly, he changed the subject. "It's time you showed me what progress you've made with your bird. Can you coax the goshawk to eat from your hand as the Master of Falconry taught you? Will it come when you call it back?" he asked her. "Let the jesses go, and we shall see."

But inwardly, he was more disturbed by Catherine's confidences than he would admit. As the goshawk soared skyward, then returned to Catherine's lure, he scowled in thought. Was the Gypsy a spy in disguise? he wondered. And if so, for whom and for what purpose? He had had his suspicions all along. He should have brought her in for questioning long ago. But it was not too late to track her down. There was a powerful faction at court opposing the king's French marriage. If she were working for them, there would be the devil to pay!

Chapter Nine

Crispin spread his nets far and wide, searching out the Gypsy, but it was Catherine who found her first, quite by accident.

She was not even looking for her; indeed, she had all but put the matter out of her mind. Crispin's reaction—his mockery and mild ridicule—had stung, as had his barbed comments on her awkward handling of the goshawk. Resolving to distinguish herself the next time he took her hawking, she relegated the Gypsy to the back of her mind and spent long hours in the mews, trying to tame her bird, stroking its feathers, and filching delicacies from the kitchens for its delectation. If chopped chicken heads could be termed delicacies, she thought with a little grimace of disgust as she trained the hawk to come at her call using the chicken heads as lures.

By the time she saw Crispin again, she was well on the way to becoming an expert bird handler.

Negotiations for the king's French marriage had dragged on, the king had gone on a royal progress to distant parts of the country, presumably to win public support for the French marriage and his peace plans, and Crispin had been in his train.

There were those who objected to the marriage, not because the bride was French and the daughter of England's enemies, but because she was a child. Even in five or six years she would not be the proper age for a wife, they argued, and until she was a woman grown, she would not be able to provide the king and the kingdom with an heir. To which King Richard stubbornly replied that every passing day would remedy the deficiency of her youth, and that he could take charge of the education of his child bride and bring her up to be a good Englishwoman, more at home with the manners and customs of the English than any adult foreign princess would ever be. Moreover, as a relatively young man, still in his twenties, he was young enough to wait for her to grow up.

Catherine herself couldn't see what all the fuss was about. The marriage documents were already signed and sealed, and a proxy wedding had already taken place. It was official, in her opinion, and she was beginning to find the long delay tedious in the extreme. Though if Crispin had been closer at hand, she was sure they could have found ways to while away the time together most pleasantly! She found herself a trifle melancholy, yearning for his presence. Even his black moods were an improvement over not seeing him at all!

Keeping busy was a palliative, and Catherine applied herself to her lessons with diligence. She was hurrying in from the mews one day, and was late for her lesson with her music master, but the pompous little man was nowhere to be seen. In his place was a handsome youth with glistening black curls worn a little longer than fashion decreed. He had a well-turned leg—clad in fashionable particolored hose, Catherine noticed with appreciation—and his face was half concealed by his curling black locks as he bent his head to tune her lute.

The lad lifted his head and turned to face her, smiling a mocking smile that teased and taunted.

"You . . ." Catherine gasped. "What are you doing here?"

"I have come to give you a music lesson," the Gypsy said calmly.

"Where is Maitre Jacques?" Catherine demanded. "What have you done with him?" She looked about her wildly, as if expecting to see the body of her music master stuffed into a chest, his short stubby legs protruding from it, or at the very least sprawled on the floor.

"He cannot be with you today," the Gypsy announced. "I have come in his place." She strummed a few notes upon the lute. "Your instrument was badly out of tune," she said severely. "I have mended it for you. Listen!" she commanded. "Does this not sound better to you?" She played a lively little ditty, humming the tune in accompaniment.

"You have many talents, I perceive," said Catherine coldly, for she had now had time to gather a measure of composure. "Teller of fortunes, tuner of lutes, player of lutes . . ."

"Singer of songs . . ." suggested the Gypsy with a grin.

"Sing me this song, Gypsy," Catherine commanded. "Tell me what you are doing here masquerading as a boy."

"I make rather a pretty boy, do I not?" said the Gypsy complacently, stretching out her shapely legs in their particolored hose and preening with satisfaction. One leg was striped in blue, the other in forest green.

Catherine was fast losing patience. "I want to know what you are doing here," she demanded. Her voice was growing a trifle shrill, she noticed.

The Gypsy pouted prettily. "I already told you. I have come to practice music with you."

"I need no practice with such as you!" snapped Catherine in exasperation.

The Gypsy smirked. "The king thinks otherwise."

"The king! What do you know of the king?"

"I know it is not wise to defy him." The Gypsy jumped up and began to stroll about the room, idly strumming the lute.

"Does the king know who you are . . . what you are?" Catherine was dumfounded at the Gypsy's effrontery.

"He knows that I am a skillful player of the lute." She stepped closer to Catherine, strumming a few more chords. "More skillful than you."

"That remains to be seen!" snapped Catherine.

The Gypsy extended the instrument to her with a mocking smile. "Show me," she teased.

Catherine thrust the instrument away angrily. "Does the king know you are a woman, disguising yourself as a boy?" she demanded.

"The king knows what he needs to know." The Gypsy's face darkened. "As for you, my lady, you know too much. I warn you, you would be wiser not to meddle with the affairs of your betters."

"You . . . my better!" Catherine hooted. The notion was absurd. Chantal was a Gypsy wench who, for who knows what reason, had donned boyish garb. Was it to spy upon the court? Upon the king? Or upon her?

Catherine moved decisively, sidestepping swiftly and reaching toward a bell rope to summon help. "You are absurd," she blustered. "I shall tell—"

The Gypsy stepped closer. "You will tell no one." Her voice was menacing. "No one." Bringing her face close to Catherine's, she said, "I warn you, if you meddle with me, you meddle with more than you know. Far better for you to accept things as they are, for I tell you, lady, things are not always what they seem. And this is a lesson you have yet to learn, though you need to study on it." Picking up the rejected lute, she said, "Now, let us have our lesson in peace, for I have come to make music with you." She sat down in a window seat, and Catherine, subdued, sank down beside her.

"Chantal . . ." she began weakly.

The Gypsy shook her head, and her tangled curls danced on her shoulders. "Charlot," she said, correcting Catherine. Pushing the curls back from her face, she began to pluck the lute. "When I am dressed in this guise, I am known as Charlot. You will remember that," she commanded.

Catherine felt as if she had stepped into a maze of intrigue which she could neither understand or comprehend. Had Crispin been available, Catherine would have confided in him, despite the Gypsy's prohibitions to tell no one, but he was not at hand, and since she did not know whom to trust, she wisely held her tongue, biding her time.

From then on, she frequently saw Chantal moving freely about the palace in her male guise as Charlot, and she smarted at the recollection of her humiliation at the Gypsy's hands, for she felt that she had not distinguished herself during their confrontation. But as time passed and Crispin did not return, the very familiarity of the sight of Chantal dulled her apprehensions.

The king returned from his royal progress, but Crispin did not accompany him, having been detached from the king's retinue for special duty in the north, or so Catherine was told when she made discreet inquiries. Then the court moved to Windsor for the rest of the summer, and Catherine saw Chantal no more. Occasionally, she wondered what had become of her, but the duty of readying the little queen's apartments for occupancy had fallen to Catherine, and she threw herself into the task with enthusiasm which left her little time for idle speculation.

By the time Crispin returned, the court had moved back to Westminster again and Catherine, on the eve of her departure for France, was in a flurry of preparations. And what with her preoccupation, and the sheer unexpected joy of seeing Crispin again, Catherine forgot all about the Gypsy.

She was in the garden, having discovered a secluded spot where cooling fountains splashed and flowering plants and shrubbery were especially beautiful. It was a retreat she made a beeline for whenever her duties permitted.

Reluctant to go back inside on such a beautiful day to resume her packing, she lingered, and unable to resist the temptation, knelt down to pull a few stray weeds that the gardeners had overlooked, her gardener's fingers fairly itching to till the soil.

"Cat!"

She glanced up in surprise. Nobody ever called her "Cat" except . . . except . . . "Crispin—oh, Crispin!"

Awkwardly, she scrambled to her feet and dusted off her hands. It was her misfortune, she thought ruefully, that he should come and catch her all unawares, with her hands grubby with soil and curling tendrils of unruly hair straying from her headdress. She put up her hands to tidy her hair, and then thought better of it, fearing to smear dirt from her hands to her face.

But it didn't matter, after all. Nothing did. For he was beside her in two long strides, or so it seemed, and then she was caught up in his strong arms. And she was glad to be there, happier than she had thought possible.

He was leaner and browner than ever, after a summer spent on the roads and byways of England, and his tawny hair was bleached white-gold by the sun. His eyes were even a more piercing blue as they roved hungrily over her face and form.

"Cat, I missed you."

"And I you," she blurted out with her incorrigible honesty, too happy to make a pretense of playing the coy court lady. "I expected you back with king."

"Richard, curse him, had me chasing all over the country, from the Scottish borders to the Welch marches. He wants to be sure our borders are secure before he leaves the country," Crispin explained. "And on my way home, I made a personal detour that took me more than a few miles out of my way." He grinned teasingly. "Now, where do you suppose I went?"

Catherine looked at him blankly, shaking her head. "I have no idea."

"Clifford Manor, of course." He opened his tunic and pulled forth a packet of letters. "Your mother is well and sends her love, as does your old nurse. Your mother also sends these letters to you. The blotches at the bottom of the page represent kisses sent by your old nurse, or so I understand."

"*Oh!*" Catherine's eyes grew wide, and she instinctively made a grab for the letters, but on a sudden whim, Crispin held them above his head far out of her reach.

"Not so fast." He shook his head. "The price of these letters is a kiss, my beauty." He teased her with a mock leer, laughter in his eyes.

Catherine pouted. "I am not so free with my kisses, sir." Though her heart beat faster, she took a step backward. Then another.

Unwisely, Crispin lowered his arms, and Catherine seized the advantage, dancing round him, then making a sudden leap and snatching at the precious missives. But they were still out of her reach, and colliding with Crispin, she nearly lost her balance.

He put out a strong arm to steady her, and then held her fast. "Cat . . . Cat," he murmured huskily, "I went far out of my way for you. May I not claim my reward?"

His face, bent downwards, hovered over hers, and she felt his warm breath, sweet on her face. He also smelt, not so sweetly, of horse and sweat and saddle leather, but Catherine did not mind, for she knew it meant that he had come straight from the stables to her, and moreover, she was reminded of his long journey, which in part he had undertaken for her sake. And indeed it was a man's odor, strong and lusty and wholly male, quite unlike the perfumed courtiers to whom she had grown accustomed and whom she held, to a certain extent, in contempt.

"Oh, very well," she said crossly, but she was making a pretense of ill humor, and they both knew it.

A kiss was nothing, she told herself stoutly, as she raised her face to his. A token of affection between friends, a forfeit in a game of Hoodman Blind, or a penalty exacted by the Lord of Misrule at Christmas revelries. That was all. It was not as if she had never been kissed before.

And yet it was, for Crispin's kiss was like no other she had ever experienced. It was surprisingly gentle, his lips pressing tentatively against hers, then tenderly covering her mouth.

As he moved his mouth over hers, Catherine shuddered with delight, her lips instinctively parted, and she succumbed to his forceful domination as his tongue grew increasingly bold, exploring the inner recesses of her mouth.

158

She moaned, feeling a spate of wild, sweet longings ripple through her, strange longings that she could not identify, and which left her weak and breathless and shaken. As her knees buckled, she swayed against him, savoring the hard lean strength of his body, drawing her strength from his, and twining herself about him, as a vine will twine about a stout oak tree.

Crispin uttered a groan deep in his throat and, as he felt her respond to his caresses, savored her kisses as the headiest of fine French wine. The kisses did not slake his thirst for her; they merely deepened and intensified it, warning him that nothing but the final intimacy ever would.

In their total absorption in each other, the packet of letters was forgotten, and somehow the packet came undone, and letters drifted down about them as falling leaves to lie unheeded at their feet.

"That," said Crispin with satisfaction, "was worth the saddle sores and blisters on my backside."

"Ooh!" Catherine pulled away, her face flaming. How could he be so crude! So coarse! To talk about saddle sores at a time like this!

"I was merely jesting, dear heart," Crispin said penitently.

Catherine, who had yet to learn that a man will sometimes hide behind an ill-timed jest to conceal his deeper emotions, walked away haughtily.

She sat down on a garden bench to sort her letters as Crispin retrieved them from the ground and handed them to her. One had fluttered into the fountain and was virtually illegible, but the others, dated consecutively and written in her mother's neat hand, were a sweet breath of home, and she buried her nose in them and began to read, ignoring her companion.

Which was just as well, as it gave Crispin a chance to sort out his feelings for her, feelings that he now realized, too late, went further than he had supposed.

He had missed her unspeakably while he was away, more than he had expected or even thought possible. It was his deep-seated yearning for her that had sent him miles out of his way to bring her back letters from home.

Seeing her bright head, with its elaborate coils of burnished hair, bent over her letters, he wondered for the hundredth time how it was that this simple country girl had captured his heart when more worldly beauties had left it untouched for so long.

To be sure, she no longer gave the appearance of utter simplicity. She was richly dressed, and in accordance with current fashion, the hair on her forehead had been plucked back from her brow to make her forehead appear broader and to enhance the oval shape of her face, according to the prevailing standards of feminine beauty. Her eyebrows had also been plucked into fashionable narrow arches, in a way that he found unappealing on other women, but endearing on Catherine.

But inwardly, he was sure that nothing had changed; she was still an innocent with her rich inner beauty still shining through.

As for himself, nothing in his circumstances had changed either. He was still a landless knight, with no fortune and no prospects and nothing to offer her. He was no more than the king's bastard brother, whom the king chose to employ as no more than an errand boy. His sovereign's treatment of him sorely galled the man who, but for an accident of birth . . .

Catherine's voice broke into this reverie. To bridge the deepening silence, she remarked, "My mother writes that the harvest is good this year. She says that she will follow your advice about the crops and thanks you for it." Her mother had written more, all in praise of Sir Crispin, but that Catherine chose not to divulge.

She sighed. "I wish I might go home for a visit before we go to France," she said wistfully.

"You know that cannot be," Crispin said gently.

"Oh, I know, but that does not make it easier."

She looked melancholy as she folded her letters and tucked them carefully away in their pouch. "Do you go with us to France?" she inquired, hoping that the answer would be in the affirmative.

"I do, though more from necessity than by choice."

Crispin's face set in stern lines, and Catherine looked at him inquiringly, wondering why he suddenly looked so grim. "The king leaves Henry of Bolingbroke in charge of the realm while he is in France, and once again I asked leave to serve under him, but was refused," he said shortly.

"Oh . . ." Catherine had been hoping that Crispin would be included in the king's pretinue, for it was not especially large and, inevitably, she and Crispin would be thrown much together. It was a prospect that filled her with delight, and she felt more than a little piqued that he did not share her anticipation. She had been looking forward to enjoying the festivities attendant upon the royal wedding with him, and was deflated that he so obviously preferred duty in England to acting as her escort at the various functions she would be expected to attend.

Irked, she said boldly, "If I were king, I would not trust Henry of Bolingbroke so far. King Richard may find he has no realm to come back to!"

Crispin looked startled. "Bah! Women's gossip!" he retorted, nettled.

"Not so," Catherine declared. "I have observed with my own two eyes how Henry courts the people, who hail him as 'Bluff Hal' or 'Good Harry.' And many a time I have seen him look upon King Richard with envy when the two dine with the rest of us in the Great Hall." She tossed her head. "Mark my words, Crispin, Henry has his eyes on Richard's throne."

"Well, well, you have become quite the political expert while I've been gone," Crispin sneered.

"I have eyes in my head," she snapped. "Crispin, it's as plain as the nose on your face." An unfortunate turn of phrase, Catherine reflected, regretting the words as soon as they were out of her mouth, harking back as they did to their stormy initial encounter.

"Such talk verges on treason," said Crispin abruptly. "By now, you should have learned to guard your tongue, Cat," he warned her. "A word in the wrong quarter could do incalculable harm. You would do well to remember that the Lancasters have been kind to you," he added sternly.

"So they have," Catherine agreed readily. "That is, the Duchess Katherine has been kindness itself. But Henry of Bolingbroke is not her son but only her stepson, and he . . ." Catherine floundered to a stop, with a feeling that she was only digging herself in deeper.

Oh, dear, she thought miserably, how had she gotten herself in such a coil? Crispin's face was black as a thundercloud.

"I will heed your warning," she said meekly.

"See that you do." He glanced up at the sky, which had become overcast in the course of their conversation. "It looks like rain. Let me escort you back to the palace, my lady," he said formally, offering his arm.

Mutely, Catherine rose from her seat. Peering at his dark and thunderous face, she knew that there was no possibility of winning him back into good humor. Would she never learn to guard her tripping tongue? she thought despairingly. Silently castigating herself all the way, she accompanied him back to the palace.

Chapter Ten

The royal wedding was the stuff that dreams were made of. Girlish dreams, at least.

The splendor and opulence of the French court met and far exceeded Catherine's expectations, even though she had grown accustomed to the lavish bachelor court of the widower English king.

She was bedazzled nonetheless by the sheer magnificence of her new surroundings: by the velvet hangings and the silken tapestries, the carpets so thick that she felt she was floating on air rather than setting foot on solid ground, the gold plate and precious Venetian goblets and bejeweled salt cellars.

The wedding guests were likewise very grand, magnificently clad in rich raiment and glittering with gems, but none was so grand as the mother of the bride, Isabeau of Bavaria, Queen of France. She was a famous beauty, possessing flawless alabaster skin, magnificent dark eyes and hair, and a shapely bosom whose decolletage was extreme, even by the standards of the French court.

Her daughter, Isabella, the bride, was a young replica of her magnificent mother, though Catherine devoutly hoped that the resemblance was only superficial, for the Queen of France was reputed to be rapacious and greedy beyond belief, as well as utterly amoral, numbering among her lovers the Duke of Burgundy, her husband's uncle, as well as his younger brother, the Duke of Orleans. These two were mortal enemies, each plotting to seize royal power from the King of France when it fell from the sick man's feeble hands.

For the King of France was afflicted with a debilitating mental illness that at times utterly incapacitated him. His reign had had a brilliant beginning, and his loyal subjects had given him the nickname Charles, the Well Beloved, but while still a young man he had become liable to bouts of insanity during which, among other things, he imagined he was made of glass and might break. During these periodic bouts of insanity, he also expressed an extreme aversion to his wife, which, in view of her reputed excesses, Catherine found not at all peculiar!

At the moment, the king was enjoying one of his rare periods of lucidity, which enabled the royal couple to present a united front on this festive occasion, the marriage of their eldest daughter.

Prior to the wedding ceremony, the kings of France and England met with great pomp and ceremony at Calais. Catherine, who was lodged on the outskirts of town at a very fine hostelry which was taken for the less important wedding guests, was not present at their ceremonial meeting, but Crispin was, and he obligingly described the scene to her in great detail. She listened avidly, wishing she had been there to see it for herself, but since she had not been, she was glad of the chance to see the grand spectacle through his eyes.

She was glad he had sought her out for more than one reason. Ever since their quarrel back in England, there had been a certain constraint between them, a constraint she did not know how to bridge.

She bitterly regretted taunting him on that never-to-be-forgotten occasion, wishing she could take back her hasty words which had been inspired solely by pique. On the other hand, what kind of relationship could they build, she wondered moodily, if they could not be frank and open and honest with each other? She had a mind of her own and was entitled to her own opinions.

Nevertheless, in subsequent meetings, she had taken care to keep her own opinions strictly to herself! They had met several times since then, on a casual basis; he had even taken her hawking a few times and complimented her on her improved handling of her bird. But still, there was that awkward constraint. They had never quite gotten back to that easy friendliness that had characterized their relationship; he had been correct, and distant and polite, no more than that.

She had hoped that their friendship might ripen on board ship, but she had seen little of him during the voyage to France. Instead, she had thought of him a good deal, delicious thoughts in which he had rescued her from shipwreck.

But annoyingly, the Channel had remained as calm as a mill pond, and the voyage had passed without incident. To pass the time, she had taken to needlework, embroidering a pair of gloves intended as a gift for the little queen. She'd been scowling over a tangle of embroidery silks in the inn parlor when, most unexpectedly, he was announced.

"You've gotten those silks into a hopeless snarl," he said good-naturedly. "Let me pick it out for you."

Catherine watched and listened as he sorted the bright silk into neat skeins. Not for worlds would she have him guess how much her body hungered for the touch of his hands, nor how the sound of his melodious voice affected her so powerfully. With a little effort she dragged her attention back to the gist of his words, and then found herself caught up in it.

"The two kings slowly advanced towards each other," Crispin was saying, "between two lines of four hundred French knights on the one hand and four hundred English knights on the other. It was a magnificent display," he said enthusiastically. "The King of France was escorted by the Duke of Lancaster and the Duke of Gloucester, while the King of England was escorted by the Dukes of Burgundy and Berry."

"The Duke of Berry?" said Catherine thoughtfully. "Isn't he the royal duke who collects all those objets d'art and commissions so many illuminated manuscripts?"

"He is." Crispin looked a little annoyed at the interruption. "The duke is reported to have seventeen castles full of such objects, and as you may

167

imagine, he and Richard got on famously. Richard even promised him a pair of unusual greyhounds available only in Scotland to add to his collection of rare dogs."

"I must admit," Crispin continued meditatively, "Richard surpassed himself at the meeting of the kings. Charles of France is an ailing, fretful invalid, pallid and spindly and not much to look at. But Richard was superb, looking every inch a king. Handsome, debonair, and memorable."

"I know," Catherine agreed, smiling fondly at King Richard's handsome half brother, whom she secretly felt far surpassed the king. But she was glad that Crispin was able to forget his bitterness and animosity and ungrudgingly take pride in his sovereign. Crispin's admission was as close to an apology as she was likely to get, she realized suddenly, with a sudden rush of gladness.

"What happened then?" she prompted.

"At the instant the two kings met, in the middle of the avenue of knights, the eight hundred men fell to their knees in salutation.

"The two kings saluted each other by kissing on both cheeks in the French fashion," he went on. "Then, they went into the pavilion specially erected for this occasion, followed by the royal dukes. As they disappeared into the tent, the eight hundred knights sprang to their feet and brandished drawn swords that glittered in the sunlight. It was an intensely moving sight," he assured her.

Catherine breathed a long satisfied sigh of contentment. So well had Crispin described the scene to her that she felt as if she had been there herself, seeing it with her own eyes. She felt happy that he had wanted to share this intensely moving experience with her, happy and humbled. And somehow, during his recitation, she had felt the constraint between them dissipate, as if by magic.

Crispin hesitated, then taking a deep breath, continued his narrative. "Immediately after the ceremony, the king singled a few of us out for special honors," he went on in a different tone.

"Oh?" Catherine pricked up her ears.

"Cat, I am to be Governor of Windsor," he announced with pride.

"Oh, Crispin, I'm so happy for you!" Catherine's eyes glowed. It was a great honor, she knew. Moreover, she was well aware how much he had resented being kept at court as the king's messenger, subject to his half brother's sometimes erratic whims.

And Catherine was happy for herself as well, for Crispin's new appointment inevitably meant that they would see more of each other, for she would be in attendance on the queen at Windsor. It was the royal residence deemed most suitable for the little queen, for in view of her extreme youth she would keep her own household, entirely separate from the king's until she came of age to be a wife in fact as well as in name.

That is, Catherine would be at Windsor with the little queen *if* she passed her next test. The happy, confident look faded from her face, to be replaced with a worried frown. "Tomorrow I am to go to St. Omer," she remarked. "The Queen of France wishes to interview me to determine if I am a suitable companion for her daughter. What if she doesn't like me?" she fretted. "Will I be sent home in disgrace?"

"Which 'she'?" asked Crispin, amused. "The mother or the daughter?"

"Either . . . both . . . I don't know." She picked up her neglected embroidery and began to push the needle through the linen, scowling nearsightedly at it. "I'm terrified," she confided, pulling impatiently at the tangled silk thread.

"You needn't be," Crispin assured her, trying to bolster her sagging spirits. "From what I hear, the Queen of France is hardly a model of maternal solicitude. The younger children go hungry and neglected, while Isabella is made much of ever since the marriage negotiations began."

"Then she will probably behave like a spoiled child, difficult and impossible to please," Catherine prophesied glumly, jerking at her embroidery silk, which had tangled itself into a knot.

"She will not," Crispin predicted confidently. "You have nothing to fear from Queen Isabella," he assured her. "She is an enchanting little girl."

Firmly, he took her tangled embroidery work from Catherine and set it aside. "You are making a mess of this, Cat." Catching up her now-empty hands, he squeezed them encouragingly between his own. "Would you feel better about it if I accompanied you to St. Omer?"

"Oh, Crispin, *would* you?" There was nothing Catherine would like better. She knew his presence would give her renewed confidence in herself, even as his hands, lightly clasping her own, sent little jerks and tremors through her flesh.

But though she appreciated his offer of support, she thought better of it. "No," she decided reluctantly. "This is something I must do on my own.

And Queen Isabeau is sending a litter and an escort of soldiers for me. But it is good of you to offer," she added hastily. "Extremely good."

"There is much that I would do for you, Cat, if you would let me," he said huskily.

Catherine, who did not quite know what to make of this unasked-for declaration, smiled uncertainly and hastily changed the subject.

Crispin was right, Catherine found the next day, to her everlasting relief. The little Queen of England, for so she had been styled ever since her proxy wedding earlier in the year, was as exquisite as a beautifully dressed doll and just about as animated. Tall for her age, and slender, she was a miniature replica of her mother, but there the resemblance ceased, for while Queen Isabeau's dark eyes contained the smoldering challenge of a courtesan, Isabella's eyes were gentle, with a sweet expression denoting, Catherine hoped, a placid disposition. She was also, in Catherine's opinion, too thin, too pale, and far too solemn. When she remembered the mischievous girl that she had been at that age, Catherine's heart ached for the overburdened little queen, and she vowed then and there to follow King Richard's advice: "to make my bride merry," even if she had to to play the fool in order to do so.

Receiving the royal nod of dismissal from Queen Isabeau, Catherine curtsied, first to her and then to the little queen, and backed out of their presence, as etiquette demanded, receiving a small smile of acknowledgment from the little girl, but none from her formidable mother. From the questions the woman had put to her, and her responses, Catherine could not tell if the mother was satisfied, but she left St. Omer resolving to find a way to gladden the heart of the little girl, if she were given the opportunity to do so. As she rode back to Calais in the litter that swayed so sickeningly, her head danced with plans and schemes for entertaining and amusing her new little mistress.

And for the first time she wondered what it must be like to be a royal pawn in the game of politics, to marry, not for love or even for liking, but at the behest of others, because one must. And she began to realize anew how lucky she was to be simple Catherine Clifford, with a heart free to bestow on whomever she chose. It was a heady prospect. Even if she had been burdened with great estates or enormous wealth, she might have ended up a king's ward, to be sold to the highest bidder. But as it was, she had unusual freedom of movement and choice, and she meant to make the most of it!

Neither by word or expression had Queen Isabeau indicated her opinion of Catherine, and it was not until the next day, with Catherine still on tenterhooks as she dressed for the wedding, that she received an indication of royal favor. Queen Isabeau sent word that the little queen wished Catherine to share in the honor of carrying her train.

Catherine's heart leaped up into her mouth. She was totally unprepared for such a contingency, and feverishly went over in her mind the proper procedures so that she might not stand when she should be kneeling, or kneel when she should be standing. And horror of horrors, what if she should drop her end of the heavy garment? She went to church praying that this or no lesser catastrophe should befall her.

Mercifully, it did not. Her prayers were answered, and everything went according to plan. The little queen was even paler than on the previous day, if that were possible. But garbed in scarlet velvet and ermine and bedecked with jewels, she played her part to perfection. She was led to church by her father, the King of France, who, with a final fond caress, turned her over to her bridegroom, King Richard.

After the ceremony, the queen was presented to her new English ladies; to the Duchess of Lancaster, who, after making her obeisance, bent and kissed the little girl's cheek in a motherly fashion; to the Duchess of Gloucester, whose husband was head of the English war party and bitterly opposed to the French marriage; to the Duchess of York, the Lady of Namur, Lady Poinings, and others in the English entourage.

All the other ladies outranked Catherine, whose formal presentation came last. Weary as the little queen was by this time, she summoned a special smile for Catherine, her face lighting up in recognition of her train bearer. For a moment, her dark eyes glimmered, as if she and her new lady-in-waiting shared a special secret. Turning to King Richard, she tugged at his gold-embroidered sleeve to get his attention, and when he bent his golden head down to her, she whispered something in his ear which made him chuckle a little and bestow on Catherine a nod of approval, followed by one of his devastating smiles. Dipping low in her final curtsy, Catherine floated from the dais as if on a cloud, ignoring the envious glares of less-favored ladies.

Crispin had contrived that they be seated together at the banquet that followed the reception, which naturally meant that they should share a plate. Awed by the splendor of the assembled company, and by the table settings of gold plate on cloth-of-gold adorned by fleurs-de-lys, Catherine could only pick at the elaborate dishes, though Crispin had a hearty appetite.

There was a great peacock, its tail artfully spread; suckling pig and hares with pike; quails and partridges; entremets of swans; pasties of venison; bream poached in ale and flavored with saffron and almond milk. To finish off, there were pears, comfits, medlars, peeled nuts, and a great castle made of marchpane that was a work of art.

The royalty and guests of highest rank sat at high tables on raised platforms, each under an individual canopy of cloth-of-gold. From where she sat, Catherine could see that the little queen too could only pick at her food, eating but little. She looked so alarmingly pale that Catherine felt anxious for her.

Queen Isabeau, on the other hand, ate enough for two. At this rate, she would not keep her lovely figure for long, Catherine thought spitefully, for she did not like the little queen's formidable mother, who had flaunted her bare white bosom even in church, who flirted with all men impartially, even her new son-in-law, and who was as smug as a cat in a cream jar now that she had succeeded in marrying off her daughter so advantageously, for it was she who had promoted the English match.

Beside her, King Charles looked as wan as his daughter, and Catherine wondered if the imminent parting from his favorite child might not bring on another of his recurrent bouts of madness.

King Richard, the new bridegroom, looked distracted, and Catherine wondered if he were remembering another wedding day and his much-loved first wife, though he was attentive to the needs of his second, plying her with sweets and cutting bits of meat for her with his own hand.

When Crispin had satisfied his appetite, he began pointing out some of the assembled nobility to her.

"Thomas, Duke of Gloucester, now he's a wily one," Crispin muttered in her ear. "The king's uncle, and so, I suppose, my own, loath as I am to admit it." He shook his head. "Note with what an avaricious look he regards all this gold plate—as so much booty. Gloucester has been known to say that France is still a very rich country and that peace ought not yet to be made."

"How did the king get around his objections?" asked Catherine, for she knew that the Duke of Gloucester wielded much power in council.

"With a bribe. Richard paid him an enormous bribe—fifty thousand gold nobles with an earldom and a pension of two thousand nobles a year for his only son, Humphrey. Yet still the French marriage sticks in his craw."

Catherine made a small exclamation of horror.

"That fish-faced female beside him is his wife," Crispin went on. "She was Eleanor de Bohun and a great heiress in her own right."

Catherine nodded. "I've met her already," she said with distaste. "I don't think she likes me. At least, she has slighted me on every possible occasion."

"Don't take it to heart. The de Bohuns all think they are greater than God."

Crispin went on pointing out others of note— pretty Maude Holland, the king's niece who was married to the French Count of St. Pol; Tom Mowbray, the English Governor of Calais. . . .

"What can you tell me about that lady?" Discreetly, Catherine gestured to a handsome but haughty woman who was seated very near the high tables. "She is to be the queen's governess."

"Philippa de Coucy?" Crispin whistled through his teeth. "A poor choice. The lady bears a grudge against the king. She was once married to his great friend, the Earl of Oxford. But Queen Anne arranged for a divorce so that Oxford could marry one of her Bohemian ladies with whom he fell madly in love. It caused a great scandal at the time, and is no doubt why Richard insists that Isabella brings no French ladies with her. I suppose he couldn't very well turn down Lady de Coucy, though. She is half English, for her father married into the English royal house, and she has spent much time in England, though she went back to France after her divorce."

He shook his head in warning. "You'll do well to watch her, Cat. Try to make sure that she doesn't take out her spite on the little queen."

Finally, the hippocras was served, the wine laced with honey and delicate spices which marked the end of a banquet. Throughout the meal, John

Camuys, King Richard's head minstrel, had played for the assembled company. Now he retired, presumably to sample some of the rich viands and fruit, and was replaced by a slender figure, gaily dressed and strumming a lute.

Catherine gasped and grabbed Crispin's arm, so that the hippocras sloshed from his goblet and spread an ugly stain on the elaborate tablecloth.

"What the devil . . ."

"Never mind that," Catherine said urgently to Crispin, who was furiously scrubbing at the stain on his finest tunic as well as on the tablecloth. "Look!" She pointed excitedly at the minstrel. "It's Charlot!"

Chapter Eleven

"*Who?*" Crispin, still scrubbing hippocras stains from his best tunic, looked at Catherine as if he thought *she* had suddenly gone mad.

"Charlot!" she said impatiently. "Umm . . . that is, Chantal!" Recalling that, what with one thing and another, she had completely forgotten to tell him about the Gypsy's dual identity, and how she came to be privy to the Gypsy's secret. Catherine excitedly began to fill him in.

"Now let me understand this." Crispin held up a restraining hand to stem the flow of words that tumbled from Catherine's lips. "The Gypsy girl, Chantal, is really a boy disguised as a girl?" Crispin knew better; in fact, he had proof that such was not the case, though he naturally could not reveal how he'd come by such knowledge! "My dear Cat," he said. "That simply cannot be."

"No . . . no, Crispin. You've got it all wrong," Catherine said in exasperation. "Chantal is a girl disguised as a boy . . . as a minstrel. That one over there, in fact. Oh, why can't you *see*?" she wailed. "She . . . she came to my chambers and *threatened* me, Crispin." There, that was the gist of it, and Catherine felt she had finally gotten to the heart of the matter, the essence of the thing. She sat back, satisfied.

"And you told no one about this?" Crispin looked incredulous.

"Who was there to tell?" said Catherine simply. "You were away at the time, on the king's business. And I . . . I simply did not know whom to trust. She warned me specifically to tell no one . . . or . . . or it would be the worse for me." Her voice faltered.

"I see." Crispin heaved a sigh and bent a dark and brooding look on the gaily dressed minstrel who cavorted about, very near the high tables. He, or rather, she wore a short coat of fine Flemish cloth fitted tightly to the body. Impossible to believe that the tightly fitting garment concealed feminine curves, but if the breasts beneath it were bound with a cloth, Crispin conceded that it was just possible. Especially as the minstrel held the lute in such as way as to conceal the chest and nipped-in waist. The short coat also possessed long full sleeves, lined in pink and maroon, which flowed over the minstrel's wrists and hung downward, providing covering of a sort.

Crispin's eyes traveled downward to the shapely legs, encased in maroon and pink tights in a diamond-shaped design, and he gave a start of surprise. He would know those shapely legs anywhere; he had had an intimate acquaintance with them, he thought wryly. He did not need to see the minstrel's face, which was partly concealed by a hood lined in bright pink silk, to know who she was.

"It's her," he admitted.

"Well, what are you going to do about it?" Catherine was afire with impatience.

"At the moment, nothing." He remained in his seat, considering his options and intently studying the extravagant little figure who capered about in shoes with fashionably pointed toes which curled up to the point that they had to be banded at the knees. She was strumming her lute and singing a gay little ditty that had the guests at the high tables convulsed with mirth.

Unheard of that a spy should so flaunt herself under the very noses of royalty and before them all, he mused, and yet, was that not the essence of Chantal's particular style? Her bold and brazen effrontery was, in itself, a form of audacious disguise, he supposed.

Having determined on a prudent course of action, Crispin rose from his seat. "Wait here, Cat," he commanded. "I've got to set some inquiries in motion. And for God's sake," he muttered in an undertone for her ear alone, "calm down and try to look inconspicuous if you can. We are attracting undesirable attention."

Catherine, belatedly becoming aware that curious glances were coming their way and probably had been for some time, nodded. Trying her best to look unconcerned, she picked up a small silver knife and, with unsteady fingers, began to peel a peach that she had no appetite for and no intention of eating.

Crispin was gone for some time, and when he returned, Chantal had blended into a group of motley dressed minstrels and jongleurs and disappeared.

"Where have you been?" Catherine hissed. "She's gone. I was looking right at her," she said, vexed, "and then, in the blink of an eye, she . . . she simply vanished."

"No need to worry," Crispin said comfortably. "I've put one of my best men on her trail. He's skilled in all sorts of intrigue. He'll track her down if anyone can, and then . . ." Crispin's jaw hardened, and his piercing Plantagenet eyes grew dark and steely. "Then Mistress Chantal will answer to me."

Though his words were mild enough, his tone boded ill for the Gypsy, and hearing the implied threat, Catherine shivered in her seat.

"Don't fret, Cat," he assured her, seeing her shiver but misinterpreting it. "Everything is under control." He patted her hand comfortingly.

Normally, by this time at a wedding feast, even a royal wedding feast, the jests grew broad and the humor bawdy, but this was a special occasion in which the bride was too young to take to bed—would indeed be too young for bedding for a number of years. It put the pranksters and jesters at a disadvantage, and the evening was dying away.

Moreover, the little bride was already rubbing her eyes and striving to suppress her yawns. She should be put to bed, Catherine thought indignantly, and not a marriage bed either. Fervently, she hoped that someone besides herself would take notice of the little girl's exhaustion before very much longer.

Someone did—King Richard himself—which Catherine thought must surely be a good omen for his future kindly treatment of his child bride. Catherine saw him lean towards his newly acquired father-in-law, bypassing Queen Isabeau entirely, and murmur in his ear. Immediately thereafter the little queen was whisked away, and shortly afterwards, the royal family took its departure en masse. As etiquette decreed that none of lesser degree could leave before the royals, this was taken as a signal for a general exodus.

As Catherine was not to take up her duties until the little queen was actually on board ship, Crispin escorted her back to her hostelry. Though she was not very important in the general scheme of things, still, she was important enough to command a bedchamber of her own, for which she was thankful. The great chambers that she had shared with others on the journey were usually noisy with rustling, whispering, giggling, and even the occasional snore.

She wondered idly if Crispin snored—an odd thought to pop into her head, surely, and one which made her smile.

Seeing the fleeting smile flit across her expressive face, Crispin teased, "A penny for your thoughts."

"I do not sell my thoughts so cheaply, sir," she retorted smartly.

"A shilling then."

Smiling again, Catherine shook her head.

"Still too cheap? One gold noble, then," he said

boldly. "It's my best and final offer."

Catherine let her eyes go wide. "Ten shillings. You must prize my thoughts highly, sir!"

"I prize *you* highly, Cat," he said huskily. "And I think you know that, do you not?"

Catherine dropped her eyes. Suddenly, the teasing game she had so lightly embarked upon held serious overtones.

"I . . . I do not know," she whispered.

"Oh, my foolish Cat." Slowly and inexorably, he drew her into his arms. She could feel his uneven breathing on her cheek as he tenderly held her close. "You must know I do. Why are you so loath to admit it?"

"I don't know," she murmured dreamily, for how could she be expected to know anything, to be sure of anything, with her senses whirling? She knew only that she loved the taste . . . smell . . . touch of him as his mouth came down on hers.

His lips, as they closed over hers, tasted faintly of wine and spices. His scent was a spicy fragrance, for he preferred the clean sharp odor of herbs sprinkled sparingly into his bath to the heavy cloying perfumes and pomanders used by most of the nobility.

Catherine's nostrils quivered slightly in appreciation of his aroma, so different from the occasion of their last kiss, when he had come straight to her from the stables in his haste to see her and bring her letters from home. Tonight, she relished the clean sharp masculine scent of him, so different from the smell of horse and saddle leather, but no less manly or virile. Inhaling deeply, she felt drugged by it.

The feel of his strong arms about her had the same effect as on that previous occasion, or perhaps it was even more potent. His touch was sending little darts of pleasure through her flesh, and her heart was hammering wildly, so that she was sure he must be able to hear and feel it.

Would each embrace improve upon the one before it? she wondered, growing more intense as their desire for each other grew, until they were consumed by fire—a fiery passion that knew no bounds and demanded physical fulfillment.

Through the fullness of her skirts, she could feel his passion rising as he pressed the lean hard length of his body ever closer to hers and his kisses plundered her mouth of its sweetness.

With a little moan, she gave herself up utterly to sensation, drinking deeply of his mouth, which tasted better than the finest hippocras.

The winding corridor was dimly lit and, for a wonder, no one was about. Catherine's back was to the wall, and Crispin, in his urgency, pressed her against it, his engorged manhood, swollen to its fullest capacity, strained against her thigh, and she whimpered, feeling its heat and power, even through several thicknesses of cloth.

He groaned, and little drops of sweat beaded on his forehead. It cost him the utmost self-control to resist the compulsion to whisk up her skirts and take her then and there, standing up with her back to the wall, as he had done on numerous occasions with other willing wenches, easing himself with quick sharp thrusts in dark corridors.

But Catherine was not just any willing wench to be lightly tumbled, and much as he longed to sheathe his manhood in her soft moist flesh as naturally as he would sheathe his sword in its scabbard, he denied himself, and her, that voluptuous pleasure. For this was the woman he not only wanted to bed, he realized with a sudden jolt, but to wed. He wanted her not for a moment's pleasure, nor for a night, glorious as that night might be, but forever and for always.

And wanting her so, he would not, he told himself with gritted teeth, violate her virginity, no matter how much he longed for her, or how much she herself might want it.

And want him she did. His instinct and his experience told him that. She was pliant and yielding in his arms. If he chose to sweep her up and carry her into her chamber, there to lovingly divest her of every stitch of her clothing, he knew she would yield herself up to him willingly, gladly, generously, giving him everything he desired.

For a moment, for an eternity, he was sorely tempted to do just that. He longed to bare her long naked limbs, to remove her headdress and take down her glorious hair, freeing her curls from the plaits in which they were bound. He ached to make love to her warm sweet body until she squirmed with pleasure and cried out for fulfillment.

But he could not, not now, not knowing that this was the woman he wanted for his wife, and he must cease tormenting himself with these fantasies, or he would lose his iron self-control and turn fantasy into reality.

The delicious fantasy had but fueled his ardor, and he ached and throbbed for release. "Cat," he groaned. "I want you."

Her eyes half-closed in an ecstasy of wanting, she whimpered a wordless response.

"But I . . . I would not take your virginity," he said hoarsely. Lord, how he wanted to do just that! To kick open the door of her chamber, carry her across the threshold, and ease her onto the waiting bed, there to find fulfillment for them both in the most divine ecstasy two human beings could experience together.

It was a tempting prospect, and for a fleeting moment his resolution wavered, but only for a moment. He had, he told himself, the most powerful of reasons for self-restraint. "Being baseborn myself, I would not risk having you bear a bastard, Cat," he said simply. "We must be wed."

Chapter Twelve

"Wed!" Catherine squeaked. She stiffened in his arms, and her eyes popped open. His words had brought her back down to harsh reality. Suddenly, she remembered who she was . . . what she was . . . where she was . . .

Clutching her headdress, which had slipped down over her ear, she pushed it back into position, and then, twisting in his arms and arching her body, she slithered out of his grasp.

What on earth had possessed her? she wondered frantically. It was as if he had cast a sensual spell over her, a spell in which she had forgotten everything but the touch, taste, and feel of him. In which he had utterly and completely filled her world.

"Wed?" she repeated experimentally, sampling the word on her tongue, as she would a fine wine.

"Yes, wed," said Crispin impatiently. "You want to be married, don't you?" *He* did. Urgently. If he could have found a priest willing to perform the ceremony on the spot, he would have married her then and there.

It was unthinkable that she might not want to. In his experience, all the women he knew were either already married or wanted to be.

"We-l-l." Catherine temporized. She had not really given the matter much thought. In an age when girls were usually brides at 14 and young matrons with a child or two at 15 or 16, she had, as she was well aware, been given unusual freedom. It was a freedom that she treasured and meant to make the most of.

While she was thinking his proposal over, Crispin spied a convenient bench farther down along the wall and, hooking his foot around it, dragged it over and straddled one end of it. Catherine, whose knees were feeling shaky, thankfully sank down at the opposite end, a cautious distance away, for she felt too shaken to risk a repetition of their passionate interlude.

Crispin was looking at her expectantly, and she gathered her scattered wits about her and voiced the first objection that came to mind, for she really did not wish to marry—not yet. No matter how powerfully she was attracted to Crispin, she valued her freedom, and marriage was a form of bondage.

"How can we marry?" she asked, dodging the question of whether or not she wished to. "I am committed to the queen's service."

"That need not be an insurmountable obstacle," he responded promptly. "It is not at all unusual for a married lady to serve in the royal household. Geoffrey Chaucer's wife served Richard's grandmother, Queen Philippa of Hainault, loyally, both before her marriage and after it. And after the queen's death, she went on to serve the Duchess of Clarence. She is dead now, but the Chaucers had a good affectionate marriage for many years, though they served in separate households."

The term "good affectionate marriage" had rather a lukewarm sound, hardly indicative of a love match, and Catherine made a little grimace of distaste, which Crispin, in his enthusiasm, did not notice.

"We need not even be separated, as the Chaucers so often were," he reminded her. "Now that I have been appointed Governor of Windsor, we will be serving in the same household. What could be more convenient?"

Convenience was not a word that appealed greatly to Catherine either. And so far, he had breathed not a word of love. Oh, he had said that he *wanted* her, but not that he *loved* her.

Crispin went on, blissfully unaware that he was taking the wrong tack altogether. "As Governor of Windsor, I will have a generous stipend so that I will be able to support you, Cat. Though not lavishly," he warned. "Our expenses will be minimal, though, for we need not seek other lodgings, and you already have a fine new wardrobe, provided by the king."

He frowned. "Of course I am still a landless knight, with no estates of my own, but you have a fine property, though small, and with improved management, I daresay it can be made more profitable."

A chill went down Catherine's spine. Her lands . . . he wanted her lands! She was an heiress and he wanted her lands. It was as simple as that. Why hadn't she noticed the acquisitive gleam in his eye when he was kissing and caressing her?

· She stifled a sob. Only a few minutes ago, he had been making passionate love to her, kissing and caressing her with every evidence of enjoyment. And now the man was calmly and cold-bloodedly sitting across from her discussing stipends and wardrobes, lodgings and land like a . . . a lawyer, rather than a lover. And without a word of love. Oh, it was not to be borne!

Catherine rose with dignity and said, "I'm feeling rather tired. I fear I must go to bed."

"To bed?" Crispin was startled.

"I'm very tired," she said faintly.

He looked at her searchingly. She did look rather wan and white, come to think of it. Furthermore, it had been a long day and, fresh from the country as she was, she was unused to the tedium of court ceremonials, topped off by a heavy dinner with wine at every course. No doubt she was not feeling quite well.

So he opened her chamber door and ushered her in, though he could not resist dropping a chaste kiss on her brow. "Good night, my dear."

"Good night," she said coolly, not offering to return the kiss, and shutting the door firmly behind her.

Crispin, baffled, went to his own lodgings, wondering if he had said or done something to offend her. Surely, his proposal of marriage should not have had that effect. But it was not until his declaration that she had become so withdrawn, had gone so white. No, he couldn't think what had caused her sudden withdrawal from him, unless . . . unless it was the stain of bastardy on his escutheon, the shame of his bastardy that had offended her. And she too tactful to tell him so, in so many words.

He shook his head, still puzzled, for tact was not one of Cat's more endearing qualities. She was blunt, and forthright and honest, sometimes alarmingly so. Well, he would not pursue the matter further, he decided. He would wait in patience and take his cue from her.

Catherine had been dreading the embarkation on the next day, and she was even less prepared to deal with a distraught and tearful royal child than she otherwise might have been, since she had cried a good part of the night away herself. But to her intense relief, the little queen was calm and composed, displaying little emotion at parting from her family.

Not that one could expect anything else, Catherine reflected. The detestable Queen Isabeau was not, she felt sure, the kind of mother one parted from with tears and lamentations. And Isabella's father, though kind and well meaning, was a remote and inaccessible figure, especially when his spells of insanity were upon him.

The little queen only expressed regrets at parting from the small sisters and brother she was leaving behind, Joanna, Marie, Michelle, and Louis, the Dauphin. Wistfully, she spoke of sending presents to them all when she reached her new home. "And you, Catherine, will help me choose a doll for each of my sisters, and perhaps a toy soldier for my brother, will you not?" she asked, graciously

191

including her new demoiselle in her future plans.

"Of course I will." Catherine assented enthusiastically to this scheme as it was likely to be one that would give the little girl something pleasurable to look forward to. "We will pick out a fine doll for each of your sisters, madame," she promised. "And for your brother, perhaps an English archer, complete with longbow and other accoutrements." Though she did just wonder if such a present would be considered suitable for the heir to the throne of France, considering that it was the English longbow that had won the great English victories at Crecy and Poitiers.

Noticing that the little girl stumbled over her name, trilling the "r" and pronouncing it in the French fashion, Catherine diffidently suggested that she shorten it to "Cat," as Sir Crispin was wont to do.

Isabella smiled delightedly, trying the new designation on her tongue. "Cat—I like it," she pronounced, a spark of mischief lighting her dark eyes as she cocked her head at Catherine. "And, with your ginger hair, it suits you, I think. Assuredly, you shall be Cat henceforth."

Catherine congratulated herself on having brought a smile to the queen's preternaturally solemn little face. The casually bestowed nickname stuck, and before long, even the king himself was whimsically referring to her as "the queen's cat."

They had a fair wind from France, and in less than three hours disembarked from the *Isabella*, the flagship named in compliment to the queen.

From then on, all was a dizzy round of pomp and pageantry, from Dover to Rochester, from

Rochester to Eltham, and thence to London.

Isabella was dressed in a sumptuous red velvet gown, embossed with birds of goldsmith's work that sat upon simulated branches of pearls and emeralds. She rode perched upon a high white palfrey so that she would be visible to the crowds who came out to see her pass by, holding up their children for a good look at the little queen, who was not so very much older than themselves. People hung from the windows of their houses and climbed the parapets of London Bridge when the queen passed through Southwark, smiling and waving graciously at her new subjects. Catherine, who had dressed her for the great occasion, and who knew how tired she was, marveled at the little girl's royal demeanor.

That night she lodged in the royal apartments of the Tower of London, and Catherine, who was familiar with the history of the great pile of stone and how it was used as prison as well as royal residence, shivered as they passed beneath its portals. She wondered if its royal tenants were not, in some measure, as much prisoners bound by golden chains of circumstance as those who clanked in chains far below the royal apartments. But she kept such speculations and her unwelcome knowledge of the bloodstained stones to herself, and reflected thankfully that at least the royal apartments were bright with great fires burning to dispel the gloom and warm with carpets and tapestries to keep out the drafts.

The next day the queen passed in procession through London itself, and the fountains ran with red and white wine and the houses were decorated with banners and tapestries of cloth of gold in her honor. Multitudes threw flowers before her, and the Lord Mayor himself was presented to her in a colorful ceremony before she made her formal entry into Westminster through the King's Gate, where Richard was waiting in his palace to receive her.

The queen was to lodge at Westminster until her coronation, which was not to take place until Epiphany Sunday, and for some time Catherine was kept busy supervising the unpacking of her extensive wardrobe, for Queen Isabeau, in her pride, would not send her daughter to England without the most lavish of linens and laces, the most exquisite of undergarments, the finest of furs.

Of the many magnificent gowns in Isabella's trousseau, Catherine's favorite was a sapphire velvet gown embroidered all over with pearl roses. She was also very partial to a cape and hood lined down the sides with miniver and with a mantle lined in ermine. Dressing the little queen in her finery was like dressing an exquisite living doll, thought Catherine, and was the most enjoyable part of her duties.

Isabella also brought many jewels with her, and Catherine was in charge of the many necklaces, coronets, rings, collars, and clasps. She endeavored to make a lively game of dressing up and choosing which jewels to wear with what outfits, to lessen the tedium of ceremonial dressing for the little girl.

Nor had Isabella's parents sent her undowered to England. She brought a dowry consisting of 800,000 gold franks to be paid in yearly installments. That should have answered the carping critics, chief among them the Duke of Gloucester, who complained of King Richard's extravagance in welcoming "the French king's daughter" with ceremonials and processions. It should have, but it did not. Catherine, who deplored them, tried her best to keep the complaints and criticism from the queen's ears. The processions and ceremonials were no more than her due, thought Catherine indignantly, and surely the festivities honoring the queen whose marriage brought peace between the two countries cost far less than the arming and outfitting of companies of soldiers for war. It was certainly more economical in terms of human lives and human suffering.

The next great occasion, and the last, was Isabella's coronation. Catherine combed out Isabella's long black silky hair and dressed her in the great heavy robes of state—in velvet and ermine and cloth of gold—and accompanied her to Westminster Abbey, where she was crowned by the Archbishop of Canterbury.

Through all the pomp and circumstance of the royal processions and ceremonials, Catherine had seen almost nothing of Crispin, and busy and preoccupied as she was, she had nevertheless missed him. But now, with the final magnificent ceremonial brought to a successful conclusion, she and Isabella went to Windsor, which was to be the queen's chief residence.

Catherine rode behind the queen, who was as always performing her royal duty, smiling and waving at her cheering subjects. And as she rode, Catherine could not help but feel a deep upsurge of joy and longing, and a great singing in her heart that nearly burst forth upon her lips. For she was riding home to Windsor—and home to Crispin.

Chapter Thirteen

Catherine and her royal mistress were equally tired of processions and ceremonials and state occasions, however much honor these might bestow, and were glad to settle down in one place for a while. Catherine was especially glad to be free of the incessant packing and unpacking, free of the constant worry that a particularly valuable coronet or pendant or necklace might be forgotten and left behind or mislaid altogether. It was with a sigh of relief that she locked away the jewelry and other finery, for her responsibility for these valuables weighed heavily on her slender shoulders.

The queen's apartments at Windsor had been newly refurbished in red and white satin, her own colors, and were bright and gay enough to delight the heart of any child. The tapestries were embroidered with falcons, her own emblem, and the king's Master of Falconry presented her with her own bird, a pure white falcon, her own emblem in living flesh and blood.

Isabella delighted in hawking, declaring it was almost as good as flying yourself to gallop over the hard ground, unhood the bird, let the jesses go, and be at one with the bird as it took flight, soaring into the frosty air. Catherine concurred, for that was what she herself most enjoyed. What she objected to was the bird's retrieval of its prey—the blood-soaked feathers of grouse or pheasant. But Isabella, though tenderhearted, took it with a child's matter-of-fact acceptance of things as they are.

When the weather grew too cold for sport, she and Catherine settled down by a roaring fire to make music or play at chess. To Catherine's consternation, the little queen far surpassed her at the game, for she was far too apt to make a hasty ill-thought-out move and find herself checkmated.

Isabella also excelled at her lessons, which were part of the daily regime, for the Queen of England had to learn to speak English like a native, insisted the Lady de Coucy, her governess. She would not allow Isabella to speak French in her presence, and since she superintended all the child's lessons—in reading, writing, arithmetic, music, and needle-work—the little queen was forced to recite and respond to questions the sour-faced lady put to her in English, not in her native tongue, or risk a sharp and humiliating reproof.

The little girl was sensitive and eager to please, and Madame de Coucy's sharp reproofs and criticism stung, but Catherine never saw her lose her temper or her patience, no matter what the provocation. Catherine had grown to love her little charge, and her heart ached for the little girl.

"Is there nothing to be done about her?" Catherine asked Crispin in despair. He had, of course, in his capacity as Governor of Windsor, formally welcomed the queen to her new home, but he was busy and preoccupied in the performance of his new duties, and Catherine saw far less of him than she had expected to. Was he avoiding her? she wondered. Sometimes, it seemed so.

"Madame de Coucy?" Crispin shrugged. "You can complain of her to the king, I suppose. Though what will come of it, I don't know. I *did* warn you about her," he pointed out.

"There's nothing to complain of exactly," Catherine admitted. "Nothing specific, that is. It's . . . oh . . . just slights and snubs and petty restrictions and . . . and most of all a lack of caring and affection. Children need love," she said with conviction.

"You will have to make the best of things," Crispin advised. "After all, the child gets plenty of love and affection from you, at least."

And she did. Crispin marveled at how devoted Catherine had become to her young charge. He had looked on as she wracked her brains to entertain and amuse the lonely little girl, whose brother and sisters were so far away, and seemingly gave her whole heart to the task. If ever Catherine loved a man with such depth and with such devotion, he would be a lucky man indeed, Crispin reflected.

He himself had been circumspect in his relations with her ever since that night in France, which now seemed very long ago. On that never-to-be-forgotten night they had both been carried away by their emotions, by their undoubted physical attraction for each other, by the atmosphere of the wedding feast, and perhaps by too much wine! Thus, he rationalized her rejection of his too precipitate proposal.

At this point, she was totally absorbed in her new duties and wrapped up in the child-queen, but the novelty would soon wear off and the time would come for them—he was convinced of it. Thrown together by circumstance, as they were bound to be, their relationship would have time to grow and develop, he was sure. All the time in the world.

After a long dull spell of cold weather, it had warmed up, and there was a touch of spring in the frosty air. For several days, Catherine had been cooped up with the queen, who was sick abed with a feverish cold. Catherine had dosed her with the same sort of nostrums with which her old nurse had plied her under similar circumstances, but when her home remedies proved ineffective, she sent, in a panic, for the royal physician.

The royal medical man was escorted to the queen's chambers by Crispin himself.

"You're looking peaked yourself, Cat," he commented. "Come and ride with me in the fresh air. You need an outing."

Catherine assented gladly enough, for she knew the physician would be some time making his examination of his royal patient, and Isabella, between spasms of coughing, urged her to go.

"I shall be quite all right, Cat," she croaked hoarsely. "And the king has given his physician some letters for me." She waved the missives gaily. "When the physician is done, I will take his medicine," she made a wry face, "and read my letters from Richard until you return."

Judging that the king's letters might be the best medicine of all, Catherine went off with Crispin with a lighter heart than she had had in days.

It was delightful to be riding out again, she reflected, stealing a sidelong glance at her handsome escort as they jogged along. Though she saw him on an almost daily basis when he made his formal report to the queen, and occasionally at other times as well, they had had little chance to be alone all that long dull winter, with correspondingly little opportunity to discuss personal matters. And no chance at all for him to renew his wooing of her, should he wish to. Sometimes she wished he would; sometimes she was glad he didn't, and wished that things could go on as they were indefinitely, with no hard choices for her to make.

Even though they had had little chance to talk privately, she was uneasily aware of how she was beginning to look forward to their daily meetings. The hour in which he customarily made his report to the queen had become the high point of her day. And that he was ever there in the background, a source of support and strength, meant a great deal to her.

If only she weren't convinced that he was attracted to her lands as much as to her! And yet, as she knew very well, most marriages were based on such practical considerations—wealth, land, and property, or political considerations—rather than on sentiment.

She pondered much on this on long winter evenings when she had put the child-queen to bed, reflecting how pleasantly she and Crispin could while away the long tedious evening hours if . . . if only they were wed. At such times, her traitorous body grew warm and languorous, and she regretted her too hasty rejection of his marriage proposal.

And at other times, with the perversity of womankind, she did not!

The bridle path along which they were jogging grew more and more narrow, so that they could no longer ride side-by-side. Crispin took the lead. "Follow me," he urged. "I have something to show you."

Wondering where he was taking her, Catherine trailed after him, ducking her head, for low-hanging branches of tall trees threatened, were she not careful, to sweep her from the saddle.

After a few minutes, they came out in a little wooded dell where, in a sheltered spot, a carpet of delicate white snowdrops covered the ground.

Uttering a small wordless exclamation of delight, Catherine slipped from the saddle, handing her horse's reins to Crispin, who likewise dismounted.

"Oh, Crispin, a harbinger of spring!" she cried, turning a glowing face to him. "It reminds me of home."

"I thought it might." He smiled with quiet satisfaction.

"I used to go out in the early spring and pick bouquets for my mother," Catherine recollected.

"Though they did not blossom as early there as here." She knelt to pick the fragile white blooms, and in a moment her hands were full of flowers. "I must take a nosegay back for Isabella. They will brighten the child's room."

"You will need something to tie them in bunches with," Crispin, ever practical, remarked.

"What? Oh, I know." Thrusting the bouquet of nodding white blossoms at him, she commanded, "Here, hold them, please." Then she shoved back her hooded cloak and pulled a ribbon from her loosely tied back hair. The hair gleamed brightly in the weak winter sunlight as she tossed it impatiently back on her shoulders.

"Your hair shines in the sun, bright as a new penny." Crispin said hoarsely, relishing the sight. He had long wished to see her gleaming curls set free to tumble on her shoulders, instead of tightly bundled into a caul or totally concealed by one of the elaborate headdresses that were de rigueur at court.

"Oh, yes, the queen calls me her ginger cat, you know," said Catherine with an unsteady laugh. She made a great business of twining the ribbon around the stems of the bouquet, and when her hands brushed Crispin's, they trembled at his touch.

To cover her confusion, she said, in a too-bright tone of voice, "There, that should do it." She gave the ribbon a final tweak and took the bouquet from him. "Now, if you will help me into the saddle, sir?" she said with false cheeriness.

His hands reached out to clasp her around the waist and lingered there. Her waist was so narrow, he could nearly span it with his two hands, he marveled.

Slowly, inexorably, he drew her into his arms. The very air seemed to vibrate with their intense physical awareness of each other. Catherine's heart was thumping erratically, and her breath came in little gasps.

"Cat," he whispered into her hair. "Cat, it's been so long. . . ." Winding a hand in her hair, he let it slip between his fingers, toying with her ear and caressing her soft throat. Then, his head bent and he fastened his mouth on hers.

Catherine stood within the circle of his arms, her hands clasped before her holding the bouquet of flowers. At any moment, she could have pushed him away, or stepped back, but she did not. Instead, she shifted her bouquet into one hand and with the other reached up to clasp him around the neck and draw his face even more firmly down to hers. "Oh, Crispin, I've been such a fool," she murmured brokenly.

"Shh." His finger reached out to rub caressingly over her lips and reduce her to silence. "Hush, my love," he murmured. "We were both at fault. We were going too far, too fast, and you were not ready. Let us begin again, shall we?"

"How do you mean?" asked Catherine dreamily between little nibbling kisses.

"There is to be a tournament on St. George's Day when the king and court move back to Windsor. Will you give me a token so that I may wear your colors in the lists?"

"Oh, Crispin, there is danger in these mock battles. I do not like them," she said foolishly, though she thrilled at the thought of him wearing her colors and proclaiming himself her knight, for all the world to see.

"Better a mock battle than a real one, my sweet," he assured her, laughing away her objections. "The lances will be blunt-tipped."

Catherine shook her head doubtfully. She knew it was not uncommon for serious injuries and even fatalities to occur in these mock battles. How could it be otherwise when mounted opponents crashed in collision at full gallop while brandishing 18-foot lances at each other?

"I don't want any harm to befall you, Crispin," she said worriedly.

"Fond little faint-heart," he teased. "Whatever happened to the warrior-woman who attacked a bandit with only a staff?"

Catherine smiled wryly. "She has become a coward for your sake."

"Do you really care so much, Cat?" he asked soberly.

Catherine lowered her eyes. "I do," she whispered in confusion.

Crispin's heart leaped at her confession. "Well, then, give me your token and a kiss for good luck, and I shall promise to take no unnecessary risks for your sake."

Catherine shyly lifted her lips, and they sealed the bargain with a long lingering kiss.

As it happened, the court came back to Windsor well before St. George's Day, for the king was concerned about the health of his little queen and as soon as he could shake off his Parliamentary

Advisors and Councillors, he returned to Windsor to cheer her through her illness.

"It is but a slight indisposition," Isabella assured him from the depths of the great bed where she lay, propped on pillows, her slight body scarcely molding the heavy bedcovers. Delicately, like a little kitten, she sneezed and then sneezed again.

The king whipped out his own embroidered handkerchief, and holding it to her nose, commanded her to blow. "They call me a fop for inventing the thing," he said whimsically. "But it is a convenient device nonetheless." And Catherine and Isabella could not but agree with him.

He treated her with all the indulgence of a fond father, and Isabella blossomed at the unexpected attention that she was receiving, worshipping her handsome husband. And in turn, the king basked in her open adoration and in her pretty manners.

In a day or two, Isabella was up and about again, looking better and stronger and brighter in spirits than Catherine had ever seen her. Her lessons were suspended for the time being, as the king kept her at his side, playing chess with her, making music with her, and taking her riding and hawking.

It was a happy time for both couples, for the king's preoccupation with the queen set Catherine free to spend precious time with Crispin. They sometimes went riding and hawking with the other courtiers, but more often dallied behind, exchanging thoughts and stolen kisses, and even making cautious, tentative plans for their future.

But all too soon, the king was needed back in London for a Council meeting, and the happy interlude was over.

After he left, Catherine had her hands full trying to console the queen, who was not to be consoled on any account.

"Be of good cheer, madame," Catherine advised. "The king will be back for St. George's Day and that is not so very far away. In the meantime, we will practice conversing in English every day, and you will be so much more proficient by then. The king was so pleased at the progress you have already made," she reminded her cunningly.

"Yes, that is so." The little queen looked pensive. "The king will take me with him everywhere when I am a woman grown, will he not, Cat?"

"I am sure he will, madame." Catherine spoke soothingly.

"And when I am a woman, he will love me as a man loves a wife?" she pursued. "As Sir Crispin loves you, dear Cat?"

"Loves me? Sir Crispin?" Catherine was astounded.

Isabella's dark eyes widened. "Has he not spoken to you yet of the great love he bears you, Cat?" She looked puzzled. "But how is it that you have not seen it for yourself? It is there in his eyes whenever he looks at you, Cat. Such depth of emotion . . . such great tenderness . . ." Her voice trailed off. "I hope one day Richard will look at me as Sir Crispin looks at you," she said wistfully.

Catherine said automatically, "I am sure he will, madame." The queen was but a child, she thought, bemused. And yet children, in their honesty, simplicity, and directness of approach, quite often perceived things that adults, with their greater worldliness, did not. Children were often extra-ordinarily perspicacious about people, and none more so than the sensitive Isabella.

He loves me? thought Catherine. She turned it over in her mind, bemused by the notion, examining it from all angles. And then, with greater certainty—he loves me! And her heart began to sing.

Chapter Fourteen

The day of the tournament dawned bright and clear, though the lists were muddy after a week of spring rain. But the wet weather did not discourage spectators of high and low degree from pouring into Windsor well in advance. From the streets of the village to the castle gates, crowds thronged—crowds in which poor peddlers jostled prosperous merchants, and whores in scarlet-striped hoods rubbed elbows with respectable matrons marshaling clamorous children. But the populace was in a holiday mood, and a general atmosphere of good will and good fellowship prevailed.

The great cobblestone courtyard was as crowded as the streets with mounted knights and their squires, servants and pages running hither and thither, and late-coming noblemen arriving with a flurry and flourish of trumpets.

Most knights had arrived at Windsor earlier in the week, and had filled the available accommodations to capacity, so that the late arrivals and those of lower rank were forced to encamp in muddy fields below the castle walls in a bivouac of multi-colored tents. In similar fields, roasting pits had been dug for charcoaling the numerous oxen slaughtered for the occasion. Barrels of beer and ale were provided for the common folk, while casks of malmsey wine were more to the taste of knights and their squires.

Unlike the tournament grounds at Smithfield, which customarily doubled as a slaughtering ground when not required for tournaments, the lists at Windsor were permanent, and durable loges had been built in tiers for the more noble spectators to enjoy the contests in relative comfort.

The common folk jostled for positions of advantage, perching on the stockades that enclosed the 150-yard field and munching loaves of barley bread that had been distributed among the crowds.

The royal loge itself was placed so that the sun would not glare into royal eyes. Another royal prerogative, thought Catherine, smothering a giggle, as she followed the queen to her seat and piled cushions on the great throne-like chair so that the little girl would be high enough to view the spectacle.

High above the loge, which was canopied in gold and scarlet-striped silk, floated the royal lily and leopard flag, signifying that the king himself was present.

The Lancastrian loge adjoined the royal loge, and the grizzled Duke of Lancaster and his still-lovely wife came by to pay their respects before the tournament commenced. Accompanying them was the duke's son by his first wife, Henry of Bolingbroke, Earl of Derby.

Not for the first time, Catherine observed the enmity between the king and his cousin, Henry. Close in age, the two men had been raised together, and each, she shrewdly suspected, envied the other for what he himself did not possess. Henry coveted Richard's crown, as well as his good looks and great charm of manner, while the king resented Henry's martial prowess, popularity, and enormous wealth, which had come down to him through his mother, Blanche of Lancaster, and his wife, Mary de Bohun—wealth which made the king's privy purse pale into insignificance.

Henry took pleasure in goading Richard, she noticed, taunting the king over some boyish rivalry at the quintain, at which he had bested Richard, on a long-ago occasion better forgotten.

Tactless, stubborn, stolid, and humorless, so Catherine summed up John of Gaunt's first-born son. She'd supposed that King Richard had supported the duke's efforts to legitimate his children by Katherine Swynford out of affection for his uncle. Now she wondered, with unwonted cynicism, if the king's true purpose was not to humiliate his cousin and to decrease the considerable inheritance Henry could expect to receive from his father, the duke.

The heralds blew a fanfare of trumpets, a roar rose from the crowd, and a marshal, waving a white baton, shouted, "In the name of God and Saint George, come forth to do battle!"

The Lancasters made a hasty departure for their own loge. And none too soon, thought Catherine, watching the king glower after his obnoxious cousin.

Trumpets sounded another peal, at either end of the lists squires loosened bridles, and the two great destriers thundered towards each other down the field. Clods of mud were thrown up by their pounding hooves, and their armored riders rode with lances poised at the horizontal, each aimed at his opponent. Each rider's helmeted head was lowered, and each rider braced himself for the shock of combat.

The crash of wood and metal and splintering lances was deafening, and before long, Catherine's head began to ache from the din, the dust, and the nervous tension of waiting for Crispin's turn to come up. By the time he appeared in the lists, her hands were clammy, and little beads of sweat had popped out on her forehead, though the spring sunshine was fitful and only pleasantly warm.

"There he is." The little queen nudged her. "Look, Cat, there is your knight."

"I know," Catherine murmured. She had eyes for no other.

He was superb in full tournament regalia. His brightly polished armor shone like a mirror in the sun. Over it, he wore a covering skirt of green silk, embroidered with the White Hart emblem, denoting he was a king's man.

Like his armor, his horse shone like a newly minted coin from much brushing and currying. The saddle was high-pommeled, to decrease the likelihood of his being unhorsed in combat.

From his helmet fluttered a green silk scarf, the favor that Catherine had given him. And because it was customary for ladies to shower small tokens—gloves, scarves, ribbons, flowers— on deserving knights who distinguished themselves during the tournament, she had also given him a more personal and permanent token of her favor, the brooch her mother had bestowed upon her when she left home. It secured her scarf to his helmet, and she herself had pinned it on earlier that morning.

"It is too valuable an object to wear in the lists," Crispin had objected, turning the little gold brooch about in his hands to examine it more closely. He smiled over the motto engraved on the back, "Love Conquers All," but made no comment.

"It has little real value," Catherine responded. "And it was very nearly lost once. The night we were attacked by brigands. Do you remember?"

Crispin nodded.

"I thought the bandits had made off with it, but later, I found it snagged on one of my gowns." She took it from his hands and proceeded to attach it and her silken scarf to his helm. "I want you to have it; it will bring you good fortune," she insisted.

"I have something for you too, Cat," he announced. "Though it is but a trumpery bauble by comparison." And he produced an exquisitely contrived love knot, the symbol of constancy between two lovers.

Catherine had never seen one of such delicate workmanship. "It's beautiful!" she cried out in delight. "And now, we each have a token from the other."

"That was my intention." He smiled. "Let me

fasten it on for you, Cat." He bent his head to the task, frowning in concentration, and his tawny-gold hair brushed Catherine's chin, tickling it.

Laughing, she buried her hands in the thick thatch of hair and grasping handfuls, tugged playfully.

"Ow!" he complained. "Is that any way to treat your champion, my lady? I demand more respect," he growled.

With a lightning move, he reached up and grasped her arm, his hand sliding down it and tightening round her wrist. She felt the controlled strength of his lean, tough warrior's body as he pulled her into his arms and held her fast.

"But your hair was tickling my chin," she said to justify herself.

"I'll tickle more than your chin, woman," he growled, falling upon her and tickling her ribs unmercifully.

She twisted and twined about in his arms, laughing and begging for mercy, and their delightful love-play might have continued indefinitely had not Elwyn, Crispin's squire, blundered in just then, interrupting their private moment together.

"Oh, pardon me, my lord, my lady," the young man stammered, backing hastily out of the room, his face covered in confusion.

"It's all right, Elwyn. You may stay," said Crispin easily, reluctantly releasing Catherine. "You must go, m'amie," he said regretfully. "It is time that Elwyn helps me don my armor and prepare for the joust."

"And I should be with the queen," Catherine said, suddenly recollecting her own neglected duties.

"She is very excited about attending her first tournament in England."

A blare of trumpets sounded, recalling Catherine to the present and to the tournament field.

A herald issued the ritual call to arms, identifying the combatants by name for those who might not recognize the heraldic devices. Catherine caught her breath and wiped her clammy hands on a handkerchief borrowed from the queen as she whispered a prayer.

The combatants were evenly matched. Crispin's opponent, chosen by lot, was the hotheaded son of the Earl of Northumberland, Henry Hotspur, so called for his fiery disposition. He was a warrior of renown, having won his spurs in battles against the marauding Scots in the much-fought-over border country to the north.

The two knights pulled down their visors, and when the marshal threw down his white baton, the squires loosened the destriers' bridles. The combatants thundered down the lists, lances poised and at the ready, bearing down upon each other. They were all but standing on the backs of their mighty chargers, each contestant rising in his stirrups to get the whole weight of his body behind the blow he was delivering.

They met, and each man's lance, correctly foiled as the rules of a pleasance combat decreed, clashed with the other's, as the chargers, impelled by their own momentum, pounded past each other.

Crispin's lance was shattered by Hotspur's blow, and Catherine sighed, for now she had to sit through the whole nerve-wracking business over again, as each knight was entitled to lose three lances before he was considered defeated.

The combatants separated, and each trotted back to his own end of the list. Crispin's squire handed him up a fresh lance, and the combatants prepared themselves for the second course.

"Hotspur is a ferocious fighter, but Crispin has the better technique," the king said judiciously. "They are evenly matched. Courage, ma belle," he murmured into her ear.

Catherine glanced up in surprise, taken aback as she so often was by King Richard's perceptive powers and unusual empathy.

The queen smiled sympathetically and quietly retrieved her crumpled handkerchief from Catherine, whose nervous fingers, plucking at the embroidery, had nearly denuded it of finery.

For the second time, the combatants thundered toward each other and braced themselves for the shock of collision. But the impatient Hotspur rose in his stirrups a trifle too soon and launched his thrust at Crispin with poor timing and poor judgment. And at the moment of collision Crispin's lance met its mark, glancing off Hotspur's shield to lodge in his hauberk, prizing the impetuous warrior off his horse and out of the saddle.

The crowd cheered. Hotspur's squire came running to his assistance, for an unhorsed knight could not get to his feet unaided. Crispin, raising his visor and gracefully acknowledging the applause of the crowd, cantered to the royal loge to receive his reward.

The excited little queen bestowed on him a small golden medal, the king voiced a gracious compliment, and Catherine, standing up and leaning over the balcony, tossed him a flower.

Crispin rose in his stirrups and executed a short bow in acknowledgment. "Sire," he said, "I thank you, but I crave yet another reward."

"And what reward might that be, sir knight?" the king asked indulgently as one pair of blue Plantagenet eyes met the other. Never had the two men, brothers in blood, appeared more alike than they did at this moment, thought Catherine, though the king was growing a short beard and Crispin was clean-shaven.

"I claim a kiss from the queen's lady and mine own," he responded, "for I wear her favor and she mine."

"That is not in my power to grant, sir knight," King Richard replied. "It is a boon that only the lady herself can grant you." He turned to Catherine and looked at her quizzically.

For answer, Catherine, crimson with blushes, leaned over the parapet and offered her lips to Crispin, whose mailed arms reached up to steady her around the waist as he caressed her soft mouth with his lips.

The crowd broke into applause, the king remarked approvingly, "Very prettily done," and the little queen reverted to French in her excitement, exclaiming, "Tiens, Catherine, vous avez un chevalier preux!"

The remainder of the single-combat part of the tournament passed in a daze for Catherine. It was a blur of blows given and received, fanfares of trumpets, clods of mud churned up by heavy steel-shod hooves, and heraldic ceremonies that grew increasingly tedious as the day wore on.

The king, whose interest in the martial arts was minimal, grew bored, and the little queen restless. By the end of the day, everyone was waiting impatiently for the grand melee, in which a like number of knights chose sides and fought each other for the glory of Saint George and the king.

Crispin was to participate in the final event, fighting under the banner of Henry of Bolingbroke, for Henry had specifically requested Crispin to take part in the melee under his command, and the king had given his permission for an exchange to be effected.

As that part of the tournament drew near, Catherine's anxiety level began to rise again, for the grand melee was, in effect, a minor battle in which, though swords were blunted with heavy lead foils, virtually anything might happen. Despite precautions, heavy blows, even with a blunted sword, could cleave a skull or slice off a limb at a stroke. The losers could expect broken bones or severe bruises at least; for the winners, prizes would be distributed in the great hall that evening.

Since this was her first tournament, Catherine listened intently as the marshals explained the rules for this particular combat. It was to take place on horseback but might be pursued on foot with the flat of the sword as the weapon of choice. If a knight lost his helmet, lost his weapon, or if any part of his body touched the wooden stockade surrounding the lists, he would be declared hors de combat.

The marshal finished shouting the rules and flung down his white baton, the heralds shouted, "Laisser aller," and the gates were raised at either end of the field.

218

Then 40 horses, 20 contenders on one side and 20 on the other, came pounding down the field towards each other. Their collision made the loges reverberate in a tumult of horrendous sound as bloodcurdling battle cries tore from contenders' throats, stallions screamed, lances crashed and splintered, and steel rang on naked steel. Catherine clapped her hands over her ears to lessen the din.

Not a few of the knights were unhorsed in the opening collision, but they were hoisted to their feet by squires, who came running onto the field to their rescue, and continued the mock battle on foot. Others, not so fortunate, were helped off the field by their squires if they were wounded or disqualified by losing shield or weapon. Very soon the field became a tangled mass of neighing riderless horses, armed fighting men, broken lances, splintered wood, blood, mud, and lost or broken shields and swords.

Catherine strained her eyes trying to spot Crispin in the aptly named melee, but she did not spy him until the field had thinned out even more.

His side had taken the brunt of the charge, and he and Henry of Bolingbroke, both unhorsed, were fighting back to back against a host of contenders.

They were badly outnumbered, yet continued to slash away, hewing their opponents down in an awesome demonstration of coordinated swordsmanship.

Bolingbroke was a skillful swordsman, but he lacked Crispin's dash and fire, thought Catherine critically. Nevertheless, she had to admire the man's staying power, as his stolid body absorbed blow after blow without flinching, even as Crispin whirled, slashing and parrying, dodging his opponents' blows with greater agility, while protecting his partner's back.

This winning combination had whittled the opposition down from seven or eight against two, to five against two, and then evened the odds. But then Crispin's sword went spinning out of his hand from the force of a massive blow by a heavy blade, a blow that must have made his whole arm go numb. Rubbing his arm, swordless, and thus disqualified by the rules of the tournament, he left the arena, and Bolingbroke stood alone.

But Catherine didn't care what befell Henry of Bolingbroke. In a fever of anxiety, she sent a page scurrying to the physician's tent to ask after Crispin, and could not breathe easily again until the boy returned with the welcome information that Sir Crispin, apart from a sprained wrist and a few bruises, was unharmed.

Queen Isabella squeezed her hand sympathetically, and King Richard gave her a quizzical look. "Well, are you satisfied, ma belle? Your knight is unhurt and unharmed," he teased her, not ungently.

Catherine blushed in embarrassment, but the king was pleased to find that an affaire de coeur had developed between his handsome half brother and the queen's newest lady. For Catherine was devoted to his little queen, of that he was sure, and Crispin's love for her would bind him even more closely to the royal faction and assure his continuing loyalty in the hard times that were coming. For King Richard could foresee a time when he would need all the loyal adherents he could get, and he would bind them to him by whatever means necessary.

There was feasting that night in the Great Hall at Windsor, and much merriment. As governor of the castle, Crispin took his place at the High Table, as did Catherine, who was in attendance on the queen.

After the banquet, prizes were bestowed on deserving knights who had distinguished themselves, and then a troupe of mummers put on a play in honor of Saint George, depicting his valor in slaying a mammoth green dragon with scales and fiery red nostrils from which smoke belched forth at intervals.

The lovely maiden whom Saint George was to rescue from the fire-breathing dragon was tied to a boulder-like prop. She was played by a pretty boy in a bright yellow wig who wrung his hands, wept, and shrieked most convincingly.

When the dragon was slain, with appropriate histrionics, and his scaly green skin lay on the floor in a heap, three men who had worked the prop emerged to make their bow, alongside Saint George and his maiden. As the maiden swept a deep curtsy in acknowledgment of the applause, her bright yellow wig slipped askew and a wiry black curl poked forth.

Catherine gasped and clutched Crispin's arm. The pretty "boy" who had taken the part of the rescued maiden was none other than the Gypsy, Chantal!

Chapter Fifteen

Catherine was thunderstruck. She thought she had
seen the last of Chantal long ago, and now here she
was, bold as brass.

Catherine turned an accusing gaze on Crispin,
whom she thought had taken the matter in hand
ages ago.

To be sure, she hadn't asked; she had taken it
for granted that he would investigate the spy as
he had promised to do. And if she were honest
with herself, she really had not wanted to know
the means he'd employed to track down the Gypsy
and to question her. The rack, the thumbscrew—
both were common means to make a reluctant spy
reveal his or her secrets.

Of course, she didn't think Crispin would employ
such devices himself in person, but . . . there it was,
she didn't ask because she really did not want to
know.

But Catherine had plenty of questions now, and

they tumbled to her lips, fairly trembling there. She had actually opened her mouth to give them voice when Crispin grasped her arm and gave an almost imperceptible shake of his head in a gesture so fierce she felt daunted.

To forestall her impetuous blurting out of things better left unsaid in such company, he squeezed her arm even harder, as a signal, and then rose to his feet, pulling Catherine after him.

"Sire, I crave a boon," he addressed the king boldly. "My lady is feeling faint from the heat of the Great Hall. Will you give me leave to escort her to the battlements to take the fresh air?"

The king looked amazed at this unprecedented request, but the little queen tugged at his sleeve to get his attention and then whispered in his ear, at which he smiled broadly.

"To be sure, Sir Crispin. It is a fine evening, an evening made for lovers. We will excuse you," he said indulgently.

Every eye was upon them as they made their exit from the Great Hall, and Catherine's face was aflame with embarrassment as they passed through the whispered buzzing of the ladies and the louder ribald comments of their menfolk.

"Was that necessary?" she hissed, as soon as they were out of earshot. "You have made us a laughingstock!"

"It was necessary," said Crispin grimly, dragging her along by the arm.

"Ow, you're hurting me," she complained.

"Sorry," he apologized, easing his grip on her arm, but still retaining a firm grasp, as he marshaled her up first one pair of iron stairs and then another, until they reached a secluded place upon the battlements where they could talk in private. In the distance, Catherine could hear sentries marching their posts, the clink of their armor, and the giving of the password.

Crispin cast a glance around to make doubly sure they were alone. "I could see you were about to blurt out secrets not your own," he explained in a low voice. "Secrets that would put Chantal in danger."

"Chantal *is* a spy, isn't she?" Catherine demanded.

"Hush, keep your voice down . . . sounds in the night air travel farther than you think." He sighed. "I wanted to keep you out of this; it does not concern you, and up to now, you have had no need to know. But now"—he shrugged—"unwittingly, you might blurt out something that would put Chantal in danger . . . and ultimately and indirectly the queen."

"The queen?" Catherine was astounded. "What has the queen to do with this?"

"Chantal *is* a spy in the queen's service, though Isabella does not know of her and does not need to know. So, you must keep a still tongue in your head," he cautioned.

"And you took *her* word for this?" Catherine asked skeptically.

"I took no one's word, except that of the King of France, who employs Chantal and others like her to safeguard his daughter in a foreign land. He assured me, before ever we left France, that Chantal is one of his best spies."

"And was he in his right mind?" said Catherine impudently. She was still skeptical.

"At the time he was," Crispin assured her, knowing that the French king had since relapsed into one of his recurrent bouts of madness. "It is because of his erratic health that King Charles is particularly concerned about Madame—because of his health and because of a secret clause in the peace treaty that guarantees Richard support from France in the event of rebellion in this country. I believe the exact wording is, 'to aid and sustain King Richard with all their power against any of his subjects.'"

Catherine's eyes went wide in shock. "Rebellion!"

Crispin put his hand to her lips and his mouth to her ear. "Even now there is a plot afoot to depose Richard and imprison the little queen."

"Imprison . . . !" Catherine gasped in horror.

"Chantal got word of it and the plot was foiled," Crispin said rapidly. "We know the Duke of Gloucester was at the bottom of it. Did you not notice his absence at the tournament? He lurks at Pleshy, his country estate, where he has virtually established a rival court."

"And Lancaster? And Bolingbroke?" said Catherine, her mind moving fast.

"Have nothing to do with this as far as is known," Crispin assured her. "The Duke of Lancaster, though he once hankered after the crown, is loyal. He has been the prop and mainstay of the throne for years."

"And Bolingbroke?" Catherine persisted. She mistrusted the man.

Crispin sighed. "What do you have against Henry? He is the loyal son of his loyal father, as his presence here today proves."

Catherine thought it proved nothing, but she forbore to say so.

"Cat, all this must not be revealed to anyone," he cautioned her. "Do you understand?" He caught her chin in his hand and looked earnestly into her eyes. "Much rests on your silence. Richard will move against Gloucester in his own good time. Meanwhile, Chantal will keep her ears open and pass such information as she garners along to me, or to another, in good time, I trust, for other plots to be foiled. But I fear hard times ahead. And," he said softly, "I fear for you."

"For me? Why?"

"Because you are too open, too candid, too honest to cope with such intrigue, although that same honesty and directness served you well when . . ." He broke off suddenly, as if he had already said too much.

"When . . . what Crispin? What are you saying?" Her troubled eyes searched his face, and she cast back in her mind over her encounters with the Gypsy. Then she caught her breath sharply.

"That very first meeting on the day she told my fortune at the village fair . . . that was no accidental encounter, no chance meeting . . . it was intended . . . is that not so?"

"It was no accident," he agreed. "It was indeed intended. I thought there was something strange about that encounter from the first," he admitted. "The way in which Chantal singled you out, and then foisted herself upon our company the rest of the way to London. It did not quite ring true. I should have seen that for myself," he admitted, chagrined at the clever way in which he had been duped by the Gypsy, who had had no scruples in getting what she wanted by any means possible.

"Chantal's first mission in England was to contact you, assess your character, and report back to the King of France. Remember, at that point, although your mother was a member of the French royal house, you yourself were an unknown quantity." The man shrugged. "Fortunately, you showed yourself 'My Lady Blunt and Outspoken,' and thereby saved yourself."

"From what?" Catherine demanded. "From being sent back home in disgrace?"

"From poison or the dagger," he said bluntly. "This is a dangerous game you are involved in, Cat. I've told you that before," he said more gently. "You would have been killed, m'amie, had you shown yourself any less candid and open and honest than you are."

Catherine paled. "And that day she came to my chambers to threaten me . . ."

"She didn't threaten you, Cat, not exactly," said Crispin wearily. "But you were being far too inquisitive. She was merely trying to warn you off. Before you had to be silenced forever."

Catherine felt a shiver go down her spine.

Seeing her shiver, Crispin reached out and pulled her roughly into his arms. "The night wind blows sharp off these battlements," he said, "but before we go back inside, we must give anyone who may be lurking about a view of what they expect to see. What we allegedly came out here for . . ." He grinned wickedly. "A little lovemaking by moonlight."

"Oh, and we must give them an eyeful, must we?" said Catherine with spirit, feeling a slow burn of excitement beginning to infuse her.

"An eyeful indeed." He folded her in his arms, marveling at the way in which the soft supple lines of her body melded to his. "I trust you will not find that a hardship, my lady?" he murmured huskily, nuzzling her neck.

"No hardship at all, my lord," she whispered, intensely aware of his male vigor and of the warmth and strength of his flesh. Recklessly, she threw her arms about his neck and pulled his head to hers, so that she might tantalize his mouth with kisses. "No hardship at all."

The king, who knew when to bide his time, also knew when to move swiftly. With the installments paid on Isabella's dowry, he had raised his own small private army of Cheshire archers, all of whom wore the White Hart badge and were completely loyal to him. At the head of this picked band of men, he rode to Pleshy Castle, the Duke of Gloucester's country retreat, and with fair words—the request was couched as an urgent need for the duke's presence in Council—he rousted the older man out. When they were well away from Pleshy Castle, the Duke of Gloucester became, in effect, the king's prisoner. He was immediately shipped to France and imprisoned at Calais Castle, whose governor, Tom Mowbray, Earl of Nottingham, was a long-time friend of the king. And there, in Calais, shortly afterwards, Gloucester reportedly died, under suspicious circumstances, and at a very convenient time for the king.

When she heard the news, Catherine's blood ran cold. That the handsome, smiling king, that kindly indulgent man beloved of Isabella, had so deceived his own uncle, taken him into custody, dispatched him to France, and then . . . she refused to speculate further, but in her heart she knew it was murder—cold-blooded murder.

"Judicial murder, if you like," Crispin conceded. "At any rate, England is well rid of Gloucester."

"But to kill his own uncle . . ." Catherine waved away Crispin's objections before he had a chance to voice them. "Oh, very well . . . to order it done . . ."

"That cuts both ways, Cat," he reminded her swiftly. "Richard was his own nephew, remember? Yet he plotted against him."

Catherine frowned.

"Would you rather Gloucester's plot had succeeded?" he asked her ruthlessly. "Picture the results to yourself, Cat . . . Richard deposed . . . dead perhaps . . . the country in anarchy . . . Isabella imprisoned . . ."

"Well . . . since you put it that way . . . no," Catherine admitted reluctantly.

"Well, then." Crispin shrugged.

Catherine bit her lip. "If . . . if Gloucester had been imprisoned here at Windsor, what would you, as governor, have done?" she could not resist asking.

"The fact is, he was not," said Crispin shortly. It was a question he had put to himself a score of times, without coming up with any satisfactory answer. He was a king's man, who owed the king fealty, but how far should that loyalty extend?

The king, who moved swiftly to silence malcontents and traitors (for the Duke of Gloucester was not the only plotter to be purged), moved with similar swiftness to reward his loyal adherents.

Five new dukedoms were created, which was perhaps intended to minimize the fact that Tom Mowbray, who had acted as King Richard's sword-arm, was made Duke of Norfolk.

Was that Mowbray's price? Catherine wondered. She was sure the question was raised in minds other than her own and trembled on other lips than hers, for she was at last beginning to learn discretion.

The outraged citizens of London were far less discreet and coined a nickname for the new royal favorites, the "dukettes," and made up scurrilous songs about them.

With King Richard's popularity waning fast, he found it advisable to keep a troop of Cheshire archers about him at all times—a handpicked bodyguard. And with Londoners so hostile, he decided to hold Parliament in Shrewsbury instead of London, packing the Parliament with his own supporters. Rapidly passing a series of bills, the new Parliament gave Richard the power to rule as an absolute monarch, with a large percentage of all national revenues for himself and a subsidy guaranteed for life.

Crispin, who had seemingly taken the suspicious death of the Duke of Gloucester in his stride, was outraged by this maneuver. "By God, Cat," he sputtered, "Richard has virtually succeeded in revoking the Great Charter, the Magna Carta that King John's barons forced him to sign nearly a hundred years ago! Henceforth, Richard will rule as no King of England has done for a hundred years—by divine right!"

Catherine couldn't see what Crispin was so excited about. "But Richard *is* our anointed king," she said placidly. "And perhaps his way is the right way. He has brought us peace, after all," she pointed out, for like most women she cared far more about individual people than principles, be they ever so weighty.

"But at what price? And does the end justify the means?" Crispin argued.

Catherine shrugged. She'd been far more shocked by the Duke of Gloucester's suspiciously timely death than by what, to her, was a murky point of principle. And she had no intention of wasting what little time she had with Crispin these days arguing over a point of principle.

When the king and court returned to Westminster after the tournament, he had taken the queen with him, and where the queen went, Catherine went also. Sometimes, she felt less "the queen's cat" than her faithful shadow. But she supposed that, given the far-reaching implications of Gloucester's plot and the current unrest in the country, Richard felt the queen safer with him at Westminster, and he exerted himself to the utmost to amuse and entertain her. There were feasts and tournaments, hunting parties and hawking by the river, mummers and minstrels—all kinds of entertainment, for the court was almost frenetically gay. Isabella basked in Richard's attention, but Catherine soon wearied of the incessant gaiety, which seemed to her forced and artificial, and longed to be back at Windsor— with Crispin.

She and Crispin had come to a kind of quiet understanding in which they had agreed to put their personal lives aside for the interim, for the times were unsuited for lovers and the pressure of public events superseded private plans and desires.

Even after she and Isabella returned to Windsor, there was an uneasy feeling in the air of a calm before the storm; it was as if everyone was on tenterhooks, waiting for the storm to break.

It came, finally, from a most unexpected quarter. Seemingly out of nowhere, a quarrel broke out between Thomas Mowbray, the new Duke of Norfolk, and Henry of Bolingbroke, Earl of Derby and Duke of Hereford.

What the quarrel was about, Catherine couldn't quite ferret out, and she suspected that nobody else could either! In essence, each man made wild accusations, accusing the other of being a liar and a traitor.

That there was more to it than met the eye, everyone was sure.

King Richard decided that an open hearing in which each man could present his case would take place at Windsor. And in the days prior to the hearing, Crispin was most often to be found closeted with the chamberlain, the seneschal, and the sergeant-at-arms. In view of Richard's waning popularity with nobles and commoners alike, Crispin was vitally concerned with security and doubled the guard with his own handpicked men. He wanted no untoward incidents to occur while the king was in residence, and Catherine could understand and sympathize with his preoccupation.

The crowds that flocked to Windsor for the hearing were not the good-natured holiday-makers of tournament day, as anyone could see. There was a feeling of breathless anticipation in the air, as if no one, either courtier or commoner, could predict with any accuracy what was going to happen next.

What actually happened at the hearing was inconclusive. The two principals in the dispute were brought before the king, and with much panoply, heralds presented their respective cases. Bolingbroke's herald stated that Mowbray was a "false traitor to your royal majesty and the whole kingdom." Mowbray's herald denied the accusation and beseeched the king to "allow him combat against the accuser."

At that point, Bolingbroke threw down his gauntlet and Norfolk picked it up. A date was set for the combat to take place at Coventry, not combat à pleasance, as at the tournament, but combat à l'outrance—to the death!

Crispin was glad of the change of venue. Tempers were at fever pitch, and he had had enough of adjudicating disputes between the adherents of Mowbray and those of Bolingbroke and of sending his men-at-arms around to break up drunken brawls between the servants of one faction or the other.

Catherine thought it a great piece of nonsense and said so, in her usual blunt fashion. What good did it do for two of the highest-ranking noblemen of the realm to go at each other with sword, mace, or battle-ax until one or another of them was mashed into a pulp on the field of combat? she demanded of Crispin. It didn't prove anything, did it? It didn't establish the truth of the matter. It didn't serve the ends of justice. It was a stupid, obtuse masculine way of arriving at a decision. And finally, answering her question, she declared roundly that it proved neither man's guilt or innocence—it proved nothing at all!

"Each man feels his honor has been impugned," Crispin explained wearily. "By all the laws of chivalry there is but one solution: a duel to the death."

"A fig for chivalry!" cried Catherine. "And a fig for honor too!" She wasn't unduly concerned about the fate of either man; she detested Bolingbroke, and Mowbray, who by all accounts, as Governor of Calais, was responsible for Gloucester's death, was hardly any better!

No, what incensed her about the unsavory affair was the grief it brought to the little queen, who held her head high through all the gossip, innuendo, and speculation that inevitably swirled around her. Catherine tried to keep it from her as much as possible, but she was foiled by the spiteful Madame de Coucy, who as Isabella's governess insisted that it was her duty to make the little queen politically knowledgeable. Against this line of reasoning, Catherine had no recourse at all.

She wondered that the king permitted the little queen to accompany him to Coventry, for this was no chivalric spectacle, but a duel to the death. She herself was feeling rather squeamish at the thought of watching these two pigheaded boors pound themselves into a pulp, but if the queen must, then so would she. Though, if they succeeded in beating each other's brains out, perhaps the country would be better off! she reflected.

Seeing Isabella's ashen face as she dressed her in her finest gown and set a thin gold chaplet on her dark silky hair, Catherine felt quite savage herself.

Ironically, though Catherine, who dreaded the spectacle, had to attend, Crispin, who wanted very much to be there in person, could not. Bolingbroke had specifically requested him to be one of his attendant knights—a signal honor, so Crispin informed her—but the king had withheld his consent, refusing to release Crispin from his duties at Windsor.

"Never mind," Catherine consoled him. "I'll give you a detailed account." She made a little grimace of disgust.

"More likely you'll cover your eyes until it's all over," Crispin grumbled.

"Indeed not! If the little queen can stand to watch, then so can I!" retorted Catherine spiritedly.

Coventry, a midland city strategically located between the estates of the one protagonist from the north and the other from the east, was bulging at the seams, for spectators of high and low degree came flocking in from near and far. The tilting field had been outfitted with a lavish splendor, befitting so dramatic an event. Above the field, the colorful royal pavilion had been set up with a gold dais for the king and queen. Tiers of seats, rising one above the other, were packed with people of substance, while the grounds were jammed with spectators of lesser degree, though finely dressed merchants rubbed elbows with rabble in dusty jerkins and sweat-stained tunics who had tramped in from the surrounding countryside for this once-in-a-lifetime spectacle.

The crowds were eager and expectant, laying bets on the outcome. From what Catherine could tell, Bolingbroke was favored, though Mowbray, a doughty warrior, had his votaries as well.

The Duke of Hereford, as challenger, was the first to enter the lists. He wore Italian armor, and was mounted on a white charger with blue and white velvet trappings on which swans and antelope were embroidered.

The Lord Marshal met him at the barrier, ceremonially demanding his name and station.

"I am Henry of Bolingbroke, Duke of Hereford and Earl of Derby, and I come hither to do my endeavors against Thomas Mowbray, Duke of Norfolk, so to proclaim him a traitor against God, the king, and the kingdom." He raised his naked sword, which glittered in the sun, and swore on the cross of its hilt that his cause was just.

The Duke of Norfolk, his opponent, then galloped up on a steed caparisoned with crimson velvet and richly embroidered with silken lions and mulberry leaves. He went through the same ceremonial ritual and swore his oath in a convincing manner.

When the Lord Marshal had examined their lances, and other preliminaries were concluded, the two combatants lowered their visors and galloped to their respective ends of the field.

Trumpets blared. The combatants spurred their steeds and, lances couched, thundered down the lists, bearing down on each other.

Seizing the dramatic moment, King Richard leaped to his feet and threw down his warder, signifying that the combat, which had barely begun, was over without a blow being struck.

The heralds cried, "Halt! Halt in the name of the king!"

The combatants fought to rein in their great destriers, pulling the animals back on their haunches, so that they slipped and skidded and nearly went down.

The heralds blew a long quavering note on their trumpets.

It was unheard of; it was unprecedented; and it was over.

Chapter Sixteen

"What happened then?" Crispin asked. He had the sorry tale from other sources, but he wanted to hear it from Catherine's perspective.

They were back in the gardens at Windsor. Catherine had left the weary little queen to nap, for she was quite worn out by the combined effects of heat, stress, and emotion. Catherine felt similarly fatigued herself, but at the same time, she was all agog to share the experience with Crispin.

"Disappointment," Catherine said slowly after thinking it over for a moment. "A tremendous, overwhelming sense of disappointment."

"I should think there must have been," Crispin interjected with feeling.

"There were loudly voiced complaints on all sides," Catherine resumed, picking up the tale where she had left off. "Much grumbling—and those who had come primarily to see a bloodletting were absolutely livid," she recollected.

"Not surprising," Crispin grunted.

"There was a long, long wait, while the king, who had left the field, took council with his advisors," Catherine remembered. "Chairs were set up right there in the lists for the combatants—a green velvet chair with blue and green hangings for Bolingbroke, and a red velvet chair for Mowbray with—"

"Never mind the chairs, get on with the story," said Crispin impatiently.

Catherine was piqued. "I was just trying to show you how it was," she said, annoyed. "Anyhow, they dismounted and took their seats," she continued, "and there they sat, as though carved in stone, in the blistering sun, in full view of everyone, for *two solid hours*, waiting for the king to come back and announce his decision."

"It was dreadful," Catherine went on. "That awful expectancy. The tension was so thick you could cut it with a knife. And it was so hot, but nobody, of whatever degree, was willing to leave his seat, for fear of losing his place. And the rumbling and the grumbling grew louder and more pervasive. The queen was white as a ghost. I feared she might collapse, and I tried to persuade her to retire to the pavilion to rest and refresh herself, but she refused."

Catherine sighed. "Finally, the trumpets blared again"—she was beginning to hate the sound of trumpets—"and the king and his counselors reappeared.

"The king sent Sir John Bushy, his secretary, to take up a central position in the lists, and he read the verdict from a long scroll."

"What did it say?" Crispin asked.

"Both contestants were banished," Catherine said succinctly. "Henry of Bolingbroke for ten years and Thomas Mowbray for life."

"Ten years . . ." said Crispin bleakly.

"If, within that time frame, he sets foot in England again, he is sentenced to death."

"How did he take it, Cat?"

"As you might expect, he was stunned. And so was Mowbray. Mowbray went down on his knees to the king, and, oh, Crispin, he gave him such a piteous look, like a poor whipped dog that can't understand why its master is beating it. It was heartbreaking to see a proud man so humbled," said Catherine with a little tremor in her voice.

"But Bolingbroke"—she gave a little shiver—"he will humble himself to no man, not even the king, perhaps not even to God himself." There was awe in her voice. "He just turned his back on the king and walked away."

"He is a Plantagenet, after all," said Crispin, with pride for his cousin and his lineage.

Catherine nodded. Just so, she knew, would Crispin have behaved, had he stood in his cousin's shoes and their situations been reversed.

"He will not go alone into exile, I think," Catherine ventured after a little pause. "His admirers will follow him." She stole a glance at the man sitting motionless beside her on the carved stone bench. "Crispin . . . you . . . you would not . . ." She faltered.

He looked at her in surprise. "Go with him?" He stretched out his arm and draped it around her shoulders, pulling her close. "Nay, Cat, my place is here. My heart is here. Surely, you know that."

With a small wordless murmur, she nestled closer to him for comfort, and he pressed a gentle, tender undemanding kiss upon her brow.

"Oh, Crispin, what is going to happen now?" she whispered. "What is going to happen to us all?"

"I don't know, Cat." He pondered briefly. "Richard will ride high for a time," he predicted confidently. "Henry has long been a thorn in his side—he is too popular, too wealthy . . ."

"And too ambitious." Catherine could not resist the barbed comment.

"So you say," Crispin, unruffled, refused to be drawn out. "I suspect Richard does not yet realize that by making a martyr out of Henry, he has created a new hero for the country."

"I heard John o' Gaunt tell the queen that he would rather see his son dead than so dishonored," Catherine recollected.

"There is no dishonor, no shame in this for Henry"—Crispin shook his head—"but rather for the king."

"That is so," Catherine admitted. "There was a great outcry among the spectators when the king's verdict was announced. The common people, especially, made no bones about voicing their scorn and derision. And there were many," she recalled, "of both high and low degree, who made their way through the crowds to kiss his hands and wish him 'Godspeed,' calling him 'Sweet Harry' and the like."

Crispin nodded. "The king may find, in ridding himself of a rival, he has created a monster."

"As for Tom Mowbray . . ." Crispin dismissed him with a snap of his fingers. "Exile is as good a way to silence him as any. He knows too much about the circumstances of Gloucester's suspicious death."

"They say he goes on pilgrimage to Jerusalem to expiate his sins," remarked Catherine.

Crispin mediated briefly. "Cat, do you suppose Richard had this in mind all along?" he asked. "Or was it a sudden impulse?"

Catherine frowned. "I suppose he must have had it in mind," she said slowly after a moment's thought. "In fact, I am sure of it," she added with more certainty. "I was puzzled at the time that he allowed, no, encouraged, the queen to be present at a duel to the death, which was bound to be a sight quite unfit for a child. It was not like him, you see; he has always had such care and concern for her."

"That would explain it," Crispin said thoughtfully. "Since he knew all along that there was to be no carnage—no bloodletting—and her presence in Coventry would enable her to bear witness to his triumph in judgment, his mercy and great magnanimity. Ah, but Richard is a crafty fox," he mused in a tone in which distaste was mingled with reluctant admiration. "Let us hope he has not outsmarted himself this time."

"It is the queen I am worried about," Catherine fretted. "All this stress and strain is so bad for her."

"She is a child still. She will forget about it in time," Crispin consoled her. "Do not fret overmuch about her, my lady of the loving heart."

"She is not such a child as you think," said Catherine in a troubled voice. "She is growing up fast. Who would not, under such circumstances?

She has such dreams—such nightmares, that I have taken to sleeping on a pallet by her bed, to be there to comfort her when she wakes screaming in the night," Catherine confided.

"Which is not at all where I would have you sleep, m'amie," said Crispin meaningfully. He judged this doleful conversation had gone on quite long enough, and he chose the ambiguous statement to deliberately jolt Catherine out of her doldrums.

"I can't imagine what you mean," she said primly, though the blush suffusing her face gave away the lie.

"Can't you, my dear?" His arm was still draped negligently about her shoulder, and now he began to play with the golden chain around her throat which supported a heavy pendant resting on her breast.

The pendant was an intricately carved, ornate affair, given her by the queen, and from it dangled a perfect large white pearl, which nestled snugly in the cleft between her breasts.

"Oh, to be a pearl and find oneself at home in such a beauteous valley," he said huskily, experimentally tugging on the chain and pendant so that the milky white globe rolled gently back and forth between her breasts.

With deep interest, he watched as her breathing quickened and her breasts began to rise and fall in a faster rhythm, their tautened peaks upthrust, straining at the cloth of her bodice.

Catherine sat up straighter, trying to ignore the teasing, tantalizing feel of his hand as it caressingly brushed her neck and throat and breasts, toying with the ornament, lifting the chain and dipping the pearl in the hollow between the soft white mounds of flesh.

She felt fiery little ripples and tingles darting through her whole body, even in hidden places that he had never touched, while her breasts themselves began to ache and throb, swelling with an almost unbearable yearning to be fondled and caressed.

And then, as if he knew and understood the yearning even better than she did, he responded to it, slipping a hand into her low, square-cut bodice, thumbing the jewel-hard nipple to a fever peak, and spreading out his hand and fingers to cup the heavy fullness of her breast, kneading and manipulating it so that near-pain mingled with exquisite pleasure.

With a little sigh, she leaned back against his shoulder, threw back her neck, exposing the slender white column of her throat to his kisses, closed her eyes, and gave herself up utterly to the delightful sensations he was evoking within her. Her whole body quivered in response to his heated touch, and unconsciously she wriggled even closer, craving, though she was only dimly aware of it, the ultimate closeness, the ultimate intimacy, and the ultimate release.

Their breaths were coming in ragged gasps, and she made a little moan of protest when, with a final fond caress, his hand left off cupping and squeezing her breasts. But the hand's absence was only momentary, as he pulled her half onto his lap, her spreading skirts billowing out across their legs. She felt his male hardness, straining against its trusses, and then she felt his hand, now caressing and stroking the bare flesh of her silken thighs.

She gasped, and her eyes popped open. In all the teasing love play in which they had hitherto indulged, the stolen kisses and caresses, he had never yet been so bold.

"Shh—open yourself to me, m'amie," he coaxed her with gentle insistence.

She found it easy to obey him, for her body did so of its own accord, acting on age-old instincts. She found herself whimpering with an exquisite sense of anticipation as his hand fondled and caressed her thighs, creeping ever upward to the swollen mound of their joining. And then his exploring fingertips teased and toyed with her, and she moaned in a kind of exquisite agony.

Sweat beaded on his forehead, but he kept his own arousal under stern control as, careful not to tear the band of flesh that proclaimed her maidenhead, he brought her to fever pitch and kept her there, fondling, stroking, and caressing, until she went rigid against his hand and slumped against him in relief as he freed her from all tensions in a bursting of sensations she had never before experienced.

"Ohhh!" she cried, letting out a long breath in wonder, hiding her face against his shoulder as his arms went round her and his lips brushed her flushed face with the tenderest of kisses. "Oh, I had not thought anything could be . . . be like this."

He smiled at her innocence. " 'This' is but a prelude to greater joys, m'amie. When we are wed, as we must and shall be, we will no longer have to content ourselves with stolen moments and secluded spots."

Catherine glanced around her nervously. They had come to a secluded part of the garden where intruders rarely ventured for the express purpose of talking freely without being overheard. But one thing had led to another and, overcome by passion, she had not given a thought to their being seen or spied upon till now. Her face flamed.

"There is no one to hear or see," he said soothingly, interpreting her swift glance around and reddened face aright. "But Cat, we cannot go on like this indefinitely. Each time we snatch a stolen moment, one or another or both of us is left wanting."

She made a small ineffectual gesture toward him. He seized her hand, and turning it palm upwards, kissed it lingeringly. "I take my pleasure from yours, m'amie,' he said fondly, "but in these uncertain times we must snatch our happiness when and as we can. Will you not wed me, Cat, and give me the right to protect you and yours, whatever may befall?"

Catherine looked troubled. She loved him; she was as sure of that now as she was of anything, and she was sure he loved her in return. Indeed, he had so woven himself into the very fabric of her existence that she could no longer imagine life without him.

But neither could she imagine life without the little queen, who had also made her way into Catherine's heart and nestled there, with a child's innocent demands for love and care and nurturing.

"But what of Isabella?" she cried. "I cannot desert her now, Crispin. Not while she has need of me. And she has no one but me. The king . . ." She made a small futile gesture. "The king is . . ."

"The king is mad," said Crispin harshly. "As mad as Isabella's father, the French king, though in a different way, I grant you."

Catherine paled. "Do you really think so?"

"I do."

"Then that is all the more reason for me not to desert her," said Catherine resolutely. "Let us wait a little, Crispin, and see what happens." She bit her lip. "And if you do not wish for us to meet again like this . . ."

"God help me, I cannot do without you, Cat!" he burst forth.

"Nor I you." She seized both of his hands in hers and brought them to her lips. "Be patient. Give me a little more time," she begged.

Reluctantly he nodded. "As you wish."

She rose, shaking out her skirts. "I should get back to Isabella; she will be wakeful by now and asking for me."

"Till tomorrow then."

"Tomorrow," she promised, hurrying away with a rustle of skirts, then pausing to look back and blow him a kiss, as if she could not bear to part from him.

Moodily, he watched her departure, then settled back on the bench to put his mind to icy baths in cold mountain streams and knightly vigils on cold stone floor slabs—anything to distract him from the memory of her soft, warm, willing body.

Chapter Seventeen

As Crispin had predicted, King Richard was riding high these days. With Gloucester dead and both Bolingbroke and Mowbray banished from the kingdom, he must have felt his enemies were vanquished and that he had nothing and no one left to fear.

Extravagance at court reached new and unprecedented heights, and the king, whose expenses by now far outstripped his Parliamentary revenues, was forced to resort to ingenious and (some said) diabolical methods of extorting money from his groaning and overburdened subjects through a series of forced loans, dishonest pardons, and blank charters. Under threat of torture, wealthy citizens were forced to sign bonds, blank bonds, with the amounts only filled in afterwards when the king's minions had conducted a thorough investigation of each citizen's accounts and were satisfied that this much and no more could be squeezed from the groaning taxpayer's coffers.

"Is it right," Queen Isabella, on a visit to court, asked the king in perplexity, "for a man to put his signature on a bond when the amount is not filled in and he does not know how much he is signing away?"

The king said shortly that it was justified as the only way to make sure that a rich man was taxed to the ultimate for the good of the realm. "The bond is blank," he explained, "to allow time to discover exactly how much the man is worth and how much he can afford to pay." And then he sent her back to Windsor.

Geoffrey Chaucer himself ventured to criticize his patron in verse, sending a poem to the king in which he was advised to "Cherish thy folk and hate extortion."

The king, when he had read the verses his court poet had courageously sent to him, crumpled up the parchment in a fury, so Catherine heard from a reliable source.

John of Gaunt, the old Duke of Lancaster, might once have held up a restraining hand to curb his nephew, but when his son went into exile he had retired from court, and according to all reports, his health was failing fast.

Isabella had developed a lively affection for the old Duke of Lancaster, looking upon him as a kind of surrogate grandfather, and Catherine took her several times to visit him and cheer his sickbed. King Richard occasionally joined them at the old man's bedside. Out of pity for his uncle, Richard had reduced Henry's original sentence of banishment from ten years to six, but everyone, including the old man, knew he would not live to see his son in England again. Everyone also wondered what would happen to the vast Lancastrian possessions when the old man died. Richard had promised that Henry could claim his inheritance in absentia, with a lawyer to act as proxy and handle his affairs for him, but by now, everybody knew that Richard's promises were written on the wind. Had he not already sequestered Tom Mowbray's estates to the crown?

The atmosphere was tense and strained, and were it not for her secret trysts with Crispin, Catherine really did not know how she could have gotten from one day to the next. She lived for their stolen meetings and snatched moments of privacy, and she was convinced that Crispin shared her feelings to the utmost. He often declared as much, and his loving words were sweet to Catherine's ears. But sometimes little niggling doubts crept in, and she wondered if he were only playing the game of courtly love with her, the game which was considered to ennoble a man, making him more valiant and inspiring him to greater deeds of chivalry.

Still, she continued meeting with him at every opportunity, in their favorite secluded spot in the gardens or high on the battlements, and with each stolen assignation they drew a little closer to the ultimate act of love and commitment. He taught her ways to pleasure him, and played sweet tunes of love upon her body, as a talented musician would a treasured instrument. But though their love play gave them the easement of physical release, it fell far short of final consummation, and Catherine fantasized an even deeper ecstasy when they could fully and freely share with each other the complete and ultimate expression of love.

And sweet as their secret assignations and stolen trysts were, something in Catherine's nature, her basic honesty and integrity and forthrightness, was offended by the clandestine nature of their meetings. She loved the man, and she wanted to proclaim that love for all the world to see.

And so, when Crispin, in late autumn, issued an ultimatum, declaring that at the Christmas revels he intended to ask of the king a Christmas boon, her hand in marriage, Catherine consented gladly, though with a little trepidation. The current situation, unsatisfactory as it was, was yet preferable to other alternatives she could think of.

"What if Richard withholds his consent, Crispin?" she asked with a troubled frown.

She had been half sitting, half reclining in his arms, on a bench in a seldom-used room of the castle, reached only by a hidden passageway and known only to a select few. It was their refuge from the blustery autumnal gales blowing outside. Now, she sat up straighter and turned to look at him with anxious eyes.

"Let's not borrow trouble, Cat," said Crispin, nuzzling her neck playfully.

"But what if he does?" Catherine persisted.

"Then we will run away together," Crispin recklessly proposed. "Henry of Bolingbroke is in exile in Paris. I will take service with him, and you can throw yourself on the mercy of your French relatives."

Catherine shivered at the thought of being at the mercy of Queen Isabeau of Bavaria, though she was only a relative by marriage, Catherine supposed. The King of France might be more mercifully inclined, she reflected, if he were in his right mind at the time. Though what either of them might have to say to a poor relation who had defected from their daughter's service, Catherine trembled to think of.

"How can I possibly leave the little queen?" Catherine protested. "Isabella needs me."

Crispin sighed. Cat's almost excessive loyalty to the child-queen tried him sorely at times. He had even toyed with the notion of getting Cat with child, as a means of binding him to her, for with her belly big with their babe, surely she would be less obsessed with the well-being of a child not her own.

But Crispin's sensitivity to his own baseborn status precluded his taking the easy way out. He was too scrupulous to risk getting his love pregnant with his child until they were safely wed.

"I need you, Cat," he said roughly. "In my bed, in my arms, at my side. Do I count for nothing?"

"Oh, Crispin, you know you count as everything to me—well, almost everything," the incorrigibly honest Catherine assured him, her green eyes glimmering with tears. "It is just that the little queen is so young, so needy, so alone. I am all that she has."

"She has the king, and before too much longer she will be ripe for bedding, for she is rising twelve years old—nearly ready to be a wife in more than name. Henry of Bolingbroke's wife was married to him at twelve and bore her first child, young Harry of Monmouth, at thirteen."

"Yes, and nearly died of it," Catherine retorted swiftly. "Richard loves Isabella well in his own fond protective way. He would not use her so."

"Well, then, what of us?" Crispin demanded. "It has been three years—nearly four!" He sighed. "*Must* you give up your youth to her, Cat?"

Catherine drew a long breath. Had it really been that long since she had first met Crispin and left home in his company? Where had the years gone?

She looked down at her hands as if she were looking down a long road of time and then spread them helplessly. "Do what you must," she whispered, for his jaw was stern and set, his mind made up, and she knew she could prevaricate no longer.

The Christmas festivities at Windsor were more than usually lavish and King Richard was in an unusually benevolent frame of mind. He readily gave his consent to their betrothal. Queen Isabella was, at first, understandably downcast at the prospect of no longer having her favorite lady-in-waiting within call day and night, but she soon grew reconciled, and entered excitedly into making plans for a lavish wedding in which King Richard himself would give the bride away.

But before a wedding date could be set, events of a public nature intruded into their private lives and upset all their plans.

The king's cousin and legitimate heir, Roger Mortimer, who was serving as his viceroy in Ireland, was slain by Irish rebels, and the court was plunged into mourning.

And then, at the turn of the year, John of Gaunt,

the time-honored Duke of Lancaster, breathed his last. It was a not unexpected blow, but no less distressing for all that.

But the final crushing blow that brought their wedding plans to a complete standstill, causing them to be postponed indefinitely, was something that Catherine, inadvertently and indirectly, brought upon herself. It just went to show, she reflected afterwards, how a person's slightest actions could change her life, for good or ill, and even affect the course of history.

She had quarreled violently with Madame de Coucy. For three years and more Catherine had held her impetuous tongue, biting back numerous sharp retorts. In part, she'd succeeded in keeping her temper for so long because Crispin was there, ever counseling restraint. "Don't get into a shouting match with Madame de Coucy, Cat," he warned her on one occasion. "You cannot possibly win, and the lady is notoriously bad-tempered and vengeful. What's more, she still has powerful connections both here in this country and in France. You must endeavor to keep your temper if you value your position at court."

"But Crispin, she is so unkind to the poor little queen. Her insolence knows no bounds." Catherine knew his advice was sound, but she was troubled.

"Then it is for the queen to complain of her insolence to the king," he replied.

Catherine shook her head sorrowfully. "She won't do that—she claims it is beneath her dignity to take notice of such affronts, poor little mite."

"Perhaps Isabella fears to put Richard's affection for her to the test," Crispin suggested shrewdly.

"Whatever . . ." He shrugged. "My advice to you is to keep your distance from Madame de Coucy whenever possible, Cat. And to keep your temper and guard your tongue."

Catherine took his advice to heart, struggling to do just that no matter how sorely she was tried. On the whole, she bore Madame de Coucy's insults to herself (and there were many) better than she could bear seeing the little queen slighted or mocked and ridiculed. And ridicule and mockery were Madame de Coucy's preferred forms of punishment. The governess goaded the sensitive child with her tongue as with a lash, and both Catherine and Isabella cringed under it, the former trying to protect the latter as best she could.

Early in the new year, letters and Twelfth Night presents came from France, and Isabella, who seldom heard from her family, was in a transport of delight. Her uncle, the Duke of Orleans, had sent her a little monkey, a pet she had frequently expressed a desire for, ever since Catherine had told her of the monkey she'd seen on that long-ago market day.

The queen and her favorite lady were both watching the monkey cavort about the room and laughing heartily at its antics when Madame de Coucy swept in with a rustle of silken skirts. Her face was drawn into a scowl of ill-humor, and Catherine, who could read the danger signs, hastily scooped up the monkey and thrust it behind her back, well out of sight.

But the monkey wouldn't stay put. It clambered up Catherine's back and perched on her shoulder, clinging to her neck with its little arms. From its safe perch, it chittered and gibbered at Madame de Coucy, from whom it sensed hostility.

"What have you there?" asked the governess frostily.

"A monkey, Madame," said Catherine, struggling to detach it from her neck and hand it over to a page.

"Ugh, what a disgusting little beast!" The governess shivered in an exaggerated manner. "Where did it come from?"

"From France, Madame," Isabella chimed in, trying to divert Madame de Coucy's attention from her new pet. "My uncle of Orleans sent it me, along with a number of other gifts. Wouldn't you like to see them? There is a pretty silk scarf from my sister, Michelle, embroidered with her own hands." Isabella displayed a grubby square of silk clumsily embroidered with her initial. "And here are miniatures painted on vellum of my baby sister, Katherine, and my little brother, the Dauphin."

The governess cast an indifferent eye over Isabella's treasures. "Trumpery baubles," she said with a disdainful sniff. "Is there nothing from the king and queen?" she added with an acquisitive gleam in her eye, for Isabella was wont to appease her by passing on trifling gifts of jewelry, French finery, or perfumes.

"The king, my father, is ill again," said Isabella. "And the queen is busy with affairs of state."

"Which means nothing, I suppose," the governess sneered.

At that point, the monkey, finally detached from Catherine's neck and insecurely held by the little page, tore loose from his grip and began to gambol about the room, chittering and gibbering. Catherine and the boy tore after it in hot pursuit, cornering it upon a table to which it leaped. The table was littered with wrappings and ribbons and small gifts, among them an opened box of comfits and glace fruits, with which, in high glee, it began pelting the governess.

The fine lady shrieked, dodging the volley of sticky sweets, rendered even stickier because the monkey sampled each of his missiles before spitting them out and using them as weapons in his arsenal.

The page boy emitted an unwary yelp of laughter, and even Isabella succumbed to a fit of the giggles.

Oh, no-no! thought Catherine, aghast. She knew Lady de Coucy, like many people who derive enjoyment from ridiculing others, could not herself bear to be the butt of a jest. Frantically, she dived for the monkey, grabbing it by its long, sinuous tail and then scooping it into her arms. She turned it over to the page, with a stern admonition to take it and go, though she could barely be heard over Madame de Coucy's shrieks of rage.

"Get that animal out of here!" Madame de Coucy shrieked. "At once, do you hear! Get rid of it!" As the frightened boy, bearing his mischievous burden, ran out of the room, the governess, her face suffused with rage, marched up to the table and, with a sweep of her arm, cleared it of wrappings, ribbons, gifts, and candies. "And get rid of this trash as well!" she shouted after the boy.

Isabella, all merriment fled, rushed in to secure

her treasures that were among the clutter. "Madame . . . madame . . . my sister's gifts, my brother, the Dauphin's miniature . . ." she expostulated.

"Your brother, the Dauphin, indeed!" the governess sneered, picking sticky bits of glace fruit from her elegant gown and elaborate headdress. "Your brother is no more rightful Dauphin than I am, but is one of the bastards your wanton mother has foisted upon France. I doubt if she herself knows who his father may be, for all Europe knows she is the whore of the world!

"Though who can blame her?" the lady ranted in her fit of hysterical rage. "With a madman for a husband! Madness is in his blood; the de Valois stock is accursed, as King Richard will find if ever he takes you into his bed to bear him sons as witless as their grandsire!"

Isabella went white to the lips, and Catherine, stunned and appalled, at last found her voice and broke into the governess's hysterical diatribe. "How dare you! How dare you!" she shouted, stepping in front of the little queen, as if she could protect her with her body from the woman's verbal assaults.

"I dare because it is the truth, which none can deny!" the woman blustered.

"This time you have gone too far, madame!" Catherine stormed. "The king shall hear of this, I promise you."

"Oh, the king . . . the king . . ." sneered Lady de Coucy contemptuously. "The king is my own cousin, through our mutual grandfather, King Edward the Third. Think you he will take the word of a nobody like yourself? A jumped-up country wench brought in to amuse a whey-faced brat!"

Catherine drew herself up. She seldom traded on her de Valois connections or, indeed, thought of them, so thoroughly did she regard herself as an Englishwoman, but she did so now. "You will do well to remember, madame, that my mother is a de Valois, as much a princess of France as was yours a princess of England." She added ominously, "We shall see who the king will believe!"

"Do not count on that whey-faced brat to back you up!" the governess warned, with a vengeful glance at the tearful Isabella. "I have ways to insure her silence, and I assure you the king will take my part."

"As he did in the matter of your divorce?" taunted Catherine, though she might better have held her tongue. But her blood was up, roused by the bitter hurt the malicious woman had dealt the child she cherished, and her unruly tongue ran away with her. "All the court titters, even now, over your husband's preference for a Bohemian lady. And it is well known that the king himself intervened, petitioning the pope for a divorce on his behalf so that he might free himself from you." As she took the sobbing Isabella's hand to lead her from the room, Catherine fired a parting shot over her shoulder. "And indeed, madame, 'tis no wonder you could not keep a husband, so foul-tempered as you are!"

Aghast at her own temerity, Catherine did her best to soothe and calm the distraught little girl, though she found it exceedingly difficult to refute Madame de Coucy's charges, so full of truth were they (though a truth far better left unsaid).

"It *is* true, is it not, Cat, that my father's illnesses are not ordinary ones? That . . . that he has spells of madness?" Isabella heaved a long choking sigh and leaned back on her pillows for she was so worn out by spasms of weeping that Catherine had undressed her and put her to bed, though it was only the middle of the day.

"So they say," Catherine, at her wit's end, answered evasively, for she did not know how much Isabella knew or suspected of her father's chronic ailment. "In truth, I do not know exactly what his illness is, madame. Only what has been reported."

"That he is a . . . a lunatic," Isabella said flatly.

"That he has spells of what the world calls madness, madame, but that at other times he is as sane as anyone," Catherine admitted reluctantly, striving to be truthful, for the child would have to know sooner or later, if she did not already.

She wiped the little girl's swollen eyes with a cool damp cloth and smoothed her tangled hair. "Come now, drink this soothing potion the physician has prescribed to ease your headache," she coaxed. "It is a concoction of poppy juice and will make you sleep. In the morning, when you wake again, everything will seem better."

But Isabella dashed the cup away. "How can anything be better, ever, when I know that in my body I bear the seeds of madness!" she said bitterly. "And that when I grow old enough to bear King Richard sons, as is a queen's duty, they will likely inherit my father's madness."

"You can not know that, madame. No one can

predict the future." Catherine groped for a note of encouragement. "Though your father is afflicted with a malady, his brother, the Duke of Orleans, is unaffected. The king's ailment may not be hereditary," she pointed out. "In any case, it is in God's hands, as are we all."

Catherine was hours soothing and calming the distraught little queen, but as soon as she had induced her to take the physician's soothing draught, Catherine left her in the care of one of her other ladies and, still simmering with indignation, went straightway to the king. Madame de Coucy had preceded her, of course, with her version of the contretemps, which naturally differed widely from Catherine's, but the king heard her out, and Catherine was careful to report faithfully and accurately all that had transpired.

"She must go," the king declared, before she had even finished her tale. "This passes all bounds." He frowned thoughtfully. "I will ask Lady Mortimer to replace Madame de Coucy as governess, but she will not be available until her period of mourning is over. I fear I must ask you, Cat, to postpone your wedding until Lady Mortimer can take Lady de Coucy's place, and until I myself return from my expedition to Ireland."

"Ireland?" It was the first Catherine had heard of a projected Irish expedition.

"These Irish rebels must be put down," the king averred. "I intend to lead a punitive expedition in person. Even under ordinary circumstances the queen would have relied heavily upon you while I was away, and now . . ." He looked a trifle apolo-

261

getic. "I fear we cannot spare you to Sir Crispin just yet.

"In token of our great appreciation for your loving care of the queen and of our great affection for you . . ." The king clapped his hands, and a page came running up with a jeweled casket. He opened it and removed a magnificent gold chain, with the links forming the king's initial. From the chain dangled a huge ruby pendant, large as a hen's egg, or so it seemed to Catherine's bedazzled eyes.

King Richard draped the chain over her head, and the pendant lay heavy on her breast, as heavy as her responsibilities, thought Catherine ironically. She murmured her thanks and, at the regal nod of dismissal, withdrew, backing out of the king's presence in a daze.

Crispin's face grew dark as a thundercloud when she told him of the proposed expedition to Ireland and of the subsequent delay in their wedding plans.

"Richard is a fool!" he burst out. "No king of England has ever been able to hold Ireland or ever will! It is an endless bog that sucks up men, money, and supplies." He shook his head. "And what does he intend to use for money to equip his troops? Despite all his exactions, the royal treasury is empty, frittered away on lavish court ceremonials, endless entertainments and amusements, and, of course, ostentatious presents to his favorites." He eyed the jewel on Catherine's breast with disdain.

But Richard had an answer for those who questioned how he would finance his Irish expedition. He simply went back on his promise to Henry of

Bolingbroke that he might inherit his father's extensive wealth, and sequestered the entire Lancastrian estates to the crown. Nor did he seize them without obtaining a legal opinion to the effect that a traitor could not inherit that which should be forfeit to the crown, a piece of legal chicanery that left even Richard's most loyal followers aghast.

"By God, Cat," Crispin fumed. "Richard is running mad. He has sown the seeds of his own destruction. No man of low or high degree can feel safe in his inheritance or look to pass his property on to his sons under these conditions. Men of whatever degree who might have cause to fear the security of their property will look to Henry of Bolingbroke as their champion."

Catherine sighed. Between Crispin's fulminations over the Lancastrian sequestration, on the one hand, and Isabella's lamentations over Richard's impending departure to Ireland on the other, she was sore beset.

On the whole, she was more sympathetic to Isabella's plight, being easily able to imagine herself in her position. She was less sympathetic to Crispin's point of view, saying crossly, "If Bolingbroke hadn't gotten himself into a silly quarrel with Mowbray, neither of them would have been exiled and none of this would have happened."

So outspoken was she in her dislike and distrust of Bolingbroke that Crispin was alarmed. "For God's sake, Cat, guard your tongue!" he cautioned her, grasping her arm and steering her out of the Great Hall, where, after a fine dinner, Madame de Coucy was making her farewells to a coterie of her sycophants. "That lady has sharp ears, and she is bound for France, where she will doubtless report to exiled Bolingbroke."

Catherine shook off his restraining hand. "Let her. I care not!" she said recklessly. She was sick of all this intrigue, and the strain of watching her every word was beginning to tell; she was worried about the young queen, who had refused to come down for dinner and had dined off a tray in her room, and she was bitterly disappointed that their wedding had had to be postponed.

All of a sudden, her whole body felt engulfed in a tide of misery and despair. A tear trickled from the corner of her eye and rolled down her cheek. Furiously, she wiped it away, but it was followed by another, and then another. They came faster than she could control them. And then, to her horror, she began to sob aloud.

Crispin put his arm around her and hurried her along the winding corridors, concealing her tearful face as best he could from the curious eyes of servants and passersby until they reached the seldom-used room that was their only refuge. When the door was safely barred against intruders, he took her in his arms.

"Cat, m'amie, what is it?" he murmured, rocking her back and forth and stroking her back with broad soothing strokes.

"I don't know," she gulped. "I'm just so weary," she wailed aloud. And then she was overcome by sobs again, deep wrenching sobs that wrenched her insides and shook her slender frame.

He held her close, making little soothing noises deep in his throat, and when the storm of tears had abated somewhat, he offered her a handkerchief to dry her eyes, saying whimsically, "One of Richard's more useful innovations."

Catherine dabbed at her eyes and blew her nose. "Thank you," she said primly. "I . . . I don't know what came over me. I'm sorry, Crispin." She felt deeply ashamed of herself. That she, a warrior's daughter, could so give way to her emotions, to her disappointment, and fall apart like this was utterly shaming.

"No one can be strong all the time, Cat," he said consolingly. "All this has been very hard on you. Richard left it up to you to tell Isabella of his Irish venture, did he not?"

"He did." She drew a long quavering sigh. "And it was quite an ordeal. The poor child fancies herself in love with him, Crispin."

"She is at a difficult age—in love with the idea of being in love. She'll get over it," he said callously. "It's you I'm worried about, Cat. You are going to need all your strength, m'amie, in the days ahead." Tenderly, he brushed away a tear that still trembled on her eyelash.

"What are you saying?" Catherine demanded, bracing herself. "Do you know something that I don't?"

But Crispin shook his head, refusing to say more than he had already divulged, and Catherine, who felt that she already had enough to cope with as it was, declined to press him further.

Richard came to Windsor to bid farewell to the queen, and for a few days she was utterly happy, with a child's ability to live completely in the present moment.

As on previous occasions when he was expected, she raced to the highest turrets of the castle when his arrival was imminent so that she could catch the first glimpse of him riding in on the London road.

The king had instructed his Governor of Windsor to arrange a grand tournament especially in the queen's honor, and Crispin had done so, making arrangements for 40 knights and their squires to participate in the grand spectacle, all of whom wore the emblem of the white falcon, the queen's own device.

Crispin himself was among the participants, and as usual distinguished himself by his valor, skill, and courage, but Catherine felt that she had had enough of tournaments and mock battles. They were beginning to seem alarmingly like the real thing.

Young Harry of Monmouth, Bolingbroke's son, who was not much older than Isabella, served as Crispin's squire. He was a handsome youth with a winning manner, but Isabella would have none of him.

Glowing with happiness and self-importance, Isabella distributed the prizes, and Richard made much of her.

Catherine admitted to herself that beside the debonair king, young Harry appeared a callow youth. He was to accompany King Richard on his Irish adventure, serving, she supposed, as a hostage to insure his father's good behavior while the king was out of the country. But Bolingbroke was a ruthless man with a brood of sons younger than Harry, and she wondered what good, if any, holding the boy as hostage would accomplish.

The happy days sped by all too fast for the queen, and all too soon came the necessity of saying good-bye to the king. On their last morning together, they attended mass in Windsor Chapel, where King Richard, his blond hair gleaming in the candles' gentle glow, chanted the Collect as a solo in his sweet true tenor voice. "Increase and multiply upon us Thy mercy . . . that we may so pass through things temporal that we finally lose not the things eternal . . ."

Pages met them at the west door of the chapel with comfits and a stirrup cup of wine, which Richard permitted Isabella to share. "Au revoir, ma petite reine," he said, embracing her so fondly that tears pricked Catherine's watching eyes.

"Adieu, mon cher mari," the little queen cried out, watching him mount his gaily caparisoned horse with such longing in her eyes that he lifted her up in front of him for a final fond embrace, saying, "Adieu, madame, adieu, until we meet again."

Gently, he set the queen down from his horse into Catherine's loving arms. Then he leaned from the saddle and clasped Crispin's hand. "Watch over my little queen," he said huskily.

"I will, sire," Crispin pledged, looking the king straight in the eye. "Whatever happens, no harm will befall her. I swear it on my life."

And then, with his attendants, King Richard rode away, making for Bristol, where he would take ship and embark for Ireland.

Within a week, word came that the king had landed safely on the coast of Ireland. Catherine unrolled a map of the country and pinned it up on the wall so that the little queen might follow the king's proposed route. Isabella pored over it, twisting her French tongue around the unfamiliar names—Waterford, then inland to Kilkenny, where Richard intended to engage the rebel King of Leinster, Art MacMurrough, in battle in the mountains of Wicklow, and then on to Dublin.

There was some fighting, they heard, and afterwards King Richard knighted Harry of Monmouth, the young son of his rival, a move which Catherine thought showed unprecedented generosity. And then wild storms on the Irish Sea closed the waters to shipping, and they heard no more.

With King Richard's communications with England effectively cut, Bolingbroke made his move.

The little queen was in the chapel, praying for the king's success in Ireland and his safe return, and Catherine slipped away to the gardens, hoping to meet Crispin there. Since the king's departure, she had rarely left the queen's side, and she was desperate for news. In equal measure, she hungered for Crispin's touch and the strength of his comforting arms about her.

But it was not Crispin she encountered but Chantal, and the Gypsy girl was so weary and travel-worn that Catherine barely recognized her. She had been lurking in the shrubbery hoping to catch a glimpse of Catherine, and she emerged from her hiding place as soon as she spotted the queen's favorite lady.

Catherine was stunned into a shocked silence by her unexpected appearance. The usually jaunty

French spy was dirty and disheveled; her face was scratched and puffy from lack of sleep, her tunic dusty, her hose torn, and her shoes nearly worn through.

"Get me some food, for the love of God," she begged. "I am nearly famished." She swayed on her feet and then collapsed in a huddle, her head between her knees.

Without further ado, Catherine hurried to the kitchens and pilfered a loaf of bread and a small jug of wine, the first items she could lay her hands on without arousing suspicion.

When she returned, the girl snatched the loaf from her hands and, breaking it into great chunks, stuffed it, chunk by chunk, into her mouth, washing it down with great gulps of wine. Gradually, the color returned to her sallow face.

"What news?" Catherine asked in a fever of impatience as the girl revived.

"Bolingbroke is on the point of breaking banishment," the Gypsy announced bluntly. "If at all possible, we must get the queen away to France."

"How do you know?" Crispin had come up behind both girls, and now he laid a heavy hand on Chantal's shoulder. She eyed him warily, but answered readily enough.

"I have been in France. I followed Arundel, the Archbishop of Canterbury, to Paris, where he met with Bolingbroke at the Hotel de Cluny. Arundel offered him the crown, and has even obtained a papal blessing on the project."

Catherine drew in her breath sharply, hardly believing her ears.

"Where is Bolingbroke now?" Crispin demanded.

Chantal looked at him oddly, a little taunting smile playing about her lips. "Why ask me, sir knight? You should know as well as I that he is in Brittany, mustering arms and men. The whole coast of England lies open to him, and he will be here within a few days."

"To claim his inheritance," Crispin stated firmly.

"To claim the crown," Chantal retorted.

"He has sworn to my Lord of Northumberland and others that he comes only to claim his inheritance and that Richard shall reign to the end of his life," Crispin said, but with less certainty.

"And you believed him?" said Chantal with passionate scorn.

Catherine looked from one to the other in bewilderment.

"Bolingbroke is breaking banishment?" she demanded of Crispin, anguish in her eyes. "And you . . . you knew of it and did not warn me?" she said accusingly. "You have been in communication with him?"

Crispin sighed. "I . . . and others."

"I care not about those others," she said brokenly. "But that you should be . . . a . . . a traitor!" She made a futile gesture with her hands. "Oh, Crispin, how could you?"

He took a step towards her. "Cat . . ." he began.

"No . . . no . . . don't touch me." She backed away. "Traitor!" she flared. "Traitor!"

Chapter Eighteen

"Traitor!" The word hung heavy on the air, as if it were a palpable object between them and not a verbal accusation.

"Traitor to Richard, perhaps," Crispin admitted. "But not to England."

"Richard *is* England!" retorted Catherine. "He is the king."

"England is more than one man, Cat. And Richard lost England long ago. He lost the love of his people, who groan under the heavy burden of his taxes; he lost the respect of the barons by ignoring the rights of inheritance, and now he has lost the support of the Church. What is left?" Crispin shook his head somberly. "By embarking on this mad venture into Ireland, I fear he has lost all."

"You may chop logic all you choose!" Catherine cried angrily. "I know where my loyalties lie." She was near to tears. "And why did you not even warn me of Bolingbroke's intentions, since you were in on the conspiracy?"

"There is no conspiracy," Crispin said wearily. "At least, none that I was aware of. I did know that Henry's intentions were to return to claim his birthright, but as God is my witness, I did *not* have any idea that the Archbishop would offer him the crown or that he would accept it and deliberately set out to overthrow Richard." He hesitated, then added energetically, "Though I believe Henry of Bolingbroke will make a better king than Richard, and by God, if he wants my support, he shall have it."

"But Richard is your brother," Catherine protested weakly.

"He has never acknowledged me as such." The lack of that acknowledgment had always rankled in Crispin's breast, Catherine knew. "And by the same token, Henry is my cousin, my father's brother's son, and almost as near in kinship."

"Enough of this." Chantal, who had been sprawled out on the grass with her eyes closed, rose to her feet and dusted herself off. "Save your quarrels and your justifications for another time," she urged. "Your personal problems are no concern of mine. What matters to me is the queen. Though Madame Isabella is queen of this benighted country, she is still Madame of France, and I would see her safely back there. My concern is all for her."

"As is mine," said Catherine swiftly, surprised that she and the Gypsy were now in accord.

Chantal turned to Crispin with a mocking smile playing about her lips. "And you, sir knight. Though you have evidently decided to turn against your king, I cannot believe you would wish the child harm. Will you cooperate with my efforts to safeguard her? Look the other way, if you must?"

"I have sworn to protect the queen with my life," he said sturdily, rising to Chantal's challenge. "If it seems best to get her away to France, I will do all in my power to help you."

"Tres bien." She spoke absently, wrinkling her brow in thought, then addressed Catherine. "Say nothing to her yet," she advised. "But be prepared to leave at a moment's notice. I shall have to make arrangements for her to travel in safety and comfort, and that will take some doing. But we have time, I think. Bolingbroke is still in Brittany, and armies are not raised in a day or even two." She meditated briefly. "It is best that you come with her, I think, both for her comfort and sense of well-being, and for your own safety as well. Your devotion to the queen is well known, and you may not be safe here from Bolingbroke's fury if Madame slips out of his greedy grasp."

"But I don't want to leave England," Catherine blurted out in dismay. "It is my home."

"Chantal is right, Cat," Crispin said. "If we succeed in spiriting the queen away, she will need you on the journey." It was the strongest argument he could use with Catherine, he was well aware. Privately, he considered that his Cat, with her outspoken ways and fierce loyalties, would be more in danger than the queen, whose rank and position virtually guaranteed her a measure of security. She was not expendable in the general scheme of things; Catherine was.

Catherine looked at him coolly. "You want me to go?"

"I think it best."

"The issue need not be decided today," Chantal declared impatiently. "It is as easy to make arrangements for two as it is for one. And that one a child. But I must be on my way. When the time is right," she told Catherine, "I will come for you both." And then she slipped away, ducking back into the shrubbery from which she had come and disappearing from view.

The two that were left behind looked at each other across the gulf that had suddenly divided them, a gulf so vast neither knew how to bridge it. Theirs was no lovers' tiff, Catherine realized with a sinking heart, but a fundamental difference of opinion that might never be reconciled. How could it—with she for the king and he taking the usurper's part?

"Cat . . ." Crispin reached out to take her arm, but she flinched away.

"No." She backed off, holding out her hands palms outwards, as if to fend him off. "Don't say anything . . . not now. I can't bear it."

"I'm sorry, Cat," he said helplessly. "But I must follow my own convictions and do what I think is right."

"And so must I, Crispin. So must I." Holding her head high, though she felt her heart was breaking, she turned and walked away.

The next few days were fraught with tension. Nothing was heard from the king, and Catherine, while making discreet preparations for a hasty departure, tried to guard her tongue and keep her unwelcome knowledge of what was going on from the queen, who in any case was anxious enough.

Catherine did not want to alarm her unnecessarily. After all, she told herself, it hadn't happened yet, and maybe it never would. Maybe Bolingbroke would change his mind at the last minute, or maybe he wouldn't be able to recruit an army or obtain the necessary supplies. Any number of things could happen. Maybe his ship would go down in the Channel with all lost, she thought hopefully.

But none of her ill-wishing did any good, and all too soon rumors began flying about—rumors that Bolingbroke had safely landed at Ravenspur, on the Yorkshire coast, within easy reach of his hereditary stronghold and of the Nevilles and Percies of Northumberland, who could be expected to rally to his assistance.

And then he was on the march, and men flocked to his standard, and volunteers enlisted under his banner, so many of them, it was said, that he was hard put to find provisions enough to feed them all and had to send some of them home again.

It was impossible to keep such news from the young queen, but whatever she felt, she held her head high and proud, even before Catherine who was heartsick for her, saying with regal disdain, "Our cousin comes to claim his inheritance and for no other reason, but it is a mean trick all the same with the king out of the country."

For the king was still in Ireland, and though his uncle, the elderly Duke of York, was regent, and had sent a frantic message re-calling him, still he did not come.

In the meantime, Henry of Bolingbroke had seized several castles, and then marched west to confront the regent's scanty forces before Richard could sail home to join forces with the old duke. York's army scattered before Bolingbroke's might, and many of the royal forces deserted to him.

Three royal councilors, fearing the worst, took refuge in Bristol Castle, but Bolingbroke routed them out and, without even the pretense of a trial, summarily executed them. He then sent their heads to London with a formal message that he had come to take up his rightful inheritance and were the Londoners with him? If not, he didn't care, as he had people enough! But the detached heads conveyed a less than subtle hint that, on the whole, it was better to be for him than against him.

"The arrogance of the man," raged Catherine, who was white-faced and sickened at the news. She was glad to see that even Crispin looked a little shaken by this barbarity. "And this is the man whom you think would be a better king than Richard?" she taunted him. "An honorable man . . . a defendor of English liberties! Bah! He is nothing but an unprincipled usurper!"

"It is war, Cat," Crispin reminded her. "And in war atrocities are often perpetrated by both sides."

But Catherine didn't care; she wanted Crispin back where he belonged—on *her* side! And she used every argument she could summon and every womanly wile she possessed to get him there.

"Face facts, Cat," he said patiently. "Richard's cause is already lost. Whether either of us likes it or not, Henry holds England in the palm of his hand. And before long, he will hold Richard there as well. *If* Richard returns."

For Richard had done the unthinkable, that which would have set his father, that old campaigner, the Black Prince, reeling in the grave. He had divided his forces, sending a part of his army to England under the old Earl of Salisbury, while he himself remained in Ireland to gather the rest of his scattered and depleted forces, for the Irish campaign had been a debacle.

By the time Richard finally crossed the seas, Bolingbroke was making a triumphal progress through the west country, his army jubilant in victory.

"I wonder you do not join him," said Catherine nastily, "since above all things you prefer being on the winning side."

"I might at that," retorted Crispin, stung by her goading, "were it not for you and the little queen."

"Don't let me stop you!" Catherine flung back at him as she flounced away.

Crispin looked after her with a frown. Ordinarily, he ignored her barbed comments and sharp-tongued remarks, for he knew they were her only outlet for venting her frustrated emotions, but sometimes she went too far. And he himself was deeply disturbed. If they were to get the queen safely away, it must be soon. And where was Chantal? She should have been back long before this. Had she been taken? he wondered. Perhaps it was time to make some plans of his own.

Before Chantal returned, the news worsened. King Richard had landed in Wales and was making for Conway Castle on the north coast, a virtually impregnable fortress, where the loyal Earl of Salisbury had assembled an army and was waiting for him to join them.

Richard disguised himself as a traveling friar, and abandoning his personal baggage and other encumbrances, made his way up the coast with only a handful of loyal friends and his greyhound, Mathe, for companionship.

He had counted on finding a small but loyal army at Conway, but when he arrived he found only Salisbury and a few retainers. The rest of Salisbury's army had melted away in the interim, disintegrating in the absence of the king and because of rumors spread by Lancastrian spies, rumors of Richard's death and of the seizure of his treasury by the enemy.

Lacking an army to fight with, Richard tried diplomacy, sending a messenger to Henry with authority to offer him his father's lands and titles if he would cease his open rebellion.

Henry held Richard's messenger as hostage and sent the rebel Earl of Northumberland to Richard, demanding a personal meeting in order to put his case before the king. Northumberland swore an oath on the cross that Henry had no treasonable intentions, and Richard agreed to accompany him to Chester to treat with Henry in person. But on the way Richard and his tiny group of friends were ambushed, and the king was taken prisoner.

Clearly Henry had the upper hand, and appalled by his ruthlessness, Crispin could find it in his heart to feel sympathy for the feckless king and even a gallant impulse to rally around him. But it was an impulse he quickly subdued. In his gallantry and dauntless courage against all odds, King Richard was a tragic figure whose plight tugged at the heartstrings. But he had sown the seeds of his own destruction, Crispin reminded himself. Erratic in his fits of brilliance, he had squandered so much early promise, so much treasure, and the love and respect of his subjects, whose patience had finally run out.

Richard, though brilliant, was basically unstable, Crispin told himself. The country needed a firm hand at the helm, a stable ruler, such as stolid, cautious, calculating Henry, who could provide stability to the realm in his lifetime, and who had a brood of sons to carry on after he was gone.

But of course, the women could not be expected to see it in that light. Young Isabella wept bitterly in Catherine's arms when she received a last letter from the king—a letter written while he was still at Conway Castle, a letter written in the form of a poem, in which he addressed her as "his hope and his consolation," and in which he lamented his fate, saying, "when I from such a height have fallen so low and lose my joy, my solace, and my consort . . ."

The same Welsh messenger who delivered the letter recounted in detail what had befallen Richard since then, how he had been lured out of impregnable Conway Castle by Henry's false promises and taken prisoner. And then the messenger recounted, in his lilting Welsh accent, how the king's favorite dog, whom he loved and had taken with him everywhere, had fawned upon Henry, ignoring the king. Henry had pushed the fawning greyhound away in annoyance, but Richard had advised him wryly to keep the dog at his side, "for my favorite greyhound, Mathe, fondles and pays court to you this day as King of England, which you will be, and that the natural instinct of the creature sees. Keep him therefore by your side, and he will forever follow you."

The report of which occasioned a fresh outburst of tears on Isabella's part, and Crispin could see that Catherine too was hard put to it to hold back her own tears, struggling to do so for the little queen's sake.

How like Richard, Crispin thought sardonically, to dramatize the incident, seeing in the defection of an old, half-blind dog the significance of his own downfall. He would have made a better poet than a king, thought Crispin ruefully.

Later, after Catherine had paid the messenger and led the queen away to put her, exhausted with tears and emotion, to bed, she sought Crispin out and, enemy though she considered him to be, wept bitterly in his arms.

"Oh, Crispin," she sobbed, "it breaks my heart to see Isabella so stricken with grief."

"There, there, Cat," he soothed her, holding her close. "She is only a child, after all. She will get over it in time."

"And Richard?" she whimpered. "What will be his fate? Surely he has not deserved this, to be brought so low that not even his own dog will acknowledge him as master!"

"It is all over for Richard, I fear. You must face it, Cat. Richard has lost all. He is certain to be deposed, if not worse. We must look ahead, and put our minds to getting you and the queen away to France.

"Come now, dry your eyes"—he set her gently from him—"and take a good look at this map I have drawn for you." He unrolled a piece of parchment and spread it out on a small table. "If you follow the route I have marked, you will do well enough."

Catherine dabbed at her eyes and peered over his shoulder, following his finger as it traced the route. "You can take shelter at the White Hart Inn," he advised. "I have made discreet enquiries, and the innkeeper is loyal to Richard still. His daughter is wed to one of Richard's Cheshire archers."

"Can you not come with us?" she asked, her heart in her eyes.

"I cannot, Cat," he said roughly. "Would you have me desert my post?"

"Yes, if it would keep you safe from harm," she said defiantly. "A thousand times yes." Verbalizing a fear that had been in the back of her mind for days, she asked, "What will Bolingbroke do to you if the queen evades his grasp? After all, she is in your charge."

"Nothing, I hope," he said soothingly, though he had some reservations on that point himself. Glossing over it to ease her mind, he said, "Make no mistake about it, Cat. When he comes, I shall have to yield up Windsor to him, whether I wish it or not. We could not possibly hold out against superior forces with only a few men-at-arms. And, when the time comes, as it will, I intend to exchange the white hart badge for the red rose of Lancaster and swear fealty to him as my overlord and sovereign." He frowned. "But at the same time, I will not soil my hands with the blood of a little girl, even if that child were not dear to us both."

Catherine turned white. "Would it come to that?" she whispered.

"I doubt it. More likely, he would only hold her hostage for whatever advantage it might bring him. Nevertheless, I would prefer that both of you were safely back in France. And so, lacking Chantal, we must make plans."

"When must we leave?"

"Tomorrow, I think. We have delayed too long already."

"Catherine drew in her breath sharply. "So soon?"

"Tonight will be our last night together, Cat. Perhaps forever."

His words sounded like a knell of doom in her heart. "No, Crispin, no . . ." she whispered, clutching at his tunic. Suddenly she knew, beyond any shadow of a doubt, that she loved him, wholeheartedly and without any reservations. She didn't care that he was for the usurper and she for the king; she didn't care that he was her enemy. That didn't matter anymore; what mattered was that she loved him with every particle of her being.

"None of us can know what the future will bring, m'amie. Stay with me tonight," he said persuasively. "Let us have one last night to remember—to carry in our hearts whatever happens. One night to last us a lifetime."

Privately he thought that his lifetime might not last so very long. Despite his brave words to

Catherine, he knew that it might be measured in days if their plan to get the queen away to France succeeded. Bolingbroke might be magnanimous in the first flush of his victory; on the other hand, he might not. Judging by the heads already adorning London Bridge, his magnanimity was not to be counted on!

"But the queen . . ." Catherine protested faintly.

"She is sleeping," Crispin reminded her. "You yourself told me she had cried herself to sleep."

"Yes," Catherine recollected. "What's more, the physician left her a sleeping draught, so that if she wakens in the night, one of the maids can give it to her."

"Well, then . . ." He drew her into his arms.

With a little murmur of assent, Catherine nestled there. It was where she longed to be. She could feel the steady thumping of his heart through his silken tunic and the warmth of his body radiating heat, which felt good, for the night air was chill, for all that it was still summer.

They stood so, wrapped in each other's arms, for a considerable time, for the night was young yet, and it was theirs.

When finally she stirred restlessly, he asked, "Wouldn't you be more comfortable without this ridiculous thing?" He tugged at the cylindrical golden caul that confined her heavy plaits of hair on either side of her head and which was attached to a gold headband over her forehead. "I would see you as I did on the day you rode your father's warhorse, with your hair flowing wild and free."

Catherine's fingers replaced his clumsy hands, and she deftly loosened the caul and released the heavy plaits, which, freed from their confinement, tumbled down on either shoulder.

He lifted a heavy braid and twined it round his throat, where it lay like a thick rusty-red collar. "You hold me captive, lady," he said whimsically. "Do with me what you will."

It was an appealing invitation, and Catherine promptly availed herself of it, teasing and tormenting him with quick darting kisses and nipping love bites, tracing his lips with her tongue and poking the tip between his lips.

He groaned deep in his throat and reached for her.

"Oh, no . . ." She twisted away, though only as far as the length of braid permitted as it lay twined about his throat. "You are my captive, remember. And captives are *not* permitted to touch their captors," she rebuked him with mock severity.

"Of course not. I beg your pardon, lady." Entering fully into the game, he assumed a military stance and clasped his hands behind him, as if tied at the wrists.

Still at a little distance, she stood back, cocking her head, and surveyed him with approval. "That's better. But don't captives usually have to yield up their swords?"

"Which sword, lady?" he inquired in a voice choked with laughter.

Her eyes widened. His quasi-military posture and slightly spread legs made clearly evident that to which he was referring. She caught her breath at the evidence of his stunning virility.

"The sword at your side will do . . . for now," she said demurely, though her heart was thumping painfully. She lay her hands upon it, withdrawing it from its sheath and setting it aside. "You don't need the scabbard either," she decided, undoing the belt at his waist. His firm stomach muscles rippled and flexed under her hand, and she gasped a little, feeling her own excitement growing.

"A merciful captor would untruss my points," he suggested. "Or permit me to do it myself. I am feeling, er, a trifle congested."

"Who said I was merciful?" Catherine retorted swiftly. Then, with a nod; "Oh, very well."

She watched with interest as he reached under his tunic and wrestled with the points of his hose, untrussing them and peeling them slowly down to reveal his firmly muscled thighs and calves.

He stepped out of his tights and his shoes, while he was at it, and stood partly naked before her, assuming his former military stance.

She drew in her breath sharply, shivering a little in her excitement. "A little more modesty, if you please, captive," she said with mock severity. Leaning forward, she reached to pull his tunic down over an interesting bulge. But as she leaned forward, her braid slipped from around his neck. The game was over.

Instantly, his hand snaked out and captured the braid, tugging her ever closer by it. "Ah, and who is the captor now and who the captive?" he growled.

"I do not know," she whispered foolishly, not wishing to admit defeat.

"I know," he said firmly, pulling her into his arms. "Is not each of us held captive by the other?"

he suggested. "I am your captive, Cat, and you are mine. And neither of us would have it any other way, m'amie."

They exchanged a long, lingering, passionate kiss, as if to seal the bond. And then, remembering his earlier wish, she untied first one long braid and then the other, unplaiting her hair and combing it out with her fingers, before shaking it down her back.

He reached round and ran his hands through it, from the nape of her neck to its ends, admiring its gleam in the candlelight, loving its sheen and soft sweet smell and texture, pulling a hank of it forward to nuzzle and caress, saying, "I would see you as Lady Godiva, Cat, clothed only in your hair."

Dropping the lock of hair, his hands went to her bodice, tugging insistently at the front lacings, and her hands joined his, impatient to help him, and then the lacings gave way, and her breasts in all their generous fullness were laid bare.

Gently, he parted her bodice and eased her garments down so that her upper torso was wholly unclothed. But playfully, she bent her head and shook her hair forward, so that it fell in waves and ripples over her breasts.

"Oh, ho, so you would play at being coy, would you, my lady," he growled. "Well, let us see what a stiff wind will do to Lady Godiva." Kneeling before her, he blew across her breasts, blowing the rippling hair away and causing her sensitive swollen nipples to tauten in stiff hard peaks. He flicked the tautened nipples with his tongue and gently nibbled them.

"Ohh . . ." she groaned, bracing her hands upon his shoulders for support, for she felt as if her knees would give way under this sensual onslaught.

He buried his face in her swaying breasts, working little miracles of sensation with his lips and tongue and teeth. At the same time, he unfastened the gold links of her belt and loosened the lacings of her skirts, so that they rippled down her thighs, falling in a silken heap at her feet.

Drawing little swirling circles with his tongue on her breasts and belly and silken flanks, he drew forth a heated response from her.

Rising, he scooped her up in his arms and carried her to the bed, easing her gently down upon it, and none too soon, for she felt she could stand no more.

Shrugging out of his tunic, the only garment left him, he joined her on the bed and aroused every inch of her flesh with burning kisses.

And then she felt a momentary pain as with one deep thrust he entered her, sheathing himself in her as he would sheathe his sword in its scabbard.

The pain she experienced was fleeting, and as she felt it ease, she closed herself hungrily around him. At long last, they were one.

He lay quiet for a moment, glorying in the moment of union, and she held him tightly, amazed at the feeling of fullness, of rightness, of completion, as if they were at home, at last, in each other.

Tentatively, he moved, exploring her inner depths with his instrument of love, as he had explored her flesh with his tongue, and she moved in unison with him, cradling his turgid flesh with her body.

And then, unable to withstand the honeyed sweetness of her flesh any longer, he groaned and reached his fulfillment, as she rose to hers, in a glorious explosion of sensations that overwhelmed them both.

Sweat-soaked, they lay together in a tangle of limbs, kissing and caressing each other amidst a welter of sweet love words, until he reached up to pinch out the candle and they fell into a deep and blissful sleep.

They roused several times during that night to slaken their thirst for each other yet again, and each time, in its own way, was sweeter and more fulfilling than the last. It was as if their bodies knew in advance of the long drought in store, and were determined to replenish and revivify themselves, giving and taking enough loving nourishment to last a lifetime.

In the gray light of dawn, Catherine woke, yawning and stretching like a satisfied cat. She turned sleepily, but his side of the bed was empty, though it was still warm from his body, and the pillow still bore the indentation of his head.

Her eyes searched the shadowy room, and found him straddling a chair, fully dressed, his eyes roving over her body as if to memorize every inch of her beloved flesh.

She smiled a good morning and wordlessly held out her arms to him, but he shook his head, smiling sadly.

"It's time, Cat. You must be up and on your way before dawn fully breaks."

Seeing her smile vanish, he rose from his seat and, crossing the room as if drawn by a magnet, bent over her, kissing her regretfully. "I feel as badly about this as you, m'amie, but it must be." Lovingly, he caressed her flushed face and tangled hair.

With a final fond caress, he steeled himself and said, "I am on my way to the stable to saddle horses for you. You must go to rouse the queen and dress her in this servant's garb." He dropped a plain and simple gown of some rough-woven material on the bed. "I think it best that she travel as your servant. Some disguise is necessary, I fear. Make sure she wears no jewelry or other adornments," he added. "When you are ready, meet me at the postern gate. And do not linger overlong," he cautioned. "Time is precious."

Chapter Nineteen

But all their plans came to nothing because the little queen flatly refused to leave England.

"Richard is my husband. I will not desert him," she declared. "Il est mon mari, mon cher mari." And when Catherine pressed her, she threw a royal fit of temper the likes of which Catherine had never before seen her display.

A half hour later, they were still arguing. "But madame, you *must* go." Catherine tried to sound severe.

"Dare you say 'must' to me, your queen?" the little madame said haughtily, stamping her royal foot. Then her face crumpled, and she threw herself into Catherine's arms like a bewildered child. "Oh, Cat, I'm sorry," she wailed. "But you must understand that I cannot desert my husband. Queens do not run away."

"But if you could help the king by doing so," Catherine suggested cleverly. It was her best argument and she had saved it to the last. "If you got away now, you could make an appeal to your father, the King of France. Beg him to intervene on King Richard's behalf."

"Oui. I have already thought of that." Isabella produced a thick document, closely written and blotched with tearstains. "But I do not need to see him in person to make an appeal. You go. You take the letter, Cat. Deliver it to the king, my father, and remind him that by the terms of my marriage treaty he is obligated to come to the aid of my husband, King Richard."

Catherine was at a loss. "But King Charles would not heed me, madame," she stammered. "You, his beloved daughter, would be so much more effective."

A discreet rap sounded on the door, and Crispin, low-voiced, demanded admittance.

Swiftly concealing the letter in her bodice, Catherine cautioned the queen to silence. "Say nothing of this letter to anyone," she warned. Then she unbarred the door and opened it a crack.

"What is taking so long, Cat?" Crispin demanded. He slipped in, followed by Chantal. She was dressed in Gypsy garb. Her pretty face was bruised and swollen, and she was missing several teeth. She made a curtsy to the queen with painful stiffness. Evidently, she had suffered a severe beating.

"Madame," Crispin said without preamble, "this is Chantal. She is in your father's service. I advise you to heed her as you would heed him."

"Bolingbroke's men are on their way here, within a day's ride, perhaps less." Chantal spoke swiftly. "They will take you into custody, madame. And they have a warrant for your demoiselle's arrest."

"Me?" said Catherine in astonishment. "But why? What have I done?"

"You are accused of plotting against Bolingbroke. Madame de Coucy is your accuser."

"But I never . . ." Catherine was indignant.

"So you merely offended the lady." Chantal shrugged. "In times like these it is enough. The easiest way to get revenge on someone is to accuse that person of treason."

"Treason!" Catherine's face paled.

"Your innocence or lack thereof is unimportant. Besides, you are half-French and a kinswoman to the queen. That is automatically enough to make you suspect," Chantal said bluntly. "You must leave now. You would not like to be a prisoner, I assure you. I have just escaped one of Bolingbroke's prisons. That is why I was delayed," she added, "or I would have been here long before this."

"How did you escape?" Catherine asked, fascinated.

Chantal shrugged. "I bribed the guards. But I think in a similar situation, you would not care to employ the coin I used . . . the coin of my body."

Catherine digested this in silence.

"Do you have word of the king?" the little queen asked.

"They are bringing him to London. He will be lodged in the Tower."

"The Tower?" Isabella's face brightened. "Do you think they will let me go to him?"

"Indeed not, madame. You must not think of such a thing." Chantal looked alarmed. "You will be placed in custody and sent to the fortress of Wallingford until Bolingbroke decides what to do with you. And the king will not be lodging in the royal apartments of the Tower, as before. He is Bolingbroke's prisoner now, and so will you be, unless you get away. That is why I have come," she added briskly. "I have information on the best route to take, and who can be trusted to help you, if you need it. Also, I have brought disguises for you and your demoiselle. You will be a nun on her way to a French convent, and Lady Catherine will be your servant boy."

Seeing the queen's mulish look, she said, "Come, madame, and try on the nun's habit. Do you not wish to see your father and your family in France again?"

"With all my heart," she answered quickly, "but all the same, I will not desert the king in his hour of need."

Crispin broke in roughly. "Cease this foolishness, madame. Bolingbroke will have your head or order you smothered with a pillow as you sleep, and none will be the wiser."

"And what of *your* head, Sir Crispin, if I escape to France?"

"My head is my own concern, madame. And I have sworn an oath to protect you. Would you have me forsworn? For surely, Windsor cannot hold out against Bolingbroke's might."

"I absolve you of your responsibility to me, Sir Crispin. But I will not run away."

Isabella remained adamant, and the combined persuasions of the three of them could not convince her to go.

"What can we do?" Catherine asked anxiously in an undertone.

"Short of bodily throwing her over a horse, I do not know," said Crispin ruefully. "But you must go, Cat. For you are in more danger than she, now there is a warrant out for your arrest."

"Yes, Cat, you must go." The queen had overheard their whispered conversation, and added her voice to Crispin's. "They dare not harm me, for I am Madame of France, but you are of no such importance, and neither Sir Crispin nor I can protect you." She drew Catherine to her side. "Go now and ask my father for help," she said in a low voice. "I, your queen, command you to do so."

"Yes, go," Chantal urged her. "I shall be here to look out for Madame," she reassured Catherine.

"But aren't Bolingbroke's men looking for you?"

"They are looking for Charlot, a minstrel, not a fortune-telling Gypsy girl. I shall follow Madame wherever they take her and get word to France if she seems in peril." She picked up the rolled bundle of clothing she had brought and thrust it into Catherine's hands. "I went to some trouble to obtain this. At least you will get some use out of it." She eyed Catherine critically. "But before you change into it, we should cut your hair."

"Cut my hair!" Catherine squeaked, clasping her hands to her ornate headdress.

"But of course. How can you expect to pass as a boy with that great mass of braids?" Chantal was scornful. She rummaged in a sewing kit and came up with a pair of shears. "Remove your headdress and stand still."

While Chantal cut away, and as heaps of russet

hair piled up at Catherine's feet, Crispin sat by, murmuring consolation. "It will grow again, Cat, thicker and more beautiful than ever. And you are not a Samson, to be shorn of your strength with the cutting of your hair," he reminded her encouragingly.

Perhaps not, Catherine thought ruefully, as she looked at her strange new self in a mirror a few minutes later, but she certainly felt a little weak in the knees.

Gathering up the bundle of clothing, she went to the queen's dressing room to change, and Isabella accompanied her, saying, "The garments may need some alteration, Cat, and I am a better needlewoman than you." While Catherine was changing, the queen snipped the seams of a cotehardie apart, inserted her letter into the lining, and sewed it up again. "The letter will be easier to carry and safer so," she advised Catherine.

Catherine, who felt as if she had been carried away and caught up in a raging flood to land who knows where, nodded in a dazed fashion. In the space of a few minutes she had been transformed from a court lady into a very creditable servant boy.

And then the queen bade her a tearful farewell, for who could know when, if ever, they would meet again, and Crispin escorted her down the back stairs and out into the courtyard to the postern gate.

"Take longer strides," he advised her. "And remember to keep your voice low and gruff when you converse with anyone."

"I'll remember," Catherine promised.

"There is still much of the day left. Do not travel after sunset, Cat, for night is the province of brigands who would slit your throat for a few pennies," he warned her.

"I'll only travel by day," she promised, stifling her misgivings.

"Now is your chance to ride astride again," he teased, trying to cheer her. "So make the most of it."

"I will," she said, summoning all her resolve. She had shed tears enough already, and she was determined to bid him farewell with dry eyes and a smile.

He led her into a little alcove formed by the angle of a storage shed adjoining the wall and took her in his arms. "Before God, Cat, I am loath to see you ride out all alone. I wish I had someone trustworthy to send with you as escort."

"In times like these, who can be trusted? I shall be all right," Catherine assured him with a confidence she was far from feeling.

"You have your map and sufficient monies?" he asked her, ever practical.

"Isabella gave me a money pouch full of coins," she nodded. "Look after her, Crispin," she urged him.

"I will," he promised. "Not only because she is the queen, but because she is dear to you."

"No dearer than yourself," she whispered as her hand stole upwards to caress the hard-boned masculinity of his handsome face, which was drawn and anxious.

He caught her hand and pressed a lingering kiss into the palm. "God help me, m'amie, I thought

King Richard's grief excessive and self-indulgent when he lost Queen Anne. I did not know then that parting with someone you love is like losing a part of yourself," he said huskily. "Believe me, I will do all in my power to insure that you can come back one day."

"Will you, Crispin?" she said wistfully.

"I swear it, Cat." He gently pressed his lips to hers as if to seal the pact, and then gave her a leg up into the saddle. "Make as good time as you can to the coast," he advised her. "The French ship of which Chantal spoke is waiting at harbor. It will take you straight to Calais. God be with you, Cat."

"And with you, Crispin," she murmured, blinking back tears, for she felt as if her heart were breaking. Clucking to her horse, she clattered out into the courtyard making for the postern gate.

At first, it felt rather good to be out on the open road, riding a fine piece of horseflesh astride, free of hampering skirts and heavy headdresses. It lifted Catherine's sagging spirits. Was this the way men felt? she wondered, going about their manly pursuits, riding off on campaign, taking control of their own destinies?

But the further she traveled from Windsor, the more apprehensive she became. It had been some time since she had been out on her own, and then only around the environs of Clifford Manor, where she knew everyone for miles around and everyone knew her. She felt strangely anonymous, which was, of course, the purpose of her disguise. But still, it was unnerving.

Crispin had written out a pass for her that gave her a false identity, should she be stopped and questioned, but she was reluctant to use it unless absolutely necessary, for it would go hard for him, she feared, if he were implicated in her escape. In any event, she had a good 24 hours head start before needing to fear pursuit, and she intended to make the most of it, riding hard but at a steady pace that would not exhaust her horse, or herself. The port at London was teeming with Bolingbroke's supporters, Chantal had advised her, and so she was making for the south coast where the French ship was at anchor. It was a longer journey across country, but was presumably less hazardous.

She rode steadily all the rest of the day, hoping to make the White Hart Inn by nightfall, but at dusk was still far from her goal. Although tired and hungry, she decided to press on by starlight, fearing bandits less than the risk of capture. She had seen several parties of men-at-arms marching to join Bolingbroke, and had skirted the main road whenever she feared to encounter such groups, which had delayed her.

The White Hart Inn was swarming with Bolingbroke's men when she finally reached it, and she took shelter behind a convenient haystack while she considered her choices. These men might not be looking for her yet; on the other hand, they might be the very ones who carried a warrant for her arrest. What course would suit her best—boldness or prudence? She couldn't decide.

She watched and waited, skulking in the shadows, her stomach rumbling with hunger, while the soldiers watered and unsaddled their horses for the night. There appeared to be a good deal of milling about in the courtyard and rough, good-natured banter among the soldiery. Half a dozen men were gathered about a plump, pretty serving wench, ogling and fondling her. Finally, she shook them off, with many a good-natured jest, and then made her way to the well to draw water, the group parting to let her through.

The well was not far from Catherine's hiding place, and as the girl neared it, Catherine drew in her breath sharply. She thought she recognized the maid from her previous visit, years ago with Crispin.

What *was* her name? Catherine racked her brains—Madge, Molly—no, it was Meg, the landlord's pretty daughter. She was almost positive.

But would Meg recognize her—especially in her present guise? And could she trust her? She had appeared to get on very well with the soldiers, jesting with them and teasing them flirtatiously.

Catherine peered cautiously around the haystack. The group of soldiers had dissipated, most of them going into the inn, calling loudly for food and pots of ale. Meg was at the well, drawing up slopping buckets of water. Catherine could hear the creak of the windlass and the splashing of water.

Dare she trust her? Catherine pondered. But while she was mulling over it, her horse took the decision out of her hands, throwing up its head and whinnying. Catherine caught wildly at the reins, pulling the horse's head down onto her shoulder and holding its nose to muffle any further outbreak.

But it was already too late. Meg, hearing a horse

where no horse should be, stopped short, and then turned in the direction of the haystack, grumbling to herself. "Pesky soldiers, leaving their horses loose," she groused. "Drat the men."

Catherine burrowed deeper into the hay, leaving the horse to its own devices. Free of restraint, it trotted up to the maidservant and, dipping its head into one of her water buckets, began to guzzle thirstily.

Meg snatched at the trailing reins to lead it back to the stables; then a wisp of reddish hair and a suspicious hump in the haystack caught her eye. She picked up a pitchfork and advanced upon the haystack. "You . . . whoever you be, come on outta there!" she demanded.

Giving up her attempt at concealment, Catherine ruefully emerged, pulling bits of hay from her hair and shaking the chaff from it.

"I'm a friend," she quavered.

Meg looked skeptical.

Hesitantly, Catherine gave the password.

Meg's eyes widened. "Are you truly for the king?" she whispered. "You have stumbled into a hornet's nest. Bolingbroke's men are here."

"I can see that," said Catherine with some asperity. "That's why I was hiding."

Meg cast a quick glance over her shoulder. "They've all gone inside to guzzle ale," she said reassuringly. "It should be safe enough at the moment."

"I need food and drink and a place to rest," said Catherine urgently. "I can pay you well."

Meg hesitated momentarily, then said, "Oh, very well. Come with me. If we are stopped and ques-

tioned, I'll say you are my brother, just back from
an errand."

"Brother?" said Catherine questioningly, temporarily forgetting her disguise. "Oh, yes, brother,"
she added, remembering to keep her voice low
and deep. Evidently, Meg did not recognize her,
and perhaps it was just as well.

Meg led her to the stables, skirting a steaming
midden heap, and turned her horse into an empty
stall. "You can sleep up in the loft." She pointed
to a rickety ladder. "It'll be safe enough, I daresay,
if you keep quiet. I'll sneak some food out of the
kitchen as soon as I can," she added.

She turned away, then came back to where
Catherine was wearily unsaddling her horse and
clutched at her arm.

"My man went with the king to Ireland. He's one
of the king's archers, Jack Bennet by name. I've not
heard from him since he left. You've no news of
him, I don't suppose?"

Catherine shook her head. "I'm sorry," she said
awkwardly.

"Ah, well, I didn't think so," said the girl with
resignation. "But my boy, Jacky—he's only a baby,
really—keeps asking for his dad and I hoped . . ."
Her voice trailed off.

Meg was as good as her word, returning a little
while later with a whole pigeon pie, bread, cheese,
and a mug of ale to wash it all down.

"Keep some by you for tomorrow," she advised.
"By the time that lot leaves at cockcrow, there'll be
nothing but crumbs left in the kitchen. As it is, our
ale kegs are near drained dry."

Catherine nodded, putting the bread and cheese

aside and devouring the hot pie, for she felt famished.

"Thank you for all your help," she said with feeling when she could speak again.

The girl shrugged. "Maybe somewhere, somebody is helping my Jack, so he can get back to his family again." She picked up a hay fork and began to pitch hay from the loft down into the stables. "I'll do this job ahead so the hostler won't need to come up here in the morning. You can lay low and keep quiet if you hear anyone moving about." She stuck the fork back in the hay and began to back down the ladder. "If I don't see you again, good luck."

After Meg left, Catherine made a nest for herself in a pile of hay and, too tired to be fussy about her resting place for the night, settled down to sleep.

It seemed as though she had only been asleep for a few minutes, but in reality it must have been hours, for dawn was beginning to streak the sky when she was awakened by a loud commotion.

The soldiers were milling about below, saddling up, and a loud-voiced captain was demanding to know whose horse was housed in the far stall. The stable boy, a witless lad, tugged at his forelock and said, "Dunno, sir. Don't look like none of ours."

"Of course it's not, you fool!" snarled the captain irritably. "It's too fine an animal to belong to a village inn."

Catherine was jerked from sleepiness into instant wakefulness, and her heart started to thump so loudly she was sure the men below could hear it. She stiffened, holding her breath. Would the captain institute a search for the unknown rider of the horse? If so, she was lost.

He did not, evidently deciding that it wasn't worth the effort and time involved. They must be on their way, he told his men.

Catherine breathed again. Then, to her horror, she heard him say casually, "Tell you what, lads. We'll confiscate the horse. And all the other nags belonging to the inn while we're at it. We can use a few extra fresh horses. And it'll be a good lesson to the innkeeper to paint out that damned white hart sign and replace it with the red rose of Lancaster. What's more, if any traitors are skulking about, well, it'll set 'em afoot at least."

Oh, no . . . no, thought Catherine, her knuckles white as they clutched a beam, holding herself silent and rigid, listening intently. This couldn't be happening to her . . . it simply couldn't be! They couldn't take her horse, her only means of transportation. They couldn't. They just could not!

But they did.

Chapter Twenty

Catherine felt like crying. She felt like weeping and wailing and tearing her hair and screaming and cursing. But of course, she could do none of those things.

She lay quietly, stealthily pulling more hay over herself and praying that none of the soldiers would think of searching the loft. The soldiers led the horses out of the stables, and at a distance she could hear the commotion the landlord roused when he realized they had rounded up the inn's horses and were making away with them. But aside from shaking his fist and cursing, there was nothing he could do either.

Catherine prudently lay low until the commotion had quieted down. Then she scrambled down the ladder and made off, having divided the coins in her pouch and left an ample supply for the landlord and his daughter, for she felt responsible for the troubles she had unwittingly brought to them and wished to compensate in some way.

Plucking up her courage, she set out afoot. She had her map, a small parcel of food, and just about enough coins left to purchase a horse, if she were lucky enough to find one for sale later on when she was safely out of the district. That is, if she were not set upon and robbed, she thought grimly.

There were few travelers about. Given the unsettled state of the country, honest folk were biding at home, hoping to preserve what little they had from scavenging soldiery.

Catherine walked until she could walk no longer, and then she rested. When she was recuperated, she got up and walked some more, always making sure to keep the sun to her left these early morning hours, lest she become confused, disoriented, and lost. There were great stretches of lonely heath to be traversed and areas of pine and woodland. She avoided such villages as there were, for fear of the inhabitants. Whenever she ran across little streams meandering through the wooded valleys, she took a drink and then took off her shoes and paddled her blistering feet in the cool sparkling water. Never had she felt such appreciation for water.

Later in the day, plowland and woodland gave way to rolling chalk downs suitable only for pasturing sheep. She might have felt conspicuous traversing this barren terrain with no cover to dodge into, but there was no one to see her except flocks of baaing, bleating sheep and the odd shepherd or two.

Late in the afternoon, a wool cart driven by an old man stopped and he offered her a ride. Without hesitation, she accepted gratefully, for her feet were sore and blistered and she felt utterly spent. The driver was not disposed to talk, and for that too she was grateful, leaning back against the tightly packed wool and dozing.

"Be 'ee on the run, lad?" the old man asked when she woke from a short nap.

Catherine was taken aback. "Er . . . umm . . . why do you ask?"

"Lotta reasons," he said vaguely. "For one thing, you're headed toward the Cinque Ports, and I miss my guess if you're not aiming for France. I'm going to Rye myself, and you're welcome to ride along with me if you're a mind to." He hawked and spat over the side of the cart. "There's a French ship in port, trading cargoes of Gascon wine for wool."

Catherine nodded.

"They do say the ports are swarming with soldiers, looking for a redheaded lass dressed as a lad," he remarked. "If you be her, you'd best get into the cart down under the wool. It'll be hot, and it'll stink some, but it'll be safer." He peered at her slyly. "If you be her, that is. If not, pay me no heed."

Catherine didn't know what to say. The old man chuckled and reined in the swaybacked nag. He waited till Catherine jumped down and, going around to the rear of the two-wheeled cart, clambered up inside, diving deep into the soft woolly fleeces.

The old man was right, she reflected. The wool was hot and smelly and greasy, but she made a little nest for herself, and actually dozed off from heat and exhaustion.

The cart jolting to a stop woke her abruptly sometime later, and she held her breath, hearing loud harsh voices questioning the old man, who answered placidly.

The wool muffled all but the sound of their voices rising and falling, but evidently the old man's answers satisfied his questioners, for presently she heard one of them, rough-voiced and impatient, say, "Pass on, pass on."

The cart clattered up steep cobblestoned streets and came to rest at what sounded like the courtyard of an inn. Her rescuer got down from the driver's perch and, under pretense of making some adjustment to his load, came round to the back and spoke in a low voice to Catherine.

"You there, lad? I got bad news for 'ee. The ports have been closed to shipping—all shipping."

"What of the French ship?" Catherine whispered.

"It crossed the bar earlier today and put out to sea while it could still get away. It may be anchored in some cove or maybe it went back to France without ye. Was I you, I'd make for some other port, Winchelsea or Hastings."

"But . . . but won't they be closed too?" At this moment, Catherine bitterly regretted her country was an island.

"Maybe . . . maybe not. But you'll have to chance it," the old man mumbled. "We're at the Mermaid Inn. You can sleep in the cart tonight, but by daybreak you'll have to be on your way." He hawked and spat. "I'll sell my wool to the landlord for a small profit but that's better than waiting around. Sodding soldiers," he muttered.

Catherine heard him grumbling to himself as he unhitched his nag and led it away. Then she heard from him no more.

Resigning herself to a long and supperless night, she made herself as comfortable as she could. All during the early part of the evening she heard coming and going, voices calling back and forth and the clatter of hooves on cobblestones. When she judged it full dark, she cautiously stretched, to ease her cramped limbs, but dared not emerge from concealment.

It was a bitter disappointment to make her way here with so much effort only to find the port closed. In addition to this, she was terribly hungry and thirsty and quite horribly uncomfortable.

To pass the time, she began to cast over in her mind who she might turn to for help in her present predicament. Both Chantal and Crispin had suggested a number of loyalists, but none of them were in Rye itself.

When the sky began to turn light, she pulled out her map and studied it anxiously. Bodiam Castle was not too far away, and Sir Edward Dalyngrigge, who had built and fortified it, was a strong king's man and had been so ever since the Peasants' Revolt about 20 years before. Surely he could be trusted if anyone could.

Catherine reviewed in her mind what she knew of the man. He was one of the most successful of the English war captains who had fought in France, bringing home a fortune in booty and ransoms that he had used in the building of Bodiam

Castle, which he had boldly erected and fortified without a royal permit. He had been forgiven his presumption by King Richard, partly because of his service in the French wars and partly because of his undeniable skill at deterring French raids on the Sussex coast.

He was reputed to be a rough and uncouth old warrior who still undertook pirating ventures of his own, and hence was likely to have a ship at his disposal. He was also reputed to be an inveterate pursuer of women, which did not deter Catherine, since, if he found her attractive, he might be the more disposed to help her.

And if the price of his help was her virtue, well, she would just have to deal with that when the time came. There was a Lady Dalyngrigge, so Catherine had heard. She had been a great heiress, and it was said the wicked old pirate locked her up whenever he went on one of his pirating expeditions.

Resolutely, Catherine folded her map and tucked it back into her pouch. Then, before full light, she crawled cautiously out of the cart, stifling little cries of pain, for her limbs were still and cramped. Keeping to the shadows wherever she could, she hobbled away.

By the time Catherine limped sore-footed to Bodiam, her shoes were worn through and she was feeling faint and dizzy from lack of food and sleep. The gray walls, towers, and battlements shining across the wide lily-starred moat appeared to rise out of the midst of a lake like a shimmering hallucination.

The main entrance to the castle faced north, and was approached only along the length of a dog-legged causeway overlooked by a great gatehouse and a huge tower.

She knew better than to expect she could approach without being observed, and as she expected, her weary, sore-footed entrance was seen from the northwest garrison next to the great gate. There was probably an assemblage of men-at-arms stationed in the barbican, but as she presented no particular threat, only one emerged to challenge her. He demanded her name and the nature of her business in a bored tone of voice.

"Take me to Sir Edward Dalyngrigge," Catherine stated in as commanding a tone as she could muster.

The man's bushy brows shot up. "What business does a vagabond such as yourself have with Sir Edward?" He guffawed. "Faugh! You stink of sheep, boy!" The man grimaced as Catherine came nearer, approaching the portcullis.

"I . . . I must see Sir Edward," Catherine insisted. "It's a matter of life and death. I . . . I have a message for him," she said desperately. "I must see him . . . I . . ."

Suddenly, her vision blurred, the shining castle shimmered before her eyes like an unattainable vision of the Holy Grail, her senses spun round in a whirl, and she sank down before the portcullis in a faint.

Catherine was revived by the stink of chicken feathers being singed directly under her nose, and came back to life choking and gagging.

"She's coming round, my lady," said a plump plain-faced matron who was in charge of the singed chicken feathers.

There was a rustle of silks and a scent of French perfume and the plain-faced gentlewoman was joined by a faded beauty, who leaned over the bed in her turn.

"Where am I? Who . . . who are you?" asked Catherine weakly.

"I am Elizabeth de Wardeaux Dalyngrigge," the lady announced. "More to the point, who are you, my dear? And why do you come to us dressed as a boy? A very dirty disreputable boy at that?"

Dirty and disheveled she might be, Catherine realized, but dressed as a boy she was no longer. Struggling to sit up, she discovered she was stark naked under the bedcoverings. She sank back down again and squeaked, "Where are my clothes?"

"Being burned, I should think," said Lady Dalyngrigge in an amused tone. "They were incredibly dirty"—she grimaced—"and they smelled foul." She wrinkled her pretty nose in disgust.

Forgetful of modesty, Catherine sat up in alarm, the bedclothes falling away from her full breasts. She hitched up the blanket and said with difficulty, "There is a message . . . a letter . . ." Her mouth was incredibly dry and felt as if it had been stuffed with cotton wool.

"You have a letter for Sir Edward?" Lady Dalyngrigge caught on very quickly. She sent her waiting woman scurrying to retrieve Catherine's clothes before they could be destroyed.

"Must see . . . Sir Edward . . ." Catherine mumbled.

"Yes, yes. He has been sent for and will be here directly," Lady Dalyngrigge said soothingly.

"Where is here?" Catherine demanded.

"The living quarters of the family at Bodiam," said Lady Dalyngrigge, amused. She handed Catherine a beaker of some herbal concoction. "Careful now, not too much at once, my dear." She took the beaker back from Catherine. "When you collapsed, the guardsmen loosened your clothing in an attempt to revive you, and in the process discovered you were not what you seemed." She gave Catherine another sip of the soothing herbal liquid. "Also, for a time, you were delirious, mumbling about the king and queen and a message. In Sir Edward's absence, the guardsmen reported the incident to me, and I had you brought here before sending for Sir Edward." She cocked her head alertly. "Ah, if I'm not much mistaken, there he is now."

An impatient male voice was heard cursing at the servants, and Sir Edward stormed into the room, complaining about being called away at a critical juncture. "Dammit, Lizbeth, can't you let a man . . ." He broke off, catching sight of the slender occupant of the big bed. "Well, well, what have we here, eh?" he inquired more genially.

"I regret disturbing you, my lord, but we have a guest," said Lady Dalyngrigge quietly. "This young lady collapsed at our gates. I would introduce you but I have not yet discovered her name myself."

"It's Catherine Clifford," said Catherine quickly. "I . . . I came to Bodiam because I need your help, Sir Edward."

"Oh?" Sir Edward Dalyngrigge, a heavyset, florid-faced man, preened and combed his large drooping moustaches with his fingers. "What can I do for you, my dear? The dictates of chivalry demand aiding a maiden in distress."

The effect of this fine sentiment was rather spoiled by his bulging eyes, which roamed over Catherine's face and slender figure, lingering lasciviously over her bare shoulders and partially uncovered breasts.

The old lecher! thought Catherine indignantly, tugging the bedclothes almost up to her neck. But mindful of her predicament, she kept her temper and explained her situation to Sir Edward.

He looked both amused and enthusiastic. "No problem at all, my dear. I keep a ship ready for just such situations. We can sail with the tide."

Catherine, quite overcome, stammered her thanks. She had not thought it would be so easy to convince him.

"I don't in the least mind tweaking Bolingbroke's nose for him," he confided, sitting down on the edge of the bed and patting Catherine's bare arm in an avuncular fashion. "Richard was a fool to go to Ireland, of course," he pronounced. "Left the country open to Bolingbroke. A cold fish if ever there was one. I never could stomach the man. Nothing of his father, old John of Gaunt, about him. Except the ambition, that is. Ah, well, we're going to be stuck with him, I suppose." He shook his head mournfully, then rose to his feet. "You get some rest, my dear. I'll make arrangements for the sailing." He patted her arm again. "Don't you worry your pretty head about a thing. I'll see you safe in France, or my name isn't Edward Dalyngrigge."

Feeling much better after a hot bath, a bowl of hot soup, and a few hours' rest, Catherine went down to dinner in a gown borrowed from Lady Dalyngrigge. Sir Edward's already bulging eyes popped out at the sight of her, and he insisted on showing her around the castle, which Catherine soon realized was his pride and joy.

"One of the noblest examples of military architecture in England," said its builder proudly as he led her on an exhaustive tour of the castle.

To the west of the central courtyard, a separate wing housed the servants, who had their own kitchen and a common hall. On the east wing were the family rooms, which had a private access to the great hall and the chapel. In the gatehouses and towers of the great fortress were guest rooms and separate suites for the gentlemen of the household, an innovation introduced by Sir Edward. On the whole, the castle was as lavish as anything Catherine had seen at court; it was ornate and ostentatious and, yes, even picturesque.

"You can be justly proud of your achievement, Sir Edward," said Catherine admiringly as he tucked her hand into the crook of his arm and led her around the battlements.

"Thank you, my dear." Sir Edward beamed. "I like to think Bodiam is the very embodiment of the chivalric life in respect to defense, adornment, and accommodations."

"Indeed it is." Catherine was properly awed.

He patted her shoulder, contriving to let his hand slide down to cup her breast, and Catherine quickly moved away, stepping lightly to a parapet and exclaiming loudly at the beauty of the Rother Valley spreading far below them.

"As beautiful as you, my dear Catherine." He moved up beside her and said, with clumsy gallantry, "You are a fine figure of a woman."

Catherine ignored the remark. "Should we not go down to dinner, Sir Edward? Your lady wife is holding it for us," she reminded him, "and if we are to sail with the tide . . ." With determination, she headed for the stairs, compelling Sir Edward to follow after his guest.

Dinner, as might be expected, was a lavish affair. Catherine's host was a good trencherman, eating his way through an elaborate variety of courses. Her hostess, on the other hand, barely picked at her food, and Catherine, whose appetite had been assuaged earlier on by a hearty bowl of soup, followed her example. She only nibbled at the spiced venison and roast swan and took small sips of the fine French wines, doubtless brought back from her host's foraging expeditions on the French coast.

Noticing Catherine's lack of appetite, Sir Edward inquired solicitously, "Is the malvoisie not to your taste, m'dear?"

Catherine forced a smile. "It's excellent." She took a cautious sip or two to please him, but she suspected it would make her lightheaded, and she feared she would need all her wits about her to deal with Sir Edward once they were underway. So she merely wet her lips and helped herself to a piece of sugared marzipan, crumbling it nervously in her fingers until the meal was over.

Finally Sir Edward rose. "I am going to arrange accommodations for you on board," he announced. "One of my men will escort you to the quay when we are ready to set sail." Bending over his wife, he gave her a rough parting kiss. Lady Dalyngrigge looked as if she did not much enjoy the salute, Catherine observed, nor did she seem in the least put out at parting from her lord and husband.

When Catherine saw her host again, he was in his sea boots and wore, to her amazement, an old-fashioned dark-stained mace hanging from his belt. She wondered if the stains were bloodstains, and fervently hoped he would have no occasion to use the weapon on this present venture.

"You are in good time, m'dear," he called as Catherine boarded the ship. "The tide is with us and we can weigh anchor any moment now."

The ship in full sail seemed to fill the narrow little river, but before long they were slipping out into the open sea, running before the wind, and Sir Edward set his course for Calais.

Chapter Twenty-One

Catherine looked across the dark rolling sea that was carrying her farther and farther from Crispin, from home, from all those whom she loved and who loved her, and her heart sank like a stone. Would she ever see her loved ones again? she wondered despondently. She strained her eyes for a last glimpse of the English coastline and breathed a prayer for all those she had left behind.

Before long, physical discomfort overtook her emotional malaise. The wind was fresh, the sea choppy, and she began to regret even her modest indulgence in spiced venison and French wine. She was fighting down incipient nausea when Sir Edward, who had given the wheel to his helmsman, came up behind her and put his arm around her.

"A fine night, is it not, m'dear." he observed, taking a deep breath of the salty sea air and exhaling slowly and noisily.

"Is it?" said Catherine faintly. She was too pre-occupied with her stomach, which began to roll alarmingly with the pitching and tossing of the ship, to notice the brightness of the stars, the soft-ness of the sea air, or indeed the close proximity of Sir Edward. Then, with sudden urgency, she pushed him away and made a dash for the rail, where, after being violently ill, she huddled, groaning, for the remainder of the voyage.

Fortunately, it was mercifully short, for that same fresh breeze that rendered the sea choppy sent them scudding across the Channel quickly.

Sir Edward, rather disgruntled, delivered a green-faced Catherine to the house of one of Chantal's contacts in Calais. It was English-occupied territory and had been since 1347, so she was not altogether out of danger of arrest and detention, but the risk was correspondingly lessened, for Bolingbroke's seizure of power was not yet complete, and his long arm did not so far extend across the Channel.

Her French contacts helped her make her way into French territory, and thence, by easy stages, for she was still weak from her ordeal, to Paris, where almost immediately upon her arrival she was summoned to court.

She had hoped to be given a private interview with the king, but was told that he was indisposed, a polite term, she supposed, for his mental malady.

She was received instead by Queen Isabeau, nor was she granted a private audience, which she had wished for. She was forced to make her way amid throngs of French courtiers to where the queen sat in state, with the Duke of Burgundy on one side of the throne and the Duke of Orleans at the other. The two men were bitter rivals and could be relied upon to give conflicting advice.

Catherine was still dressed in her borrowed gown, and her shoes were nearly worn through. Among the gorgeously appareled courtiers, she looked like a plain little wren set down in a flock of peacocks, but she held her head high with pride and ignored the jeers and tittering of the courtiers.

The Queen of France had only recently learned about the rebellion in England, and she was in a fine fury. "Where is Madame? Where is our daughter?" she demanded without preamble, her dark eyes flashing scorn. "Why did you come away without her?"

Catherine swallowed hard. She could not let herself be intimidated by this vicious virago. Nor could she let herself be baited into losing her temper.

"The little queen must be by now in Bolingbroke's custody, madame. She sent me away because I was accused of treason and in danger of arrest and imprisonment." She hesitated. "She sent me with a letter for her father, the King of France."

"Let me see the letter."

"It is addressed to the king, Madame." Catherine delayed as long as she dared.

"Am I not her mother? And Queen of France? Give it to me." Queen Isabeau held out an imperious hand.

Silently, Catherine handed over the letter she had brought at such risk into the country. She knew that if she had been taken by Bolingbroke's men, and the letter found in her possession, she would have been judged a traitor and condemned to a traitor's death. Even Crispin had not known she bore a letter imploring the King of France to intervene in England's affairs.

Impatiently the Queen of France broke the seal and scanned the letter. Coming to the end of it, she uttered a short barking laugh and handed the missive first to one duke and then to the other.

She bent a dark, inscrutable gaze upon Catherine. "Are you familiar with the contents of the letter?" she demanded.

"In general. I have not read it, but Madame Isabella has honored me with her confidence."

"Our daughter implores us to come to the aid of her 'Sweet Richard,' who is, she says, 'sore beset.'" The queen's mouth twisted into an ugly line. "Hah!" she sneered. "'Sweet Richard' indeed! 'Fool Richard' is more like it. To throw away a throne . . ."

The same fate would not befall Isabeau of Bavaria, Catherine felt sure. What that acquisitive lady had, she would keep, though she must wade in blood to her knees to do so!

"What is your advice, my lord of Burgundy?" the queen said to the duke. "What would you have us do?"

"Nothing at present." The Duke of Burgundy stroked his chin thoughtfully. "They have a way in England of thinking nothing about changing their kings when it seems convenient. Let us wait and see what happens."

The queen uttered another of her short barking laughs. "What will happen," she predicted, "is that Richard will lose his head as he has lost his throne. That much, at least, is evident."

She turned to the Duke of Orleans, the king's brother. "And you, brother of Orleans? What do you advise?"

"We must treat with the English to bring Madame Isabella home," he said promptly. "Bolingbroke has her in his power, and if we do not act quickly, he may execute King Richard and force her to marry his eldest son to cement our alliance with England. It is the politically expedient thing to do."

The Duke of Orleans himself had a son of marriageable age, recalled Catherine. Isabella's cousin, Charles, a former playmate of whom she had spoken with fondness. No wonder the duke wanted to bring her home, she thought cynically.

"Hmm . . . so Bolingbroke has a young son?" The Queen of France pricked up her ears. "And if Richard were to die and Henry of Bolingbroke takes the throne, this boy would become Prince of Wales." She smiled. "Perhaps all is not lost after all." And crumpling up her daughter's tear-blotched letter, she tossed it away, so that it wafted down the steps of the dais and fell at Catherine's feet.

So much for the letter, so much for poor Isabella's heartbroken petitions to her father, thought Catherine angrily. King Charles of France would never see his daughter's letter or hear of her pleas, of that she was sure.

The next messenger that came from England told of Richard's deposition. He had been forced to summon a Parliament, and there, in Westminster Hall, formally gave up his sceptre and his crown to Henry of Bolingbroke, who with equal formality handed each item to the Archbishop of Canterbury so that crown and sceptre might be presented to him again with the proper ceremony.

King Richard's golden hair had gone gray over night, the messenger reported, but the king's voice was still rich and gold-timbered as he spoke, "I have reigned King of England for two-and-twenty years. And now, freely and willingly, I give you my crown, Henry of Bolingbroke, Duke of Lancaster."

Richard always appeared most noble in adversity, thought Catherine ruefully, remembering how he, as a golden-haired young boy, had seized control of the situation at the time of the Peasants' Revolt. Visualizing that triumphant scene and comparing and contrasting it to that of the scene in which he, a broken man, had renounced his crown, she wept for him. She also wept for Isabella, who, it was said, was being harried from place to place, each of them more strongly fortified than the last. The little queen was a political pawn that Bolingbroke would not easily let go, Catherine feared.

Catherine herself had become a kind of hanger-on at the French court, an anomalous position in which she felt extremely uncomfortable, the more so in view of the court's depravity and licentiousness, which appalled her. King Richard's court in England seemed almost puritanical in comparison, reflected Catherine, looking back at it with longing. She did not take into consideration that in those years she had been in the household of a child-queen—a child whose innocence King Richard had prized and guarded, shielding Isabella and, by extension, Catherine from all that was sordid and degraded.

And there was much at the French court that could be so described, Catherine found, to her disgust. She didn't wonder that the nobility of France had lost the battles of Crecy and Poitiers to the English. In her opinion, the French nobles were a sorry lot, self-indulgent to the point of degeneracy, corrupt and decadent beyond belief.

The dissolute French courtiers modeled themselves after Queen Isabeau, who was herself a model of depravity. Her lovers, of both high and low degree, were legion, but as much as she was addicted to the pleasures of passion, the French queen was equally addicted to the passionate pursuit of money and power. She devoted much of her attention to amassing a personal fortune, and extracted from the poor mad king assignment of lands and revenues in separate household accounts, thereby acquiring treasures of gold coins and jewels, some of which she stored away in vaults; the rest she spent on sumptuous clothing and in lavish and extravagant displays of ostentation and in riotous living.

Queen Isabeau was equally addicted to political intrigue, and she grudgingly took Catherine into her household to further her own ends, sending for her repeatedly to question the girl on English politics, particularly as they related to her daughter. How strong was Isabella's childish affection for King Richard? Could she easily be swayed from her loyalties? How well did she know Henry of Monmouth, the young son of King Henry, and what was her opinion of him? Had she blossomed into the lovely young girl her childish beauty had given promise of when she left France? And finally, and most important of all, how likely was it that Henry of Bolingbroke, now King Henry the Fourth, could hold the crown he had seized? For already there were plots afoot to deprive him of it.

Catherine answered as best she could. The question-and-answer sessions went on and on, sometimes far into the night. Sometimes the queen called her to a private audience; at other times either the Duke of Burgundy or the Duke of Orleans or both together were present to add their queries to those of the queen.

Queen Isabeau reminded her of a malevolent black spider, spinning sticky political webs with the object of ensnaring her own daughter in them, and before long Catherine developed as great an aversion to the mother as she had affection for the daughter.

Grueling as Catherine found these protracted and probing sessions of interrogation, a summons to the queen's chamber came almost as a reprieve, for at least when she was closeted with the queen, she was spared the necessity of defending her virtue from the amorous assaults of dissolute French courtiers. Only in the queen's chamber could she draw a safe breath, for they pursued her everywhere else with their unwelcome attentions.

It was not that she was irresistibly beautiful, Catherine reflected. It was that she had the attraction of novelty, presenting a new face, a new figure, a new challenge to those gallants bored by excesses and ever craving new and different and ever greater forms of stimulation. Fending off their advances was an ordeal, and she would have been hard put to preserve her virtue intact had she not remembered rough and ready tactics of defense she had learned in the rough and tumble of play with peasant children long ago. The tactics stood her in good stead now to defend her from those perfumed and pomaded courtiers who would not take no for an answer, and after giving one a black eye and another a bloody nose, and kneeing a third in the groin, she was left severely alone. Her would-be swains nicknamed her the "Ice Maiden," a nickname that Crispin, had he known of it, could have refuted, she thought ironically.

Crispin. Where was he now? Catherine wondered, sick at heart. For such news as trickled in from England was not good. The little queen had been removed from Windsor and sent to Sunning Hill. Had Crispin ridden in her entourage, or was he still at Windsor? Catherine had no way of knowing.

King Henry—for so she must learn to think of him, she supposed—had taken residence at Windsor, and Catherine's heart ached to think of the usurper making free with the royal residence that had been theirs. Greedy Henry of Bolingbroke had robbed so many of so much. She wished him little joy of it, and was not surprised to hear that he was laid low of an illness which was attributed to poison.

And then her heart leaped into her throat for, early in the new year, word came of a revolt in which the little queen had taken part.

The rebellious nobles planned to join forces and seize Windsor in the name of the little queen, who, excited and thrilled at the prospect, went about tearing down Lancastrian emblems and replacing them with King Richard's white hart badge. She also had issued, in her name, a proclamation that she did not recognize Henry of Bolingbroke as king. And then, evading her captors, she herself rode out to join with the conspirators, one of whom was a tall blond horseman strongly resembling her king.

But the plot, ill conceived and poorly carried out, failed. King Richard's double was put to death for impersonating him, and Isabella, who was judged too young for severe punishment, was made a state prisoner and kept under even closer restraint.

Catherine's heart plummeted. Her disappointment in the failure of the short-lived rebellion was acute. She grieved for Isabella, but even more, remembering Crispin's uncanny resemblance to King Richard, she feared that the impostor might have been he. Common sense told her that he was unlikely to have taken part in a conspiracy against King Henry, but still, a little niggling element of doubt remained and gnawed at her day and night.

The abortive uprising sealed Richard's doom. Before long, word came that he was being held prisoner in grim Pontefract Castle in Yorkshire, and then that he had died there under mysterious circumstances. Of grief and melancholy, so King Henry claimed, though it was rumored the usurping king had egged his cronies on to murder.

"It is no more than I expected," declared Queen Isabeau. "Richard's death is the inevitable sequel to his deposition. For the sake of peace in the realm, it was expedient to put him out of the way." She smiled in satisfaction, for King Richard's death left her 13-year-old daughter a widow, available to be used once again as a political pawn in a marital game.

Queen Isabeau, ever quick to seize an advantage, immediately instituted diplomatic maneuverings to insure that Isabella's second husband would be Henry of Monmouth, Prince of Wales. "The new king is already a sick man, so they say; it is likely she will not have long to wait before becoming queen again," Isabeau predicted confidently.

Catherine, when she heard of it, was sickened by the woman's greed and callousness. Could she not give her daughter a little time to grieve for the man who had been her husband, if only in name, a man who had won her childish heart and had ever treated her with kindness and affection!

She could have told Queen Isabeau a thing or two about her daughter had she dared. That the girl, though young and impressionable, was fully as resolute and strong-willed as her indomitable mother. That she would recoil in horror from marriage to the son of the man who had deposed and murdered her husband. But Catherine knew she was at court only on sufferance; she had no other place to go, so she wisely held her tongue and kept her misgivings to herself.

As time passed, and as her usefulness as an informant dwindled and finally ceased with the changing circumstances, Catherine found herself wondering despondently what was to become of herself. Queen Isabeau would not tolerate her at court or maintain her out of her own pocket from the kindness of her heart; she had none. And Catherine was penniless and virtually friendless, an exile in a foreign land. For despite her French blood, she did not feel in any way at home in France. She was English to the core.

Had she been able to find a friend or two at court, her situation might not have been quite so desperate, and she might not have felt her exile quite so keenly, but her strenuous rebuffs of amorous advances at the outset had made her an object of mockery and contempt among the men. And after an episode quite early on in which she had inadvertently stumbled into one of Queen Isabeau's "Courts of Love" and revealed all too plainly her shock and disgust, the ladies had snubbed her as well.

"A friend at court is worth more than a penny in the purse," Crispin was wont to say. His voice came to her mind like an echo out of the past. The aching loss of him was like physical pain—a dull steady pain that does not go away or abate but is ever present, almost, but not quite, unendurable. When it threatened to become unendurable, she took out her memories and counted them over, one by one. One of the memories she especially treasured was of her last day home, the day she had ridden old Bayard, her father's great gray warhorse, bareback for the last time, Crispin at her side on his mettlesome blood-bay courser.

The last time she had heard from her mother, which was before she left for France many months ago, the letter had informed her that old Bayard now rested under an apple tree in the pasture, his battles over. Catherine's eyes pricked with tears. One friend was gone forever, never to be seen again. How many were left? She wondered where Crispin was now, and if he still rode his mettlesome blood-bay.

The Love Knot

*   *   *

Crispin rode the Welsh borders for King Henry, but not upon the blood-bay stallion. Its throat had been slit one dark night when the wild fierce tribesmen of the hills had slipped down to the English camp and wreaked havoc in the English horselines.

"I too have something to learn about the art of war, it seems," said Crispin regretfully to young Prince Hal. Ever since that night, Crispin had tethered his new charger, a coal-black steed named Brutus, just outside his tent.

Crispin had been sent to Wales under the command of Henry (Hotspur) Percy to nursemaid young Prince Hal. It was not an assignment he relished overmuch, but the boy was a fine lad, though not on the best of terms with his father, the king. Henry of Bolingbroke was a hard man, as those who seize power must be, and he rode his son hard.

"Do you not think Hal over-young for campaigning, sire?" Crispin had ventured.

"He is my heir and must learn to bear a man's burdens if he is to be of any use to me," the king had said brutally. "If he is old enough to tumble wenches, he is old enough to learn the arts of war." The king had frowned. "The lad has run wild long enough. And you'll be a better influence on him than companions of his own choice. For one thing, you don't go in for whores," King Henry had said bluntly. "You're fastidious. I like that in a man. I'm fastidious myself."

It seemed an opening, however slight, for Crispin to declare that his love for a certain lady kept him chaste, a lady wrongfully accused and exiled, but he decided the time was not yet ripe to plead Catherine's cause.

King Henry had his hands full defending his crown, now that Wales had risen in revolt. Moreover, he saw conspiracy around every corner, the more so since the abortive poisoning attempt, if such his illness had been, and the rebellion in which young Queen Isabella had participated. Just recently Henry had found a spiked instrument concealed among his bedcovers, and was convinced that a servant of Isabella's had concealed it there for the purpose of doing him an injury. It was ludicrous, of course, but it was a measure of the turn the king's mind was taking.

So Crispin's instincts warned him to bide his time, to wait until the king owed him a favor before asking one in return. Cat was safe at the French court, he told himself. She would land on her feet somehow. For the time being, it was better she remain in France.

By now, Catherine was so far out of touch with affairs in England that she was of no further use to Queen Isabeau as an informant. Her plight might have been desperate but, luckily, a vacancy occurred in the royal nurseries about this time, and the queen promptly dispatched her there to wait upon her younger daughters.

The little French princesses closest in age to Isabella were married and gone, but Michelle, who was betrothed to the Duke of Burgundy's heir, and Katherine, who was little more than a baby, were still at home.

If home it could be called, mused Catherine grimly, thinking of her introduction to the place.

The royal children were housed in the Palace of St. Pol, a group of buildings on the eastern edge of the city near the place de la Bastille. The palace was impressive, even to one accustomed to Windsor and Westminster. There were 12 galleries connecting its buildings and courtyards, which gave way to seven separate and distinct gardens. Those gardens beckoned so invitingly that Catherine, immediately upon her arrival, could not resist the temptation to wander around them for a few minutes, inhaling the sweet fragrance of blossoming plants, and admiring the decoratively shaped topiary and the exotic plants, few of which she could identify.

But as she wandered, she noticed that the topiary was straggly, and the plants were sadly neglected and overgrown. She paused to pull away briars and brambles that were choking out an exquisite little flowering shrub, thinking happily that she would have time to take the garden in hand while the children were playing outside on fine days. And then, remembering that her little charges had been notified of her arrival and were waiting for her, she tore herself away rather regretfully.

Once inside the palace, Catherine was in for a rude shock. It had been built during the previous reign, about 30 years ago, and evidently it had not been cleaned since, or so it appeared to Catherine's dazed and horror-stricken eyes. There were layers of grime-coated floors and walls, fine furnishings and tapestries, moldings and cornices, and gilt-framed mirrors. Broken windows had been boarded over in some cases, and in others lay open to the wind and weather.

Lifting her skirts high to keep them from dragging in the dirt, Catherine followed a slovenly servant through labyrinthine passages littered with pigeon droppings to the children's apartments.

By now, Catherine knew what to expect, and was not surprised at what she found. The royal children of France were as dirty and unkept as any beggar's brats. Little Katherine had wet herself and was toddling about in sodden skirts. Michelle, three years older than her sister, was trying to feed her a crust of bread she had picked up off the dirty floor. With the other hand, she was unconcernedly scratching her head. Catherine knew what *that* betokened.

In another room, a vacant-faced nursery maid was leaning upon a broom. "Why have you not bathed and fed the children?" Catherine called sharply.

"No wages, no work." The woman shrugged and began to push the broom about in a desultory fashion.

Catherine drew in her breath with a hiss. So it was true—those rumors she had heard and dismissed as idle gossip. That the queen withheld the servant's wages and spent the nursery budget on jewels and adornments. Catherine had not believed it until now.

The only one of her children to whom the queen paid the slightest attention was her son and heir, the Dauphin, a puny spindling boy, as sickly as his deceased elder brother whom he had succeeded as Dauphin, and as likely to die young, Catherine feared. Still, she dosed him with the herbal remedies she had learned from her old nurse, though he was not her responsibility, and buckling down to the job, saw to it that he and his sisters were kept clean, fed good nourishing food, and taught their letters. Little Katherine, the youngest of the three, was most appealing. Yet unborn when her oldest sister, Isabella, had left for England, she was a rare beauty, closely resembling her mother and with a temper to match.

The negotiations for Isabella's marriage proceeded, despite her protests in far-off England, for her mother was determined to match her daughter with Prince Hal, though both royal dukes, presenting a united front for once, stood against it.

In England, King Henry was as determined that his son marry Isabella as was Queen Isabeau. For if he had to to return the little queen to her French family, he would be honor-bound to return her dowry along with her, and he had already spent the money and distributed her jewels among his coterie of followers. King Henry was perpetually short of cash for he had discovered, to his cost, that thrones do not come cheap!

But even more to the point, King Henry of Bolingbroke desperately needed the French alliance. His grip on the crown was not as secure as he had once thought it would be, and he was learning too late that it is easier to criticize authority than to wield it. In Scotland, trouble was brewing, trouble that was largely fomented and financed by France, and Henry was forced to pull men out of Wales, which had been temporarily brought to its knees, and rush his army up to Scotland.

Crispin, for one, was glad to go. He did not like the Welsh campaign. It consisted largely of chasing the elusive Welsh chieftain, Owen Glendower, up the hills and down the Welsh valleys. Failing to lay hands on the Welsh Wizard, as Glendower was called, Henry Hotspur ordered the pillaging and burning of cottages that had given Glendower shelter. Crispin carried out the orders with the utmost reluctance, restraining his men from indulging in robbery and rape, though he had the devil's own time doing so. "Burn the cottages and barns, but spare the churches and monasteries," he ordered. "The women and children can take shelter there, until their men come down from the hills."

So Crispin was glad to see the last of Wales. The campaign in Scotland promised glory and honor and a chance to win renown in a set-piece battle, for 12 thousand Scotsmen, it was said, were on the march down upon Carlisle.

But first, he must bid farewell to his protege, young Prince Hal, for he had developed a fondness for the stalwart youth, whose reckless disregard for danger he had sought to curb. "You are the hope of England," he'd told the boy, leaping in front of him and taking in his arm a Welsh arrow that was meant for the prince.

"My father shall hear of your courage," Hal had promised. "Though in truth, I know not how much he values my life, for he has other sons, and my younger brother, Tom, has ever been his favorite."

Hal had been summoned to court at the same time that Crispin was ordered to Scotland, so the two had come to a parting of the ways and were having a final drink together before separating.

"I shall stop at Havering-atte-Bower and woo Isabella on my way to Court," the lad declared. "What think you of my chances for winning her heart, Crispin?" he asked his friend. "You must know her well, for you were governor at Windsor in the last reign."

Crispin stared into his cup of wine, swirling it thoughtfully. "Your chances are not good, Hal," he said candidly. "Isabella loved Richard well, and makes no secret of the hatred she bears your father and, by extension, any member of his family." Crispin looked melancholy, for talk of Isabella inevitably brought thoughts of Catherine to mind. He wondered if it was from her that the young queen had learned to openly and freely express her feelings, for as a rule, royal children learned early the arts of dissimulation, and Isabella's forthrightness reminded him strongly of his lost love.

"Look not so glum, my friend." Prince Hal clapped him on the shoulder. "'Tis my problem, not yours," he said. "And 'tis no great matter, after all, for her mother and my father favor the match, and both of them are accustomed to getting what they want. I shall woo her and win her love after we are wed."

"'Twas not of your situation I was thinking," Crispin admitted. "But my own." At Hal's inquiring look, he poured them each another cup of wine and said, "It's a long story. You remember the little queen's favorite lady, Catherine Clifford?"

The lad wrinkled his brow in thought. "The tall one with the red hair? She whom Richard called The Queen's Cat?"

Crispin nodded. "We were betrothed, but the wedding was postponed until Richard should return from Ireland. And then . . ." A little drunk with wine, he told Hal the whole story, including Catherine's escape to France and exile there.

"'Tis like a minstrel's tale of romance or the Roman de la Rose," Prince Hal marveled when Crispin had finished. "I could approach my father in your behalf, and I will, but he is a hard man and a stubborn one. But only wait till I am King Henry the Fifth," the boy cried, "and then, by God, you shall bring your Cat home again, and Isabella will be my bride, and we will all be happy together."

Crispin was not *that* drunk. "For God's sake, boy, hold your tongue!" he warned. "Do not anticipate your accession, even in your thoughts." He glanced around the crowded little tavern that was filled with English soldiery, for Prince Hal had the common touch and preferred to do his drinking with his men. Fortunately, ale and wine were flowing freely, and nobody was taking heed of the young prince and his companion. Nevertheless, Crispin lowered his voice, muttering in an undertone, "Your father is unsteady on his throne, as well you know, and sees traitors everywhere," he cautioned. "Take care he does not see a traitor in his oldest son. And be not too eager to assume the crown. It is heavier than you know."

"Well, let us at least drink to our ladies," the prince proposed, clinking cups with Crispin. "To Catherine and to Isabella! And to the success of our missions—yours to war, and mine to wooing!"

Crispin was still in a melancholy frame of mind when he rode off to the Scottish war, for he did not

put much stock in the promises of princes, nor was
he of a mind to wait until Hal succeeded his father
to the throne in order to claim his Cat. Henry
of Bolingbroke, though not in the best of health,
might yet live to make old bones, if he did not worry himself into an early grave with his womanish
fears, his unreasonable distrust and suspicion of
everyone around him. It was the king's obsession
with traitors that kept Crispin from suing him for
Catherine's pardon.

But if he distinguished himself in some remarkable way on the field of battle and proved his
own loyalty beyond the shadow of a doubt,
then, Crispin reasoned, King Henry might well
reward his valor with the boon he craved above
all others. And with this thought uppermost in
mind, he spurred his weary steed onwards into
Scotland.

Prince Hal's wooing did not prosper, for Isabella
refused him yet again, and he rode on to court to
pressure his father into resuming relations with
France, for if he could not win Isabella's heart, he
was determined to win her hand. The king, in an
effort to placate his heir and to secure Isabella's
dowry, resumed the off-again, on-again marriage
negotiations.

The negotiations were lengthy and complex, and
messengers began to come and go between France
and England on a fairly regular basis.

One such messenger to France brought a letter
to Catherine. She was in the schoolroom with the
little princesses when it was brought to her, and
she set them to copying exercises while she opened

it with hands that were suddenly clammy and that trembled in her eagerness.

The letter was from her mother. It was brief and to the point. Since Catherine was considered a traitor, her property was confiscated to the Crown. Thereafter, Clifford Manor, its wide lands and demesnes, had been handed over to a man of proven loyalty, to a man who had the king's ear and his complete confidence.

And that man was none other than—Sir Crispin!

Chapter Twenty-Two

Catherine was outraged. How dare he? she thought stormily. How dare he feather his own nest at her expense? Of all the unmitigated gall!

Tears blurred her eyes so that she could no longer read the closely written pages, and she laid the letter across her lap, blinking furiously to clear her vision.

All these months without a word from him and now this. Oh, it was too much to bear! After all his protestations of love, the man had betrayed her.

She choked back sobs. It must have been her lands he wanted all along, her property that he was angling after. And when he could not get them in the normal course of events, through marriage, he had waited until she was disgraced and in exile, until her property was forfeit to the crown, and then he had pounced.

How often he had expressed resentment at being a landless knight. She uttered a low, bitter laugh.

Well, he was landless no longer. He was Sir Crispin of Clifford now. And she a nobody, from nowhere. The king she had served was dead, and a ruthless usurper sat upon his throne. She had thought herself too lowly and unimportant to feel the full force of his ruthlessness, but she felt it now.

He and Crispin were birds of a feather—ambitious usurpers both. What services had Crispin performed for Henry Bolingbroke to be so rewarded? she wondered with a shudder.

Like everyone else, she had heard ugly rumors of how King Richard had met his death. That he had been set upon by Bolingbroke's men and his skull cloven to the bone. When his funeral cortege had passed through England, from Yorkshire to King's Langley, his body had been embalmed but soldered down in lead so that only his face was open to view. What terrible wounds had been concealed, and had Crispin any part in his death? Fervently, Catherine hoped not.

It did not bear thinking of. Fiercely, she dashed the tears from her eyes and hunched over her mother's letter, poring over her mother's neat script.

She was as well as could be expected, her mother wrote, and she hoped Catherine was the same. It was sad to see the property pass out of the family, but she was resigned to its loss, and she advised Catherine to bear it with fortitude. It was only to be expected when one was on the losing side.

Sir Crispin had been kindness in itself, her mother wrote, inviting her to stay on as chatelaine of the manor and making few changes of any significance.

At least he had not turned her mother out of the only home she had ever known. She supposed she ought to be grateful for his excessive forbearance, thought Catherine sardonically.

In fact, Sir Crispin was seldom home, her mother continued, being much occupied with the king's business, though he had come to the manor to recuperate from a wound received in the Scottish war, at the Battle of Homildon Hill. But fortunately, the wound, though painful, was not serious, and he . . .

The wound was not serious! What did her mother mean? Catherine clutched the letter with clammy hands, her heart pounding. *All* wounds were potentially serious. They could putrefy . . . there was always the danger of blood poisoning . . . one never knew.

Anxiously, she skimmed the rest of the letter and breathed again. Crispin had fully recovered, thanks to her old nurse's devoted care and skillful nursing, and after a short period of recuperation had been judged well enough to return to duty. Wales was aflame again, the wild Welshmen pouring out of the hills in great numbers to attack English-held castles and strongholds. Since Crispin's return to Wales, her mother had had no further word of him. She prayed daily for his safety, she wrote, for she liked him well and Clifford Manor could have no finer master.

Catherine let the letter fall to her lap. Well, she, for one, would not pray for him, she thought with a sniff. No, not one single Ave Maria or Paternoster. *She* would not develop calluses on her knees praying for a traitor, a betrayer. She would put him right out of her mind; she would tear him and the love she bore him right out of her heart forever. Or at least she would try to!

The marriage negotiations and the squabbling over Isabella's dowry dragged on and on, and messengers went back and forth between the two countries routinely, but no more letters came for Catherine.

Suddenly, miraculously, for everyone had assumed his lapse into madness was final, the King of France recovered his senses. Appalled by the unseemliness of the projected match, he demanded the return of his daughter and her dowry, declaring that King Richard's blood stood between the House of Lancaster and the House of Valois and that such an unnatural union would be accursed.

Catherine thought he would be content simply to have his daughter back, but his brother, the Duke of Orleans, had earmarked Isabella for his heir, and he liked his lilies well gilded.

The king's return to sanity also improved Catherine's circumstances considerably. He granted her a generous pension, "for services rendered our daughter, the Queen of England," and gave her a small house of her own in Paris. From being a person of no consequence, she was suddenly catapulted into a person of some importance. All of a sudden, she had suitors aplenty and the freedom she had always craved. No longer relegated to the nurseries, she still visited the royal children on a regular basis, for she had developed an affection for the neglected little girls.

On one such occasion, she walked into the schoolroom to find the children dancing about with linked hands and chanting in chorus, "Big Sister is coming home! Big Sister is coming home!" they shrieked in glee.

It was the first Catherine had heard of it. The haggling over Isabella's dowry had appeared likely to go on indefinitely. "Are you quite sure?" she demanded excitedly of Michelle, who was old enough to know whereof she spoke, as little Katherine was not.

Michelle nodded. "I'm sure. Our father, the king, has just been to see us. He told us the talking is over. Isabella is coming home at last."

"Isabella was Queen of England," chimed in Katherine. "She is coming home to marry our cousin, Charles. But then she will only be a duchess." She added importantly, "I'd rather be a queen. Someday I *will* be a queen. And you," she taunted Michelle, "will only be a duchess!"

"Yaah. You're just a baby. What do *you* know?" Michelle jeered, giving little Katherine a poke.

"Am not a baby! Not a baby!" Katherine grabbed Michelle's hair and gave it a yank.

Catherine reproved them both a little distractedly. It seemed too good to be true, after all this time.

But it *was* true. Isabella was coming home at last. The King of France had threatened the King of England with full-scale war if his daughter were not restored to him, and King Henry Bolingbroke, who had quite enough on his plate, backed down.

Catherine was in a fever of excitement. It was so long since she had last seen Isabella, so long, she sighed, since she had last seen anyone from home.

She wondered wistfully if Isabella would take her back into her service. Catherine had a comfortable livelihood now, thanks to the king's pension, and a little house all her own that even had a garden attached. She had even acquired a few French friends, though with painfully acquired cynicism she knew they were attracted mostly by her sudden good fortune.

That her startling reversal of fortune was directly attributable to the king's favor and was dependent upon it, she was well aware. But her house was deeded to her outright, and her pension was guaranteed so that her position was secure.

It amused her mightily that the ladies who had once shunned her now courted her favor. And the gallants who had once cornered her in dark corridors, intent upon depriving her of her virtue, now courted her assiduously with honorable matrimony in mind, for she was no longer penniless or homeless and the king himself honored her as his kinswoman and family friend. Moreover, as all knew, she was that rarity of rarities at the French court, a virtuous woman. And now, a woman of means.

At first, she reveled in her newly acquired prosperity and freedom. She flirted with her love-struck swains when she was in the mood to do so, and barred her doors to them when she was not, for none of them touched her heart, though they swore vows of eternal devotion, showered her with small and insignificant trifles (the only type of gift she would accept), and sang plaintive love ballads beneath her window. One, bolder than the rest, climbed a ladder to the window of her second-story bedchamber and demanded admittance. Catherine opened the window and jerked the ladder out from under him, and he tumbled into the garden below. He would be picking thorns from her rose bushes out of his backside for a week, she thought with a giggle.

She was also inclined to laugh over Bertrand de Flament, a silly young man who pursued her with amorous glances and languishing sighs, until he acquired the habit of sneaking up on her and stealing a kiss. But Catherine was sharp of eye and fleet of foot, and whenever she saw him coming, resplendent in a gold-embossed surcoat and velvet mantel with a long-tailed pocket called a liripipe, she took to her heels. Bertrand's vanity was his undoing, for his long pointed shoes of red leather Cordovan called "poulaines" exceeded the current fashion to such an extent that the tips had to be tied to his knees with chains of gold and silver and he was reduced to a mincing walk.

One particularly persistent suitor, whom Catherine allowed the run of her house because she thought him a harmless simpleton, was Damian de la Roche D'Arcy. The gentleman was a minor member of the French nobility, but though his lineage was noble, his pockets were empty, and she had heard that his estates were heavily mortgaged. He needed to marry money, but no heiress would have him, and Catherine's small but secure pension would at least provide him with spending money, could he lay his hands on it.

"You should seek out a burgher's daughter," she advised him kindly. "One whose father is willing to trade his well-filled bags of gold coins for a noble son-in-law and noble grandchildren.

"I know that," the gentleman answered despondently. "But Madame my mother won't hear of it. She vows she will have no burgher's brat as a daughter-in-law. But you are different. You are a woman of virtue, which is remarkable in this degenerate age, or so my mother says. That you own your own home and have de Valois connections makes up for other deficiencies," he recited, as if it were a lesson he had learned by rote. "What is more, your pension, though small, is sufficient to allow the three of us to live together in modest comfort." He beamed at her innocently.

Speechless with indignation, Catherine showed him the door.

Yet there was one among her suitors to whom Catherine felt drawn. A tall, fair-haired nobleman, Gaston de Foix, in whom she saw a vague resemblance to Crispin. A widower with a small daughter, Gaston had sad blue eyes and a melancholy expression. "I hear you have done wonders with the little princesses," he told Catherine candidly, obviously assessing her potential as a stepmother to his little girl.

At least he was not after her pension or her property, Catherine reflected, liking the man's candor. As she got to know him better, she found she enjoyed his company, for he was an admirable gentleman, of more mature years than her other suitors, quiet, but possessed of a ready wit and humor that she found refreshing.

That they had each loved and lost created a bond between them and an atmosphere of mutual trust in which each confided the circumstances of his loss to the other. Gaston's wife had died after a long pain-wracked illness; Catherine's betrothed had betrayed her, so she told him, claiming her manor and lands as his reward for faithful service to the usurper king. "The property was all he wanted all along," she told him bitterly.

"Not all, I think," Gaston protested mildly. "For you have much to offer a man, ma belle. Beauty . . . warmth . . . spirit." Lightly, he fingered a loose tendril of hair on her cheek, caressing it gently with his fingertips, but she seemed oblivious to his touch and, after a moment, he withdrew his hand.

"Crispin betrayed me," she said stubbornly. "He is, no doubt, ensconced in my house even now, gloating that he is a landless knight no longer."

"It may be that there are extenuating circumstances that you know nothing of," Gaston suggested diffidently.

"Pah! Extenuating circumstances! How could there be?" Catherine was scornful, but a little niggling seed of doubt in the rightness of her judgment had been planted in her mind. Or was it a ray of hope?

Whatever it was, Catherine's preoccupation with her former betrothed convinced Gaston that he could have no future with her.

On his departure, he pressed his lips to hers, and though she raised her face trustfully to his, the kiss was lukewarm at best, for some essential spark was lacking, and each of them knew it.

Thereafter, Gaston drifted out of her life as gently as he had drifted into it, and though she missed his companionship at first, she did not pine after

347

him, and indeed was relieved to hear, a short time later, that he had married again, his bride being the well-to-do widow of a burgher with a flock of young children in need of a father.

She needed no man in her life, Catherine told herself stoutly. She was sufficient unto herself, she had all the freedom she had ever craved, and if there was an emptiness, a hollowness to it, well, so be it.

Her loneliness would be alleviated, she was sure, when all the tedious negotiations for Isabella's release from her English captivity had been concluded and the little queen came home again. If Isabella would take her into her household, Catherine decided that she would serve her and her children after her for the rest of her life, for with her estate confiscated and her own life forfeit, she could not go home to England ever again.

Once, long ago, another lifetime ago it seemed, Crispin had promised her that he would see to it she could go home again, but he had betrayed her, seizing her home as his reward for backing and serving a usurper. Oh, he had an eye for the main chance, did Crispin.

Thinking of him, she dashed away a tear. She wished her manor had been bestowed on anyone other than him. It was too galling for words.

Not a word had she heard from him in all this time—though he had been her betrothed. Though she had given him her heart. He had trampled it into the dirt, for all he had ever wanted was her house and lands. Oh, it didn't bear thinking of!

So she made up her mind not to think of it—anymore than she could help, that is. Resolutely, she turned her mind to planning for Isabella's return, looking forward to the day she would see her dear child again.

All France, it seemed, was looking forward to the prodigal daughter's return with the same eager anticipation as Catherine. In Paris, the bells pealed day and night. Feasts and fireworks and festivals were planned, and an official holiday declared on the day the little queen came home.

The King of France arranged for Catherine to join the gay cavalcade of French nobility that rode out to welcome his daughter home. "For you were her friend in a foreign land, and no one has a better right to wait upon her than you," he declared. "It is fitting that you, to whom we entrusted her when she left us, be there to welcome her home again."

Leulinghen, a sort of frontier ground of English-held territory in France, was the site appointed for Isabella's formal restoration. It was en fete, decorated with greenery and flowers, banners and bunting. Pennants bearing the fleur-de-lis fluttered from every corner, as did the little banners made of red silk split into many points, the oriflammes, the royal standard of France.

As she made her final farewells to the English ladies who had accompanied her to France, Isabella distributed her remaining jewels among them, and they wept to see her go, their little queen no longer. And then, as she left the chapel of Our Lady of Leulinghen and crossed the frontier, taking her first step onto French soil in many years, her uncle, the Duke of Burgundy, who had been appointed to formally receive her, wept, hard-bitten as he was, to see his lovely young niece in her widow's black gown amongst all the glittering finery.

Embracing her and kissing her on both cheeks in the French fashion, he passed her along to Catherine, whose own cheeks were wet with tears of joy.

So were Isabella's. "Cat! My dear Cat!" she exclaimed, shedding royal reserve like an unwanted cloak and hugging the dear friend she had never forgotten.

The reunion was all that Catherine had hoped for. Her little queen had grown into a lovely young girl, nearly as tall as Catherine herself.

As soon as the formalities were concluded, the two friends seized their first opportunity for a private chat, laughing and crying over old times all through the night.

At some point, Isabella called for wine, as their throats were dry from talking. It was served by a pert servant boy with a trim figure and curling black hair.

The boy looked suspiciously familiar. "Chantal!" Catherine gasped.

"Charlot," she corrected her, with her black eyes dancing merrily. "It is Charlot when I am in this guise," she said severely. "Will you never remember?"

"So you too have come home again."

"For the moment." Charlot stepped up to pour Catherine's wine and said in a low voice, "I expect to be off on my travels again before long, for the Queen of France does not give up easily, and she has other daughters, any one of whom will do as well as the other." She grinned impudently. "A spy need not lack for employment."

From Leulinghen, Isabella was escorted to Boulogne, Abbeville, and thence home to Paris, in a grand procession celebrated with banquets, feasts, and tournaments.

When at last they reached Paris, Isabella sent Catherine home. "You are tired, Cat, with all of these festivities. You should go home and rest," she urged.

Catherine felt a little hurt. "But . . . but do you not want me to wait upon you?" she stammered. "I . . . I had thought to join your household."

"Of course you may, if you wish." Impulsively, Isabella embraced her. "There is nothing I would like better," she declared. "But you are tired, and I think you should go home and sleep before you make a decision." Isabella looked at her oddly. "In fact, I am ordering you to go home."

Her house in Paris was dark when Catherine arrived home, for the hour was late, she was not expected, and her few servants had either gone to bed or were out on the streets sharing in the festivities and merrymaking.

A sleepy servant opened the door for her, and then, with a yawn, the old man stumbled off to bed. Catherine went upstairs, divesting herself of her ear bobs and other small pieces of jewelry as she went.

In her room, she set down her small taper on the dressing table and decided not to light another. Though the room was shadowy, she decided it wasn't worth it, for she was going straight to bed.

She removed her headdress and unplaited and combed out her hair, then began to struggle with the lacings of her gown. It laced in the back, and she wondered if her maid was still up, or even in the house at all, for as usual she had gotten the laces into a tangle. Impatiently, she tugged at them, which, of course, only made the tangle worse.

"Do you need a lady's maid, madame?" a familiar voice enquired. "If so, may I offer my services. I have, er, some experience at the job."

Catherine whirled.

"Crispin!" she gasped. "What are you doing here?"

Chapter Twenty-Three

"I rode in the queen's train," he explained, advancing into the room from the shadowy corner in which he was half concealed. "Are you glad to see me, Cat?"

"Not especially," she said, steeling her heart, which leaped and danced in her breast, and striving to maintain a facade of sullen aloofness. "And not in that guise." She was referring to the red rose badge that he wore upon his breast and to the triple SSS collar of Lancaster that he wore at his neck. She obstinately refused to look higher, and so she did not at first see the jagged scar that ran from the top of his cheek into the hairline above his ear. "You have changed your allegiance since last we met," she said, sulky and stubborn, refusing to admit, even to herself, the overwhelming joy that flooded into her at sight of him.

"You knew I would. It should come as no surprise."

"Much surprises me," she retorted. "Isabella did not tell me you were in her train."

"Because I asked her not to. I thought it might intrude upon your reunion with her and dim your joy in seeing her again," he said candidly. "There is much that lies between us. Much that needs clarifying . . ."

"Nothing lies between us anymore. Nothing that can be clarified," she denied, sulky still.

"Oh, my foolish Cat . . ." He started towards her.

"No . . . don't come any closer." She backed away, in full retreat—both from him and from the deepest feelings of her heart—feelings that he aroused within her. His sensual spell had lost none of its old magic, and she feared it. She fought to keep a clear head, fought to deny their mutual attraction, fought to deny her deepest feelings.

"I . . . I don't want to see you. I don't want to talk to you. Go away!" she cried wildly. And then, almost in the same breath, "Oh, Crispin . . . *why?* Why did you steal my house and lands?" The cry was wrung from her very soul.

"I feared you would see it in that light." He sighed.

"In what other light is there to see it, my lord of the manor?" she cried in sudden spite. "You have risen high, my lord . . . for a bastard!"

He drew in his breath sharply, and for a moment the scar at his forehead glowed ruby-red and his hand dropped to his sword hilt and clenched there, the knuckles white. But he fought down his anger and said silkily, "I had forgotten my Cat has sharp claws, so often did I hear her purr."

Catherine did not like his reference to her purring in his arms. She lifted her chin and said sharply, "I am not 'your Cat' and never will be again!"

"'Never' is a long time," he said steadily. "Be reasonable, Cat. How else was I to protect your mother and your nurse and all those others you hold dear? Your property was confiscated by the Crown. If it had not gone to me, it would have gone to some other, who would have turned them out of the house to beg their bread upon the high road."

It was true, and Catherine knew it in her heart and grudgingly admitted it to herself, though not to him. Stubbornly, she maintained a sulky silence.

Crispin was fast losing patience, for her reference to his bastardly rankled within him. "I earned your house, my fine lady. Earned it fighting the Scots at the Battle of Homildon Hill, where I was wounded and left to die. And wounded again in the Welsh wars. Your house was bought with my blood."

"Blood shed fighting for a usurper!" Catherine cried out.

"Henry Bolingbroke is king. He was declared so by Parliament and anointed by the Archbishop of Canterbury."

"Richard was rightful king," Catherine reminded him, stubborn to the last.

"Richard is dead," he said brutally. "The king is dead. Long live the king."

"And are your hands stained with Richard's blood?" It was a thing she dreaded to know, yet was compelled to ask.

"Before God, they are not!" he answered wrathfully. "I had nothing to do with his death. It was a dirty business, and I took no part in it."

"Yet you fight for Bolingbroke," she retorted, near to tears. "I was true to my king, and you were false. I am in exile, and you make free with my house. Oh, it is sweet to be on the winning side, is it not!"

"I did what I thought was right. I did what I must, as do we all," he said angrily. "Do not hold me to account, Cat. I am answerable to my confessor and to God—not to you!"

A long silence stretched between them. Catherine bit her lip in thought. True, she admitted to herself, a man must do what he thinks is right. And yet, did he really think it right to take advantage of her position to seize her house and lands?

"Why did you come here, Crispin?" she said wearily, for it seemed they were getting nowhere—all that was accomplished was the hurt each dealt the other.

"To give you this." He unbuttoned his tunic and withdrew a parchment that bore the royal seal. "The king's pardon, Cat. I once promised you that you would come home again, and now you may."

Catherine's heart beat faster, but she refused to look at the document, shoving away the hand that proffered it.

"Oh, so I can go home, can I? Home to what? Now that you have seized my house and lands . . . am I expected to live on your charity?" She lifted her trembling chin proudly. "I prefer the charity of the French king, who has given me this house and all that I have."

"Not to live on charity, Cat. To live . . ." He hesitated. "As my wife." Seeing that she would not take the document, he laid it aside. "Your pardon is conditional upon our marriage. It was all I could wrest from the king. And it cost me dear," he said roughly. "It cost me the king's favor."

"But . . . but why?" Catherine was bewildered. "What have I done to earn his enmity? Only to be loyal to my king and queen."

"It is not you alone. Henry sees conspiracies everywhere," Crispin admitted reluctantly. "He is not the man I thought he was. Nor is he the man he used to be. *My* conscience is clear, but his is not. He does not sleep at night, and he has become a fretful peevish invalid, starting at shadows and suspicious of everyone, even his own son.

"I have watched him grapple with some of the same problems that beset Richard and deal with them less successfully. His ambition has brought him nothing but grief." Crispin set his jaw in a determined fashion. "More I will not say."

It was close as he would come to an admission that he might have been wrong, Catherine saw. His pride would admit no more.

"So I am to be forced into marriage?" Catherine fretted. "Never to see my home or my mother again, unless I consent to the match?"

He nodded.

"And you are to be my . . . warder?"

"In a manner of speaking . . . yes." His lips twitched in amusement, for he could see she was softening.

"Is it such a harsh fate, m'amie? I promise to be a kind and loving one. We were friends once,

357

you and I . . . yes, and lovers too. We would have been wed long before now, had not fate and the intrigues of kings come between."

He reached out and clasped her hands. "So what do you say, my lady? Will you not come home with me and be my wife and take your rightful place as lady of the manor? For I love you well, my sweet shrew, and house and lands and life itself are meaningless without you."

Tenderly, he wiped away a tear that trickled down Catherine's cheek. "Let not the house come between us, Cat. It is as much yours as ever it was, and we will live there quietly, as befits a country squire and his lady. Nor will I leave you to fight more of Henry's battles for him and thus regain his favor. I have done with all that. My only ambition now is to share a life with you."

"Truly, Crispin?"

"Truly, Cat," he averred.

She reached up and traced the scar on his forehead with gentle fingers, fingers that trembled. "Then I think I must say yes, for you have battle scars enough."

He caught at her hand and brought it to his lips, pressing a lingering kiss upon the palm. "But none of my battles have been so fierce as the one I fought and won tonight. For I have won it, Cat," he said exultantly.

She turned her hand so that the nails ever so gently raked the hard planes of his face, a face that was carved deep with new lines bracketing his nose and lips since last they had parted. "It is the last time you will feel your Cat's claws," she promised.

He laughed, deep in his throat. "Ah, that I do not expect. But I do long to hear her purr again. It is what I lived for when I was left for dead on the field in Scotland. What I have longed for all these months."

Catherine nestled in his arms. "And so you shall," she vowed, knowing that at long last she had come home.

For "home" was more than house and land, property, goods, and chattels. It was, in truth, a kingdom of the heart, where two lovers reigned supreme, meeting as equals and sharing each other's joys and sorrows in a citadel built and bounded by love, and ever besieged by the world and its woes.

For a long time he held her folded in his embrace, and a sweet, silent peace descended upon them. Then slowly, almost reverently, he divested her of her sumptuous court gown and lacy undergarments, serving as her lady's maid and expertly disentangling the knots in her lacings, breathing tender, almost worshipful kisses over her bare skin as he removed each garment, piece by piece. And she, in turn, acted as his squire of the body, unbuckling his sword in its scabbard, untrussing points, and removing his tunic to reveal a naked torso, clothed only in its scars.

"Ohh!" she breathed in indignation. How dare the world treat her lover so? For his chest was criss-crossed with a staggering array of half-healed wounds. Here, just below his shoulder and extending to his left nipple, was a jagged cut. A little lower, and the sword would have pierced his heart. There, along his side and down toward his groin, jagged scar tissue puckered. Impulsively, she bent his head and traced first one scar and then the other with her lips.

He groaned deeply, his hurts assuaged by her gentle caresses and by the kisses she lavished upon them as she ministered to him. It was an exquisite pleasure, but he by now was too desirous for the rapture of their union to endure such refinements of lovemaking for very long.

His eyes blue flames of desire, he fell back to the bed, pulling her down atop him and fitting her to his shaft. She could feel his hunger, and she met him freely, as with unabashed enthusiasm she welcomed him into her body, wrapping herself about him and matching his urgency with a lusty eagerness of her own. Each was completely in tune with the other, and each was equally desirous of fulfillment.

Within moments, it came, in an awesome, shuddering ecstasy that left them spent and breathless, but bathed in the glow of the most perfect satisfaction that a man and a woman can experience together.

For three days, they were oblivious to the world around them, and mercifully, it did not intrude upon them. They slept and woke, rousing to make love again and again, as if each could not get enough of the other, and slept again, and roused to eat and drink and talk, sharing each other's adventures and experiences since last they met. For he must hear of how she made her way through England and thus to France and of what had befallen her at the French court. She told him of Meg, the landlord's daughter, and of the old man in the wool cart whose name she never knew, and of Sir Edward Dalyngrigge. "That old lecher!" exclaimed Crispin wrathfully, but he could not help laughing when Catherine told him of her seasickness and of Sir Edward's obvious discomfiture. She told him of Queen Isabeau's relegating her to the nurseries, of the royal children, and how King Charles had rescued her from from obscurity and given her a pension and a house of her own. And she hinted just a little of her French suitors, so that his eyes sparked with jealousy.

And she demanded to know about his battles in the north and west of England, of how he received each and every wound, and of the famed Welsh leader, Owen Glendower, whose name and fame had spread even to France. Glendower's irregular tactics were still confounding the English, Crispin admitted. "Though Prince Henry grows in stature," he said thoughtfully. "One day, he will make a fine king and bind up England's wounds."

"Tell me more about my mother and my nurse," Catherine prompted, for she was not interested in the Lancastrian heir.

Crispin obliged her, telling her of how her nurse had cured him of his wounds, forcing foul-tasting potions down his throat and nursing him through a fever that had kept him bedridden for months. "She is fatter and more forceful than ever," he said with a grin. "As for your mother, she does well enough in health, though she is delicate. She is living for your return, I think, and when I left, I promised her that I would bring you back."

"I have missed her sorely," Catherine said wistfully.

"You will see her soon enough," Crispin teased her. "If ever we can rouse ourselves from this bed, that is!"

"Oh, if you are tiring of me already . . ." Catherine cried out, pretending to pout and attempting to leap from the bed.

But he held her fast, pulling her to him and growling, "Is this any sign of exhaustion or tiredness, my lady?" And sprawling against his firmly muscled body, she found solid evidence that he was not in the least tired of her.

On the fourth day of their idyll, the world intruded at last, for Isabella summoned them to court. They rose and bathed and dressed, Crispin himself combing out Catherine's tangled tresses.

"It is barely long enough to braid," she fretted, discontentedly tucking the russet curls under her headdress.

"It will grow as our love grows," Crispin consoled her, "reminding us of all we have been through for each other."

Isabella had only to look at their smiling faces to learn the answer to the question she teasingly posed to Catherine. "Well, Cat, do you still wish to come back into my service?"

And when Catherine blushed and stammered in confusion, Isabella laughed and said, a little sadly, "I think I know the answer already."

Though grieved at losing Catherine, the little queen insisted on giving the lovers a lavish wedding, with herself to wait upon Catherine instead of Catherine upon her, with the little princesses scattering flowers and the King of France himself to give the bride away.

The Love Knot

To please his bride, Sir Crispin set aside his red rose badge and Lancastrian collar, and in their place he wore instead her favor, a trumpery little brooch engraved with the motto "Amor Vincit Omnia."

And amidst her bridal finery, Catherine wore a token she had carried with her through all vicissitudes, a dark blue love knot, faded and frayed, but still tied in its intricate design, as constant as their love for one another.

Timeswept passion...timeless love

A LOVE BEYOND TIME

FLORA SPEER

When he is accidentally thrust back to the eighth century by a computer genius's time-travel program, Mike Bailey falls from the sky and lands near Charlemagne's camp. Knocked senseless by the crash, he can't remember his name, address, or occupation, but no shock can make his body forget how to respond when he awakens to the sight of an enchanting angel on earth.

Headstrong and innocent, Danise is already eighteen and almost considered an old maid by the Frankish nobles who court her. Yet the stubborn beauty would prefer to spend the rest of her life cloistered in a nunnery rather than marry for any reason besides love. Unexpectedly mesmerized by the stranger she discovers unconscious in the forest, Danise is quickly arroused by an all-consuming passion—and a desire that will conquer time itself.

__51948-8 $4.99 US/$5.99 CAN

ᴛʜᴇ ROSELYNDE CHRONICLES

ROSELYNDE

Roberta Gellis

"A superb storyteller of extraordinary talent!" —John Jakes

In an era made for men, Alinor is at no man's mercy. Beautiful, proud and strong willed, she is mistress of Roselynde and her own heart as well—until she meets Simon, the battle-scarred knight whose passion and wit match her own. Their struggle to be united against the political obstacles in their path sweep them from the royal court to a daring crusade through exotic Byzantium and into the Holy Land. They endure bloody battles, dangerous treacheries and heartrending separations before their love conquers time and destiny to live forever.

_3559-6 $5.99 US/$6.99 CAN